TILL THE END OF TIME

TILL THE END OF TIME

ALLEN APPEL

DOUBLEDAY

NEW YORK LONDON TORONTO SYDNEY AUCKLAND

TO MY WIFE,
SHARON CONWAY APPEL

PUBLISHED BY DOUBLEDAY

A DIVISION OF BANTAM DOUBLEDAY DELL
PUBLISHING GROUP, INC.
666 FIFTH AVENUE, NEW YORK, NEW YORK 10103

DOUBLEDAY AND THE PORTRAYAL OF AN ANCHOR
WITH A DOLPHIN ARE TRADEMARKS OF DOUBLEDAY,
A DIVISION OF BANTAM DOUBLEDAY DELL
PUBLISHING GROUP, INC.

THIS IS A WORK OF FICTION. NAMES, CHARACTERS,
PLACES, AND INCIDENTS ARE THE PRODUCT OF THE
AUTHOR'S IMAGINATION OR ARE USED FICTITIOUSLY.

LIBRARY OF CONGRESS
CATALOGING-IN-PUBLICATION DATA
Appel, Allen.
Till the end of time / by Allen Appel.—1st ed.
p.   cm.
1. World War—1939–1945—Fiction.
I. Title.
PS3551.P55T48   1990
813'.54—dc20   89-77761
                                      CIP

ISBN 0-385-24944-6

Thanks to Bill Garrison, Patrick Tucker, and Kent Carroll for valuable ideas; my son Allen for helping out with Charlie; Lucy Herring for cheerful, intelligent editing; and Ned Leavitt for being a good friend and wise advisor. And special thanks, as usual, to Bhob Stewart for being one of the smartest and most helpful human beings on the planet.

One civilian [on Bataan] was a saddle-shoed American youth, a typical Joe College of that era who had been in the Philippines researching an anthropology paper. A few months earlier he had been an isolationist whose only musical interest was Swing. He had used an accordion to render tunes like "Deep Purple" and "Moonlight Cocktail." Captured and sentenced to be shot, he made a last request. He wanted to die holding his accordion. This was granted, and he went to the wall playing "God Bless America." It was that kind of time.

GOODBYE DARKNESS
WILLIAM MANCHESTER

TILL
THE
END
OF
TIME

IN TIME OF WAR
THE ATTACK

Morning.

Alex Balfour walked up a low hill toward the rising sun. The day was mild and pleasant. The warm gentle wind carried the smell of rich, newly turned earth. He walked alone on a narrow dirt road that curved easily up the side of the hill. High white clouds floated in orderly lines across the bright blue sky.

A broad cultivated field stretched away on his left. He crouched down to examine one of the plants. A pineapple. Rows and rows of spike-leafed baby pineapples squatting gray-green and low against the red earth. He stood. He looked down at himself and saw that he was wearing only his blue running shorts and a white T-shirt.

It was as if he were dreaming a slow sweet dream. But somewhere within, consciousness stirred and he remembered a headache, maybe a headache, but then this thought drifted away. Too much effort to remember. He was content simply to be. He walked on. The dirt of the path was soft and warm beneath his bare feet.

In the distance a man appeared at the top of the hill. In a few moments they were nearly abreast. The man was Oriental. Japanese, Alex thought. He wondered, for a moment, if they grew pineapples in Japan.

"Good morning," Alex said, and smiled. The man bobbed his head and hurried past.

Alex turned back. "Excuse me," he called. The man hesitated, then continued on. "Excuse me," Alex called again. "Could you please tell me what day this is?"

The man turned but continued to move away, walking backward as he faced Alex. When the answer came, his voice was accented but easily understandable. "It is Sunday. It is the seventh of December." He turned away and hurried on.

Almost Christmas, Alex thought. He reached the easy summit and walked along the flat crest overlooking a wide bay. He saw a large island and a great many ships at anchor. A light wind riffled the blue water. Up on the hill there were no sounds of men and ships. Only a small wind rustling in the grass.

Alex's mind turned sluggishly, peevishly, an out-of-tune engine struggling to life on a cold morning. Slowly coming awake. He began to think. Part of his consciousness wanted to go on drifting. But another part, somewhere else, began to stir, sifting information, fitting pieces together. He looked out over the bay with new interest. Ships. *War* ships. Memory fell into place. A key slid in, clicked, turned, and a gate in his mind swung wide. He turned and ran back to the other side of the hill.

"Wait!" Alex shouted to the Japanese man, cupping his hands to his mouth. "What year is it?" The man stopped and looked at him. "What year is it?" Alex called again. The man began to run down the path. Alex watched him for a moment, knowing what year it must surely be, feeling the first cold touch of fear, knowing now when and where he was, knowing he was not on this lonely, lovely hill for the pleasure of a morning walk on a warm summer day. It could not be. It had never been.

He ran back to the crest, where he could see the ships and the harbor. Warships. Battleships. Destroyers. He looked into the sky, shading his eyes, searching, listening.

He heard it, on the wind. The tiny buzz of high, faraway airplanes. Approaching.

He looked around, feeling his body quicken to the fear. His heart was pounding. His breathing was shallow.

Nothing. No houses, no telephones, no people, no help. He could never reach the harbor in time. He searched the sky again for the planes.

High above, a wide V of dive bombers appeared through ragged holes in the clouds. Below them the ships lay quiet. Sleeping. No fighters flew up to meet them. No anti-aircraft fire puffed sudden black clouds. At that moment the Japanese commander tapped out the prearranged code that would alert Tokyo to the successful surprise attack: *Tora, Tora, Tora.*

ALEX FELT his breath catch as the tiny planes began to dive. He could do nothing. He could only stand looking up at the planes descending like hawks. He felt the heat of anger, the rage of helplessness. Alone, he lifted his clenched fists, and shouted into the rising wind.

1

THE TELEPHONE WOKE HIM. ALEX'S EYES
snapped open. He was sitting up in bed, breathing as if he'd just run
up a flight of steps. He was sweating. He reached for the phone. It
was Molly, calling from work.

"What's wrong?" Molly asked. "You sound funny. Did I wake you?"

He looked at the clock. 8 A.M. He rubbed his face. "Yes," he said.
"I . . . I was having . . . a dream." He tried to remember what it was
that had made his heart pound, that had left him sweating and afraid.
The tag end of it floated just out of reach; high clouds, the wind,
something he had to tell someone, something so urgent that—

"Alex?"

Clouds, the wind, a path. And the path led to . . . what? The thoughts
of clouds evaporated, light morning mist blown away by a strong breeze.
It was gone.

"Sorry," he said. "I guess I was really out of it. I don't know what
happened. I got out of bed right after you left and went for my run.
I must have fallen asleep when I got back." He looked at his feet.
They were filthy. The sheets were smudged. How could the floors be
that dirty?

"I'm glad I called to make sure you were up. Today's your first
class. Did you forget?"

The alarm went off, on cue. He reached over and silenced it. "That
was the alarm, see—I didn't forget. I must have set it before I fell
back asleep. I'll be ready as soon as I have a bath and a cup of coffee.
When was the last time we swept around here anyway?"

Molly laughed. "Don't ask me, taking care of the house is your department. I'm the one with a job."

"As of this morning, I also have a job. Time to split up the chores more equably. Why'd you call, anyway? Just to make sure I was out of bed? That doesn't show much confidence."

"Alex, it's a long time since you had to get up to go to work. Let's just say I was making sure."

"Oh ye of little faith. Look, I'll see you tonight, I've got to get moving."

"All right. I may be late. I've got a new assignment."

He stood up and stretched. "Anything interesting?"

"Could be. Could be very interesting. We'll talk about it when I get home."

Alex hung up the phone and went into the adjoining bathroom. He turned on the taps of his big claw-footed bathtub, took off his shorts and T-shirt, and gazed into the mirror. This was part of his morning ritual, staring at himself while the tub slowly filled. Time to tally and update his life list of strengths and weaknesses. Most mornings the weaknesses column was long and familiar, the sins unvaried, old standards that he regretted but seemed unable to change: I drink too much. I stay up too late watching old movies. I don't have any friends besides Molly. I have too much money for my own good. I do not deserve Molly Glenn. Strengths: I exercise regularly. He ran his hand down the hard muscles of his stomach, raised his arm, and flexed the muscle. *Not bad. Not exactly Charles Atlas, but not bad.* I'm a good cook, he went on. And after today he could add a new one: I have a job. He leaned closer to the mirror. Good-looking, he supposed, in a bland-blond sort of way. At least Molly said he was good-looking. She was a big-time reporter for the New York *Times* so she had to be telling the truth. He inspected the dark circles under his eyes. *Got to get more sleep.* He tried to smooth his hair down in the back, realizing that he should have gotten a haircut. His hand moved to the raised scars on his left shoulder. He was probably the only man alive who had been wounded by a bullet and an arrow in almost exactly the same place. He'd been lucky—both injuries had missed the big nerve that ran along the shoulder muscle. He had full movement of the arm, though he swore he could feel the onset of bad weather in it. He raised his arm and rubbed his shoulder. It hurt. *Gonna rain.*

Steam from the bathtub rose around him. *Clouds? Ships?*

He turned off the taps, climbed into the tub, and lay back. The water crept to within an inch of the edge. He'd taped over the overflow drain years ago. He looked at his dirty feet. The thought rose in him even as he tried to push it away. A small but insistent voice. *The floors aren't dirty. It's happening again. You were sleeping, dreaming, yes, all that. And more.*

2

MOLLY GLENN LEANED BACK IN HER CHAIR
and looked at the thin folder on her desk. By now Alex would be in
his beloved bathtub. She thought of him lying back in the steaming
hot water, dreaming his dreams. She was glad she had called. He
usually slept late. She had been surprised that he had gotten up early
and gone on his morning run. What didn't surprise her was that he
had gone back to bed after he got back. She put Alex-in-the-bathtub
out of her mind and got back to work.

She opened the file and picked up the two lone newspaper clips.
Not much to work on. Odd that there weren't more. By now she almost
had them memorized. The two stories had been filed more than thirty
years apart, but both contained much of the same information. The
first, from the *Times*, 1955, was a report of a Russian trial of twelve
Japanese war criminals captured at the end of World War II. The
trial itself had occurred in 1950. *The wheels of justice must grind slowly
in the Soviet Union.* For a moment she thought about what it must be
like to be a Japanese prisoner in Russia. Would any of them still be
alive?

The Japanese, after conquering Manchuria in 1939, had built a
bacteriological warfare factory in Harbin, Manchuria. The factory
produced toxins and research on various vectors for dissemination. She
made a mental note to find a book on germ warfare. She understood
that vectors were how you spread your toxins, but she didn't know
much more than that.

The news story reported that Japanese research at the germ factory had included plague, anthrax, cholera, and typhoid and paratyphoid fevers. Fleas and other insects had been bred in large numbers for use as vectors. *Jesus, a giant flea farm.* She felt her flesh creep. The unit had been disguised as a Red Cross installation. The Russians had stated that 1500 to 2000 prisoners had died there as a result of experiments. She put the story back into the file. Just touching the old yellow clipping made her feel weird.

"You get everything you need on that new story?"

She swiveled her chair around. Her editor, Harry Watkins, looked down at her over his half-glasses. Somewhere, probably from an old movie, Harry had learned to appear solicitous, worried, and briskly efficient, all at the same time. It had something to do with his bow ties, suspenders, and up-to-the-minute $700 suits.

"There wasn't much to get, Harry. Two clips and a lead on a Congressman."

"More than enough, Glenn. You'll let me know as soon as you come up with a game plan, won't you?" *Why have I never scored this broad? Jesus, she's good-looking. Great tits, great ass, that drop-dead red hair.* Even as he thought it, he was aware it was a perception colored by several years' rejection.

"I'll let you know, Harry. I just got the story an hour ago."

Harry held up both hands. "No hurry, no hurry," he said, smiling brightly. *Can't understand why she sticks with that crazy boyfriend. Guy's out of town all the time, leaves her alone for months at a stretch. Have to be crazy to leave a woman like this all alone. That's his tough shit. Gives old Harry room to manuever.*

He glanced around the newsroom, making sure everyone was hard at work. "Well, got to go. Let me know, right? You need any extra help, I could probably carve out the time." He turned and walked away before she had time to answer.

Molly shook her head and went back to her clippings. The other story had been published just last month. It was a syndicated column by Jack Anderson and Dale Van Atta, reporting on the efforts of an American Congressman who was investigating the same germ warfare installation. The Congressman, Rep. Pat Williams of Montana, had been contacted by a constituent who was seeking help finding medical care for health problems stemming from his imprisonment in the Japanese germ warfare camp. Williams's investigation had turned up the fact that not only had American prisoners been used as guinea pigs, but after the war our officials agreed to cover up the whole operation in return for scientific data gleaned from the research. Since most of the participants were now dead, the Congressman was having trouble getting anyone in the Bush administration interested. That didn't surprise Molly. Somehow she didn't think the President's men would go very far to turn up this sort of evidence on one of our major allies and trading partners.

She picked up the clipping and read the list of diseases injected into the prisoners: typhus, typhoid, anthrax, cholera, plague, salmonella, tetanus, botulism, smallpox, tuberculosis, and encephalitis. Other prisoners had been frozen to study the effects of frostbite. Quite a list of atrocities. Suddenly she didn't feel so sorry for any Japanese war criminals still being held in Russia.

She added this clipping to the file and closed it. She carefully placed the file in the exact center of her blotter. Her hands were spread flat on the desk top. Pale creamy skin, no freckles, nails cut short, neat and clean. Nice hands. Except the little finger of her left hand had been cut off at the first joint.

One year, she thought to herself. *It's been a year and it never leaves me. The Indian. John Raven.*

She pushed away the memory. She clenched her hands into fists.

She had lived through the experience and written the story. Only words on paper, but words that had brought her two local awards and a Pulitzer nomination. Was it worth it? She drew a deep breath. *Now this.* She'd spent the last year writing harmless little stories about minor events, and now they offered her this. She wondered if she could face it. This was not harmless. Nor minor. She could feel this one, this was important, and she wanted to work on it. She would do it, she couldn't stop herself. But she didn't want to get hurt again, there was no question of that. Once was more than enough.

3

To Alex Balfour, being a historian was a hereditary occupation. Some families begat doctors, others lawyers, a few executioners. The Balfour men were historians, both traditionally and very possibly, genetically. Some of them, Alex and his father for sure, maybe his grandfather, could also move backward through time.

This special ability was both a blessing and a curse. He was not immortal, he was as liable to harm as any man. But it gave him a *sort* of immortality; the capacity not only to see the past, but to participate in it. It was an uncertain and dangerous existence. He never knew when he would be taken back, away from the present. Or where. It was like having a hereditary disease that could come, unannounced, at any moment to cast him down, to seize him.

The first stirrings had begun when he was just past his eighth birthday. Dreams came to him in a wash of confused sight and sound. Figures, faces, images lay just beyond a pale scrim. As he grew older, the scrim faded away. Veils were lifted, and the dreams began to focus and achieve depth and dimension until finally, unexpectedly, he reached the final level. Three years ago he had gone through the barrier of the past into Revolutionary Russia. There he learned that the ability was not his alone, there he had met his father. His dead father. Alive.

A year later it had been the rough past of America, a hundred years before. He had survived these trials and travels, and found a joy in his survival and in the experience. And so he had come to live with his ability, though unable to call it forth, and equally unable to resist it when it drew him back.

As a historian, and as a teacher, he found his experiences to be invaluable. He also came from a long line of history teachers. Teaching is what most historians do. His father had broken that part of the family tradition by becoming a famous and wealthy historical novelist. Alex, even though he had inherited enough money to keep him comfortable to the end of his days, taught. He liked to teach. He had a formidable education and an impressive intellectual capacity. He also had trouble holding a job.

ALEX LOOKED OUT at the class assembled before him. The students seemed fresh out of high school, hardly old enough to be attending a university. But here they were, history students at NYU, and here he was, Professor Balfour, History 103, World War II, Pacific Theater. From Pearl Harbor to Hiroshima.

When they'd offered him the class, he'd leapt at the opportunity. Two years ago he'd been fired from his teaching job at the New School. Not that he blamed them for firing him. He'd disappeared in the middle of the semester. He almost laughed when he thought about it, yes, *disappeared* was the correct word. It hadn't been his fault, but they couldn't have known that. *Sorry, didn't mean to miss class, it's just that I had to go back and fight the Russian Revolution.*

In the three years since he'd last taught, student fashion seemed to have fragmented into a number of distinct styles. At the New School he had taught punks and intellectuals. Now, he confronted protoyuppies, retrohippies, a sprinkling of skinheads, and a whole group whose members dressed entirely in black. Those in black had the whitest complexions he'd ever seen outside of a Kabuki theater.

Most of the students lounged in their wooden chairs, looking like a tribe of sullen natives waiting for some form of authority to rise up against. But Alex had been a teacher long enough to know that appearances are deceiving and the brightest minds often lurk behind masks and costumes of indifference and reaction.

He called the roll from his official tally sheet, introduced himself, and walked around the front of his desk. The classroom was an almost perfectly preserved antique: old-fashioned wooden desks, chalky blackboards, and wooden floors weathered by years of hot summer sun streaming through the tall unshaded windows, wet winter boots, and students, generations of students.

"Why," Alex asked, "did America enter the Second World War?" He glanced around the room.

"To make the world safe for democracy," a boy with hair in ten-inch-long spikes drawled. Alex couldn't tell if the answer was intended to be sarcastic.

"To help the British against the Germans," a girl in the back offered.

"Because the Japanese attacked us at Pearl Harbor," a pale boy dressed in black sweatshirt, black jeans, and black boots answered. None of them had raised their hands. *Must not be the custom here*, Alex thought.

He nodded. "Those are all correct answers. Although there was more to it than that." *Yes, a good deal more.* He'd spent the last six weeks studying everything he could find on World War II. He'd taken courses on it in college, but his general knowledge had dimmed. He had brought home so many new books he'd had to build new bookshelves, much to Molly's amusement. She thought he had quite enough books. He had thrown himself into it, submerged in a sea of battles, heroism, and Japanese infamy and atrocity.

"Two years after the war in Europe began, the Japanese attacked America at Pearl Harbor." He walked around behind the desk and thumbed through a sheaf of maps, rolled up like window blinds, hanging above the blackboard. He pulled down East Asia. *Amazing. This looks like the same map they had when I was in high school.* He looked in the chalk tray. *Jesus Christ, a pointer, a real pointer.* He picked up the pointer and wiped off the chalk dust. He tapped Japan on the map. He felt like David Niven in some half-remembered old war movie.

"Is Pearl Harbor in Japan?" a girl asked. *What? Is she serious?* "Like, where exactly is it?" The question came from a neatly dressed young lady halfway back in the row nearest the window. "And what was it? Like a marina or what?"

She was serious. He had visions of writing one of those trendy books on the woeful state of today's youth. "How many of you," he asked, carefully keeping his voice neutral, "know the geographic location of Pearl Harbor?" Out of a class of twenty-two students, he counted eleven hands. "How many of you know the circumstances of the attack?" Five hands remained raised.

He felt a wave of anger sweep over him. *Easy now, let's not blow the job on the first day. The fault here lies not with these children, but with all their past teachers. Remember Pearl Harbor? Evidently not. All right, time to change the game plan. Back to basics.*

He turned around and used his pointer to locate Hawaii. "Pearl Harbor is in Hawaii, on the island of Oahu. Here is Hawaii," he said, tapping the map. He moved the pointer across the ocean. "And here is Japan. On December the seventh, 1941, Japan attacked our Pacific Fleet, anchored in Pearl Harbor. A strike force of six Japanese aircraft carriers, supported by battleships and cruisers, launched a surprise air attack at seven fifty-three on a Sunday morning. They heavily damaged or sank nineteen ships, some of them the mightiest battleships in our Navy." He paused for a moment. "We lost 3,457 soldiers, sailors, and civilians. The Japanese lost 19 planes and 55 men. To say that they achieved a stunning victory is an egregious understatement. Despite our government's knowledge that the Japanese were planning an attack somewhere, and that diplomatic negotiations between our two countries had broken down, the attack came as a complete surprise. The U.S. military—"

"Excuse me?" The boy with the spiked hair held up his hand. "My name is Fletcher and I have a question. My grandfather was at Pearl Harbor. He says that President Roosevelt knew the Japanese were going to attack us there. That he allowed it so we would have to get into the war and pull the Limeys' nuts out of the fire." For a moment the boy looked embarrassed. "That's his expression, about the nuts and the fire."

Alex tapped the pointer against the palm of his hand. "I'm sorry, Fletcher, no disrespect intended, but your grandfather is wrong."

"He says that everybody knew that Roosevelt did it on purpose. That it's a matter of public record."

Alex often wondered where this public record was. Amateur historians and conspiracy theorists were always referring to it. As if there was a huge book someplace where you looked up this sort of thing. A *Giant Book of Common Knowledge.* "You're right that a lot of people believe that. Then and now. But a lot of people believe a lot of wrong things. Plenty of people believe in astrology and creationism. They believe Elvis never died. They believe you can cure disease by pretending it doesn't exist. They believe in Atlantis and mysterious visitors from outer space. They believe these things because a mystery is more fun than the truth. But to claim that Franklin D. Roosevelt deliberately allowed the deaths of more than three thousand innocent people is to make him a mass murderer right up there with Adolph Hitler. Was Roosevelt another Adolph Hitler?"

"Well, Grandpa thinks so. He still calls him the Great Destroyer. Whenever anyone gave him a Roosevelt dime as part of his change, he'd throw it away." The class laughed. "It's true."

"Your grandfather sounds like a colorful character, Fletcher, but I don't think much of his historical theories. That story of Roosevelt knowing about Pearl Harbor has been around for years." Alex put the pointer back in the chalk tray.

"Here's the way the theory goes. Roosevelt knew that we were going to get into the war with Germany and Japan eventually. That he and Churchill met to hatch out a plan. Roosevelt would supply Britain with war material through the Lend-Lease program. We would cut off all exports of iron, oil, and other raw materials to Japan. This, in turn, would force Japan to declare war on America.

"Our naval intelligence had broken the Japanese code so we supposedly knew everything they were planning. Roosevelt is said to have received information from the FBI that the Germans were very interested in Pearl Harbor, on behalf of the Japanese. We did know that the Japanese were going to attack somewhere. This German interest pointed straight to Hawaii. But supposedly Roosevelt kept all this a secret because America, rife with isolationists, would have to be *shocked* into declaring war. And it all went according to plan: the Japanese attacked, America declared war on Japan, Hitler declared war on America, and we were all in it together."

Fletcher nodded. "Just like Grandpa said."

Alex smiled. "Except it didn't really happen that way. This is a good example of what is called revisionist history, fabricated through hindsight. Plausible, interesting, but wrong. While all the individual pieces may seem correct, they don't necessarily fit together to make up the correct picture.

"It *is* true that Churchill wanted us in the war. He understood that only with our industrial capability behind him would he be able to win the war. But in 1941 our army was ranked only nineteenth in the world. Just ahead of Bulgaria and slightly behind Portugal. Roosevelt wanted war, but he wasn't crazy. He knew we weren't ready for it yet." He paused, wondering just how much of this was getting through. "There is no real evidence that J. Edgar Hoover ever passed on any FBI material about German interest in Pearl Harbor. There's no evidence anywhere that Roosevelt had a clue that this was where the attack would be. The decoding of the Japanese military traffic was weeks behind, there is no evidence that anyone had read anything that should have been passed along. In fact there seems to be no real evidence for *any* of this. But those who favor the theory say that this very lack of evidence is proof. The old 'If there's no proof, it proves they destroyed all the proof' theory of conspiracies." Alex shook his head. "As far as I'm concerned, in that way lies madness.

"Now, it's certainly true that many people like Fletcher's grandfather hated Roosevelt. Sort of the way many conservatives today hate the Kennedys. But don't believe that Roosevelt was a mass murderer or a traitor. It just isn't true. Sorry, Fletcher."

"Well, I did get to pick up a lot of Roosevelt dimes," Fletcher said. The class laughed.

Alex laughed with them. "All right, it's early, but that's enough for today. You all need some background. Read the first three chapters in the textbook. And study the maps, for God's sake."

He watched them gather up their books and file out of the room. *Not bad for the first day. Now if I can only stay here through the whole semester.*

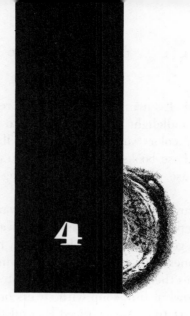

4

THE INSIDE OF THE RESTAURANT WAS
painted black. The low-backed chairs were wrapped in black canvas.
The tables were small and made of unpainted wood. Each table held
a candle and a spray of orchids in a small vase. The music was too
loud.

Alex and Molly were led to a table in a relatively quiet corner, as
Alex had requested. The restaurant, Speed Limit 55, sported both a
clever name and an appetizing entry in the Restaurant Directory section of *New York* magazine. He and Molly had been waiting for a
suitable occasion to try it out. His first day on the job seemed to suffice.
The menu was designed in what must have been considered a post-
modernist manner, but Alex found the pale pink ink annoying and
difficult to read. He ordered a Sapporo beer while he tried to decipher
the menu in the dim light, noting that each item on the list had an
automotive reference.

He leaned back and studied the interior. "Very dark, but I have
to admit, it's original."

Molly smiled. "I believe the car motif is popular in Britain. It's
known as 'motorway esthetic.' "

He chose the squid with red peppers, and Molly had chunks of
beef wrapped in green onion. The beer came and it was cold and good.
After a half a bottle he decided maybe black was not all that terrible
a decorative scheme. Molly told him about her new assignment.

"But why Japan?" Alex asked. "You know if it works out to be
anything at all you'll have to go there."

She nodded. Even in the shadows her red hair seemed to glow, catching the candlelight and gathering it to her. In the black room only the strong colors survived. "I know I'll have to. Maybe it was looking at all those books on Japan that you've got stacked and piled around the house. Besides, it's a fascinating country and I've never been there."

"Jesus, I can afford to take you if you want a vacation. You don't have to do in-depth research on prisoners of war in a biological weapons factory just to get a free trip to Japan. I'm rich, remember? I don't think the Japanese are going to take very kindly to you digging up a story that makes them out to be evil incarnate." The waitress brought them each a bowl of thin soup with slivers of green onion floating on top. For the first time Alex noticed that all the waitresses were Japanese. He felt a wave of paranoia. He'd been reading too many books on Japanese war atrocities. "Look," he went on, "it's so far away, what if something happens?" He glanced at Molly's hand.

She put her hand in her lap and frowned. "Maybe that's it, or at least part of it. It is far away, and it will be difficult." She shook her head. "It's been a year since I was hurt. Since you were hurt too. I lost part of a finger, and you had an arrow shot through you. That was bad, but it's time I got over it. For the last year I've worked on nothing but little stories that a first-year news aide could have handled. The toughest thing I've tackled has been a rent strike by upper-class whites. Damn it, Alex, the *Times* has been babying me. My editor, that jerk, keeps looking at me like I'm a slacker. If I don't stop this now, when will I? I can't go through the rest of my life being afraid. You wouldn't, would you? You've done things that are dangerous, back in the past, and I have no doubt you'll do them again. I don't like you putting yourself in danger, it worries me, but I can't stop you. I wouldn't if I could."

"I don't do it because I choose to," he said, remembering past confrontations with Cossacks and enraged Indians. "It just happens to me."

"Oh, bullshit," Molly said. "I know that you can't control it, but you participate in it. You like it. It's exciting. That comes through loud and clear every time you talk about it. It's everything that being here in the present isn't." He started to object, but she went on. "There's me, I'm here in the present, and I know you love me, but that's all you really care about. When you're not reading about the past, you're watching old war movies on your VCR, or wandering around New York waiting for something to happen. Your lawyer has instructions to pay your bills and keep up your house if you should suddenly disappear. This is not a normal life, Alex."

Well, she had him there, he thought. It wasn't so much that he enjoyed being in danger, but there *was* something addictive about it. One doesn't particularly like being shot at or beaten up or having your life constantly threatened, but he was alive back there, there was never any doubt about that. Here, he was, well, here he felt sealed inside the envelope of modern times, he saw the future as futile, he was stifled, bored, and filed away in the dead letter office. Here there was only Molly.

The waitress brought their meals and they began to eat. His squid was perfectly cooked, crunchy yet tender, with chunks of sweet red pepper. "Excellent," he said. "You know, if you cook squid for more than thirty seconds, you might as well be eating rubber bands."

"This is good too," Molly said, picking up a bundle of onion-wrapped beef with her chopsticks and putting it on his plate for him to try. "But changing the subject won't help. If I have to go to Japan to dig out this story, then I'll do it. It doesn't matter whether or not the Japanese like what I come up with. It's a job, and I'll do it the best I can."

He nodded while he ate. "I know it. That's what you should do. I worry about you, that's all. Just as you worry about me. I guess that's what people are supposed to do in situations like ours. When you're working out of town, well, I feel like you might need me."

She put down her chopsticks and looked at him. "You know, Alex, you're not the Steadfast Tin Soldier, and I'm not the Lovely Ballerina. We don't live in a child's playroom. I can take care of myself, I don't need you to rescue me whenever you think I'm in trouble. As to our situation, I'm sure that very few, if any, people are faced with situations like ours. You go back into the past and always seem to get into some sort of danger. I have to wait here not knowing if you'll ever come back. Or if you'll come back hurt." She sighed. "No, it's not a normal life. But I understand it, or at least why you do it. So I put up with it. And you put up with me. And that's why we're able to stay together. We have a history, a life. We love each other, and God knows it's seldom boring."

Alex touched the spray of orchids in the center of the table. Phalaenopsis, he thought, the moth orchid. They reminded him of his mother, who had raised orchids. And how she must have put up with his father, who could do what Alex could do, and did. Only his father was better at it than he was. His mother must have known that his father went back, but she stayed with him anyway. *And he was a real bastard.* "Maybe we ought to get married," Alex said.

BACK HOME, Molly went to bed and Alex, still on his prejob schedule, put on shorts and a T-shirt and wandered around the house, trying to decide if he should watch a movie or read a book or maybe just sit in his chair and think. He sat down in the overstuffed, purple plush easy chair.

More than ten years ago Molly had walked out of his life because she had wanted to get married and he hadn't. She had been gone a long time before she came back, and getting together again had been his salvation, in more ways than one. Now, back in the restaurant he'd asked her to marry him, and she said she just didn't know. Not exactly no, but close enough to it. She said the way they lived was too unsettled. That what happened to him was sometimes too much for her to bear. *She just didn't know.* He heard that phrase echo around in his head like a funhouse laugh, *she just didn't know*, and then it was gone. And he was . . .

. . . **RUNNING.** His body responded automatically. He stumbled, and caught himself before he fell. His senses came on-line, and his eyes told him he was on a wide grassy field. He was alone and running barefoot toward what appeared to be an aircraft hanger. The air was warm. There was the sound of a lawnmower behind him, growing louder. He glanced over his shoulder into the bright sunny sky and saw, coming in low, heading toward him, what he recognized from six weeks of reading as a Mitsubishi A6M Zero-Sen fighter.

Jesus Christ, just like in the movies! The ground beside him exploded in a line of spraying dirt as the fighter opened up. He gasped, ducked his head, and zigged to the left, away from the hanger, but also away from the dual track of bullets that stitched a path through the grass. The plane roared overhead. Alex cut hard to the right. In the doorway of the hangar several men cheered him on, as if at a track meet. An extremely dangerous track meet. He ran into the hangar and stopped just inside the wide doors. He bent over, hands on his knees, trying to catch his breath. The men outside ran in after him. He looked up and saw another plane heading toward the hangar, low enough for him to see the helmeted head of the pilot, a smiling face, white scarf whipping in the wind. The pilot waved and little lights winked on as the machine guns on the fuselage began firing.

Alex threw himself to the side onto the dirt floor and rolled behind a large piece of equipment as the inside of the hangar erupted into a shattering bedlam of ricocheting bullets and fragments of metal. The plane pulled up at the last minute. Alex stayed on the floor, listening to the receding sound of the plane's engine and the flat pop of nearby small-arms fire. He was breathing heavily. He was looking toward the back of the hangar when suddenly another Zero tore through the metal roof, nose down, appearing in a terrible shock of sight and sound, and plunged into the ground with a great metal-rending explosion. A blinding phosphorus-white flash lifted him up and slammed him down. A heavy workbench fell on top of him and the world went black.

HIS EYES were open but he could not see. His face was being pressed into the ground. He twisted his head to the side and wriggled away from the great weight on top of him. The weight stayed where it was. He could breathe again. He found himself in a small cave of wood chunks, metal sheeting, and scattered tools. He rose up and peered out through an opening onto a hellish vision of some other world. A blaze of orange flame licked out through a roiling mass of greasy black smoke. In the center of the flame the upended body of the airplane showed briefly, shimmering in the heat. Battered sheets of corrugated metal roofing lay in piles. Large machines were bent and twisted into impossible shapes that only hinted at some former function. And above the crackle of the fire were the screams, the constant screaming of injured, burning men.

He pushed up against the pile above him and shouted for help when he saw a pair of khaki-covered legs appear in front of his peephole. The pile began to shift and give as the man outside pulled at it. A table slid away and Alex stood up, free, and it was worse, more horrible than it had been in his cave. Now he could see it all, not just a piece of it, see it, hear it, feel the heat of the fire, smell the stink of burning oil, burning flesh.

"Shit," said the man who had pulled him out. He was small and wirey, a tough-looking character in a tan uniform. "You a head wound? I ain't got time for head wounds. A goddamn Jap plane just buried itself up to its asshole back there. If you got any brains left to think with, get out and give me a hand." Dazed, Alex began climbing over rubble. In a rush it came to him: memory, the dream. *He had walked up the long hill, seen the ships.* Not a dream, he realized, but a gap in the scrim, a glimpse of the past.

Pearl Harbor.

"Move it, goddamn it!" the man yelled. "If you're not dead, get your ass in gear. There's men hurt here." Alex climbed over the pile in front of him, suddenly aware with a surge of relief that all his limbs were moving freely and he was in no serious pain. Men ran by in all directions, some pulling and carrying other men, everyone shouting. He started toward the front of the hangar, toward the light, *no*, then turned back, toward the fire.

"Help me get this off him," someone called to him. Alex went to the side of the hangar and found a man crouching over a huge over-turned lathe. Now he could see that the hangar had once been a machine shop with long lines of metalworking machinery down each side. The lathe had fallen across the stomach of a man who lay pale and unmoving on the floor. Alex took one end, and the man he was helping took the other, and they both strained, trying to lift the lathe without shifting it and making it worse. The smoke grew thicker and the flames crackled closer and the goddamn greasy lathe was the heaviest thing in the world. Alex felt his muscles and joints begin to pop and tear as slowly the lathe inched upward. A surge of hope flooded him with strength, and they pulled and shoved the massive machine upright. On the floor, blood poured from the man's mouth. Alex could see that he was dead, had been dead all along, chest and waist crushed into a curiously flattened shape, the shape of a heavy metal lathe.

"Get him out."

"He's dead," Alex said.

"Get him the fuck out anyway," the man said, turning away.

Alex pulled the dead man off the floor and into a fireman's carry.

He felt a rush of warm blood down his left arm. He walked slowly and carefully away from the fire and smoke toward the light.

Outside, in the sweet clean air, he laid the man at the end of a line of other crushed and burned and bloody men. All dead. Alex felt a surge of nausea. He took a deep breath and looked away. The sky over the harbor was crowded with insectlike airplanes, buzzing in circles and diving on wounded ships. Black smoke veined with orange flame, larger versions of the hangar fire, rose in great fat columns from the ships. Through the billowing smoke, planes darted like angry bees.

"Nothing more to be done for that poor bastard," said an officer carrying a pair of binoculars. He knelt by the man Alex had carried out.

"How long's this been going on?" Alex asked. "I just got here."

The officer glanced at him and stood up. "You hurt?" He gestured at Alex's blood-soaked arm. Alex shook his head. "About half an hour," the officer said. "You a civilian?" Alex nodded. "Hell of a thing. We didn't have a minute's warning. I knew the little yellow bastards were going to do it somewhere sooner or later, but who could have guessed they could get all the way over here? On a goddamn Sunday, too!"

The man who had helped dig Alex out came up to them. "I think that's all of them, Lieutenant. At least all that we can get to. We got to get some of them to the dispensary right quick, though."

"Okay, chief. I think the panel truck came through all right. Bring it around, and we'll load it up." He looked at Alex. "You in on this?" he asked.

"I'm in."

The man nodded. The officer seemed a strange island of abstracted calm in the midst of chaos. Behind them something blew up in the hangar. "Go to it, chief," he said. He glanced up at the sky. "They'll be back soon enough."

The truck wheeled around from behind the smoking hangar and Alex and another volunteer put five wounded men into the back. All of the wounded were conscious, all young, hardly more than boys. None of them spoke or cried out as they were moved. Their faces were pale and still, their bodies black with burns, red with blood, hastily bandaged with strips of white cloth.

The three of them climbed into the truck. The chief drove and Alex sat in the middle. After a quick exchange of introductions, they started off. The chief was Chief Petty Officer Henry Tate and the volunteer on Alex's right was a soldier from nearby Schofield Barracks. "Jim Jones," the soldier said, holding out his hand. He was a small pugnacious-looking man. "They sent me over here to pick up some supplies. Hell, I never figured anything like this was going to happen. That lieutenant's acting kind of strange, isn't he?"

The chief grunted as he shifted gears. "He's all right. He's seen more in the last half hour than he ever dreamed of back in OCS school. He got everybody out of the barracks when the first bombs came in, stayed in there till all the boys was out. He's in kind of a fog at the moment. The planes come back, he'll snap out of it."

At the mention of planes, Jones put his head out the side window and peered up at the sky. They were driving along a dirt road toward the harbor. The road was full of potholes, forcing them to drive more slowly than any of them liked. The chief concentrated on negotiating potholes. Jones watched for Japanese planes.

And Alex sat in this moment of relative calm and felt fear creep over him like a cold damp fog as he tried to assimilate the confusing blur of the last hour. He pushed the fear away and concentrated. He was definitely and firmly back in the past. That part didn't surprise him and wasn't worth worrying about. He'd be here as long as he was going to be here. Experience had taught him there wasn't a thing he could do about it. Being in Pearl Harbor didn't surprise him either. He had begun to believe that it was he himself who opened whatever door he went through. That it was his purpose, his intensity, that took him back. He had read hundreds of books, had thought long and hard about the Second World War, the participants, its causes, reasons, effects, and strategies. So here he was. In it up to his neck.

"Oh shit," Jones said, drawing his head back inside. "They're coming back." His pale face caused Alex's heart to skip a beat. Even the chief looked a little perturbed as he stomped on the gas, dodged potholes, and tried to peer up through the windshield all at the same time. Talk gave way to thudding sounds as bombs began to follow them, sharper and closer. The first Zero roared overhead not more than twenty-five feet above the roof of the cab. The three of them ducked and the truck skidded sideways as the sound of straffing erupted around them.

The truck slid to a stop and they jumped out into a brush-covered drainage ditch along the side of the road. "What about the guys inside?"

Alex shouted, envisioning the wounded men piled atop one another. *Don't make me go back there, I just want to hide in these bushes.* The chief's answer was lost as two more planes thundered over, strafing the truck as they passed. The sounds of aircraft engines faded. After a minute they stood up. The planes were circling the hangar, dropping more bombs. The ground trembled with each hit. Alex and the others climbed out of the ditch and opened the rear doors. The truck had taken a line of hits. One of the injured men had a hole in his chest that welled a slow pool of bright blood. The man's eyes were closed. One of the other men was crying softly. The chief climbed in the back and spoke to the men, straightening out clothing and patting shoulders.

They got back in the front seat and drove on. As they approached the harbor and the dispensary, a stray plane made a run at them, but this time there was no stopping. They would not leave the wounded men alone again. The chief simply stomped the pedal to the floor and swerved from one side of the road to the other as Alex and Jones held on. Alex offered up a kind of formless, silent, unspecific prayer, a simple plea to be spared.

They pulled up beside a white cinderblock building. As they got out, Alex could see a man on the roof painting a large red cross. Several sailors and a nurse came out with a stretcher and helped them unload.

Inside, the long hallway was filled with rows of wounded men, their blood bright against the green cinderblock walls. The thick stench of blood and burn filled the close corridor. But this was merely a prelude, an introduction to the horror beyond. The main room was the size of a basketball court. The wounded were lying on mattresses on the floor. A few nurses, some teenage girls, and two doctors moved and knelt among the men. Orderlies were carrying away the dead. Alex stood and stared.

A low moaning murmur filled the room. A sound of pain, but pain suppressed, and fear, revealed in pleading whispers. *Help me, doctor, Make it stop, Tell them, nurse, tell them I am thinking of them, Loving them, Tell my mother, My father, My girl, My wife, My child. Tell them I love them.* The whispers massed and swirled and he could not shut them out. He turned and walked back through the long dim hallway.

Outside, through the smoke, the sky vibrated with angry flame, bursts of anti-aircraft fire from the ships, the blazing trails of tracer bullets spraying up from machine guns. And through it all the planes circled and plunged. In the nearby harbor, one of the great battleships began to heel to the side and slowly roll. Men leaped from the deck and poured over the side. The huge ship rolled over until only her gray bottom rocked back and forth above the blue water. Alex's eyes took in these sights, but his mind still focused on the men inside the building. He still heard the hushed pain. The soft, pleading, frightened sounds of men as they lay dying. The soft sounds of souls escaping. The whispers of death.

5

ALEX SAW THE SHIP EXPLODE. THE *ARI-*
zona. A large gray battleship, anchored in a double line of battleships.
All of them had taken hits, all of them were wreathed in smoke. But
this was of a different magnitude. This was direct, and final.

The death of the ship began with a flight of planes in a tight V-
formation coming in from the north. These planes began dropping
bombs, small black flecks that fell at perfect intervals. Most of the
bombs plunged into the bay, spouting huge columns of white water.
Alex watched the planes, fascinated by the process, as if the role of
observer gave him special, godlike status, a distance from the event.
He picked out a bomb to follow, the way a man will choose a single
drop of water and watch it slide down a windowpane. Alex's bomb
was lazily born from its mother plane and began its long plunge. It
disappeared into the ship and for a moment there was nothing, a
moment of absolute silence. Then the sky strobed a searing white and
the ship seemed to leap half out of the water. An enormous fireball
billowed up, spouting trailing arms of white smoke. Chunks of ship,
guns and turrets, mattresses, tiny bodies were blown into the sky.
Loose little comic-book, rag-doll bodies that flapped and flew and tumbled through the air.

The concussion knocked Alex back against the cinderblock wall of
the dispensary. He felt a sharp burst of pain in his head, followed by
a longer tearing pain that ripped at his throat as the air around him
was sucked away toward the explosion. A shuddering thumping roar
shook the earth and rolled over him in a long sustained wave. Stunned,

he collapsed to his knees and covered his head as a rain of coins, metal fragments, and chunks of flesh pattered down around him.

This is the end of the world. I am dead.

THE DOOR of the dispensary slapped open and men poured through, drawn by the thunder and light of the explosion. A solid pillar of flame rose into the sky as if sent by an angry Old Testament God, a mass of blood-red flame so great that it did not seem possible that it could have as its source something so small as the ship, the ship dwarfed by the twisting holocaust.

"Holy shit," a man said, "that's the *Arizona*. Christ, she must have taken one straight down the stack."

Alex slowly got to his feet. Everyone was staring at the blazing ship. A succession of explosions rumbled within the fires.

"Had to be the forward magazine," another man said. "Every stick of ordnance on the ship is blown. Poor bastards."

One of the doctors came out, his white coat stained with blood. For Captain Jonathan Rawlings, two months away from retirement, Hawaii had been his last duty station. *A paradise*, they'd said. *Easiest duty in the Navy.* He'd been working steadily for the last hour and had watched more men die under him than he'd lost in twenty years in the service. He looked at the burning ship. "Get down to the beach. They'll be coming out of the water."

"Ain't nothing left alive on that, Captain."

Rawlings shook his head. *I'm tired. Jesus I'm tired. I'm too old for this.* "There's always men left alive, sailor. Hurt. Near dead, maybe. But there's always men left alive. For a while. Get down there and bring them in." He turned and went back inside.

They were organized into a work party by a lieutenant with a bloodstained arm and a Spirit of '76 bandage wrapped around his head. Alex and a few others, some of them in their underwear, grabbed pants and shoes out of a stock at the dispensary. They pulled on their clothes and ran to the nearby strip of beach.

Men had jumped and been blown from burning ships. Some of them made it to the beach. Some dragged themselves farther up, to collapse on the grass. Others lay at water's edge like beached and dying sea mammals. As Alex ran up, the first from the *Arizona* were coming out of the water.

The men stumbled ashore after having been forced to swim through oil-slick water, some of it on fire. They were black from head to toe. Many were naked, clothing blown off by the blast, or burnt by the fire. Alex waded into the water to meet them, fighting back his mounting horror. *Run. The other way. You cannot bear this.* He reached out to help a man who was black from oil and burn, pink flesh and white bone peeping through fissures where skin was burnt to a crisp; crackled, sloughing off. The man stumbled toward him, zombielike, arms raised, a look of blank anguish in his eyes. Alex took the man's hand and nearly cried out when the flesh slid wetly beneath his fingers. He led the man out of the water and tried to hold him as he fell to the sand, but there was nothing to hold on to, no spot that would not tear. The man sank to his knees and fell facedown.

"Stretcher!" Alex shouted, hearing the panic in his voice. "For God's sake get a stretcher over here!" Two men ran up. The three of them rolled the burned man onto a green canvas stretcher. White sugary sand now glazed the charred flesh. The burned man watched Alex with that same unblinking dreadful stare. As they carried him away, Alex realized that the stare was permanent. The man's eyelids had been burnt off. He sank to his knees and threw up.

They came out of the water, staggering ashore in a helpless daze, and Alex and the others laid them down and tried to help them and carried them away. After the first few, a sort of deadness set in and he worked without thinking, ignoring bombs, fire, and the horrors that floated in the nearby water.

Time passed and there were fewer men reaching shore. They could see bodies floating farther out, many of them facedown, some moving weakly. Then out of the flames that licked around the hull of the sinking *Arizona*, a small boat raced toward the beach, a single sailor standing at the wheel. He cut the motor and spun the boat parallel to the beach. "I need two men," the sailor shouted.

Alex looked at the man beside him. It was Jones, the soldier who had been in the truck with him. As if on cue, they waded in and floundered toward the boat. As they hoisted themselves over the side, the motor revved and the small boat heeled over. They pulled themselves up and saw that they were heading back toward the low flames that curled up from the surface of the water, toward the gray hull of the ruined battleship. The ship that had appeared so small beneath its column of flame now seemed to rise up and become a tilting, fire-blackened cliff, shrouded by smoke. Spiked portions of ruined super-structure appeared and disappeared as gusts of wind sucked the smoke into the blaze.

"She's going down fast," the sailor shouted back at them. The boat rushed toward the flames. Alex cringed as they burst through a wall of fire. He felt it sear his skin and then they were in a small lagoon of oil-free water. "Don't bother with the dead ones," the sailor shouted to them. His voice was almost lost in the whip of air drafting into the burning ship.

Alex and Jones began pulling in the floating men as the sailor steered them slowly and carefully among the bodies. They would quickly check and see if there were any signs of life. The dead were pushed away with a long boat hook. When they found a man who moaned or moved or responded in any way, they hauled him over the side and laid him in the bottom of the boat. Alex's mind kept pointing out that they were surely leaving behind other men who were alive, unconscious men, and Alex knew it, but he was now working on some other level where common sense and the need to make quick decisions were dominant. Intelligence and facts would have to wait. They could take on six or seven wounded before they made the run back through the burning oil to shore where the injured were removed. The circling flames crept closer around the *Arizona* as she slipped lower. After four trips they stood in their small boat and watched as the water swirled over the shattered superstructure and the flames were extinguished in a great boiling hissing rush of steam and smoke.

"I'll be goddamned," the sailor said. Alex was watching the floating remains of the *Arizona*, scanning the water for movement, wondering how many hundreds of men must be trapped inside the sinking hull. "Hey," the sailor said, tapping him on the shoulder. "Look at that. That's the *Nevada*, that's my ship." The sailor hit the throttle and the boat leapt forward.

Three hundred yards in front of them, a smoking, crippled battle-ship was slowly moving into the channel. On board, Chief Quarter-master Robert Sedbury turned the wheel and the injured *Nevada* answered her helm. *Fuck the Japs. We're moving, and we can steer. If we can make open water, we can show them how we can fight.* Beside him, Lt. Cmdr. Francis J. Thomas, a Navy reservist and the senior officer on board, commanded the ship. The captain and the executive officer were somewhere on shore. *Tough luck*, Sedbury thought, knowing how pissed the captain would be to miss this one. The *Nevada* was the only sizable ship in the harbor that was moving in any direction other than straight down. She had been bombed, strafed, and torpedoed. *But by God she was moving!*

"HEY! SHIT! Wait for me!" the sailor shouted as they sped along in the wake of the battleship. "Which one of you guys can run this boat?"

Alex looked at Jones, who was kneeling in the bottom of the boat with a death grip on the gunwales. He looked a little green. "I can," he said, nodding. "If I have to. I've done a lot harder than that today."

"I ain't going to miss this trip," the sailor said, turning to Alex. "You with me?" he asked.

Alex felt his heart sink. People kept asking him that same question and he kept saying yes. He tried to remember written accounts of the *Nevada* at Pearl Harbor. Did she sink? He couldn't remember. What he really wanted to do was creep off somewhere and hide under a bush until those particular gods who were pulling the strings of his life decided to yank him back to his own time. But he found himself nodding anyway.

They swerved out and around the side of the ship. The sailor showed Jones the controls and began inching the boat toward the hull of the battleship. Someone on the ship spotted them and threw two lines over the side.

The small boat bobbed and bucked in the wash from the battleship. With Jones at the controls, they inched closer to the ropes that hung swinging and flapping against the spray-slick metal hull. Alex looked up the high expanse, at the thick wet ropes, at the narrowing surge of green water over which he was supposed to voluntarily suspend himself, and felt the cold clutch of fear and failure. Agonizing scenes of defeat as a child flitted through his memory. Year after year of humiliation in one gym class after another. Standing before hanging ropes as various Neanderthallike coaches exhorted him to get his ass up there. *Come on, sissy, you can do it. Climb the goddamn rope.* He never could. His arms were too weak, his spirit wanting.

"Now!" the sailor shouted, jumping for the rope, the word and deed shaking Alex from his reverie. He stepped up on the rail and flung himself over the swirling gap of water and grabbed for the twisting line.

He caught it. It was like clutching a thick, spray-slick writhing snake. He hung on as his momentum slammed him painfully against the hull. He dangled for a moment.

Climb, sissy.

He pulled himself up, wrapping his legs around the rope, fueled by a steady surge of fear and heart-thumping adrenaline. He was halfway up the side of the ship before he stopped to rest. As he hung there he was seized by a giddy rush of elation as he realized that *he was going to climb the goddamn rope!* He was going to actually make it to the top, and at least for this one windy, salt-sprayed moment, he was actually controlling his own destiny. In a limited way, yes, but it was up to him to get up the rope and he was doing it. Goddamnit.

The ship rolled as it wallowed to the right, struggling to miss a row of bomb blasts. Alex swung out and away, like a baby spider on a strand of windblown web, suspended at apogee for an eternity, and slammed back into the hull. He hung on grimly as stars twinkled and he gasped for breath. He could see the sailor on the other rope disappearing over the rail at the top.

Climb, dumbshit.

He pulled himself up, hand over hand, arms trembling with exhaustion, the grasp of fear at his throat and the knowledge that the middle of a war was no place to stop and smell the roses, for reflection, for savoring small triumphs. He was in control of nothing. It was only sheer dumb luck that he was still alive. He was one insignificant lump of flesh with no particular qualifications, caught up in the larger scheme of things, the rush of the past, the maelstrom of events on which he had no more effect than a useless woodtick screwed into the thick hide of a charging rhino.

He made it. He pulled himself over the brass railing and flopped down on the deck, gasping for breath.

"If you're here to help," a man in Navy whites shouted down at him, "you might get your ass off the deck and over to the Number Two starboard 40 cal."

Alex pulled himself up. His arms felt like rubber bands. His legs were shaking. "Sorry," he said. He looked around. There were men running toward a smoking fire in front of the conning tower, men running toward a fire in the stern. Machine guns rattling, bombs going off. This fury was all the more hellish because it was contained on the deck of the ship, which now seemed much smaller, more crowded, and impossibly confusing than it appeared from the shore. "What did you say?" Alex shouted.

The man shook his head and rolled his eyes. "Number Two starboard." He pointed down the rail to the middle of the ship. "Just go that way and ask anyone. It's a large machine gun you're looking for. We use it to shoot down airplanes." He shook his head again and trotted off toward the nearest fire.

Holding on to the rail, Alex stepped over hoses and sidestepped firefighters as he made his way in the direction the man had pointed. The faint sound of cheering stopped him. It floated over the water, barely heard above their own commotion. It sounded like a faraway soccer match where a point had just been scored. They were passing another ship and the men there were lined along the rail, pausing in the midst of their own battle, to cheer and wave to the *Nevada*, the only ship under way in the harbor. Alex waved back, feeling stupidly proud of something he had no part in. Yet.

He glanced up. The Japanese planes seemed to be gathering. Attracted by the movement of the ship.

A bomb plumed into the bay twenty yards away and a column of water washed over him. Alex grabbed on to the rail as the ship jumped and shuddered. He cringed, even as his brain told him that if the bomb was going to get him it would have already done so.

On his left, up on a small raised circular deck, three men stood working a large, mounted machine gun. They were stripped to the waist, covered with sweat and grease. Alex climbed up a short ladder and poked his head into the emplacement. "Need some help?" he hollered, not knowing if this was where he was supposed to be.

One of the men paused to stare at him. "Shit," he shouted to the other two, "it's a tourist." He picked up a box and set it on a platform attached to the machine gun. "Hell, yes," he yelled at Alex. "We need ammo. The lift's busted, got to haul it up by hand. You know your way around?" Alex shook his head. "Climb on up the catwalk and go straight back amidships. There are men on a fireline passing up shells. We need .40 calibers. As many boxes as you can carry. My name's Spiegle." He held out a hand as Alex came up the short ladder. Spiegle shook hands and inexplicably grinned, a good-looking young man with curly black hair, his smile white against his soot-stained pace. He turned and picked up another box and slammed it down by the gun. Another man tore off the top, lifted out a belt of shells, and loaded it into the magazine. The gun kept up a steady stream of fire, swiveling back and forth as it followed the Japanese planes. The ship rocked from another near miss.

Alex ran along the narrow catwalk until he came to a line of sweating cursing men handing boxes up through an open hatchway. He picked up two of the boxes stenciled with red .40s on the side. He was halfway back when a torpedo bomb hit, throwing him to the deck.

He pushed himself up, picked up the two boxes, and stumbled to the rail. The deck was torn and twisted where the explosion had punched through. Heavy steel plates were blown open like the petals of a rose. Smoke and the bright edge of flame poured out of the hole. Alex stood on the catwalk over the gun emplacement and looked down where the three men had been. The torpedo had hit the hull twenty feet from the gun. One man was missing, the other two were sprawled face down. Alex put the ammunition on the deck and jumped down the ladder.

He skidded on the blood. Spiegle rolled over and stared into the sky. His eyes focused on Alex. He tried to sit up, failed, and slumped back to the deck.

"Check Harris," he said, pointing in the direction of the other man.

Alex knelt beside the other man and turned him over. Harris was flayed from face to crotch. Alex looked away.

"Where's the other one? What happened to the other guy?" Alex asked, moving back to Spiegle. Spiegle waved his hand at the blood-splattered deck and gun. "Butch." He shook his head. "I think that's Butch all over the deck." He grunted as Alex helped him up and leaned him against the bulkhead. Alex unbuttoned Spiegle's shirt and peeled it away from the spreading blood. "Harris was firing, Butch was loading. Must have just blown him up, just . . ." He shook his head and shrugged. "Fucking Jap was coming right at us. Musta been a torpedo. I turned around to get another box and that's the last thing I remember."

Two near misses rocked the ship. Seawater cascaded down on them. For a moment the water washed away the blood, and Alex could see a hole the size of a quarter in Spiegle's chest. A small piece of shrapnel must have gone straight in. *No bubbles in the blood, missed the lung.* "We've got to get you some help." Another explosion. The ship trembled like a frightened animal.

"Just wrap me up. Stop the bleeding. Then see if the gun works. There's hurt men all over this ship. If we don't fight, we're going to the bottom anyway."

Alex pulled off his T-shirt and folded it into a square. He pressed it over the hole. As he worked, he could see nearby flames eating away at the paint on the deck. Other guns on the ship were still firing. He tore off what was left of Spiegle's shirt, wrapped it around and over the wound, and tied the arms tight. Spiegle looked down at the crude bandage. "Okay, okay, now get me up." Alex lifted the man, and they stood together, swaying, as Spiegle grimaced and held on to the bulkhead.

"See if the goddamn gun works," he said through gritted teeth.

Alex turned to the gun. "I don't know anything about—"

"Shit!" Spiegle leaned over and spit on the deck. "Where'd you come from, the moon? It's a goddamn .40 caliber machine gun. You grab the fucking handles, aim through the ring in front and squeeze the goddamn triggers. It takes two hands, I only got one." He held up his left arm. The hand at the end was a mass of blood. "You shoot, I'll load. I can still do that."

"We've got to get you—"

"Knock that shit off! For Christ's sake, look around. The fucking ship is on fire, we're taking water, Harris has had his face blown off, and you're whining about getting help. There is no fucking help! Now see if the goddamn gun works!"

Alex pulled the dead man away from the base of the gun. The handles were warm and sticky with blood. He tentatively squeezed the triggers. The gun blasted and slammed back at him.

"Good," Spiegle said, pulling himself over. "We got that much settled. Now I'm going to load, and you're going to shoot some fucking Japs. Don't hold on to it so tight or you'll break your wrists." He opened a box of shells and spilled out the long belt. "Kill something for your country."

The gun swiveled easily. Alex moved it up and down and back and forth. There was a large ring with cross hairs set into the shield in front of him. Two parallel barrels.

Somewhere down inside of him a little voice started to whimper. *Don't do it. Don't kill anything. You're against it, remember? You marched against the war in Vietnam.* He raised the gun. *You haven't hurt anybody yet. Don't do it.*

"There! Coming right at you!"

The Zero seemed to leap in from nowhere, wing guns firing. The plane grew in his sights, head on. Bullets whanged into the shield. Alex ducked as the plane banked and roared by. He swiveled the gun, tracking the plane.

"Shoot, you dumb shit!" Spiegle yelled, punching him on the shoulder. "Jesus H. Christ!"

Alex's hands were trembling. It was too fast. He squeezed the triggers and the gun bucked. Tracers blazed into the empty sky where there was no target.

"Not now! He's gone now."

Alex swiveled back.

"Now! Now!"

The Zero was coming in low. Straight at them. Alex squeezed and felt the recoil hammer his arms. He could see the tracers arcing high, above the oncoming plane. The plane opened up and bullets slammed into the gun shield and ricocheted around the emplacement. The noise was terrible. In the midst of it, Alex felt something break, some moral membrane that suddenly tore. Rational thought drained away. He was left with one overriding idea: *This fucker is trying to kill me!*

He leaned into the machine gun, using his body to hold it down. He squeezed the triggers. The recoil pounded into him. Blue powder-smoke filled the air. Spiegle was shouting at him. In his mind he saw a long line of dead men: Harris splayed on the deck near his feet, the gun blazed a stream of tracers into the sky, men being blown off their ships, the gun bucked against him, the wounded stumbling out of the water, the gun was hot, his arms trembled with effort, the man beneath the lathe, all the torn bleeding broken burned bodies, and the plane was still coming at him, growing impossibly large. *It's going to hit!* It banked at the last second and Alex swiveled and fired in front of the plane, and now it wasn't Spiegle who was shouting, *he* was shouting, because it was *this* motherfucker in *this* airplane who had killed all those men, and it was *this* motherfucker who was going to pay!

Red tracers sprayed into the sky and chips of airplane flew as the shells chewed their way down the fuselage. Chunks of tail assembly blasted apart as if slapped by a gigantic hand. The Zero wobbled, belched black smoke, began to spin, turned head over tail, and slammed into a huge crane on a drydock. Red-black flame burst upward and the concussion hit Alex with a thump. He was still clutching the handles of the gun, still squeezing the triggers, every muscle of his body straining, the firing mechanism clicking on empty, and at that moment he felt more alive than he had ever felt in his entire life. The gun stopped. He let go and stared at his hands; they were bloody, sweaty. His arms ached. He was breathing hard. He turned to Spiegle. Spiegle was sprawled on the deck, broken, bloody, blasted back against a pile of empty ammunition boxes. Alex heard another Zero begin its dive. *Get up, Spiegle, we're out of ammunition. Time to reload . . . time to . . . get up, Spiegle! Get the fuck up and help me!*

He looked around. The ship was dead in the water. Planes circled, beginning to descend on them. Wounded prey. Guns began firing. The world began to fade. He grabbed a box of ammunition and slammed it down beside the machine gun. "Not yet!" he shouted, scrabbling at the lid of the box. "Not yet, you motherfuckers!"

His voice, in the quiet living room, was a raw howl. Molly stood on the steps watching, horrified. Alex fell to his knees. "Get up, Spiegle! Get up and help me! For Christ's sake, get up and help me!"

6

ALEX IS LYING ON HIS BED. HE IS TEN
*years old. He feels the burning welts on his arms and his chest where the
ground bees have stung him. And where his father has hit him. He is in
his bed in the old stone house in Mexico.*

*They are here so his father can do his research, and then they will go
home and his father will write another book. But first his father will go
away into the hills. It's always the same. Even the part where his father
acts crazy before he goes away.*

*Alex was playing in the field down the hill from the house when the
first bee stung him. Then the bees swarmed out of the ground and he ran
for home, up the hill, feeling the mass of bees hit and crawl down his shirt
and sting. He outran them, was still running when he slammed through the
old screen door into the kitchen hollering and crying for his mother. But
only his father was there. His father turned from the sink and slapped Alex
to shut him up. Then Alex opened his shirt and bee bodies tumbled out and
his chest was beginning to swell and his father hit him again for being so
stupid as to step into a bees' nest.*

Later. Nighttime.

*He very carefully got out of his sagging bed and walked to the window.
He tried to hold his body as still as possible. He held his arms to his sides
like he was the Mummy. He stood at the screenless window, hands on the
smooth plaster windowsill, and looked out over the roofs of the small village.
The high full moon cast a silvery light on the white adobe houses, giving
the town a cool dead look. Pale white walls with red tile roofs gone black
in the night.*

"I hurt," he said, softly, to the starry moon-bright sky. He said it quietly so his father, asleep with his mother in the next room, would not hear.

WHEN THE grown-up Alex awoke, he did not remember the dream, the memory, the sting of bees. What he remembered, the battle, the dying, was much worse. It took three days before he could sleep again, before he felt that it would not drive him mad.

Three days.

Memory fades. It has been said that the only reason man perpetuates himself is because women forget the pain of childbirth. The edge soon begins to dull. Life asserts itself and the details of living soon separate men and women from the landscape of remembered pain.

His arms were burned from powder blasts. His chest bruised purple from the pounding of the gun. But his mind was burnt and bruised far beyond his body. For three days he lay in bed staying very still, as he felt memory slowly fade. It had broken him, blown all his internal safety valves. All the checks and balances that made life bearable had been torn away. The violence, the fear, the death, threatened to smother him. The world seemed unreal. Too soft, too smooth, too heavy, too quiet, as if waiting, rather than being.

The first day he could not speak of it. He lay on his bed with his arms not touching his sides. *I hurt.* By the third day he had told her, had to tell her, and he could see that she understood, but that she did not truly understand, that she could not, and that it separated them, drove the wedge of their difference between them, drove it deeper, but still he told her because she had to know and it eased him, made it more bearable.

"This is what I meant," she said. "When you asked me to marry you. I couldn't stand it, never knowing when you would go or how you would come back. Like this, broken. It's too much. Never knowing, waiting."

It was evening. They were going to bed, though he'd never really left the bed in the last three days. He sat and watched her as she pulled her soft nightgown over her head. The lamp on her dressing table cast a warm yellow light.

"Bent," he said. "Not broken. Not quite broken." *There is no defense here. No argument to make. The Tin Soldier is truly damaged.* Reason was on her side.

She sat at her dressing table and looked at him in the mirror. She picked up her hairbrush and ran her hand along the bristles. "It doesn't mean that I don't love you," she said. "Or that I don't want to be with you. But getting married is a step that I just can't take. Marriage is forever." She laughed flatly at the cliché. "A diamond is forever. Death is forever too. The way we are now, I have a tiny bit of distance. Being married means committing yourself totally to another person." She began brushing her hair. "It would take away my last defense. I think I'd go crazy."

He leaned back against the pillows and stared at the ceiling. He'd been doing that a lot the last few days. *No hope. What will happen to us? To me? I'm in it again, this is not over. What more can there be? Can I stop it? Would I stop it if I could?*

Life, right here, right now, seemed so normal to him. If he just didn't think. If he remembered nothing, pushed away the future, and the past, the moment seemed to glow with a kind of beauty. The steady ruffing sound of the brush through Molly's thick red hair. The warm yellow light. Preparing for bed. His body anticipating the soft touch of Molly's nightgown, her smooth warm skin, her body against his. But he could not hold the image, could not keep his mind from straying, from touching the wound. It was there, beneath it all, forever there. The sharp smell of gunpowder. The hard feel of the gun pounding against him. The heat of the flames. In his mind he saw the Zero break apart, flip, crash, blossom into bright flame. He heard the cries of the dying, the whispers of death. He drew a deep breath.

He tried to sound normal, eminently sane and reasonable. *If I act normal, I will be normal.* "That's a part of being married, isn't it? Being worried about the other person. Everybody worries." It sounded lame even to him. *Clutching at straws.*

"Alex, we're not talking about run-of-the-mill worries here. Heart attacks, muggings, getting hit by a car. This is major league stuff. For Christ's sake—Pearl Harbor?"

"All right, it's true, I'm an insurance risk. But your job hasn't turned out to be danger-free either."

She glanced at her hand. "The comparison is not even close. I'm going to Japan to research a story, and you're going . . . well, who knows where you're going? Just look at where you've been."

He ran a hand along his arm, feeling the small blisters where flecks of gunpowder had burned into his skin. "Just going to Japan to write a story? Come on, Molly. You're researching a story for the world's most influential newspaper on a major germ warfare laboratory. War crimes. *Heinous* war crimes. Something that these people have tried to keep hidden since the war." He shook his head in exasperation. "The Japanese aren't just a nation of clever little workers who build good electronics equipment. They found it in themselves to wage unprovoked war on a major portion of the globe. They were known for their cruelty, it was part of their code of life, they were savage, and brutal. They were evil. Forget your precious rock gardens and ancient temples and cherry blossoms. These people shocked even the Nazis. If you want to worry, worry about what might happen to you. I'll be worried about it, you can bet on that."

She shook her head. "That doesn't change anything. Anyway, it can't be that bad. The war was over more than forty years ago. This is a story that happened in the past. Besides, I'm writing about it, not living it. You keep acting as if I'm some sort of fragile maiden. Your little ballerina. I'm tougher than that, Alex. I come from a long line of capable women. My great-grandmother lived through several major famines back in the old country, and her daughter survived the *Titanic*. Remember, I know *where* I'm going, and *when* I'm going. You haven't any choice, or at least any that we've ever been able to discern. You don't go, Alex, you're *taken*. And you don't even know why." She turned away from him. She touched the base of the lamp on her table. It was old, made of brass with hanging crystal prisms. They had bought it one cool bright autumn day at a yard sale in Connecticut. Her hand rested on the base. When she reached for the switch, the crystals tinkled lightly. She sat for a moment in the dark, then moved to the bed.

He felt her pull the sheet back and get in. "Maybe this time I'll learn more about it," he said. "There must be a way to control it."

"Maybe." She didn't even bother to sound as if she meant it.

He could tell without looking that she was lying on her side, facing away from him. He wanted to put his arms around her, pull her into that spot in the center of the bed where she would be spooned against him, his face in her hair, at her neck in that soft place that felt and smelled of Molly, only of Molly. But there was too much between them that night. She would stay on her side of the bed, he on his. Too much between them.

. . .

A SONG DRIFTED into his consciousness: *Oh what a beautiful morning, Oh what a beautiful day* . . .

He opened his eyes. Somewhere, downstairs, Molly was playing the radio. A long rectangle of bright morning sunshine stretched across the ceiling above him. He must have slept late. *Radio?* Molly never turned on the radio. He turned his head and then held his breath.

There was an old woman in bed with him.

He lay perfectly still, looking at the wrinkled face, the sparse gray hair, the thin lips that moved slightly as she breathed. He swallowed, fighting back the urge to rip the covers off and leap screaming out of bed. He looked slowly around the room.

Where the hell was he? The room wasn't his room, but it seemed familiar. He was in a huge wooden bed—carved bedposts, dark wooden headboard. He was in bed with a woman he'd never seen before. An *old* woman he'd never seen before. He looked around the room again. It came to him. The reason the room looked familiar was because he was in his own house. He was in the third-floor bedroom in his own house. Not in the second-floor master bedroom where he'd gone to sleep. What the hell was he doing up here? *And who the hell was this old woman?* He had the sickening feeling that she belonged here, and he did not.

He closed his eyes for a minute and made an effort to slow his breathing. He looked at the old lady. She hadn't stirred. Very slowly, and very carefully, he pulled back the covers.

He forced himself to lie perfectly still while he counted to sixty. Slowly, an inch at a time, he swung his feet over the edge of the bed, and sat up.

The old lady rolled over.

He bit back a scream.

Her eyes remained closed. Her lips parted and she began to snore.

Every nerve in his body was shouting at him to run, to jump up, open the door, *and get the fuck out of there!* But he was naked. *Sure, just run out of the room, downstairs, out into the street, stark raving naked.*

He stood up. The bed creaked. The old lady continued to snore. He padded to the door, opened it, and peeked out into the hall. He heard the voice of the radio announcer, ". . . an old favorite from 1928, popular once again, Louis Alter's 'Manhattan Serenade' . . .

take it away, Harry James . . ." It sure looked like his third-floor hallway. But different. Dark rose wallpaper. Deep blue runner on the floor. Empty. *Thank God.*

He glanced back at the sleeping woman and stepped out into the hall, drawing the door closed behind him. He moved along the hall to the next doorway. The door was closed. He pressed his ear against it. He could hear nothing. Very carefully he turned the knob. For a moment he felt a rush of fear as he imagined the feel of the doorknob twisting beneath his hand. He imagined the door swinging open, a man standing inside, mouth open in surprise . . .

The door swung silently inward. The room was empty. Alex stepped in and closed the door behind him.

He allowed himself a sigh of relief. He was still in a world of trouble, but at least an old woman wasn't going to wake up next to a strange young man. A naked strange young man.

This room was the same size as the other. The bed was not as massive as the old lady's. More modern. There was a bed table with a lamp and a wind-up alarm clock. The old-fashioned kind with two little bells and strike-hammers at the top. He walked to the window, pulled back the lace curtain, and looked out. *Yep. West Tenth Street. New York City. I'm still home, sort of.*

Obviously he'd gone back while he was asleep. He used to get headaches before it happened, a few minutes' warning. No more. He wondered what that meant. He opened a closet, filled with women's clothes. There was a large-mirrored dressing table, top covered with crystal perfume bottles, brushes, round powder boxes, and crumpled facial tissues. He tried a tall armoir. He opened the narrow door and inhaled sharply as a thick metal coat hanger clanged against the back of the door. He waited. Nothing. He let out a breath and reached into the rack of clothing. He found dark pants, a white shirt, socks, and underwear. He hesitated, feeling a moment's revulsion at wearing someone else's underwear. He shrugged and pulled on the boxer shorts. They were too big, all of it was too big. No belt for the pants. He put the clothes on as quickly and quietly as possible, feeling immediately better once he was dressed, even though he wore a stranger's stolen clothes. He found a pair of black dress shoes under the bed, also the wrong size, but by now he just wanted to be out of there. He stuffed the shoes into the oversize pockets of the jacket.

Oh Jesus, someone coming up the stairs. He crept to the door, which was backed with a full-length mirror. He stared at himself. A guy in baggy old-fashioned clothes with a look of stark terror on his face. The footsteps stopped somewhere down below.

He took a deep breath. *Time to do it, time to get out of here.* He opened the door, looked out, stepped into the hall. All he had to do was go down the stairs to the second floor, around a corner, down that hall, down the next flight of stairs, and out the front door. *Yeah, sure, nothing to it, as long as you don't get caught.* He went to the stairs and began to creep down. He stopped halfway. He could hear someone doing something on the second floor. Silverware, maybe. Yes. Someone moving silverware around. Cleaning it? Putting it away? Setting a table? Dishes. A cabinet door closing. He went down until he could peek around the corner. At the end of the hall, where his bedroom should be, was a dining room. He could see the end of a table and a large sideboard. A woman walked by the doorway. He stood without breathing, the shock of seeing her freezing him in place. She moved out of sight. He was afraid to move and afraid not to move. He forced himself to walk quietly along the hallway, turn the corner, and tiptoe down the stairs. The stairs creaked, as they always had, but the melodic "Manhattan Serenade" masked his footsteps. At the bottom he looked back at the kitchen, right where it was supposed to be, and to the right at the living room. The furniture was different, but the rooms were the same. He quietly opened the front door. He stood for a moment, turned, and walked back into the house and lifted a newspaper off the same small table that stood in the hallway of his own house. The Sunday New York *Times.* Reassuringly thick and heavy. Just like home. He put the paper under his arm and walked out the door, down the steps, and without looking back, out to the sidewalk. He worked up enough moisture in his mouth to whistle a feeble little tune.

Oh, what a beautiful morning, Oh, what a beautiful day . . .

AND IT WAS a beautiful day. The sun was bright and the sky was blue and the air was cool. He stopped and slipped into the shoes, tied the laces, and glanced around him at the familiar and yet subtly different homes on the same street where he'd lived for ten years. Almost the same street. He breathed deeply, feeling relief flow into him as pure and clean as the air itself. He had overcome his first hurdle, the first few minutes of danger. He was almost light-headed with relief.

The houses didn't really look any newer . . . it was something else. He almost snapped his fingers as it came to him. No bars. No bars on the windows and doors. These people were not under siege from an army of drug addicts, burglars, mass killers, and rapists. He walked past Abingdon Square toward Greenwich Avenue. Small businesses, drugstores, more houses, guys in aprons out sweeping the sidewalk, moms with children and morning shoppers. The clothing styles prompted him to glance down at the newspaper—June 6, 1943. Ike and a man he didn't recognize, both in uniform, were pictured under the lead headline. Ike was smiling and he still had a little hair. Alex tucked the paper back under his arm. The familiar weight was comforting, a reminder that some things might be strange, but the New York *Times* is a constant.

Actually, it was hard to tell what *was* different. It all looked so ordinary that it was difficult to remember what it looked like in his own time. He would see a shop, notice that it was a hardware store, try to remember what it would be in forty years, and not be able to come up with much beyond the fact that he was pretty sure it wasn't a hardware store. A mom-and-pop grocery store would eventually become a hardcore sex shop; but the rest of it was vague, and growing vaguer. Somehow it didn't seem so important to figure out what was different. What he needed to do was figure out how to survive.

He walked down Fifth Avenue toward Washington Square, past a church where women in three-quarter-length dark-colored dresses and pillbox hats stood with men, most of them in uniform, chatting on the steps. Most of the men on the streets wore uniforms. There were many more women, though, than men. Women and children.

The white marble arch over Washington Square was the same, though if he remembered correctly, parties were still being held atop the arch. Or at least they had been, before the war. The fountain in the center of the park was functioning; that was a surprise. Children rollerskated, skipped, and ran down the radiating concrete pathways. No drug dealers, no spaced-out junkies, no bums, no filthy shambling shouting crazy people. The park had a wholesome look, a G-rating as compared to the X of his own day. He sat on a bench and smiled at a pretty young mother as she passed, pushing a huge old-fashioned perambulator. *No, not old-fashioned, not here, not yet.* The pretty mom smiled back at him.

He opened the paper on his lap and read the major headlines: "U.S. Hits Three Italian Battleships; Marshall at Africa Conferences; Rawson Heads Argentine Regime." He contemplated the smiling Ike for a few minutes, then began reading the smaller headlines. A coal strike had been averted. The Soviets had made some raids on Nazi bases. Milk deliveries and meat rationing made the front page, along with a summary of the current war news from around the world.

The page layout was pretty much the same as his own Sunday *Times*, but as he read the actual stories, the differences began to show up. After finishing several of the articles, he realized, in a general way, he didn't have a clue as to what they were about. He could read them, make sense of the words, but the meaning escaped him.

"Milk Deliveries Tardily Resumed. Drivers Leave Loading Plants Several Hours Behind Their Regular Schedules: Resumption of milk deliveries in the metropolitan area got off to an encouraging if shaky start yesterday morning, following acceptance Friday night of the Office of Defense Transportation's skip-a-day delivery order by officials of the Milk Wagon Drivers' Union, an affiliate of the American Federation of Labor.

"In most of the milk plants, trucks had pulled away from the loading platforms carrying double loads by 10:30 A.M., which is several hours later than the regular scheduled starting time.

"The one exception was the Riverside plant of the Borden Company . . ."

His eyes skipped on down the column, searching for clarifying details and some background. It seemed the Riverside workers were finally prevailed upon by Mayor La Guardia, who appealed to their higher instincts by reminding them, "not only as good sports, but as good Americans," that the children of the city depended on these deliveries. Alex read the whole article, but never figured out why the deliveries had been suspended in the first place, and what the schedule would be in the future. He moved along to another story, an impending strike by the nation's coal miners. The miners had threatened to strike twice, each time calling it off when the War Labor Board promised reprisals. Roosevelt had sent a telegram ordering them back to work, a new deadline had been set. The miners' complaints seemed to center around "portal to portal" questions, whatever those were.

He decided to forget the smaller stories for the moment, and go to the major pieces. "U.S. Hits Three Italian Battleships" was pretty straightforward, an account of a major Superfortress raid against the harbor of Spezia. "Marshall at African Conferences" was a report on a conference between Churchill and the Allied chiefs, George C. Marshall and Eisenhower. The account was so bland that it was obvious that any news of substance must have been kept secret. The last lead story told of a *coup d'état* in Argentina that overthrew an isolationist government and replaced it with a military government friendlier to the interests of the United States. None of the names of those involved in this story were familiar to Alex.

He put the paper down. On the far side of the fountain two orators on boxes shouted at each other. A small laughing crowd had gathered around them. A soldier with a guitar sat on the edge of the fountain, strumming and humming a song.

Alex felt isolated from the activity around him, as if he were sitting in a bubble looking out at someone else's world. The paper had taken away his first feelings of euphoria. A newspaper is like a friend; you read it knowing details, bringing common knowledge that assumes familiarity, a shared background. Here the subtleties and details were denied him, and he felt cut off, a stranger in a place that *looked* friendly, that *appeared* to be his home, but wasn't. He was alone.

He didn't need to take inventory. He owned nothing besides the clothes on his back, and he had stolen them. The only thing he possessed of any value was his knowledge of the future, and right here and now, that seemed of little use. What was he going to do, snag a passerby and sell him the idea of transistor radios? *Excuse me, soldier, the war will be over in a couple of years. Can you spare me a dime?*

He glanced through the newspaper, hoping that something would spark an idea. Longchamps Restaurant was having a special on sliced filet mignon sauté, fresh broccoli, and hollandaise potatoes for $1.50. His stomach growled. He turned the page. Saks was having a sale on Elizabeth Arden's Velva Leg Film. The drawing of the model looked a little like Molly. Leg Film, the ad promised, was soft, smooth, and water-resistant. Obviously a wartime substitute for nylon stockings. He looked at the drawing of the woman painting her legs and felt an odd mix of conflicting images: absurdity, loneliness, with just a touch of sex. Molly, Molly, where are you now? Absurdity won out over self-pity and he laughed at himself, mooning over a drawing of a woman painting her legs. *Time to take control, Alex. You are alone. The long slide into self-pity will get you nowhere. You may be here for the long haul.* He had a momentary image of a stern Alex Balfour slapping sanity back into a weak, sobbing Alex Balfour. *Get a grip on yourself, man!*

He opened the paper again, this time to the want ads. He found his eyes wandering back to the Longchamps Restaurant ad and the filet mignon. Get a job in a restaurant? He noticed they had a branch on Twelfth Street. He stood, folded his newspaper, and headed back up the avenue to find work.

7

ALEX WAS GONE. SOMETIME IN THE MIDDLE
of the night, he had left her and gone away; back. In the morning she
awoke and touched the bed where he had been. And as she touched
the empty bed and felt his absence, she knew that the argument of
the night before, her reasoned rejection of marriage, had been an
intellectual decision, a judgment of the mind rather than a reflection
of her heart. It was a problem she had, overcompensating for what
she feared were gender frailties by relying solely on her intellect. It
often led her down paths she didn't wish to travel, to destinations she
hadn't intended on visiting.

And he was truly gone. She could feel it in the house, could always
feel it when he was in the past, a difference in magnitude, a special
emptiness that made her feel as if she should go around and cover the
furniture with sheets, stand at the doorway for one last look, turn out
the lights and lock the door behind her. The house was *his* house,
even though she lived there. When he was away, it felt as though the
soul had gone out of it.

She shook off these thoughts. *It's just a house. I live here too.* He
had always come back. Usually injured in some way, mentally as well
as physically, but he had always returned, and she would have to
believe he would do so again. It was belief, and trust, that bound her
to him, that drew him back. And love.

She dressed quickly, trying not to look at the empty bed, trying
not to think about how they had left each other the night before. She
felt the burden of fault, knowing that she had been right, but that

being right wasn't necessarily the best thing to be. Now that it was upon her, his absence, she found that it was worse than she remembered, and that being married, having that last commitment, like emotional money saved, might have eased her loss.

The house was so quiet. The small clatter of her teacup on the saucer seemed harsh. A square of sunlight warming the bare-wood countertop seemed out of place. She drank her tea, rinsed the cup out, gathered up her things, and went to work. She did not pause at the front door and look back.

FOR A WEEK he washed dishes at Longchamps. The first day, instead of money, they gave him a turkey dinner with dressing, mashed potatoes, and giblet gravy, fresh asparagus with hollandaise sauce, and a bowlful of candied sweet potatoes. They were very big on hollandaise at the Longchamps, and by the end of the week he had grown to hate it. But the food was good, filling, and plentiful. And they let him sleep in a storage room behind the kitchen.

He found that he could have hired on almost anywhere. New York was booming and able-bodied men were at a premium. They were, in fact, so rare as to cause comment. He found that from the very first he had to have a story ready to explain his civilian status. His first thought was to claim a Pearl Harbor–related disability, but while that would have given him a certain panache, he would have had to come up with a wound serious enough to have demobilized him, but not serious enough to show. It seemed too complicated. After reading the newspaper he decided to say he was a coal miner from West Virginia, come to New York to see the sights before enlisting. Because the coal miners were reviled by the public for disrupting the war economy, Alex posed as a man who had quit the job in disgust. This cast him in a favorable light, and explained his lack of spare clothing and money. Coal miners, especially those from West Virginia, were supposed to be poor, and stupid. Which explained his many lapses when it came to some piece of common knowledge that any New Yorker would know. "Don't ask Balfour," they'd say. "He's from West-by-God-Virginia."

He spent his spare time walking around New York. He read the newspapers every day, familiarizing himself with his environment.

They locked him in at night. A dishwasher was too lowly to have his own key to the restaurant, so he was locked in with no one for company other than a few mice he'd found nesting in the fifty-pound bags of rice. He made a crude bed for himself out of a pile of empty potato sacks. He lay in the stuffy storage room in the harsh light of a bare light bulb, surrounded by cans and boxes and bags of food. Loneliness settled over him like a heavy blanket. All the old questions that he'd never been able to answer would present themselves in insistent ranks, marching forward, one after another. He saw himself as the sorcerer's apprentice, faced with row after row of implacable broomsticks and legions of unstoppable buckets filling the small room with question marks. Only in his case there was no wise magician to break in and reverse the damage. *Why am I here? How long will I be here? How can I escape? Should I try to change anything? Is it possible to change anything? Why? How? Where? When?* There were still no answers. He stared at the wooden shelves of his prison and felt as if he should be drawing little lines on the wall, marking off time served.

And he thought of Molly. The advice columnist, Dear Abby, always warned: *Never go to bed at night when you and your wife are both angry.* The same advice applied to girlfriends. This was the result. You might be taken back in time without a chance to apologize. Where was Molly now? What was she doing? Was she still angry? There were no answers on the shelves of canned beans, tomatoes, corn, and beets.

If he was here, in 1943, for the foreseeable future, what was he to do? Building a career as a dishwasher was hardly an answer. He had to do something. He had always felt that he was drawn to other times for a reason, for some specific purpose. To think anything else was to see it as a purely random act, some enigmatic quirk of nature that struck him only because of a genetic flaw. He could not believe that, or would not believe it. If it were true, his actions counted for nothing, he was reduced to a purposeless wandering, without destination or intent.

It was the war, it had to be. The war surrounded him, as it surrounded everyone. All actions were based on one's interaction with the war. It was as much a presence as the wind, the rain, the bright sun. The horror of Pearl Harbor still clung to him like some unforgettable pestilential odor. He would awake at night, the echo of the battle still sounding. It had to be the war, but what was his part in it?

He began to hammer out a plan. Or at least a course of action. Using the back of an old grocery bag, he made a chart of people who were alive in this time.

His father and mother were alive, though not yet married. His father would be twenty-nine, probably already teaching at Ohio Wesleyan. Alex wondered if that was a deferred occupation. He knew little of his father's background, other than the canned bio that was handed out to journalists in later years. From family conversation he gathered that the bio was almost as much a figment of his father's imagination as were the historical novels that he wrote. What his father did during the war was a mystery to Alex. His mother would still be a teenager, just beginning college. During graduate school she would fall in love with her English teacher, his father, and in 1952 they would marry. Late that same year he would be born.

His paternal grandfather would be alive, teaching at Yale, too old for the draft. There were no uncles or aunts on his father's side, and none that he knew of on his mother's. As he sat in the storeroom reviewing the bare skeleton of his family tree, he saw that his past was largely unknown. His father had consumed them, he and his mother, leaving them with little opportunity for family outside their own small nucleus. The cold bare limbs of his spindly family tree were patterns of his own life, his lack of a past.

The answer was there all along, so close that he had only to look beyond the family tree to the man standing beside it. Surrey. Maxwell Surrey. The man who had been his family's only real friend, and after his parents' death, almost his own father.

In 1969, Alex's father and mother had disappeared in a small plane while flying to Newfoundland to research one of his father's novels. The plane had gone down over the ocean and the bodies had never been recovered. His mother's had undoubtedly sunk beneath the waves to become part of the ocean, but his father was quite probably still alive, somewhere in the past, having been taken from the pilot's seat of the plane and thrust back to another time.

He thought about going to his father at the college where he taught, confronting him, telling him he was his son from the future. What good would it do? None. He had learned years ago that his father was not someone to trust.

But Surrey was different. He and Surrey had been friends, shared a time of danger. Surrey had been a brother to him then, a father later. Surrey was the only man alive who would understand who he was.

He worked long enough to buy a new set of clothes and a ticket to Princeton. He turned in his apron and boarded the train for New Jersey and Surrey. He didn't know what he would say when he got there, or what he would do if Surrey was somewhere else. But at least it was a plan. Movement. A purpose.

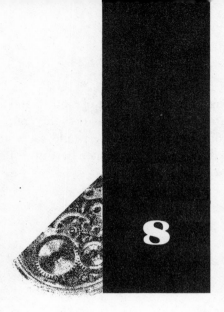

8

DURING THE FIFTIES AND THE SIXTIES,
Alex had shuttled between Manhattan and Princeton more times than
he could remember. As a child, he was often shipped from home in
Connecticut to Surrey in Princeton, via Manhattan. When he was
older, he was allowed to get off the train in New York and wander
the streets before continuing on to New Jersey. His usual itinerary
was to hang around Greenwich Village and eat sausage sandwiches
and egg rolls while watching the endlessly fascinating panorama of
hippies, aging beatniks, and assorted bums, begging in the parks,
drinking in the bars, playing chess, arguing, muttering to themselves,
and being preyed upon.

After the death of his parents, he went to Princeton to live with
Surrey. He stayed on through college, and then bought his West Tenth
Street townhouse in New York. The trips continued, New York to
Princeton, to visit the old man as he grew even older. In 1986, it had
ended. Surrey had died.

And now, in 1943, he was going back again, to find Maxwell Surrey,
alive, forty-six years old, teaching at Princeton. He would have not
yet met Alex's father, but he would know Alex. In 1917, in revolutionary Russia, he and Surrey had fought together. Now he was going
to have to explain to Surrey why he, Alex, was only three years older
than he had been in those dangerous days while Surrey had aged
twenty-five years in normal fashion.

The familiar train ride was only slightly less familiar than he remembered it. The landscape was primarily industrial in either case, lines of smoking factories and skeletal refineries interrupted by acres of flat wetlands.

He opened up his New York *Times Magazine*, saved from the Sunday before. He had been reading all the articles carefully, working on assimilating the details of the culture so he wouldn't appear stupid. He paged back toward the crossword puzzle. Along the way he scanned various articles, all war-oriented. Profiles of the men leading the American Army. What the average soldier liked to eat. Was Churchill a better painter than Hitler? He stopped at the food section, a feature he always read. The subject of the piece was what the thrifty homemaker could do with her leftovers. The recipes showed a pre–James Beard lack of sophistication. Leftover meat, the article advised, should you have been lucky enough to acquire a piece of meat in the first place, could be nicely turned into a veal curry. The ingredients were meat, of any variety, onion, celery, apple, curry powder, salt, pepper, water, Worcester sauce, and molasses. One simply mixed all the ingredients together and heated them. This dish was accompanied by Victory Garden Ring, which incorporated leftover vegetables bound together by a white sauce and egg whites, and baked in a ring mold. Dessert was Cereal Dessert: leftover cereal, milk, eggs, sugar, and vanilla, stirred and baked for thirty minutes, served hot or cold with thin cream. Not exactly *haute cuisine*, but as everyone said, *Don't ya know, there's a war on.*

He was surprised by the comfortable hominess of the New York *Times*. The entire newspaper was laced with it, giving it a local-paper sort of charm, as opposed to the "Newspaper of Record" image the *Times* would assume in later years. Here was a section devoted to poultry and poultry equipment, with how-to articles on raising your own chickens. A large advertisement on this page announced that fourteen-week-old pullets could be purchased at Macy's in their fifth-floor Barnyard Department. Alex made a mental note to check out the barnyard at Macy's.

He turned to the crossword puzzle and stared at the black and white checkerboard.

CROSSWORD PUZZLES

WITH CLUES FROM THE NEWS
By Willard N. Jordan

ACROSS

1 Most northern town in Africa.
8 Angarita's capital.
15 Huge Allied-Jap naval arena.
22 Sweet-smelling.
23 One of our newest 35,000-ton battleships.
24 Democracy's staunchest supporter.
25 Sub base blasted by Allied bombers.
26 Men trained at Quantico.
27 Slackening agent.
28 Central Asian river, 800 miles to Lake Balkhash.
29 Lapse.
30 Made wrathful.
31 Ancient Hebrew coin.
33 The Cotton State: Abbr.
34 Worthless.
36 Betray.
38 Cape or headland.
40 Arabian seaport guarding Red Sea gateway.
41 Sudden trial: Colloq.
43 Tiny water-locked area.
44 Soft friable limestone.
46 Advocate.
48 Roman goddess of horses.
49 Expiatist.
51 Stroll aimlessly.
53 Legal holder on property.
54 Carry too far.
55 Petitioned.
57 Inventor of our Army's new automatic rifle.
59 Presignification.
60 Furnished with wooden shoes.
64 Obstruct.
65 To wave weapons menacingly.
69 Key Black Earth city.
70 Jap chief of Military Affairs Bureau.
72 Nile Valley dweller.
74 Nautical rope.
75 Old Greek dirge.
77 Slip or blunder: Slang.
79 Pert. to Persia.
81 Old Dial.
83 Wealthy Arkansas Indians.
84 Precious.
85 Measure in any way.
86 Army follower selling provisions and liquors.
88 Hungarian Commune
89 Sea between Greece and S. Italy.
91 Whiten.
93 Gaselle-like antelope of Somaliland.
94 Dollar bills.
96 Fit for plowing.
98 Heavily bombed Nazi-held airfield in France.
100 Slope or bevel.
101 Birth.
103 Plodder.
105 Daughter of Cadmus: Gr. Myth.
107 Iroquoian Indian.
108 Large wax candle of France.
109 Yugoslav river.
110 Province having Sarajevo as its capital.
113 Unit of metric weight.
114 Apiece.
116 Producing agreeable impressions.
121 Ocular.
122 Maker of counterfeit specie.
124 Sudden bombing.
126 Gladly or willingly: Dial.
127 Secular.
128 "Jean ____," French battleship.
129 Tortoise beak.
131 Old road to Rome.
133 Mineral tar.
134 German city in Danube circle.
135 U. S. bomber.
137 Military opposite of van.
139 Bewilderment.
141 Noxious.
143 Greenish-blue color.
144 German industrial center razed by Allied bombs.
146 Dominican port settled by Columbus in 1493.
148 State formally.
149 Sea forming part of Indian Ocean.
150 Repairer of telegraph wires.
151 Upper House member.
152 Excess of liberty.
153 Stout Allied nation.

DOWN

1 La Paz is its capital.
2 A great admirer.
3 The Cape polecat.
4 Assam silkworm.
5 Filled with fish eggs.
6 City of 219,000 population, near ancient Carthage.
7 Great regard.
8 Sicilian lord in "Winter's Tale."
9 Winglike.
10 Less frequent.
11 Residence.
12 Item on the ration list.
13 Archaeological shaping cores.
14 Skipped lightly: Slang.
15 U.S. writer of satirical verse.
16 Confidential agent in India.
17 Hermit's hut.
18 Major Gen. Baker's first name.
19 Fastening device.
20 American outpost since July, 1914.
21 Philippine water buffalo.
32 Britain's Foreign Minister.
35 Geological time division.
37 This costs red points.
39 Consideration paid.
41 Disburses.
43 Critical examination.
45 Sorcerer.
47 Weasand or trachea.
48 Uniform.
50 French streets.
52 Tunisian rail junction.
54 Natives of Southeast Arabian State.
56 Kind of Dutch cheese.
58 Overmastering wrath.
59 Seaport of Algeria.
60 Islands east of New Guinea.
61 Battleship sunk in Pearl Harbor.
62 Sacred Indian city.
63 Swan genus.
64 Resembling American Beauties.
65 Baptista's daughter in "Taming of the Shrew."
66 Romance language.
67 Gulf on west Italian coast.
68 Combine with water.
71 In neat fashion.
73 Ecstasy.
76 Glider used in Winter sports.
78 Allied soldier.
80 Lionet.
83 Cossack cavalry squadron.
85 Blacksmith's hammer.
87 Mexican Indian of pre-Spanish conquest period.
90 Nazi-fortified seaport on Mediterranean.
91 Obscure.
92 Give audience to.
95 Dramatic.

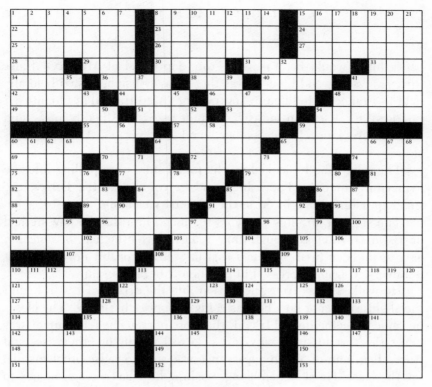

97 German city making Focke-Wulf planes.
99 Votaresses.
102 King of Sweden, 1560–1568.
104 Household stuff.
106 Chinese money of account.
108 Censorious.
109 Forward girl.
110 Large veterinary pills.
111 Iridescent.

112 U. S. Secretary of War.
113 Former Malta commander.
115 Resident of Egypt's capital.
117 Pen point.
118 Cranelike Brazilian bird.
119 Designating the filbert or hazelnut.
120 Pasture or meadow.
122 Profession.
123 Array again.
125 Narrow passage between hills.

128 Italian bank.
130 Commence.
132 Colophony.
135 Fabricate.
136 A purple seaweed.
138 Mallard genus.
140 Criminal group.
143 Philippine dyewood tree.
145 Sealing wax ingredient.
147 Bengal quince.

In his own time, he was usually able to finish the puzzle, with help from Molly. But here many of the clues were so war-related he was finding it rough going. He squinted at the tiny clues, trying to come up with answers as the train clacked along through a large reedy wetland. He lowered the paper and glanced out the window. In these stretches of New Jersey he always half expected to see wild swamp men appear, wraithlike, out of the mists, poling narrow home-built skiffs and wearing strings of dead muskrats bandoleered across their chests.

He went back to his puzzle.

Some of the clues were easy. "Huge Allied-Jap naval arena" was obviously PACIFIC. "Democracy's staunchest supporter" was AMERICA. But he hadn't the slightest idea what "One of our newest 35,000-ton battleships" would be. Likewise, the "Jap Chief of Military Affairs Bureau" was beyond him, as was the "Heavily bombed Nazi-held airfield in France." He filled in MARINE for "Men trained at Quantico," COLOGNE for "German industrial center razed by Allied bombs," and then got stuck on "U. S. bomber," and " 'Jean———,' French battleship."

The next time he looked up, he found they were pulling into the Princeton Junction. There he found he could take the Dinky, the small spur line, straight on to the university campus.

The sight of strolling students reminded him that by now he had missed his own class enough times to ensure that he had, *in abstentia*, once again been fired. The fact that he would probably never teach at a university again depressed him. Then it began to rain.

He walked away from the station into the drizzle. He still hadn't the slightest idea of how he was going to approach Surrey. The closer he came to seeing his old friend, the more nervous he felt. Surrey was never the sort to suffer any sort of a fool, gladly or otherwise, and Alex's Fountain-of-Youth appearance was sure to cause problems. To say the least. He slouched along, wishing he'd had enough money to buy a decent jacket, aware that he probably looked like nothing more than a fairly well-dressed bum.

Mercer Street, where Surrey lived, appeared little different than it would in the future. The houses were all wood frame or brick, solid, well-built structures owned by well-to-do professors. The trees were full and thick, maples mostly, bright green against the rainy gray sky. Alex stood, halfway down the block, staring at Surrey's white frame house with the deep blue trim. Rain trickled down his shirt collar in the back. His feet were damp, his socks sponging up puddled water through the holes in his stolen shoes.

"Nice house, isn't it? You want to buy it or what?"

Alex turned to the man at his side. It was Surrey, unmistakably Surrey. He was carrying a brown paper grocery bag and an umbrella. His expression was a mixture of curiosity, impatience, and irritation.

"It's got oak floors, two fireplaces, and a fresh coat of paint. Well, fresh two years ago. Wait a minute! For Christ's sake, don't I know you?" He was frowning.

Alex cleared his throat. "Well, Max . . ." Now that he was here, face to face, he still hadn't come up with a rational way to broach the subject. His usual method in these situations was to stumble around a lot and try to lie as little as possible. There really wasn't any good way to do it, so he just did it. "It's me, Alex. Remember me?"

Surrey nodded. "Christ on a crutch. Twenty-five years ago. Russia. We almost got killed together. How could I forget?" He shook his head. "I don't believe it. You're too young for the Alex I know."

"Yeah, well, it's true. Believe it, Max. It's me."

Surrey shook his head again. "So, come on, let's get in out of the rain. You can explain it to me inside. This ought to be good."

Max's study was a room Alex had always loved. The heavy wooden desk was piled high with books, the long red Morris sofa was in its usual position against the wall, facing the desk. The tall French windows looked out on a garden with small staked tomatoes and other vegetables lined in neat rows. In his own time, the vegetables would be flowers. Still in neat rows.

Surrey sat down at his desk. Alex took the sofa. Each of them had assumed the same positions in this room they would take throughout the rest of their lives. "Explain," Surrey said, with a wave of his hand. The wave was meant to include Alex's appearance, his arrival, his purpose, and all attendent details.

"I arrived in New York a few weeks ago," Alex began. He gestured at himself. "I lost all my clothes. I haven't had time to get new ones." *Lie number one.*

"All right," Surrey said, waving again impatiently, "that explains the clothes. Now, you."

Alex found himself contemplating Surrey. The man's flyaway fox-red hair was just beginning to show traces of gray. In old age, Surrey's hair would be completely white, a shaggy aureole. This Surrey, though, seemed anything but old. He appeared to be in the peak of health. He was shorter than Alex, around five-seven, solid but in no way fat. His complexion was ruddy. This particular Surrey was disconcerting to Alex, neither young nor old, neither the man that he had known, or the man he would know.

Surrey sat back in his chair. "A long time ago," he said, "you told me that someday I'd understand what was going on. You remember that?" Alex nodded. Back in Russia. They'd been about to take on a contingent of the Red Army. He'd said it just to get out of telling Surrey more lies. Surrey went on. "We were just about to do something that no one in this world knows we did. Or almost no one. We both got shot for our trouble, some other people died. Maybe we made a difference, maybe we didn't. I don't know. *But I still don't know what the hell is going on!* Now more than ever. No more, Alex. Please. This time I want to know the truth."

Alex nodded. This time he was going to tell him. And damn the consequences. "Have you ever read Wells? H.G., not Orson."

"Of course. *The Outline of History.* Bunk, most of it."

"Not the history. The science fiction. *The Time Machine.*"

Surrey snorted. "Not recently. As a child, yes, *Time Machine, The War of the Worlds.*"

"Ever read Twain's *A Connecticut Yankee in King Arthur's Court?*" He was almost afraid to mention that one. His association to Twain was closer than Surrey could ever guess.

"Yes, yes. What's the point?" He stopped for a moment. "Wait, let me guess. You're about to tell me that you've just breezed in from the past."

"The future," Alex said.

There was a long silence. Surrey stood up and went to the windows that looked out over the garden. "All right, say your piece. Give it to me straight."

"I come from the future. When we knew each other before, twenty-five years ago, it was the same thing. Then, I was in the year 1984 and I found myself unexpectedly in 1917. Now I've advanced to 1990 so it's a shock to suddenly be here with you in 1943. I don't know why I'm able to go back into the past. It just happens. I can't control it."

Surrey stood looking out the window, hands clasped behind his back. "I guess that would explain a few things," he said grudgingly, almost to himself. "Goddamn. I always knew there was something peculiar going on. You always had too many answers. And look at you now, you don't look any older than I can remember. Hell, I'm middle-aged, and you're young. Relative to me, anyway." He shook his head. "I don't believe it, but I can't *not* believe you. It explains too many things. All right, prove it. Who's going to win the pennant this year?"

"Jesus, I don't know. I don't know who won the pennant this year in my *own* time."

"Who's going to win the war?"

"The Allies. In 1945."

"Anyone could guess that. Playing Twenty Questions isn't going to prove anything." He turned around and contemplated Alex. "There's one person who can get to the bottom of this. Time. That's the question. We'll go see a friend of mine."

"No," Alex said, alarmed. "No one else can know this. I shouldn't have told you. I shouldn't even have come here." He started to stand up.

Surrey held up a hand. "This man's a scientist. He'll understand."

Alex had a vision of being strapped to a chair, alligator clips attached to his scalp, wires running to machines, blinking lights, sparks flying. Angry villagers gathering outside. He got to his feet. *Time to go, my mistake. Sorry, Surrey.*

"No," Surrey commanded, reading the look on Alex's face. "This man will understand, and he's a friend. If you don't want to tell, then don't, but I think you *will* tell him."

SURREY KNOCKED on the door. Alex thought he knew what to expect, but he was still surprised. The past was always taking him by surprise. Just when he thought he had it figured, knew what was going to happen, or what had already happened.

Albert Einstein. With the sweet basset-hound eyes. Einstein of the college posters, the T-shirts, and the *Life* magazine photographs. Eccentric, absent-minded, kindly old Einstein. Here he was at the front door, dressed just like Alex had always read: shapeless gray sweatshirt with a fountain pen stuck in the collar, nondescript pants, shoes without socks. Shock of white hair, thick gray mustache. But the overall impression he'd expected was wrong. The eyes *weren't* sad. What came across as sadness in photographs was in fact a deep, profound intelligence. Large, soft, brown eyes that seemed to understand. Eyes that encouraged you to speak, that promised answers. Sharp, wise, humorous, honest, and humane. All at once. *Amazing.*

"Yes, yes, Max, come in," Einstein said, backing away from the door. They had walked the two blocks from Max's house. Einstein's was similar, white frame, but with green trim. Tidy hedge, well-kept lawn. They stood inside the door while Einstein introduced his sister, a heavy plain woman dressed in a dotted Swiss dress. "Upstairs," he said. "For talk." Einstein's words were thick with German consonants. They trooped up the stairs and down a hallway to a study at the back of the house.

They settled into chairs. Einstein picked up an old pipe. "I'm not

ʾpermitted to smoke," he explained, "but I still like to hold my pipe. The old are allowed only small pleasures, the devil has put a penalty on all of the things we enjoy. Either we suffer in our health, or we suffer in our soul. Or we get fat." He looked at Surrey. "Now, Max, tell me how it is that I may help you. You said on the telephone that you have a problem. This concerns your friend?" he nodded at Alex.

"Yes, Albert." Surrey sat up straight in his chair. "Let me tell you first of all that Alex and I are old friends. He and I shared an adventure many years ago. Sometime I'll tell you about it, an interesting story. But for now, I have an even more interesting question. Do you think time travel is possible?"

Einstein smiled. He looked at the pipe in his hand. "Yes. A very interesting question. But very inelegantly put. Are you asking if I believe that time travels or that we travel through time? That time itself is an entity that performs some sort of movement? Please, Max. More information. Expand, Max."

"This is the way he always talks," Surrey said to Alex. "Expand, Max, expand." He settled back in his chair. "Well, it's true, I don't have your scientist's precision. I'm a historian." He turned to Alex. "This is an old argument. Anyway, Albert, you're always dealing with what might be. I deal with what has been. Let me put it this way. Very simple. Is it possible for a man to move forward or backward in time? From the future to the past?"

Einstein put the pipe in his mouth, took it out, looked at it, and sighed. "I think better when I smoke. For twenty years I am looking for a big theory, a field theory. I think I could find it if they would let me smoke." He looked out a large window into a maple tree. "Time," he said softly. He looked back at Alex and nodded. "I am the expert, yes? Einstein, the man who has liberated the world from the unbreakable rule of before and after." His laugh was a short burst. "Somehow people think that my relativity theory has given them special dispensation from their allotted three-score ten. It is amazing to me how these notions begin, they have no basis in anything *I* have said. And so now comes Max"—he smiled at Alex—"a reasonable man, to ask me about temporal displacement. Let me say, first of all, that this is not so ridiculous a question, at least in theory. If I were forced to answer, I would probably say yes, that it is possible, at least on an atomic level. But if you were asking me, as you seem to be, if it is possible for a man to do so, I would have to say no. What you must remember is that relativity is a theory that measures events at the speed of light. Since it is impossible for man to travel at the speed of light, then it is also impossible that he may take advantage of the special circumstances that occur there. This is only common sense, Max."

Surrey looked at Alex with raised eyebrows. "So you would not believe a man who came to you and said he was either from the past or the future?"

Einstein sighed. "That is a different question. People are always asking me to believe something. Do you remember that man Reich who came here and bothered me? The one who sent that silly box? We use it now to store potatoes. Believe this, he said. What is so important about my belief? What difference could it make? I may believe something today and then next week change my mind when I learn some new fact to change that belief. Now, if your time traveler came to me, I would listen to him with interest. The same way I listened to Mr. Reich. I would hear what he had to say. If it was useful or interesting, then it would be good for me to hear it. Whether or not I believed him would be another matter. It is like my belief, or my lack of belief in quantum theory: it explains much, but I do not like it. Even if I *must* believe it, I won't believe it." He put his pipe down on the cluttered table at his side. "And you," he said to Alex, "are you the man from the past?"

Karma time, as we used to say back in the old days. How can I lie? Of course there were a hundred good reasons to lie, reasons he'd been over a hundred times before in different circumstances. *I'm sick of lying. Sick of the bullshit.* If there was one virtue that Einstein seemed to embody, it was trust. Truth.

"The future," Alex said. "I come to you from the future."

Einstein sat back in his chair and smiled. And then, unexpectedly, he laughed. "Good." Einstein nodded, his eyes bright. "Very good. I have many questions to ask."

The door opened and Einstein's sister appeared with a plate of sausages, cheese, and bread. She pushed a pile of papers to the side on the low table and put the plate down. "Eat," she said. "No more questions for the professor this evening. We must not tire him." She left the room and reappeared with a pot of tea and cups. Alex and Max made themselves sandwiches while Einstein poured the tea. "Eat, Albert," Einstein's sister said, "the doctor says you must eat."

"Yes, yes," Einstein said as he loudly sipped his tea. "I must eat.

No candy, no spirits, no pipe, no cigars. As if any of it made a difference. Or as if I cared."

"You don't fear death, Albert?" Max asked around a mouthful of sausage. "No one wants to die."

"Wants? Who said wants? I said it made no difference. I am a part of life. Death is also a part of life. My molecules will simply be distributed in another way. Please, Max, no metaphysics. I am too old and too weak for such discussions." He turned to Alex. "Besides, we are talking of time, of the future. Tell me, Alex, do you have a prediction for us?"

Alex could see that Einstein was joking. That the man thought that Max was playing some elaborate practical joke on him. That Einstein didn't believe him. Probably thought him, if not joking, crazy. He didn't really blame him. Einstein had to turn down audiences from every crank with a pet theory, from advertisers and merchants, from students and teachers. The scientist was badgered and baited because he was thought to be the smartest man in the known world. So Einstein didn't believe him. They could sit around this room and joke about the past, about time, or the future. But unless he was able to convince Einstein that this was no joke, that he was not another Wilhelm Reich with an Orgone Box, there was no point in being here. And he *was* here, sitting in the same room with the one man in this world who could possibly cast some light on his ability, might possibly even give him a clue on how to control it. Besides, there had to be a purpose to his being with Einstein. If there wasn't purpose, then it all was pure chance, a roll of the dice. He had to make Einstein believe.

"There will be an atomic bomb," Alex said. "It will be made by America, is being made right now. It will be dropped on the Japanese. Thousands, many thousands, hundreds of thousands will die." *And the world will live in the shadow of this bomb forever and ever, Amen.* Alex felt himself flush. If ever there was a moment when the hand of fate, or God, or the big Nobodaddy in the sky, should strike him down, this was it. Max sat frozen, sandwich half-raised. Einstein stared at him. There was no trace of humor now.

"What the hell are you talking about?" Surrey asked.

"Do not ask," Einstein said, his eyes still on Alex. "Forget what he has said, please, Max. It is a matter of importance that you do not discuss this with anyone. You have made your point, Alex. I will see you tomorrow. First thing in the morning. We will talk, just the two of us. I was wrong to make a joke. Tomorrow. We will talk, yes?"

Alex nodded.

"Now I must be alone. I need to think." He waited while the others stood. He spoke, almost to himself. "I will think about time."

THE RAIN had cleared off and the evening sky was turning from dusky gray to a pure deep blue. The stars had not yet begun to shine. It was cool. Maple leaves rustled and dripped in the light evening breeze. Once again Alex wished he had earned enough money to buy a jacket.

Max noticed him holding his arms. "I have a spare jacket you can use. The sleeves will be too short, but it will be better than nothing." They walked for a minute in silence. "I understood some of what you said back there. Enough to know that it would be better that I understood nothing. Why did you do it?"

"He thought I was some sort of buffoon. Or that we were playing a joke on him. I had to change his mind."

"It's true? What you said?"

Alex nodded.

"No wonder Albert looked like you'd just slapped him in the face."

"He'll take me more seriously now."

Max laughed. "There's no question of that." They turned onto Max's walkway. "Albert is a gentle man, a man of great humor. He is not much with us in the real world. Lives in his head. Back there, when you told him . . . well, it's the first time I've ever seen him afraid."

They sat down on the porch, Alex on a green and white canvas-covered glider, Max in an old wooden rocker. The glider slid silently back and forth. Alex hadn't been in a glider since he was a boy. Long ago, in the future.

"You know," Surrey said, "when he told us he would think about time, he wasn't joking. That's exactly what he'll do. He'll sit in that chair and think, for hours at a time. He doesn't sleep or eat unless his sister reminds him. He focuses his brain on a problem, and he's in another world." They both rocked in silence for a moment. "Newton was the same sort of man, they say. Maybe Kepler. Totally absorbed. Self-effacing. Most great physicists are."

And some aren't, Alex thought. By his time, many in the world of physics would grow combative, tired of the popular conception that their science was somehow personally responsible for the nuclear bomb and the ensuing arms race. Alex had read an article in a science magazine about an American physicist, Murray Gell-Mann. It concerned Newton's classic answer when asked how he had come to know so much. "If I am able to see far," Newton responded, "it is because I am standing on the shoulders of giants." Gell-Mann, on the other hand, on the occasion of receiving his Nobel Prize, was heard to remark, "If I am able to see so far, it is because I am surrounded by dwarfs."

"I was with Albert one afternoon," Surrey went on. "We were talking about something. He had this big pile of papers in front of him. He was looking for a paper clip. His desk is as full of junk as a child's pockets. He came up with bits of string, old cigars, used train tickets, pennies, all manner of junk. Finally he found a paper clip, but it was all bent up. Wouldn't work. So he decided to make a tool to straighten the paper clip. Back to the drawer. Pretty soon he came up with a box of unused paper clips. All the time he was talking about physics. I was listening, not saying much."

Alex closed his eyes. The glider rocked gently. "So he took out a new paper clip and started bending it up. For a minute I couldn't figure out what the hell he was doing. Then I got it. He was bending up a *new* paper clip, to make a tool to straighten out the *bent* paper clip." Surrey laughed. "I said, 'What the hell are you doing? Just use one of the new paper clips.' He looked at what he was doing and comprehension slowly dawned. 'Once I start, Max, I find it hard to stop. Very hard.' " Max laughed again. "It took him ten years to work out the theory of relativity. That was just the special theory. Ten years. No experiments, no laboratories, no assistants. Just thinking."

The only sound was the thump of the rocker on the wooden floor. A cricket near the front steps began to sing. Others joined in.

"When he says he'll think about time, you can believe it."

They sat, looking into the evening. The street was empty. Lights began going on in houses. "Something else, Alex," Max said, quietly. "I believe you. Don't have much choice, the physical evidence is obvious. We went through a lot together, that other time. I don't know what you're here for, but I'll help you. I may not sound like I will all the time, but you can count on me."

They sat on the porch. The sky darkened into night. Soon Alex could see that the sky was filled with stars.

9

MORNING. ALEX SAT IN EINSTEIN'S STUDY,
drinking a cup of strong, black coffee. The house was quiet. Einstein
was in the kitchen finishing his breakfast. Alex stood and scanned the
rows of books on the floor-to-ceiling shelves. Most of them were in German and looked to be incomprehensible even if they were in English.
The one wall without books had three small framed black and white
portraits. Alex leaned close and read the names inscribed beneath the
pictures: Michael Faraday, James Clark Maxwell, Mahatma Gandhi.
He straightened up and thought back to his History of Science class,
taught to him right here at Princeton. Maxwell, he recalled, was a math-
ematician and a physicist, famous for linking light to electromagnetic
waves. Faraday was the physicist who built the first primitive electric
motor and offered the first theories of electromagnetism. Both of the
men were brilliant theoreticians, precursors of Einstein's own work.

Gandhi. Now he could never see a portrait of Gandhi without also
thinking of Ben Kingsley's movie portrayal. Gandhi was Einstein's
hero. Einstein, the pacifist. Einstein, the man who in 1939 sent Franklin Roosevelt a letter urging him to study the possibilities of an atomic
bomb. What would Gandhi have thought of that?

Einstein. Complicated. Unfathomable in many respects. And yet
most of the world could recite a capsule biography of the man. Or at
least most of the world could do so at one time. Alex wondered what
today's students knew of Einstein. He always assumed that they knew
the basics of history, but he was also always being surprised—"*Pearl
Harbor? What's that? Like a marina or something?*"

Einstein. Sixty-five years old. Father a failed businessman, mother a minor intellectual. As a child, he didn't talk until he was three years old. A late reader, and in general an extremely slow learner, once classified as retarded. When the boy was five years old, his father showed him a pocket compass. Watching the needle swing, the child had a revelation, or at least this was the story Einstein told in his later years. At that moment the boy decided to devote his life to discovering the unseen forces in the world of nature. As a teenager, Einstein transferred from school to school and finally received a diploma, learning along the way to detest the Prussian educational system. When he was sixteen he renounced his German citizenship for the first time. He acquired Swiss citizenship, completed his first scientific paper, and was rewarded with a job in the Swiss Patent office. And then there was the magical year, 1905, when in an incredible burst of mental acuity he published three papers on Light Quanta, Brownian Movement, and Special Relativity. In 1917 scientific tests proved the theory of relativity correct and the world went Einstein-mad. He became the most famous scientist of all time. Mothers named their children Albert, and cigar brands were created in his honor. He was a man for all history. When he died, his brain was saved, and for some curious reason now resides in a jar of formaldehyde stored beneath the desk of a doctor, Thomas Harvey, of Weston, Missouri.

"Good morning, Alex, you have the most curious look on your face." Alex turned. Einstein was smiling at him.

That's because I have been contemplating your death. More correctly, the eventual disposition of your brain. "Just thinking," he said. *If I told you, you would probably find it amusing.*

"Yes, thinking," Einstein said, lowering himself into his leather chair. "That is something I, too, have been doing." He twirled a lock of hair over his ear. "I thought long last night about what you said and about Max's questions. I'm afraid I have no answers."

"Time?" Alex asked.

Einstein nodded. "Yes, space and time. Questions that usually concern only children. Dreamers. I do not know where you are from, Alex, it may be, as you say, from some other time. That does not really matter so much, though it is fascinating to me. Perhaps I could come up with the equations to explain it, but it is the biology that is the stumbling block. Is it possible?" He shrugged. "I do not know. Maybe we should bring in my friend Godel and ask him. He is here at the

Institute, and he has an interesting theory of time. He feels that time is not a linear sequence of events, but that it bends around the universe in a great curve. Godel says that if you have a rocket ship it would be possible to move in a sufficiently wide curve to eventually travel any-where in time. Do you have a rocket ship?" Alex shook his head. "Neither does Godel." He sighed. "But what we do have is a more serious problem, and it is not theoretical. You possess information that should not be yours. These things you spoke of last evening. Even I am not supposed to know of them."

"But you do?"

"Yes, a little. I am a scientist, a member of the international scientific community. It is really a small family, closer than those outside would suppose. We talk, that is the basis of science. Now, with this terrible secret, we are not supposed to even whisper."

"Terrible?"

"Yes, of course. These are terrible times, our enemies are evil in the purest sense of the word. A few of our men have come to me for technical advice. Bush was here with a problem of diffusion. Others have been here, some with questions of a more elemental nature."

"And you have helped them?"

"When I am able. I am not much use on pure technique. I am a thinker, not an experimenter. Do you know the idea of nuclear fission never even occurred to me? In 1921 I was once approached by a man who said he wanted to speak to me, that he had thought it possible to produce a weapon from nuclear energy based on $E = mc^2$. I told him to calm himself, that the foolishness of such a proposition was evident at a glance." He paused. "I sometimes wonder whatever happened to that man. Once the idea was properly presented, it was obvious, but until then, it never entered my mind. Now it seldom leaves it. Bohr was here recently and it was all we talked about, of what would happen after the thing is built. He is very worried. He is helping to build it, he understands the danger of the Germans. But after they are de-feated?"

"If he is so worried, why does he help build it? The war can be won with conventional weapons. Why do any of you help with it? That's what I can't understand. You, a pacifist, you above all others. It was your letter to Roosevelt recommending the government begin a project into atomic energy that began it all. And Bohr? He is a great scientist with much influence. If he is against the bomb, then why does he help?"

"Because he knows the Germans. He knows what they are capable of. He has only recently escaped to America. Earlier, when the war first began, he gave up many chances to leave Denmark. He stayed, even though it meant being in constant danger from the Nazis. He stayed to help our scientist friends, mostly Jews, to escape. Finally the Germans decided that he would be arrested so that he would build for *them* an atomic bomb. Do you understand?" Alex nodded.

"They came for him," Einstein went on. "The Gestapo. He was warned, but he had only minutes. The British were there to help him escape. The Nazis were breaking down the front door of the apartment while Bohr was going out the back. He grabbed out of his ice box a beer bottle full of heavy water, deuterium, that he was using for his radiation experiments. The British took him to an airfield where he was strapped into a small airplane. They flew very high to escape the enemy guns. His oxygen mask fell off, and he fainted. He was unconscious for the entire flight. Only when they landed did he regain consciousness. He is a very courageous man. And now he has come to America to help us. Only this is not all he does. He has come and gone many times to England to talk to Churchill. In this country he has spoken with Roosevelt. He has warned them repeatedly that if the technical problems are overcome, then we will be opening a Pandora's box that will never contain these demons again. He wants me to help him with this work, with what must be done *after* the weapon is built. I have pledged to him that I will help."

They both sat quietly. The long speech seemed to have drained the old man. Alex put his coffee cup on the table. "I don't mean any disrespect," he said. "It's just that I don't understand. I need to be very clear on this matter. How can both points of view be reconciled? How can you help build it, and at the same time want to stop it?"

Einstein leaned forward. New life seemed to flood into him. "Stop it? You don't understand. We don't want to stop it. This is not something that can be patented, or hoarded by one country. This is not a secret that can be kept. This is a fact of nature, a part of the natural world, and as such it will eventually be discovered by all countries. We want *everyone* to know how to do this thing. How else can it be defused or disarmed? Your great inventor, Thomas Edison, foresaw this moment. He once wrote that there would one day spring from the brain of science a machine so forceful, so fearful in its potentialities, so absolutely terrifying, that even man, the fighter who will dare torture and death in order to inflict torture and death, will be appalled and abandon war altogether. We are at this moment, Alex, but if all countries own the secret, possess the knowledge, and understand its true power, then no one would ever dare use it. This is part of Bohr's theory of complementarity. Within the common threat there exists common promise. In this type of war, no one can win. The very necessity of forestalling war will offer unique opportunities to bridge international differences. Bohr says that Churchill will not let the secret go, will not give it to the Russians, that we cannot trust the Russians. Churchill is wrong. Stalin is a realist. He would not use a weapon of this magnitude. *No sane man would do such a thing!* Now do you understand?"

Alex would have laughed if the man were not obviously so serious, and just as obviously if he did not believe so deeply in what he was saying. "What about the Germans? Are you going to let them have the secret?"

"You are joking. That is the reason we are proceeding with such urgency in this country. All indications are that the Germans have their own nuclear program. We must be the first to build the weapon. If they are first, they will surely use it. Eventually, they will build this weapon, if they possess the resources after the war. I foresee that the world will be split into two camps, with the free world on one hand and the Germans on the other. They have proved throughout history that they will always oppose us. We have only two choices: annihilate them, or arm ourselves to the point where the potential for annihilation prevents them from attempting to take over the world."

"Who decides what countries will have the plans to make a bomb?"

"The scientists, of course. Those who have produced the knowledge. Science is a product of openness, and it accomplishes openness. It reveals error and abuse. Now, you must know that the problem is not simply the bomb, but the inequality of men and nations. A weapon such as this does not destroy one particular class of people, but all classes, rich and poor, democracies and dictatorships. There can be no winners. It follows complementarily that the opening of the world to prevent such destruction will expose and alleviate equality. It will be a new order. A world government for the protection of all nations will evolve out of common danger. This is why we work to build the weapon. For nothing less than the salvation of the world."

Alex looked into Einstein's serious, guileless face and saw that he believed everything he'd said, believed it implicitly. And evidently others believed it as well. He tried to see it from their vantage point. From where Einstein sat, Stalin was a respected ally. The great pogroms, the gulags, the mass murders and genocide were in the future, or at least the world would not know of them until the future. Germany, who had proved her intent by starting two world wars, was the common enemy. The complex and radical shifts in alliances in his own time would be inconceivable to these people. The Common Market? Japan and America? Germany as one of the leaders of the economic free world?

Jesus, they've got it all fucked up. "Look, I know it sounds reasonable to you, but it won't work. I hate to be blunt, but it's all wrong. It just won't happen that way. People and nations are too selfish, too full of self-interest. Their memories are too short. They are too uneducated, unskilled, unsophisticated, and underdeveloped to follow your logic."

Einstein sat back. "But what other possibility is there?" He was genuinely perplexed. "The only other option is an arms race that would end in the mutual destruction of the world."

Yes. Unfortunately, you are absolutely correct. "Do you remember what I said last evening? About the Japanese?"

Einstein nodded. "How could I forget it. You said we would build the bomb and use it on the Japanese. I want you to explain. How do you mean 'use it'? And why the Japanese?"

"Because the war with Germany will end without it. We will beat them with conventional weapons."

"But I did not know the Japanese were building a bomb. It is possible, I suppose, but their research has not been in that direction."

"That's not why we'll do it. The reasoning is that it will save lives, that more people will be killed in an invasion of the home islands than will be killed if we drop a bomb on them. At least more Allied lives will be saved."

"But I never imagined it would be used on civilians. Even on Germans. I assumed we would set up a demonstration of the bomb's capabilities, that this would be sufficient. After they have seen the destruction, no nation would risk having it used against them. But to drop it on civilians? No, never."

"Two bombs. Two of them will be dropped on civilians."

Einstein's face turned pale, with spots of flush on each cheek. "If this is true, it will be a fatal error. Men quickly accustom themselves to believing that a weapon that was used once can be used again. It cannot happen, it will be the end of the world. If this is true, if *you* are true, we must stop them. We must get a message to Roosevelt. He must not do this."

Alex felt himself being drawn further into the quicksand of truth and detail. *Once you start telling, where do you stop?*

"It won't be Roosevelt. Truman will be president."

Einstein looked blank. "Truman? But how?"

"Roosevelt will die. Just before the war with Germany is finished."

Einstein shook his head. "It is terrible to hear this. Even if you possess this knowledge, I cannot bear to hear more of these revelations."

"I'm sorry," Alex said, leaning forward. "It's not my fault that I know these things. I know more, much more, most of it no better. I know enough to tell you your scheme of world government guiding all nations away from nuclear confrontation is impossible. Hopelessly naive."

Einstein stared at him. "How can you live with such knowledge? Knowing. You are so calm. You see the destruction of the world and you sit in your chair and drink your coffee as if nothing is wrong. The house is burning down around you and you do not attempt an escape? To save the lives of others who live there with you?"

Alex felt himself flush. "Look, to me this is history. It has already happened. In my world we *do* live with this threat. One grows used to thinking what to you is unthinkable. To you, it's the future, you feel that there are choices to be made, many possible futures. You feel as if events may be averted. To me, these events have already occurred. They are in my past, unchanged and unchangeable."

Einstein was on the edge of the chair. "No!" He gestured violently with both hands. "You are *here*. These events *are* in the future. It must be possible to change them. Is the future immutable? Are you saying that we are condemned to act out this tragedy no matter what? That there is no free will, that all the world is preordained? And who has set us on this course? God? There is no such thing. And if there were, he would not play dice with our lives in this manner. He would not be malicious. I ask you again: How can you stand it? How can you simply allow these things to occur, to allow events that will result in the deaths of thousands of innocent people? To allow these same events that will effect the lives and future of our entire race?"

Alex looked at his hands. *There are no answers to such questions.* "I am one man. Is it right for me to decide such things? Who gives me the right?"

"*Mein Gott!* Who gives any of us the right? *Ich bin fever und flamme dature.* We should be fire and flame for it. It is the right and duty of every man to make moral decisions, to be ethical. To attempt all that is humanly possible to save lives, to take whatever action is necessary for the common good. It has always been thus. You are one man. I am one man. Together we are two." He stopped for a moment to catch his breath. He smiled slightly. "Only two, yes, but perhaps that is enough. Besides, we can do nothing else, as responsible moral men we have no choice. We must make the attempt. We can do no less."

Einstein pulled a pad of yellow paper from under a stack of magazines. "We will begin. We will write a letter to my friend Franklin D. Roosevelt. If my first letter set all of this in motion, as you say, then my second letter may bring it to a halt. It must be a very careful letter. We will not tell the President you are a man from another time. I am afraid that is a direction he will not understand. When we have finished, you will take the letter to him. Max will go with you. He has friends in Washington. I would go, but my doctors will not allow it. My frail body would not allow it." He stopped for a moment and looked quizzically at Alex.

Don't ask. Don't ask when you will die. I'm enough of a ghoul just knowing that your brain will be kept in a jar. Don't make me tell you.

Einstein read the expression on his face. "Don't worry, Alex, I'm not going to ask you when I am to die. I admit, the thought crossed my mind, but it would complicate matters. That is one secret you may keep. My life has been an interesting one, but I do not want to skip ahead and read the end of the story." He was searching through the papers on the table for a pen. He stopped and looked at Alex. "Which reminds me, I never told you the end of the Niels Bohr story.

"You remember he had escaped the Nazis and fainted from lack of oxygen in the British airplane. When he arrived in England, he was revived. He was still clutching his beer bottle of heavy water. Didn't spill a drop. When it was opened, however, it was discovered that Bohr, in his haste, had snatched the wrong bottle and brought out only a bottle of very good German beer." He patted his pocket and pulled out a fountain pen. "There is a moral there somewhere," he said. He picked up the pad of paper. "You unearth it, I leave it to you. I have a letter that must be written."

10

WHILE MAX AND ALEX WAITED, EINSTEIN studied the sky, searching the few high clouds for signs of rain. He never wore his hat in the rain, he told Alex. He found it much easier to dry his hair than his hat. He decided the clouds were benign. He wore his hat, and even though the day was warm, his leather jacket. They walked to a park where children played, and squirrels hopped in the trees.

"No, Max, you cannot escape us," Einstein said. "All men must enlist in the war against war. You are no exception."

"I'm busy," Surrey growled. His face registered his impatience. "I don't have time for your elevated games, Albert. You're going to make me know things I'm neither supposed to know nor want to know." He turned to Alex. "Did you put him up to this? This is your fault, isn't it?"

Alex shrugged and smiled noncommittally.

"*You*, Max, brought him to *me*," Einstein said. "He is your friend. If there is a first link in this chain, then it begins with you. Besides, you know that responsibility lies with all of us. So enough, we'll have no fence straddling. Now, what we need from you is to shepherd a letter we have written." He reached into the breast pocket of his jacket and retrieved a folded paper.

"Letter to whom?"

"Franklin D. Roosevelt," Einstein said. He sat down on a black, wrought-iron park bench beneath a tall oak tree. A squirrel leaped from branch to branch, chattering and scolding.

"Hah," Surrey laughed. "Roosevelt is *your* friend. You're the one who has dined at his table, slept in his home. I am only a poor history professor."

"Enough. I am quite aware that you have powerful friends in the administration. I could put this letter in the mail and it would be read by perhaps fifty underlings before it reached the President. Probably it would be thrown in a wastebasket as the ravings of a madman pretending to be Professor Einstein. So you must take it to someone in whom you have the utmost confidence. Someone who will put it into Roosevelt's hands without reading it first. To do this, to convince you of the importance of the letter, *you* must read it. Otherwise you may lack the proper commitment. This is important, Max. Very important."

Surrey stared down at Einstein for a long moment and held out his hand. Einstein gave him the letter. Alex read the letter over Surrey's shoulder.

Albert Einstein
212 Mercer St.
Princeton, N.J.

F. D. Roosevelt,
President of the United States
White House
Washington, D.C.

Dear Mr. President,

New information has come to my attention concerning the matter under consideration at our meeting last year. At that time I subsequently spoke with our congressional leaders on the importance of our undertaking. Though in no way privy to official information, I am aware that our efforts in this matter have been proceeding and have met with some initial success. That we will eventually produce the weapon is now almost assured.

My concern at this point lies with our use of the weapon. It has long been my thinking that any use should be confined to a demonstration of the weapon's capabilities. This would surely be enough to bring our enemies to the negotiating table. In no circumstances should it be necessary to actually use the weapon on a civilian population. To do so would lower our country's standards to the level of those we are currently resisting. Further, it would be a crime which future generations would condemn until the end of time. As a free, moral nation, we cannot commit such a crime.

In view of these concerns, I am sending to you a man with whom I have recently become acquainted, a man who has interesting and original ideas concerning our options for a postwar world free from the danger of our new weapon. He is a scientist with knowledge of our systems far in advance of my own. As I know that you are a man with a mind open to all possibilities, I urge you to apply your vast powers of reason to this problem. In all our history we have never faced a challenge or a danger that is as crucial as the one now before us.

Yours very truly,

Albert Einstein.

Albert Einstein

Surrey folded the letter and handed it back to Einstein. "Scientist?" he asked with raised eyebrows, turning to Alex.

"Well," Einstein said, "that is not exactly the truth." He took off his hat and ran his hand through his bushy hair. "But in this case truth must take a back seat to expediency. What matters is getting our friend Alex in to see the President."

"And what do you have to say about all of this?" he asked Alex. "Have you any idea what might happen?"

Alex shook his head. "I guess there could be problems."

"Jesus, problems? I think Roosevelt will have you arrested on the spot. Nobody is supposed to know what's in this letter, this talk of a secret weapon. I'm sure of that, and now you two have got me roped in on it. They'll probably put me in an adjoining cell. What do you hope to accomplish?"

Alex looked up into the oak tree and wondered how much he dare tell Surrey. The squirrel, sitting on a limb over Einstein, dropped a twig onto the old man's head. Einstein didn't seem to notice. "Accomplish?" Alex said. "I don't really know. How much background do you want? I don't blame you for not wanting to get involved."

Surrey gave him a disgusted look and waved a hand. "Jesus, too late for that now. Give me the bad news."

"Life is about to change," Alex said. He looked around the small park. The summer sun was bright on the trees and grass. "The world will look pretty much the same, but underneath, it will be fundamentally different. They're going to build a bomb, Max, they've already just about done it. The biggest goddamn bomb you can imagine. Bigger, actually. Bigger than even *they* can imagine. Then they're going to use it, and after that everyone is going to build them and they'll build more and more powerful bombs and the world will spend its time waiting for someone to get angry enough at someone else to use one of them, or be stupid enough, or crazy enough. And that will surely be the end of life, or at least life as we know it. The professor thinks if we can get them not to use the first one, or at least not to use it on people, we'll be able to defuse the escalation."

Surrey frowned. "Wait a minute. Even if the bomb isn't used, it will still exist. What you need to do is to keep everyone from building one in the first place."

"And that is impossible," Einstein said, shaking his head. "The theory exists, the technology is virtually complete." Einstein stood and began walking along the cement path. Alex and Max fell in behind. "Our only hope is to show that the power of this weapon is too great, that the danger to everyone is overwhelming. By not letting the bomb be used on people, we will create a precedent." He turned around and faced them. "You see, it is blood and death that seizes the mind. Once men are immersed in blood, you cannot cleanse them. When they overcome moral resistance, when they find it is possible to perform acts of evil without immediate retribution, then they will continue. They forget or disregard whatever scruples they once had. A new paradigm has been established and they will act within this new set of parameters. A weapon invented is a weapon that will be used. The Germans proved that with poison gas in the First World War. But in this case the weapon is too horrible to be allowed. Its use will mean the eventual destruction of the world. If our government, or any government, is allowed to use it on human beings, then the world is truly doomed."

"And what is Alex going to say to Franklin Roosevelt that will assure the world a future?" Surrey asked.

Einstein stopped and contemplated a group of children playing on a rope swing. Alex and Max stood at his side.

Yes, Max, Alex thought, *very good question*. What had seemed possible in the rarified intellectual and moral air of Einstein's study the day before now seemed, in the clear summer sun, impossible. He thought that Einstein's letter, if properly presented, would quite probably get him in to see Roosevelt. But what he said once he was inside was the problem. They continued on down the path.

What will I say? What words can accomplish this task? And what do I think I'm doing anyway?

He knew at least the general outline of A-bomb research. By now the atom bomb was in its middle stages of completion. Could the seemingly inevitable arms race be defused as Einstein thought? After hearing the physicist's original nuclear arms theories, it didn't seem likely. And yet, didn't he *have* to make the attempt, even though the outcome was doubtful? That part of Einstein's philosophy had to be correct; a moral man must attempt moral change. But what if what he was doing made everything worse? What if he threw the delicate balance of nuclear stasis off kilter? After all, the application of mutual destruction that existed in his own time had achieved its purpose: no bombs were ever used after the first two. And now he was going to tinker with this infinitely delicate machine. Would he eventually go back to a future already blasted off the face of the planet? He shook his head, knowing that if he allowed the questions to pile up, he would quickly founder in them. If there were no answers, then the questions were moot. He must go on. He must *try*.

"I don't know what I'll say to Roosevelt. He'd never believe I was from another time. They'd just put me away if I tried to convince them of that." He turned around and faced the other two. The twig was still balanced atop Einstein's snowy head. Alex half expected a family of birds to flutter down and begin building a nest. Einstein put on his hat, covering the stick.

And it all comes to this. This moment. My life has led to this moment where there is a chance that the future can be changed. And I have tried to change the past before, to make a difference, to use this gift in ways that have meaning, but I have always failed. But it is this old man, and other old men before him, who have taught me that there is no failure, that the morality of a thing is in the search, the attempt. That we can only try. And maybe this time I will succeed. And maybe this time we will succeed. And it rests with me, and I accept it, and it rests with this old man in whose wild hair the birds build their nests. It rests with all of us.

11

THE NEW YORK TO WASHINGTON TRAIN
was hot, slow, and crowded. Uniformed servicemen and suited businessmen jockeyed for the rare empty seat. The few women who were
traveling were automatically offered the first seats available. The cars
were nearly filled before they left New York. By the first stop in New
Jersey, men were standing in the aisles and between the cars.

The conductors opened the doors at either end of the car to encourage the movement of air down the aisle. Most of the windows
were open, but only when they were running at top speed was there
actually a breeze strong enough to carry away the accumulated cigar
and cigarette smoke. Beneath the smoke lay the sharp oniony odor of
sweating men in unwashed wool clothing. Moments of speed were
rare. Much of their time was spent idling on sidespurs, sweating,
waiting for the more important rail traffic to roll by.

"Freight," Surrey said, watching a long line of boxcars pass. "Material has priority. Food, ammunition, coal, steel, any raw material
has priority over men."

"Lots of soldiers on this train," Alex said, gesturing at the crowded
seats and aisles. "You'd think the government would want to get them
wherever they're going."

"Most of them are on leave. Heading home for a week or so. Soldiers
on leave are very low priority." Surrey was sitting in the aisle seat.
He nodded toward the window beside Alex. Outside a string of tankcars
rolled by. "Gasoline. There's your top-of-the-line item. Lack of gasoline
is the reason this train is so crowded. Most driving is forbidden."

Alex watched the long line of gray tankcars. For a moment it seemed as if the train were rolling backward and the tankers were stationary. The heat, the smoke, and the stale dead air were affecting his brain, he thought. "Looks like a hell of a lot of gasoline to me."

Surrey nodded. "The amount's not the problem. Most people think we don't have enough in reserve, but we do. The problem is moving it around, across the ocean, up the coast. The German U-boats sit offshore all up and down the East Coast and knock off tankers like clay pigeons. Or maybe clay ducks. The ships are big and slow and defenseless. You can go down to the beach pretty much anywhere along the Atlantic seaboard and see the dead sailors roll in with the morning tide. People sit on the beach at night and watch tankers get torpedoed. They say the explosions are quite beautiful. New York is blacked out because of the same problem. Every city along the coast up to twelve miles inland is blacked out or at least dimmed out."

"I read that we were blacked out because the Defense Department thinks the Germans are developing a plane capable of flying over here to bomb." He knew this would never happen, but he couldn't say so, especially on a crowded train. The "Loose lips sink ships" signs were everywhere.

Surrey shook his head. "They'd love to be able to do that, but so far they haven't succeeded. The only hits we've taken have been on the West Coast. A Jap sub surfaced off the coast of California and tossed a few shells in the direction of Santa Barbara. Up in the northwest a Jap sub brought in a collapsible airplane and bombed a forest. Not much damage and no casualties in either case. This is different. At night the lights of the cities cast a glow against the clouds. The U-boats spot the tankers against the clouds. We lost quite a few ships before someone finally figured it out."

The train jerked forward. For all of his reading on World War II, Alex hadn't known that America had actually been physically touched by the war. He knew that the Japanese were floating over firebombs attached to thirty-foot paper balloons, but most of the few that actually made it across the Pacific Ocean fell into uninhabited forests in the Northwest. One did make it all the way cross-country into rural Maryland, but it turned out to be a dud. If it hadn't been, and if it had flown a few more miles, it might have dropped on Washington, D.C. That would have made a hell of a headline: JAPS BOMB CAPITOL! No way to keep that one out of the papers. The press wasn't supposed to print anything about the bombs that made it across the ocean, the idea being if the Japs didn't know they really worked, then they'd probably eventually stop trying. At the same time, everyone was supposed to know about the bombs. The few deaths that had occurred came because people found them and fooled with them, setting them off. To the public, the whispered message was: *Don't touch. Call the authorities.*

The idea of paper balloon bombs was difficult to think of as a danger. But the thought of U-boats sitting right off our beaches like killer sharks waiting for unwary vacationers was different.

The train rumbled onto a long bridge. "Where are we?" Alex asked, imagining enemy periscopes sliding silently toward them. "Delaware," Surrey said.

Alex looked out at the wide blue-green water of the empty bay. In the distance he noticed two speed boats. They were aimed at the train, which had now slowed to a crawl. As he watched, the boats drew closer. The train groaned and ground to a halt in the middle of the low bridge. Other men on the right side of the train were looking out the open windows. The boats were coming so fast that the bows were reared high out of the water and a cockscomb of spray arced into the sky behind. The railroad car gradually fell silent as even the men in the aisles bent over to watch.

The boats were coming head on, side by side, straight toward the train. The wake spray and the sleek gray hulls gave the impression of great speed. Alex found himself holding his breath. He knew that the boats were going to pass beneath them, under the bridge, that there had to be room between the pilings. The roar of their engines grew.

The boats flashed beneath them with a blast of exhaust. A thick spume of water smacked into the windows and into the train. The men in the window seats flinched back as if slapped. There was a moment of uneasy self-conscious laughter, and in the silence that followed, Alex heard someone mutter, "PT boaters. Crazy fuckers."

The train jerked and began to move.

WASHINGTON, D.C. The Willard Hotel. Mark Twain, Alex recalled, once walked the long main foyer of the Willard. Resplendent in a white flannel suit, he would enter through the F Street doors and saunter along the elegant interior hallway, nodding to his admirers, and exit onto Pennsylvania Avenue. Then he would dash around the block and go through again.

Surrey signed them in at the ornate front desk. The plan was to spend the afternoon outfitting Alex with a decent suit for his appointment with Roosevelt. *White. White flannels*, Alex decided. *The perfect summertime suit. Next to white linen.* He'd always wanted a white suit. *Mark Twain white.*

The lobby was full of businessmen, government workers, and servicemen, though the servicemen were of higher rank than those on the train. A few women in smart-looking suits perched in the plum-colored plush lobby chairs. Most of them were sitting with men, or looked as if they were waiting for men.

Reserving a room at the Willard had been almost as difficult as setting up an appointment with the President. Washington was crammed from basement to attic with transient workers, ranging all the way from beginning government clerks and secretaries, to the highest level of program administrators. Businessmen, in town angling for lucrative wartime contracts, fought for *any* hotel space, decent or otherwise, with the same dogged determination they used in securing contracts. Generals and admirals issued orders and planned assaults on the hotel. Very Important Persons from all across the United States stormed the ornate front entrance of the Willard, seeking a room, any room, for as long as they could get it.

Surrey had pulled governmental strings which appeared to be a good bit longer and stronger than the gossamer threads he claimed. An appointment with the President and a double at the Willard in only three days must have set a record. The Einstein letter did the trick with the President, but it hadn't gotten them a room at the hotel.

"A FORTY-TWO LONG, I believe. Am I correct, sir? Maybe something in a nice white flannel?" The elegant, black-suited salesman ruled over the suit department of Lewis and Thomas Saltz, a priest in his pulpit, a captain on the bridge. Saltz was *the* men's clothing store in the nation's capital.

"Yes," Alex said, envisioning himself strolling the lobby of the Willard.

"Are you crazy?" Surrey snorted. "This is Washington in the summer. It's a swamp out there. Flannel is hot and scratchy. Besides, do you know what you have to do to keep flannel looking decent?"

"No," Alex said, "not really."

"Tell him," Surrey said to the salesman.

The salesman gave both of them his down-the-nose headwaiter look. "Actually, sir, white flannel can be nicely maintained if one extends a modicum of effort. Here in Washington, Mr. Vine at the Sunshine Cleaners does a very reputable job. At his establishment, each suit is disassembled at the seams, hand-washed and bleached, sun dried, and then stitched back together and pressed. All for the reasonable price of ten dollars. It takes about a week, depending on the weather."

Surrey rolled his eyes. "Well," he said sarcastically, "that puts the lid on that. One week is definitely too long to have a suit cleaned."

"Perhaps," the salesman said, with a small bow. "But allowances must be made. Sacrifice is in order. After all, there is a war on."

They settled on a lightweight, gray, double-breasted suit, black wing-tip shoes, a plain white shirt, and a dark blue tie. Alex looked at himself in the mirror as the tailor measured and marked, and realized that in the few weeks he'd been in this time he'd grown exceedingly seedy. He needed a haircut and a decent shave. The razors of the 1940s with their inferior, rationed blades and turned his face into a minefield of scars and cuts. To say nothing of his shabby clothing, all of which was either stolen or borrowed. Once in a real suit, the defects in his grooming stood out like an unruly wino sprawled snoring on the Persian carpet in the front lobby of the Willard.

A trip to the hotel barber did wonders. The suit was delivered that evening. After a meal of fresh seafood at O'Donnell's, a dark, below-ground restaurant with terrific rum buns and mildly authentic ship's decor, Alex felt that he was at least physically prepared. He tried to keep his mind off the meeting with Roosevelt, scheduled for the next morning. Tried to keep his mind off all the possible foul-ups. He had worried all these worries before, in other places and other times.

THE NEXT MORNING, they walked the few blocks from the Willard to the White House. Alex's new shoes hurt and the bright summer heat began to wilt him even before they crossed Fifteenth Street. But in general, he felt fine. He didn't really know what he was doing, but that was, under his unusual circumstances, almost unavoidable. The fact that he was doing *something*, moving forward, at least attempting a course of action, was enough, at least for now.

"I spoke with Pa Watson, Roosevelt's appointments secretary, last night and again this morning," Surrey said. "The President has read Einstein's letter and is willing to talk. We'll get about a half an hour with him. Don't let him bullshit away all your time, which is what he'll try to do. He'll start out the meeting with a lot of chitchat that makes it sound like he's your best friend. He'll take you into his confidence, he'll pat you on the back, he'll smile and nod and next thing you know your time is up. He doesn't want to hear what you've got to say, he just assumes that you're bringing in some sort of trouble. If you're going to accomplish anything, you've got to capture his interest and intelligence immediately; otherwise you'll just get one of his fireside chats." Alex stopped inside the White House gate, expecting a full pat-down search, but Surrey simply nodded to the guard and walked through. Government workers from nearby offices were scattered around the close-cropped lawn, eating early lunches and reading newspapers. Soldiers looking out of place in flat World War I helmets and obsolete battle gear patrolled the perimeter of the grounds. Alex marveled at the lack of real security. "Don't they know there's a war on?" he asked. Surrey looked at him. "Not here. Who should they be expecting? Tojo? Hitler? Wild-eyed anarchists? The army is marching around the lawn because it gives the home front the proper spirit. None of these old guys have any bullets, and neither do any of the anti-aircraft guns on the roofs."

Surrey gave their names to a uniformed Marine at a desk in the front hall. After a brief wait, they were shown up the red-carpeted steps to the second floor. A large man with a florid complexion and a wide grin charged down the hall toward them, hand outstretched.

"Pa Watson," Surrey said, "I'd like you to meet my friend Alex Balfour."

Watson beamed at Alex and pumped his hand. "Any friend of Max's," he said, turning to Surrey. "Does this mean you're coming back to us, Max?" Surrey smiled and shook his head. "One of the biggest brains in the Trust," Watson said to Alex. "We tried to keep him on, but he wasn't having it. Had to get back to his ivory tower with the other eggheads. Even the President couldn't convince him to stay and help us win the war."

"He running on time, Pa?" Surrey asked.

"Pretty near, Max. You boys have a seat, and the lieutenant will send you in when it's time." He nodded to a Navy man at a desk nearby. "When he gives the go-ahead, why don't you come in and jaw with me, Max? The President wants to see your man alone." Alex and Max sat down and waited. Alex felt as if he were waiting to see the Principal of the World. Which in a way, FDR was. He could feel his stomach tightening.

The President's door opened. Alex felt an electric shock of recognition at the man who came out of the office. A very young, thin, and handsome Orson Welles stepped jauntily through the door. Then, as if making a stage exit, Welles leaned back into the President's office and said, "Your obedient servant," in his deep, immediately recognizable voice. Alex heard light laughter from the office. Welles said goodbye to the Navy man, nodded at Alex and Surrey, and strode down the hall. Alex turned to Surrey, but before he could get a word out, the Navy man was in front of them. "You're next, sir. Right this way." They both stood and Max shook Alex's hand. "Good luck. I'll be in Pa's office when you're through." Alex was ushered into the Oval Office.

He stopped inside the doorway. Then he almost laughed. Somehow, he'd been expecting everything to be in black and white, like an old wartime photograph. Roosevelt was behind his desk, studying a sheet of paper, looking just the way he did in old *Life* magazines. Except he was in color. The entire room, yellow walls, gray rug, brown desk, paintings, all of it was in color. Of course. Roosevelt looked up and smiled.

Alex walked to the desk and held out his hand. Roosevelt reached up and they shook. "Sit down, Alex," the President said, gesturing to a straight-backed chair in front of the desk. "Where do you hail from, Alex? Max didn't say."

I'll bet he didn't. "New York."

Roosevelt nodded. "Don't get up to New York much these days. I guess they're bearing up under the privations of war?"

"Yes sir. New Yorkers can bear up under pretty much anything."

"That's right. Hitler wants to bomb them, you know. Fiorello

LaGuardia called him a perverted maniac in the newspapers. That did it. Goering has been ordered to produce an airplane that can carry a five-ton bomb across the Atlantic." He grinned at Alex. "You don't want to mention any of this to anyone. We came across a map, can't say how, that Hermann's boys had drawn up. Map of New York. Had a big bull's-eye drawn at the corner of Bowery and Delancy Street. Notation said they expected destruction from Rockefeller Center as far south as Governor's Island. We've got defenses set up all around the city, spotters on the roofs, but I don't expect that we'll need them."

Alex sat silently. This obviously was the routine that Surrey had told him to expect from FDR.

When Alex didn't respond or go away, the President picked up the piece of paper he'd been reading. Alex recognized it as Einstein's letter. "Now what the hell is this all about, Alex?"

At that moment, Alex felt the current of history that had been carrying him along, the swift stream of time, spin him around and cast him up on the riverbank, leaving him shivering and cold. And alone. He understood that we are all, in the end, alone, and that there is little to do but plunge ahead. *Dear God, here I go.*

"It's about the atomic bomb, Mr. President. It's about how it will be used and how it will affect the world."

Alex watched the President's friendly smile of camaraderie disappear. He remembered Surrey's instructions: *You've got to engage him immediately.* Mission accomplished. For better or worse.

"Mr. Balfour, how do you know about this bomb?"

Once again, he was in the land of lies. "I'm a scientist, as it says in the letter. Many scientists are aware of the possibility of nuclear fission."

"But to you it seems a certainty. How will we build this bomb? How will we use it, Mr. Balfour? When will all of this happen? Can you read me the future?" Roosevelt's voice now sounded cold, mocking.

Alex shook his head. "No, I can't tell you the future. No one can do that. But I can give you a scientific extrapolation based on probabilities. I know that America is putting all her intelligence and technological effort into this research. We will succeed. We're bound to. And the weapon will be used since we are in a war. People will die, tens of thousands of people. I can look ahead and see that, deduce it from the available facts. I can also see that not so many years from now the world will have thousands of bombs and there will be little to control their use. We could destroy the planet earth, and it begins right here." He touched the arm of his chair. "In this room. It isn't a matter of telling the future. It's a matter of inevitable consequences."

Roosevelt leaned back in his chair. Alex wondered if it was a wheelchair. "You know too much," Roosevelt said. "I should call the FBI right now. Hoover would put you away for a hundred years."

"I don't doubt it."

"And why shouldn't he?" Roosevelt pulled a pack of Camels out of his desk drawer. He picked up a cigarette holder and inserted a cigarette. His hands were trembling very slightly. He lighted the cigarette and blew a jet of smoke at the ceiling.

For the first time, as Roosevelt was fooling with the cigarette, Alex noticed the desk top. It was covered with junk. Little pipe cleaner donkeys roamed among pen sets and toy globes.

"If you lock me up, I can't be of any use to you. Surrey tells me you are a pragmatic man, that you don't throw away opportunities." Roosevelt contemplated Alex in silence. Clouds of cigarette smoke wreathed his stony face.

Alex looked down, itemizing the desk top while Roosevelt made up his mind. *A bronze lamp with blue shade. Four toy donkeys, no, five, there's one made out of hazelnuts. A clock shaped like a ship's steering wheel, a small bust of Eleanor . . .*

"What is it you propose?" Roosevelt tipped the long ash of his cigarette into a brass ashtray made out of an artillery shell. He asked the question casually, a poker player with a winning hand and a good pot.

"I can help you," Alex said, knowing that this was his answering bet, that he must push in all of his chips, call the pot. On a bluff. "We are going to win the war. You know that we will—"

"Just a moment," Roosevelt stopped him. "I admire your confidence, but I don't know that we will win the war. My scientists tell me that the reason we are building this bomb is because the Germans are doing so. That we are in a sort of race with them. If they build theirs first, they'll use it on us. Or on our allies." He clenched his cigarette holder in his teeth and the cigarette angled forty-five degrees skyward. "From where I sit, we may be winning the war, yes." He paused. "But too slowly, and we are paying one hell of a price." He rested his arms on his desk. The anger seemed to drain out of him. Alex noticed that Roosevelt's shirt collar looked several sizes too large.

His skin color was tinged an unhealthy gray. *He's got what? Two years?* Once again, he felt the ghoulish chill of knowing when the man he was talking to was going to die.

"I am aware," Alex said carefully, "that I don't have your perspective. I am not in possession of the enormous amount of information that comes to you. I know that what I am saying sounds premature. Even so, my point is this: I'm afraid that all of our thinking and effort will go into building this weapon. That we will use all of our resources on that phase, and have little left for the problems of the bomb's use, that the problems of the future will be neither clearly seen nor properly addressed." *An American dilemma. We bludgeon a problem into submission with our massive economic and technological prowess, but all the planning is short-term. The future is left to take care of itself. Maybe.* "It will be a mistake to drop the bomb on innocent Japanese civilians, Mr. President. We don't need to do that. If we study the alternatives, we can come up with better solutions."

"The Japanese?" Roosevelt sat up straighter. "Innocent civilians? I must confess, Mr. Balfour, you amaze me. My advisors tell me that I entertain the notions of far too many crackpots. My answer to these advisors is that one never knows when one of my crackpots will turn out to be a visionary. With useful information. I will go to any lengths, entertain any ideas, that might shorten this terrible war. But you are beginning to strain even my credulity. You know too much, Mr. Balfour." He smiled slightly. "Eleanor would be better equipped to deal with you. But you are skating on thin ice as far as I'm concerned." He frowned. He picked up Einstein's letter. "I'm going to send you away while I think about this. Be back here in two hours. Tell Surrey to come in. He's dumped this on me, maybe he can straighten it out."

ALEX SAT in a booth in the Blue Mirror Grill, eating a club sandwich. The restaurant was two blocks from the White House. The walls were floor-to-ceiling mirrors tinted a strange metallic blue. He sat and watched a silvery blue Alex chew on his sandwich, reflected back and forth from wall to wall, on and on, to infinite regress. *Be back in two hours. Time. Always time. How many Alexes? How many times?*

12

frowning. And as Alex was shown through the door, he couldn't tell
from either expression which way the verdict had gone. A hundred
years in jail, or . . . what? He didn't even know what the options were.
Whatever direction Roosevelt decided to push him in. He was a piece
in a war game, not a pawn, he hoped, but a piece with a certain
inherent power. Knowledge. Enough knowledge, possibly, to influence
the outcome. By coming here, by placing himself in Roosevelt's hands,
he had given up any possibility of simply hiding out until his connections to his own time grew strong enough to take him back.

"Sit down, Alex," Roosevelt said, gesturing to a chair that had
been drawn up beside Surrey's.

*Back to first names. Surely you don't send a man to prison while you're
calling him by his first name.*

"We have come to an agreement here, Max and I, on your status
and potential." Alex glanced at Max, who was staring straight ahead.
"I have not consulted my advisors on this matter. They would tell me
I was off my head to even consider it, so from this moment on everything
that I have to say to you must be top secret. I'm taking a hell of a
chance, but any man who comes as highly recommended as you do
deserves an opportunity to prove himself." Roosevelt settled back in
his chair. "Now, you'll have to forgive me if I ramble around the barn
here. I'm sort of in the position of the stray horse with the bad eye
who's on the wrong side of the barn. I may wander around for a while,
but eventually I'll find the door."

Roosevelt pushed his chair farther back and rested both hands on the edge of the desk. "In our earlier conversation you very emphatically told me that we were going to win this war. You're correct. It has been clear, both to the majority of my military men and to myself, that from the beginning both of our principal enemies, Germany and Japan, were fighting the sort of war that had to be decided very quickly if they were to be successful. By the end of 1942 to be exact. Obviously they have not met that schedule, which has meant a long slow battle of attrition, which they cannot win. But by which they hope to wear us down and discourage us into more advantageous, for them, terms of surrender." He stopped and inserted a Camel into his cigarette holder. A breeze brought the scent of magnolias through the open windows. Outside, in the heat-hazed distance, Alex could see the Potomac River.

"What this means is a long and continuing roll call of death for our boys. As well as our allies. In the midst of this, and because of it, I have seen our possession of this super bomb as a means not simply of victory, but of speedy victory. While we might predict the end of the European war, providing the Germans are unsuccessful in their attempt to build a bomb, in a year or so, victory over Japan is sure to be long and very costly. If a demonstration of our bomb is necessary to prove to Japan that our forces are indeed superior to theirs, then they shall have their demonstration." He raised his eyebrows. "Do I note a look of surprise on your face, Alex? Perhaps it is my use of the word *demonstration?*"

Alex nodded. Roosevelt put his cigarette holder in the artillery shell ashtray and leaned back. "I must say, and I include Max and the absent professor Einstein in this, I was disappointed to find in your letter and proposal so little confidence in my planning and my decision making. All of you have assumed that I have every intention of dropping our bomb, if and when we complete it, on a large concentration of civilians. Innocent Japanese civilians, as you put it, although I'm not sure there is any such thing. You doubt any humane considerations I might have for the future. Believe me, gentlemen, this is not so. You have shown me that your knowledge in the matter of this bomb is great, too great, I might add, but your understanding of my own planning and motives is deficient. This is as it should be, I suppose." He stopped and looked up at the ceiling, as if thinking. "You know,

I am a juggler of sorts. As part of my show I have added the difficult condition of never letting my right hand know what my left is up to. I may have one policy for Europe and one diametrically opposed for South America. I may be entirely inconsistent as far as general knowledge is concerned. And furthermore, I am perfectly willing to mislead and tell untruths if it will help win the war. That is why I'm talking to you, Alex, rather than witnessing your exit from this room in manacles, on your way to a long and very hard life in one of our more obscure federal prisons." He smiled a little sadly, as if sorry he would miss this spectacle.

"I have found that being President is quite a bit like being on roller skates. Sometimes you go where you want to, and sometimes you go where the roller skates take you. I am willing to work with that aspect of the job, and even to exploit it." Alex tried to conjure up an image of Franklin D. Roosevelt on a pair of roller skates. Even if you forgot about the wheelchair, the vision would not come.

"This also accounts for my acceptance of the more serendipitous occurrences that come my way. Such as you. Though even I have my limits." He smiled his wide grin. "You scientists will appreciate this story. Just last week Eleanor sent me a note with a scheme from one of her California acquaintances. The two of them had decided that we might have an effective weapon if we were to go out and collect as many bees, hornets, and wasps as we could possibly get. We would keep them in hives and load them on an airplane. We would then have the plane fly as low as possible and drop them over the enemy lines. Eleanor then foresaw total retreat and utter confusion among the enemy." He chuckled. "Eleanor's grasp of military strategy is as weak as your grasp of my military goals." His face grew serious. "It has never been my intention to murder masses of civilians. To accuse me of that would be no less a matter than to accuse me of, say, inflicting Pearl Harbor on our own Navy. As some idiots have suggested. They would cast me in the same mold as Tojo or Hitler. They, and you gentlemen, in your own way, do me great injury."

Alex felt himself blush. "Mr. President," Surrey said, "we meant nothing of the kind. If we have overstated the case, we have done so in light of the gravity and scope of the consequences. No one would accuse you of such things. On the contrary, it's because we are confident in your planning and decision making that we have come to you.

We understand that the knowledge we have admitted to is no small matter, and we are aware of the possible repercussions. And yet we are here."

Roosevelt nodded. "Yes. And now the one-eyed horse has finally found the barn door. Let me tell you what waits inside." He shifted his chair so he was looking straight at Alex.

"In Professor Einstein's letter, and in our conversation, you have made the point that the decision we come to as to the use of our bomb will be of utmost importance to the future. I agree. Given, for the moment, we have other plans for the European war, we are left with Japan." Roosevelt pushed away from the desk and rolled toward the wall behind him. He reached up with a stick and pulled down a map of the Pacific Ocean. The areas under Japanese control were marked in red. There was a lot of red on the map.

"Doesn't look too good," Surrey said.

"We've been running a half-assed war out there. Unfortunately, it couldn't be helped. Churchill has demanded all along that Europe be our primary front. We've been fighting like hell on those godforsaken islands, but we're hampered by all the usual problems of fighting a long-distance war. To tell you the truth, I really don't have a clear idea of what's going on in the Pacific. The Navy tells me what the Navy wants me to hear, the Army does the same thing. The two are almost never in agreement. I understand that each service is promoting its own program, but that doesn't help in making strategy. I've got good men working for me, but I always need more. I need men I can trust to give me objective information."

Alex felt a little sick but he knew it wasn't the club sandwich he'd eaten. It was what was coming next.

"What I want you to do, Alex, is head on out there and study the situation. Later, when we get within striking distance of the home islands, we'll have some hard facts to base our plans on. You know what the options are, and what we'll need to do. I can't really send out anyone else because this whole thing is top secret. You'll go because you already know. It's either use you or lock you up."

Alex cleared his throat. "With all due respect, sir, I think I could be of more use to you right here. I can talk to people who know the area. Use the information that's already available." *Besides, I already know what's going to happen. If I go out there, there's a good chance I won't be coming back. And that won't help anyone.*

Roosevelt looked determined. "Well, now, Alex, I'm sure you could do good work right here in Washington, but the point is, you've not been seasoned. To me, and eventually to my advisors, you're just one more egghead scientist with crackpot notions. Now, if I had a man who had been on site, who really knew the straight dope, well, that man would carry some real weight. What I'm going to do is give you some first-class credentials. You'll report only to me and you'll have the right to stick your nose in just about anywhere. I'll draw up your orders with all the go-aheads you'll need. You can expect further orders once you're in place. I've got a rather remarkable string of free-lance people working for me—they'll keep us in touch with one another. Meanwhile, you'll have some of the best help I can offer."

Alex waited for Roosevelt to continue.

"Me," Surrey said to Alex, his voice tight with anger. "I'm the help. He's sending me along with you. We leave day after tomorrow." Alex looked at Roosevelt. The President smiled and nodded his head.

"Have a good trip, boys. We'll be in touch."

13

MOLLY IMMERSED HERSELF IN HER WORK.
A call to Washington to Pat Williams's office set up an appointment
for the following day. The legislative assistant, Art Noonan, the man
in charge of the POW camp atrocities, seemed pleased that the New
York *Times* was taking an interest. She made her hotel reservations
and went to tell her editor, Harry Watkins, that she would be out of
the office for several days.

"You don't mind going?" Harry asked, his tone solicitous. He leaned
back in his chair, arms folded over his chest. His Irish tweed jacket
was hung neatly on a hanger behind his office door.

"Harry, I'm only going to Washington, D.C. I think I can handle
it."

Watkins nodded. "Alex out of town again?" he asked casually.

"Yes," she answered, before she could catch herself. She knew
Harry didn't like Alex, could care less whether he was in town or
not.

He nodded again. The movement rocked his chair slightly. He
pursed his lips. "If you need help on this one, I could maybe get away.
Just for the day, of course. Maybe overnight." He looked at her steadily.

Ah, the leopard shows his spots. Good old helpful Harry. "No thanks,
I can manage on my own. I'll let the desk know where I'll be once I
get there. I'll be staying with friends." She was lying, but she didn't
need Harry following her to a hotel. Just to help out, of course. Harry
had been trying to get next to her for several years now. He was easily
deflected, his overweening pride kept him from asking anything out-

right, but he was persistent. She had to work with him, so she didn't come right out and squash his frail hopes.

"Go for it," Watkins said. His clichés often approached malapropisms in their misdirection. As if he studied some popular text on how to be a regular guy, but he was always several years behind the times. The odd part was, when it came to the written word, he was an excellent editor.

Molly stood up and smoothed her skirt. As always, Harry found it difficult to take his eyes off her chest. "I'll see you in a couple of days, Harry. If Alex should happen to call, tell him I'm in Washington, and I'll call the house every night." Harry nodded. She hated to pass a message along through Harry, but she hated even worse to miss Alex. She'd leave a note at home, but she never knew where he'd be calling from, or when.

SHE WORKED LATE that evening, and ate out before going home. But finally she had to face the empty house, which was indeed empty. Quiet. When Alex was there, he always had something running: the television, stereo, radio, or some kitchen appliance. Alex created noise, he whistled, sang, hummed, or talked to her, or the TV. He filled the house with himself. If he had simply been away, she would have enjoyed the quiet. It wasn't that she was afraid, or even very lonely. She just missed him.

She packed her bag. The bed seemed too wide that night, too big for just one person. In the night, in her sleep, she stretched out her leg to touch him, but he was not there.

THE TAXI ACCELERATED out of the airport onto the George Washington Parkway. The District of Columbia lay across the river on her right, low buildings punctuated by distant, familiar monuments: the Capitol, the Washington Monument, the Lincoln and Jefferson Memorials. Traffic thickened as they crossed the Fourteenth Street bridge into downtown Washington. The taxi moved slowly down Pennsylvania Avenue toward the Capitol, which was gleaming white in the late-morning sun.

She had an hour before her appointment with Representative Pat Williams's legislative assistant, Art Noonan. She had the driver let her out at the Botanical Gardens, just at the foot of Capitol Hill. Williams's office was in the Rayburn House Office Building, almost directly across the street.

She had always loved the Botanical Gardens. She and Alex had come to Washington many times over the years, especially during college, when it seemed as if they were taking the train down at least once a month for various peace demonstrations. The Gardens were situated right in the middle of Washington's monuments and museums, but they were neglected by the vast majority of tourists. A huge building of ornate glass and stone, modeled on the airy style of the Crystal Palace of London's Great Exhibition of 1851, it held a vast collection of trees, shrubs, and flowers from all over the world. The building was divided into connecting rooms, each with its own climate and type of plant: desert, forest, and tropical, with a main hall of rain forest humidity and luxuriant trees and undergrowth. She particularly liked the hundreds of blooming orchids. Alex's mother had been an orchid grower, and Alex had inherited her plants and ability. Molly spent a calm forty-five minutes wandering among the plants, strolling from desert to jungle, inhaling the mixture of fragrances. The building was quiet and almost empty, and she was sorry when her time was up. Outside, she felt a slight shock at the return to the noise and rush of the world. She crossed the street to the huge bunkerlike Sam Rayburn Building. She stood on the wide steps of the Rayburn, looking at the Capitol through a skein of flowering trees. It was whiter and cleaner than she had ever seen it, just having emerged from its first facelift and repair in many years. The facade had begun to crumble and a Puerto Rican terrorist bomb had blown a hole in the outer wall, necessitating a major overhaul.

The interior of the Rayburn, though, did little to alter the overall bunker image. The entrance area was small, cramped, and mostly filled with a walk-through, metal-detecting security arch. The building itself was laid out in a simple cube with an interior courtyard. The halls were wide and long, the ceilings so high they seemed built for a race of giants. It resembled an enormous hospital. Any moment she expected to see a ten-foot-tall orderly race around the corner pushing a gurney the size of a Buick. The halls were lined with large wooden doors, each leading to a conference room, committee area, or congressman's office. She studied a schematic while she waited for the elevator, finding Pat Williams located on the top floor.

Williams's office looked just like every other congressional office she had ever been in, larger than those in the older buildings but just as chopped up with partitions and bookcases. Congressmen tended to collect legislative and administrative assistants the way a squirrel collected nuts, in the hope that more had to be better, and more than enough could be the hedge one needed to survive either a tough winter or a hard campaign.

One of Williams's receptionists greeted Molly and buzzed Art Noonan. Noonan was burly and young-looking though he had streaks of gray showing in his curly blond beard. He was dressed in khakis and a short-sleeved plaid shirt. He smiled and shook her hand and asked about her trip. He peered into the conference room and found his boss at work, which left them the cafeteria in the basement as the only other place they could sit and talk.

The cafeteria served cafeteria food: overdone meat smothered in brown sauce, tired fillets of pale nondescript fish, breasts of chicken breaded and fried, and watery beans and tired corn endlessly cooking on the metal steam tables. Several large black women with serving spoons waited to dish up one's selection. Molly examined the heavy, greasy food and understood why most of Washington's government workers seemed to harbor an air of gloom and defeat. It wasn't the massive budget deficit, it was the cafeteria food. She ordered a salad and Noonan had a large Coke. The tables were placed far enough apart that conversations were not easily overheard. They put their trays on a six-person table. Molly positioned her pen and her opened notebook beside her salad bowl.

"I was back in Butte, in Montana," Noonan began. "I was the district office. Just me, all alone, when this guy walks in raving about how his father was a World War II vet, an ex-POW, how he had these terrible fevers and the VA down in Oklahoma wouldn't do anything for him. He wanted us to see if we could do something for the old man. I started asking questions. The story that came out was hard to believe. POWs being used as guinea pigs by the Japanese, our government trying to cover it all up after the war." He shook his head. "That was the beginning. There aren't any of us who've worked on this who hasn't wished at one time or another that this guy hadn't come in, that we'd never been singled out for this mess. It's gone a hell of a lot farther than that little office back in Montana. We get calls from the Japanese, calls from the Russians, from the Chinese. Everybody's got an angle or an ax."

"Wait," Molly said, writing in her notebook. "Give me some names."

"The first guy's name is Greg Rodriguez, Jr. His dad was the POW. Rodriguez Jr. was the head of Public Health Services on the Flathead Indian Reservation from 1974 to 1978, so he's no novice in these kinds of health problems. See, all we ever wanted to do, at least at first, was to get a change in the VA policy. The Canadians have a Social Safety Net program of automatic compensation for Far East POWs and their wives. We wanted a program like theirs. And we wanted the Veterans Administration to locate, identify, and track down the fevers of unknown origin that were plaguing this man and other vets. If the VA had gone along with us, this whole business wouldn't have mushroomed the way it has."

"Why wouldn't they go along with it?"

"Lots of reasons. The primary one was the United States government won't admit that they know anything about what happened to these men. They say there's no background material, or if there is, it's top secret. The VA doesn't want to set up a program that caters to one special segment of veterans because they're afraid that all kinds of special interest groups will start lobbying for their own programs. The vets themselves aren't very good at pursuing their own interests. They're a conservative bunch. For years they've pointed their fingers at other people. You know, 'Stop tearing down our government. America, love it or leave it.' Now they're faced with a government that won't even admit it knows what happened to them. *These* guys know what happened. They were there. But the government is stonewalling, waiting for them to all die. Of the sixteen thousand Far East POWs who made it back, there're only four thousand still alive."

A man in a suit put a tray down at the end of their table and smiled at Molly. She glared at him and shook her head. The man shrugged, picked up his tray, and moved away.

"What did Rodriguez Sr. say had happened to him?" she asked.

"Well, his experience was typical, if you can call such things typical. We had a hearing on this whole question back in 1982. Rodriguez was too sick to attend, but we had a guy there, W. W. "Pappy" Whelchel, who was a former POW. He's from Tulsa. What happened to him was pretty much the same as Rodriguez.

"Pappy was in the Philippines when the Japanese attacked, and he was on Bataan when the American forces surrendered. The first horror was the Bataan Death March which killed several thousand of our guys—this was in July 1942. After they finished the march, they were loaded into boxcars and sent to a camp at Cabanatuan in the Philippines."

"How do you spell that?"

"I'll check it when we go back upstairs. So they loaded the prisoners, one hundred to a boxcar with no food or water. A lot of men suffocated before that trip was finished. Then in October, two thousand of them were taken to Manila and shipped to Japan and Manchuria. Conditions on these ships were terrible, much worse than you can imagine. Finally they made it to Pusan, Korea, where a hundred and fifty of the sickest were taken off and put into a kind of hospital. The rest of the Americans off the boat were shipped by rail to a camp in Mukden, Manchuria. Eventually the ones in the hospital were also taken to Mukden.

"Pappy was one of the guys in the hospital. When they first got to the camp, they were sprayed in the face with some sort of chemical. They were given shots and carefully scrutinized over the following months. The Japanese were real careful not to get near these men. Some of the prisoners got sick and died and some of them didn't. At least not then."

Molly pushed her half-eaten salad away. "Didn't the government keep any records of this when they were demobilized?"

"Most of the men wouldn't admit to what had happened after they were freed. You've got to see it from their point of view. They'd been in the camps for three and a half years. All they wanted was to get home and start their lives over, to forget the bad parts. They lied about their health problems so they wouldn't be detained. So"—he shrugged his shoulders—"no records."

"So Pappy gets screwed," Molly said.

"Yeah, well, he's dead now. What happened to him then was terrible, but at least he came out of the camp alive." Noonan's eyes narrowed. His voice was even, devoid of emotion. "There were three groups of men at Mukden, each one forced to participate in a different type of experiment. Pappy and his group were the bacteriological warfare guinea pigs. The Japanese were looking for vectors, ways to get the disease from the lab out to the enemy. They used feathers, dust, gas, all sorts of things. They finally settled on fleas."

"I read about their flea farms," Molly said.

"The second group was subjected to freezing experiments. The Japanese wanted to know what happened to men under conditions of extreme cold. They would freeze, say, one limb, an arm or a leg, then thaw it out and see what the damage was. They'd dip guys in freezing water for varying periods of time and see how long it took them to die.

"The third group was used to test new types of explosives. They'd put a bomb in a field and then stake men around it at varying intervals. They'd explode the bomb, then go around and check the damage to the men."

"Jesus," Molly said.

"Yeah. Like I said before, there've been a lot of times when I wished I'd never gotten into this. You read this stuff, talk to these guys, it's just goddamn hard to believe men could do this to other men. But in a way that's not the worst of it. In some ways what we did was worse."

"We?"

"The Americans. We knew two years before the war was over what was going on at Mukden. At least part of it. At the end of the war we were ready. We were there in a matter of days."

"And got them out," Molly said, hoping that was the end of it, somehow knowing that it wasn't.

"Sure, we wanted to liberate the camp. We rescued everyone left alive. Got them out of there and eventually back home. But what we really wanted was information. The Japanese had done a lot of experiments and compiled a lot of data. We wanted our men, but we also wanted that data. And we were ready and willing to deal to get it."

Molly stared down at her salad bowl. The iceberg lettuce was brown around the edges. "Was it that important?" she asked, the anger evident in her voice. "Was it all that important?"

"They thought it was, Molly. The United States government thought they were making a very good deal."

"Screw the GIs."

"That's about the size of it."

14

THE LUNCH CROWD IN THE CAFETERIA
thinned out. Busboys cleared tables onto carts filled with mounds of
dirty dishes. Molly slid the remains of her half-eaten salad down to
the end of the table, where it was picked up and thrown away. Noonan
brought over another Coke for himself and a coffee for Molly.

"See," he said as he sat back down, "we, the Americans, knew
what was going on at the Mukden camp. At least generally. We also
knew we had to get there before the Russians, who were poised on
the border of Manchuria, ready to sweep down on the Japanese and
grab as much land as possible before the war was over. Years before,
Stalin had promised Roosevelt and Churchill that he would join in the
war against Japan. That was part of the Potsdam Agreement. For that
promise, he received help fighting the Germans. And he did go in
against the Japanese, in August 1945. He just waited until he was
sure he could do it in a manner that would maximize his gains without
seriously endangering his forces. They were in the war against the
Japanese a total of five days.

"Russia also knew about the camp. They said that the Japanese
were mustering what was left of their forces to launch a germ warfare
attack on Russia. By then the Japanese weren't about to attack
anyone—their primary goals were getting their information and their
butts out of there. It's one thing to be taken prisoner. It's another to
be taken prisoner by the Russians." He stopped and sipped his Coke.

"Anyway, there was going to be a race to get to Mukden as soon
as the shooting stopped. Comparable to the competition between the

U.S. and Russia for the German rocket scientists. But this time we won. We got there first. And what we did was make a deal. Essentially, we let their researchers, starting with their number one guy, General Ishii, go free in return for all the material they had amassed during the course of the war."

Molly stopped writing and looked up at him. "You make it sound almost reasonable," she said.

"In the eyes of the military, it was a good deal. Of course the Japanese burned a lot of information. Smuggled a lot back to Japan. Some of their guys escaped before we could get there. But still, we ended up with a load of information that we could have never come up with any other way. Our army had been doing research on biological and chemical warfare as well. But we didn't test it on humans." He stopped for a moment and looked out over the room. "At least as far as I know, we didn't. So when the opportunity came to get some sort of genuine data, we jumped at it."

"At the expense of our democratic morals and our national honor."

He shrugged. "You and I may see it that way, others didn't then and wouldn't now. I don't think you'd see any hesitation if the same deal were offered to our chemical and biological warfare departments today. Under Reagan we increased our expenditures on C&B studies, George Bush voted twice in the Senate to increase funding, and you'll notice he hasn't abandoned this sort of research since he became President. But we've got the same old problem: how do you test the agents you come up with? You can gas only so many beagles and infect so many monkeys. At some point you're going to want live body experiments. You're going to want to try it out on a 200-pound soldier."

Molly put down her pencil and sat back in her chair. "Let's leave that part of it for a minute and get back to 1945. Let me be the devil's advocate. Just what harm came out of what we did? Aside from the moral implications."

He smiled. "The moral implications are pretty hard to avoid, but all right, I'll go along with the question.

"First of all, as far as we're concerned—by we I mean the Congressman and his staff—there was no real way to prove what happened to the men so they would be eligible for advanced benefits today. Plus, we couldn't retrieve the records of what was actually done to them. These records exist. The Japanese were meticulous about keeping records. Somewhere there are papers saying prisoner number 1394,

Pappy Whelchel, was given x units of xyz toxins and this is what happened to him. There were slides of tissues, rectal smears, throat cultures, charts of temperatures, a whole range of documentation. This is what our government traded for, and this is what they now say they never had, or they 'sent back' to the Japanese. We, the Congressman, thought if we could locate those papers, and especially the tissue slides, we'd have our smoking gun. The slides were carefully categorized, and each patient was clearly identified on the slide itself. This is valuable information: I don't think anyone threw them away or simply lost them. Or even 'sent them back.'

"This whole question has been discussed in Japan for several years now, discussed publicly because of a documentary made by the Tokyo Broadcasting System, 'A Scar Left by the Devilish Unit 731.' They unearthed some of the former members of the 731 and questioned them, and substantiated nearly all the allegations concerning the camp and the testing. Some of these individuals are not only alive but are still profiting from their knowledge. The Japanese Green Cross, roughly equivalent to our Red Cross, has done extensive work with the manufacture of artificial blood and other blood products. It's thought that these lucrative and potentially lucrative projects are a direct outgrowth of the 731 studies."

Noonan leaned forward and clasped his hands. "The thing that really gets me is that we know exactly what our government did. We *know* that they traded freedom for information. We *know* that the information existed, and it very probably exists today. We *know* that having the information would help save the lives of former POWs. *But the United States government refuses to acknowledge any complicity or wrongdoing, or that the situation ever even existed!*" He stopped talking and leaned back. He carefully unclasped his hands. "Sorry. I've been working on this for years, and it still makes me angry. I just can't understand why no one seems interested. We have press conferences, committee hearings, and nobody picks up on it. Where's the probing eye of the mass media when we need it?" he said with a half smile.

"Right here," Molly answered. "Drinking too much coffee and getting writer's cramp. Have you got documentation on all of this?"

"Not all of it, that's the point. But we have plenty of background. The proof exists, it's probably sitting in cardboard boxes in the Archives warehouses out in Suitland, Maryland. Tons of papers came in after the war—reports, documents, exhibits, the Tokyo War Crimes records—it's all there, and hardly anyone has gone through it. A couple of writers, nonfiction and fiction, have been working the boxes. The Army went in and took some of them back after we started asking questions. They said they were reclassifying them top secret." He laughed and shook his head. "Can you believe it? Sure we've got plenty of documentation. You can have it all. I want you to help us find what we need to get this thing out in the open, to help our constituents. Constituent, there's only one left alive. And personally, I want you to hang not only the bastards who did this, but the kinder, gentler bastards who are right now covering it up for the first bastards."

Molly gathered up her notebook and put it in her purse. She stood up and looked down at Noonan. His anger was still obvious.

"With pleasure," she said. "Now show me your proof."

In the empty elevator, Noonan cleared his throat. "It just came to me, I know who you are," he said.

Molly glanced at him. "Yeah? Who?" she asked.

"You're the reporter who broke the big Indian story. Last year, when that Sioux over on the Pine Ridge Reservation went nuts and shot those two power company guys. And then made his last stand. Everybody in Montana read the story. You did a hell of a job. It must have been rough."

The elevator doors opened and they walked out and down the wide hall. "Yes," she said, "it was rough." She kept her voice carefully neutral. "Thanks for the compliment."

He stopped before they reached the office door. "Look, I'll collect all this stuff for you, but it's going to take some time. I could get it to you tonight if you want. Maybe we could have dinner?"

She looked at him. She was in for a long night in a strange town and he was a nice guy and she needed the material. She could pick it up tomorrow on her way out of town, without any problem. But she hated to eat alone in hotel dining rooms. "Sure," she said. "I'm checking into the Willard as soon as I leave here. Seven o'clock in the lobby?"

He nodded. "I'll be there."

15

MOLLY TOSSED HER SMALL OVERNIGHT
bag onto the bed and kicked off her shoes. She looked around the hotel
room with more than usual interest. The Willard had only recently
been refurbished and reopened after years of neglect. One time a
Washington landmark, the hotel had fallen on hard days after the
Second World War, settling into old age and decrepitude as the neighborhood around it disintegrated, victim of the riots of the late sixties
and the fear-fueled flight of neighborhood businesses to the white
suburbs. After years of lawsuits and threats of demolition, the property
was bought and the hotel reborn. Now a showplace, both the hotel
and the hotel's restaurant were enjoying a new era.

Molly made it a point when traveling, whenever possible, to stay
where it was interesting and comfortable. Too many times she had
had to make do in cheap, seedy motels and broken-down hotels because
there were no other choices. When the *Times* would not accept her
expense accounts, she made up the difference out of her own pocket.

The room was small but nicely furnished in what looked to be
original late 1800s period furniture. But which she suspected would
turn out to be reproductions if she looked closely. She didn't bother
to look closely, content that the room was pretty and comfortable.

She lay down on the bed and thought about Alex. She wondered
where he was and what he was doing and if he was well. She tried to
pretend that it was the worry of a wife for a husband off on a sabbatical
or extended business trip, only it was worse than that, and pretending
didn't help much. And then there was the way they had left each

other, which added a layer of guilt. The combination was unique and painful and for some reason particularly pronounced. She had been through this before, and had learned to push it into a corner of her mind that was reserved for Alex-worry. He had always said that their love was the cord that not only bound them to each other, but secured him, when he was in the past, to the present. And while the cord might fray, she knew it would never break. And she wanted to tell him that, but it was too late.

Noonan was in the lobby right on time, looking mildly out of place. She liked him for that. The lobby was crowded with a mix of staid businessmen in town on government work trying to decide where to eat dinner, and wealthy-looking women and their bored husbands arriving for an expensive meal in the hotel's famed restaurant. Molly glanced at the crowd as she walked to where Art was sitting, and it struck her that while the upper classes of Washington might be just as rich as their New York counterparts, they had little of the New Yorkers' style.

Art was wearing a sport coat and tie, and wearing them as if these particular articles of clothing were occasional acquaintances rather than close friends. Molly smiled at him and steered him to the restaurant, where they were taken to their table by the hostess.

"Just like back in Butte," Noonan said, looking around the dining room. It was paneled in walnut from floor to sky-high ceiling. The room sparkled with etched glass, gleaming silver, and pure white cloth. Their table was partially hidden behind an elegant service area, the sort of table that was perfect for conducting a discreet affair. Art looked around at the glistening chandeliers and the tuxedoed waiters. "We eat in places like this most every night, back in Montana."

"Me too," Molly said. "But only when the *Times* is paying. You bought the coffee today, this is the least I can do."

Noonan grinned. "We Westerners generally frown on letting a woman pick up the check, but if it's at the expense of the big-city, liberal press, I'm willing to make an exception."

The menu was large and heavy. Molly studied it for a few moments before she realized that the appetizers were not the entrées. The only way you could tell was by price: appetizers were the price of whole meals, entrées were the price of small automobiles. They ordered a fresh trout stuffed with salmon mousse on a bed of watercress for an appetizer. Molly had a veal chop as an entrée and Art ordered venison. They toyed with the silverware and ate fresh whole wheat rolls while they waited for the food. Their conversation was mostly about their respective jobs, pleasant but neutral.

"I've been thinking," she said, "about what you told me this afternoon. Thinking and looking over the material you gave me at the office. It may not be courtroom proof, and I hope you have more of it, but it looks pretty impressive to me. I don't quite understand how the government keeps insisting that there's no proof, when you have what seems to me to be very good documentation."

They stopped talking while the waiter served them.

"You're right when you say that our proof looks pretty good. It *is* good. But around here good isn't good enough. You've got to have complete documentation that's been signed by everyone involved. We have no actual evidence of the involvement of U.S. armed services personnel making deals with the Japanese, or destroying existing medical records in the Mukden camps. We do have the testimony of those men still living who were there, but people and what they claim aren't really proof in Washington. People lie, and around here they lie a lot. The actual *paper* proof doesn't exist. That's because those responsible have either hidden it, or given it back to the Japanese as part of their deal. When we held our hearings a couple of years ago, the State Department sent over some second-echelon functionary who sat in the witness seat and said, over and over, that they had no knowledge of what we were attempting to establish. We did score a hit with one witness, a writer, William Triplett, who had written a book on one aspect of the germ warfare studies. He testified, with a stack of papers six inches high in front of him, that not only was there proof, but it was right there on the table for everyone to see."

"Where did he find it?"

"Out in Suitland, Maryland. That's where the National Archives stores their uncataloged files. He got in under the Freedom of Information Act. He spent years going through boxes, but the story was there."

"What story? And what does it have to do with the Congressman and your attempt to get health benefits for his constituents?"

Noonan glanced aside as the waiter poured them more water. "I'm not sure you want to hear about it while you're eating."

Molly remembered how his recitation of the Mukden atrocities had effectively killed her appetite at lunch. But she was working. This was no time to be finicky. "Go ahead, I'm pretty tough."

"All right," he said. He leaned forward, elbows on the edge of the table.

"In 1948, January twenty-sixth, a Japanese man entered a bank in Tokyo, after closing time, and convinced sixteen employees that he was a doctor sent by the American Occupation authorities to inoculate all of them against dysentery. He said that a nearby well was infected and causing sickness and death. He had them gather around with their teacups while he gave a small lecture on the disease and the special innoculant he had brought. He then parceled out a dose of liquid into their teacups and showed them how to drink it. They did, and twelve of them died in a matter of minutes. Four others survived. The liquid was potassium cyanide. The doctor made off with 160,000 yen." Noonan stopped, picked up his fork, and began eating his venison.

"Jesus," Molly said. "That's a pretty complicated way to rob a bank. Here in America you just load your gun and write a note."

"That's right," Noonan said. "Which is an interesting point. Bank robbery is a Western crime, almost never encountered in Japan. And this was a damn complicated and brutal way to go about it. A product of either fiendish intelligence or brilliant insanity, depending on what theory you have of the case."

"Did they catch whoever did it?"

"They caught a man, a painter named Sadamichi Hirasawa, who was convicted of the crime and sentenced to death. He's still awaiting his punishment. He's ninety-five years old and has been in a prison cell for the last forty years."

"A fascinating story, but I don't see what it has to do with VA payments to ex-POWs."

"I'm getting to that part. There are a lot of people in Japan and elsewhere who don't think Hirasawa committed the crime. The fact that he was never put to death testifies to that. Triplett, the man who wrote the book about it, *The Flowering of the Bamboo*, doesn't think he did it."

"Again, what's the point?"

"The way the murders were enacted was indicative of someone who had extensive knowledge of poisoning techniques. Here's the way it went. The perpetrator, let's call him the doctor, gets all sixteen of the employees together and asks for them to bring their teacups. He has two bottles of medicine. He takes a pipette, draws a little from the first bottle, and puts a few drops in each of the teacups. Then he demonstrates the correct way to take the medicine. Because, he says, it is extremely strong, one must protect one's teeth and gums from direct contact. He takes a few drops of liquid, sticks his tongue out and drips the fluid into the back of his mouth. All sixteen employees pick up their teacups and follow his example." He broke off when he noticed that Molly wasn't eating. "Should I shut up?" he asked. "It would be a shame to waste this." He gestured at their plates.

Molly shook her head. "No, go on. The story is more interesting than the food."

"Okay. Some of the employees complained that the liquid was very strong, that they wanted a drink of water. Not allowed, the doctor says, first they must drink the second liquid, but not before sixty seconds have elapsed. He pours a dose from the second bottle, gives them the go-ahead, and they swallow it. That much is known, exactly, because of the four who didn't die. What happened next is a matter of conjecture, but by the positioning of the bodies it seems fairly straightforward. Some of the victims collapsed on the spot. Some of them tried to make it to a sink where there was water. One of them, a young girl, managed to crawl outside and get help. When the police arrived, there were bodies everywhere, but everything else was in perfect order. Including 300,000 yen stacked near the table where the people took their poison."

"I thought you said the robber got away with 160,000 yen."

"I did. That's one of the mysteries. If your motive is robbery, why leave behind more money than you took?"

"What other motive could there be?" she asked. A waiter appeared and, at her nod, removed her plate.

"Before we get to that, let's answer your other question. What does this case have to do with our interests? Care to make a guess?"

"Well," she thought about it for a moment. "You said the man they caught was a painter, not a doctor. If the man had the ability to administer poison in such a complicated manner, he must have learned how to do it somewhere. Maybe at the Unit 731 camp in Manchuria?"

"Very good."

"But what if they got the wrong man? It could have just as easily been a real doctor, or some other health professional with this sort of knowledge."

"Possible, yes. But while the method of administering the poison could be attributed to other professions, the exact proportions of the poison and its properties would be known to very few people. The 731 employees had extensive practice in administering poison and figuring exact dosages as well. And don't forget, the 'doctor' siphoned off a few drops himself and drank it."

"Yeah, I was wondering about that."

"Cyanide, or prussic acid, settles to the bottom of the liquid it's mixed with. He probably took his dose off the top. You've really got to know your poisons to trust yourself to be able to take a chance like that. He made them wait sixty seconds before giving them the second dose, which was probably harmless. That made sure they didn't run around or cause trouble while the poison was taking effect. This is indicative of a man who *poisons* people on a regular basis, not one who hands out medicine intended to make people well."

"So why did they choose this . . . what did you say his name was?"

"Hirasawa. They came up with him for a number of excellent reasons. One of the primary being that he confessed under questioning. Then there was a matter of name cards, the Japanese are very big on handing out their name cards, and his turned up under suspicious circumstances. When they searched his house, they found a large amount of cash equal to the money taken from the bank, cash that Hirasawa was never able or willing to account for. There was plenty of evidence. But there were also snags, chief among them that the four survivors never positively identified Hirasawa as the culprit."

"Again, fascinating, but it still doesn't answer my original question: where's the connection?"

"The actual crime has little to do with our interest in the matter. It was the *investigation* that was important. The Japanese police looked into the possibility that the killer might be a member of the 731 Unit. Someone on the investigative staff knew of the unit's existence during the war and made the connection. But inquiries in that direction came smack up against a stone wall. A wall built by the American Occupation forces. Triplett, the writer, found memos from SCAPE, the Supreme Commander for the Allied Powers, MacArthur's headquarters, saying that the Japanese police were getting too close to the 731 business and needed to be headed off. Remember our top dog, General Ishii, chief administrator of the 731? A meeting was set up by SCAPE between the police investigators and Ishii so they could question him about involvement by 731 personnel. But after that one meeting, in which Ishii admitted to nothing, all contact was withdrawn. Because of the criminal investigation, however, we know how nervous SCAPE and the U.S. Army were about letting *anyone* near Ishii or anyone else from the unit. Don't forget, the deal with the Americans was information on BW to be given in exchange for *complete immunity for all members of 731*. And 731 wasn't just in Manchuria. We have indications that there were divisions just like it scattered all over the Far East. So the Occupation couldn't let anyone near 731 or their nefarious deal might be discovered. The government today tells us it's all simply a story, and yet there's this information that Triplett dug up while working on his crime angle. They're afraid now and they were *really* afraid back then. They thought the Russians might find out about it, or the Chinese, even though at the time both of these countries were our allies. I'm not sure we can understand how valuable the Army thought that bacteriological warfare information was. Even today it's probably extremely important. And I'd bet that it's still around, probably in a vault buried in the bowels of Fort Detrick where they do our BW and chemical studies."

"I thought we stopped all of that. Didn't Nixon do away with it?"

Noonan laughed. "Yeah, well, he did cut off most of the funds. That crippled them for a while, but then we had Reagan-Bush put back all the funding and more. Bush was the tie-breaking vote twice when Congress was voting funds. No one seems to remember that. His mother came out at the time and said how ashamed she was of George for doing such a thing. Reagan called her up to explain how important it was that we have a strong arsenal of these kind of weapons. Later on, around election time, Reagan mouthed some pieties concerning the abolition of such weapons, and his puppy dog George chimed right in, but both of them love chemical and bacteriological weapons. Bush still won't stop making them, even though the Russians have agreed to quit."

"Gee, do I detect a note of bitterness?"

Noonan laughed again. "You might say so. A word from either one could have cleared up all of our concerns right at the beginning. But these guys don't have the brains to see that they could have made a deal, helped out our Vets, and the whole nasty business would have remained their dirty little secret. So, if they're that stupid, then I'm just stubborn enough to want to see it all come out where we can rub their noses in it. Which leads us to you."

"Hmmm. You want me to rub their noses in it, right?" He shrugged, looking embarrassed. "You're not the first," she went on. "People are always complaining about the press digging up dirt on various hapless victims. In most cases, the original tip comes from someone with an ax to grind."

"Some axes need to be ground. The sharper the ax, the easier it will cut through hypocrisy and evil." He spoke with some cynicism, but Molly could see he meant what he was saying.

"I know it. That's why I allow myself to be used as a grindstone. At least in some cases. Those cases that I agree with. So much for the objectivity of the press."

Noonan smiled. "You don't need to apologize for having a conscience, or good sense. If you do good in the course of your reporting, where's the harm? If objectivity stands in the way of good, then objectivity is not a desirable attitude."

"I agree. But there are plenty of journalistic theorists who wouldn't. They seek to work and exist on a higher level than I am able to attain."

Another waiter wheeled up the dessert cart. It resembled a small iron lung. Neither of them wanted dessert so she asked for the check, and paid it.

"It's getting late," Molly said. "I've got some work to do yet tonight. Did you bring me any more material?"

"It's in my car, right down the block. I'll go get it. I brought you copies of the hearings we had in Montana and the one that was held here in Washington. Also Triplett's book, and an excellent chemical and BW warfare book, *The Killing Winds*. Then there's a lot of miscellaneous stuff that's self-explanatory. Want me to go get it now?"

She nodded and stood. "I'll meet you in the lobby."

MOLLY SAT on a round settee and studied the decor. The lobby was overstuffed with ferns, white marble, and fluted columns. It was what she imagined hotels in Victorian India must have looked like in the last days of the Raj. Noonan came through the revolving door and handed her the parcel of books and papers. "Would you like to go somewhere and have a drink?" he asked.

"I don't think so," she said. "I should get to work on this right away."

"Are you a married woman, Molly?" he asked.

She smiled. "Sort of."

He nodded. "You need anything else, just call. I'll be here or in Montana. If I'm out of town, the office will tell you where to get in touch with me."

"I'll be calling, Art. Thanks again for all the help."

He turned to leave, then stopped and turned back. "Be careful, Molly. This is serious business."

She picked up the bundle of papers. "I know it. And I will be. Don't worry about me. I'll be all right."

16

Tommy Fellows was a legend in the
New York *Times* newsroom. For years he'd held down the far-corner
desk in the busy international section, canny survivor of countless
office purges, consummate master in the Byzantine world of newsroom
politics. Chain-smoking, coffee-drinking, massively overweight,
Tommy would arrive about eleven o'clock in the morning, fire up a
Camel, take a swig from his oversize, chipped-enamel mug, the coffee,
a blend of African beans prepared by his own personal news-aid, and
swing into action.

He worked the phones relentlessly, calling on his international
army of sources and tipsters, beating the pertinent bushes until whatever story he was working on began to shape up and come to life. Then
Tommy would lean back in his chair and study his notes, committing
everything to his computerlike brain. After allowing the material to
percolate while he consumed a couple of jelly doughnuts, his usually
brilliant lead would bubble to the surface and Tommy would settle
down and work, unfolding his scrupulously researched tales of terror,
power, greed, and corruption, working on into the night, living on
coffee and king-size bags of Chee-tos, until it was finished, almost
always in one marathon of superhuman effort, almost always a model
of journalistic beauty. Tommy Fellows was legend, and when Molly
arrived at the office the day after her trip to Washington, she knew
that Tommy was the man to show her the path through the dangerous
and uncharted woods of germ warfare.

She lugged in the box of material that Art Noonan had given her and dropped it on her desk. She waved at her editor, Harry Watkins, visible through the large glass front wall of his office. Harry was on the telephone. When he spotted her, he began a series of frantic hand signals that seemed to indicate that he wanted to see her as soon as possible. She took her pad and pen out of her pocketbook, locked the pocketbook in her desk drawer, and trekked over to Tommy's corner.

"Is this a good time or a bad time, Tommy?" she asked.

Fellows swiveled his chair so he was facing her, and smiled. The man weighed nearly three hundred pounds. He had once become stuck in his bathtub until his landlady responded to his cries for help and had him hoisted out by the building janitor. All of which Tommy found enormously amusing. "Me and President Harding," Tommy would say. Harding had once had the same problem with a bathtub.

Tommy beamed at Molly. "For you, sweetheart, it's always a good time. Come sit with Uncle Tommy. Tell him what's troubling you."

Molly sat down. From anyone else, Tommy's line of blarney would have been annoying, but coming from him it seemed to fit. He was always helpful and unfailingly kind to the younger reporters who came to him for advice.

"Germ warfare, Tommy. Chemical weapons, biological weapons, I'm in it up to my neck, I need an overview, or background, or a disinterested observer, or something."

"Did you read my article on binary weapons last month?"

"Yep. That's why I'm here. I figured you had the material I need. The library doesn't have much in the way of clips, which is very odd. I was sure we would have more on this than we do."

Tommy frowned, closed his eyes, and pursed his lips while he thought. After a moment he opened his eyes. "Let me take a guess. Your editor is Harry Watkins."

Mildly surprised, Molly nodded. "Yes, but what's that got to do with anything?"

"More than you might imagine, my dear. You've fallen prey to one of Harry's dirty tricks. He has obviously been struck by your many charms. What he has done is nothing new. He assigns a reporter to a story, but only after he has requisitioned the appropriate clips from the files. After the reporter has worked this barren vineyard to the point of desperation, in comes yon Harry with a vast stack of material, saving the reporter's sanity, not to say his or her ass. Gratitude flows and overflows, all in the direction of Harry Watkins, savior and friend."

Molly began to steam. It fit. Perfectly. *That sleazy fucker.* She stood up. "I'll talk to you later, Tommy, I'm going to go let him know I don't have time for his games."

Tommy lifted both hands, palm up, looking shocked. "No, no, my dear, absolutely the wrong move. In this business one must learn patience, which is the primary virtue in the art of war. Blasting Harry might make you feel better, but in the end it would accomplish nothing. What you must do is utilize the information I've just given you for your own ends. Harry doesn't know that you are now aware of his scheme; turn it against him. Make use of your knowledge, don't throw away your advantages."

Molly looked down at Tommy's Buddha-calm face and knew that he had some tactic in mind. She sat back down. "Okay. How?"

"I have all the pertinent information on my files," Tommy said, hands flickering over his computer keyboard. A page of type, neon green against a black background, came up on the screen. "I consolidated the binary weapons research with my last terrorism piece. It's slugged under the code name TommyTer, feel free to call it up and use it. That should take care of your background problems. Now, tell Tommy what angle you're working on."

"I've got a Congressman with an interesting constituent problem that's blown up on him. Pat Williams."

Tommy nodded. "Yes, I attended his first hearing. He has indeed opened up a can of worms. Astounding, isn't it, that he hasn't received more notice? We've noodled around with this issue for years, Seymour Hersh picked it up back in the sixties, but couldn't get anything to stick. The Japanese continue to slip out from under it, though now that Hirohito is dead, that may change. Our government simply forts up and waits it out until the press and the public lose interest. This particular biological baliwick is as thorny as the proverbial briar patch. Japanese germs and Japanese bugs, Molly, nobody wants to talk about them, nobody wants to read about them. The public is able to take in any amount of horrendous detail if it concerns the Holocaust, but the Japanese remain almost off-limits. The Germans have been able to accept the enormity of their crimes, to dwell on them at a national level, but the Japanese will admit to very little. And the Holocaust, as terrible as it was, is over. Germ warfare continues, or at least the development side does. This stuff could break out at any moment. Consider the effects of a severe accident in one of our secret labs. A killer virus loosed upon an unsuspecting world. The public does not like to confront such a dangerous possibility."

"That doesn't seem to have deterred you."

Tommy bowed his head. "I find the deadly fascinating. Perhaps I'm jaded. I'm old and fat, and earthly dangers hold few terrors. You, on the other hand, are much too beautiful to be dealing with such evil. I must warn you. In all my years I've never worked on a story with such potential for harm. Not to me, personally, but to the world. The historical foundations are fascinating—the Japanese and their devilish Unit 731, the monstrous General Ishii—but it is the hidden world of the terrorists and their limitless capacity for malefaction that frightens me."

"Come on, Tommy," Molly kidded. "You, frightened? You couldn't tell it from your last series on the weapons of terrorism. Besides, you're a—"

"—legend in the newsroom. And the bathtub. Yes, I know," Tommy said, finishing her sentence. "But I am not playing with you now, child. This is the worst I've ever seen. I have turned over the rocks and the things that have crawled forth are abominations. Loathsome."

Molly could see, for all his usual repartee, Tommy was as serious as she had ever seen him. And that was more frightening than anything he could have said. "Will you help me with it, Tommy? I'm not going to turn it down because it might be dangerous. This is my job, I'm going to do it."

Tommy leaned forward. His chair squealed as it returned to an upright position. He rested his forearms on the desk. Molly knew that he could work on anything he wished. The managing editor allowed him to choose his own stories and set his own deadlines. "Yes, I'll help you with it. I'm interested in the connections between our present-day practitioners to the early masters, the thread that binds Abu Nidal to the Japanese and General Ishii. But we must be careful. We must use our advantages. And, I'm afraid, we must travel." He sighed. "Though I hate it. Why don't you convince Harry that it's time we made a pilgrimage. To the source."

Molly stood up. "I'd be glad to." She smiled grimly. "Harry's dug his own hole on this one. Let's see if he can climb out of it."

She walked to her own desk and picked up the original file with the two lone clips Harry had given her when he had assigned her to the story. She rapped on his door jamb and stepped into his open office. Harry was wearing his heavy tweeds with a lemon-yellow bow tie and matching suspenders.

"Molly," he said in greeting. "How was the trip? Productive?"

"Yes, Harry, it was. I picked up a mountain of material. Everything I need, actually. I think I can work out most of the questions on this end. I'm going to need to go to Japan, though."

Harry looked surprised. "Well, now, I don't think that's really necessary. I'm not sure I could get that past the higher-ups. Maybe if you had more information, you could write the piece without doing much in the way of travel."

"No, Harry, I've talked to Tommy and he's got all the background we need. Funny you should mention it, though, I think we've got a real problem right here at the paper."

Harry frowned. "What sort of problem?"

"Someone's stealing clips. I don't know if it's carelessness or by intention. It could have to do with the nature of this whole story. Someone may not want us to be working on it. Whatever it is, I'm going to spend some time looking into it, on the quiet, of course. Tommy said he'd see what was up, and you know Tommy. Once he gets his nose on the trail, he doesn't quit until he's got his man. We're going right to the top with this, I think they'd want to know."

Harry held up his hands. "Easy now, girl. I agree, this could be a problem, but there's no need to jump right in on the blind. Tell you what, why don't I look into it. No need to take up your time. And I'll work on getting you your trip to Japan. I guess we could manage it if we keep the costs down."

"And Tommy," Molly said. "He needs to go with me. We're going to work together."

Harry looked as if someone were driving a bamboo splinter under his fingernail. "Tommy? Jesus, Molly, I don't know if I can swing *two* trips to Japan. It's as expensive as hell over there. A goddamn orange costs fifty bucks."

"I'm sure you can work it out, Harry," Molly said brightly. "Once you solve this clip thing, they'll be so grateful they'll give you two weeks in the Bahamas as a reward. Why don't you just try and see what happens?" She tossed the thin file folder on his desk. "You can start with this. Nothing much there, but maybe you can get to the bottom of it. If you need me to back you up, I'll be glad to do it. I can tell them how all we could find was two lousy clips. Of course, if I'm in Japan, I won't be around to look into it."

Harry crossed his arms over his chest. "All right, you win. I'm not stupid, you know, I see what you're doing."

Molly stood up and smoothed her skirt. "No, Harry, you're not stupid, but you've got a lot to learn." Her voice was flat and hard. "Two trips to Japan and we forget the clips. I'll get your story, Harry, and it will be a good one. But don't ever try to fuck around with me again. Got it?"

She left his office without waiting for an answer.

17

ALEX LEANED AGAINST THE BULKHEAD AND
stared out the thick round window of the airplane. Below, the rising
sun reflected brightly off the surface of the calm sea, creating a broad
path of sparkling brilliance. The Pan Am Flying Clipper droned west,
toward Hawaii, toward the sun.

He stretched. The seats were almost twice as wide as any airline
seat in his own time. The lumbering seaplane was slow, but it was
large and relatively comfortable. A stewardess, dressed in a military-
style skirt and jacket, smiled at him as she walked up the aisle. He
glanced at Surrey, asleep in the seat beside him. Surrey in his light
tan uniform shirt and pants. The same as his own. They had donned
them for the first time in San Francisco the day before, much to
Surrey's disgust. They were the same uniforms worn by Navy officers,
minus any insignias or markings. He and Surrey were soldiers in
Roosevelt's private army of quasisecret agents whose job was to amass
information and send it back to the President. As such, they warranted
no badges or rank. At the same time, they were granted a freedom of
movement that few in the Army or Navy could command.

Puffy white clouds began to appear beneath them in the clear sky
between the airplane and the sparkling sea. The clouds reminded Alex
of Einstein's fly-away, puff-ball hair. The professor had seen them
off, several days before, standing on his porch in his leather jacket.
Hatless.

"Max," Einstein had said, "remove that scowl from your face. You cannot remain angry forever. Think of yourself as a soldier in the Army of Good. You are not being sent off to fight, but to learn. Knowledge, Max. You understand the value. Bolster knowledge with imagination, and there are no difficulties that we may not overcome."

"Yeah, except I'm the one who's being sent three thousand miles across the Pacific. I'll be out there, and you'll be right here. Eating cheese and drinking tea."

"True." The old man put his hands in his jacket pockets. "But remember our cause. It is important."

Max had been angry ever since they'd found out that Roosevelt was sending both of them to the Pacific. Max blamed it on Alex. Max was profoundly unmilitary and generally uninterested in the war. He was also skeptical of their influencing the outcome of anything.

"Yes, you are upset," Einstein had said, "but there seems no other way to go about this. We are only following the logical progression of inevitable events. I will work here with Bohr and a few of the others. You and Alex must do what is being asked of you. You will establish our credibility. They, those who make policy, will not listen to us, the scientists. Is this not correct, Alex? Then you must go forth. We are engaged in a mighty endeavor; we must strive for the utmost morality in our actions. Only morality can bring dignity and beauty to life. And safety to the future of the world." They had parted then, and near the end of the block, Alex had turned to look back. The old man had remained standing by his porch. *So frail.* A small breeze stirred Einstein's hair. Cottony clouds of hair.

ALEX HAD BEEN in the seat for seventeen hours. His body was sticky with old sweat and his joints were stiff.

Surrey stirred and opened his eyes. He looked at Alex for a long moment, awaiting memory. Comprehension and recognition began to dawn. He wiped his face with his hands and sat up to look out the window. "Nice view," he said sarcastically. He motioned for the stewardess and asked for coffee. After his first few sips from the china mug, his face relaxed from irritation into resignation.

Alex held up a manila envelope that he had found, torn open, between the seats. "Our orders," he said, "I see you opened them while I was sleeping. We were supposed to wait."

Surrey waved a hand impatiently. "I'm not going along with that military horseshit. Franklin loves to play the Commander-in-Chief. It's the real reason he keeps running for office. He doesn't care about being President. He's tired of that. His addiction is military power—playing with soldiers, toy ships, and cannons. It was his passion as a boy and his passion as a man. He's maneuvering us around the board just as he used to maneuver his little lead playmates. All this is so much horseshit." Surrey took the envelope and waved it. "I hate the self-important pompousness of it. The impenetrable jargon. Jesus, read it, it doesn't say much of anything, nothing specific. A couple of directives to base commanders that will immediately mark us as some sort of staff spies sent out to cause trouble. They'll put our asses on line as often as possible in the hope that we'll be wounded or killed and shipped back to whatever rock we crawled out from under in the first place." Surrey handed his empty coffee cup to the stewardess. "Do you know how much longer it will be before we get to wherever it is we're going?" he asked her. "No sir," she answered. "It depends on whether or not we've been diverted. That often happens. I'll ask the captain, though." Surrey nodded.

Alex pointed at the envelope. "Anything in there about our studying end-phase strategy? That's what we're supposed to be doing."

Surrey raised his eyebrows. "You know, for a man who's supposed to have all the answers, there's a streak of naiveté in you as broad as Kansas. You're correct. That's the official reason we're being sent out here. But nothing is ever really spelled out that clearly, not in written orders. If we come up with anything, fine. But if we happen to get killed in the process, that's all right too. Roosevelt doesn't care much one way or the other. Either way it solves some problems for him. You, in particular. If you're dead, then you won't be blabbing secret information to the enemy. Barring your demise, my job is to see that you keep your mouth shut and stay out of trouble. Look." He shifted forward in his seat. "Franklin's got legions of little spies just like us. It's one of the reasons I quit working for him. He's got informers in every branch of the government. But he's so damn personable about it, everyone thinks they're special, doing important work, reporting directly to the President of the United States." He shook his head. "Franklin's a pragmatist of the first water. Once you lose your usefulness to him, you're gone. And he can be a hard-hearted son of a bitch, he doesn't care much how you go. Once I caught on to all of this, I quit. I don't like being anyone's errand boy, not even the President's."

"Even if the end result is worth the injury to your dignity?"

Surrey flushed. "Jesus, I'm getting tired of these insults to my integrity. You and Roosevelt and Einstein keep trotting out these appeals to my higher nature. Maybe I can't attain the rarefied spiritual heights where you fellows operate. I can't help thinking that this whole mess—the war, the bomb, all of it—somehow grows out of just the same sort of fuzzy, idealized, horseshit philosophy that you all keep throwing in my face. I just don't buy it. I neither desire death at the hands of the Japanese, nor do I wish to deal it. I have no military or heroic fantasies. We did that already, you and me against the Russians, remember? It didn't really change anything then, and I don't think it will now."

The odd part was, Alex thought, he could hear himself in what Surrey was saying. Hear himself back in his own time, back before Pearl Harbor, back before the war had become personal. He heard himself echoed through years of peace marches and protests in college, ban-the-bomb rallies over the years. And he knew Surrey was right. It *was* fuzzy idealized thinking that often became the basis for righteous nations to fight their God-sanctioned wars. But in those cases, the philosophy was the excuse, the vindication for expansionist-political-religious warfare policies. But that wasn't the fault of the philosophy, nor did it diminish the validity of the ideas. That was the fault of the men who used the ideas for their own purposes.

"Let me tell you about the future, Max. This is what you are going to live to see. Maybe I shouldn't tell you. Maybe I'm breaking all the rules, if there are any rules, but I don't give a shit. I understand your position, and I sympathize with it. But sticking one's head in the sand, no matter how intelligent the head, is an act of complicity. In my time, I'm a teacher. Just like you. I memorize things and teach them to students. Right before I showed up back here, I was teaching a course in World War II, ending with the atomic bomb. I did my homework before I started the class." He held up a hand. "Don't interrupt. In 1945 the United States arsenal will consist of two atomic bombs. We will drop one on Hiroshima, Japan, and the other on Nagasaki. The Hiroshima bomb will kill 110,000 people almost immediately. In three months the number of dead will be 130,000. In Nagasaki, we will miss the center of the city, so casualties will be lighter than expected.

Still, 30,000 will die in the initial blast, 40,000 more over the next three months. The largest percentage killed will be in three groups: the elderly, women, and young girls. Lots of kids. Only three percent of the dead will be members of the armed services."

"I don't want to hear this."

"Tough shit. Get your goddamn head out of the sand. Jesus, you're the man I've looked up to more than anyone in my life. Unless both of us get killed out here—which is a distinct possibility—this is what you're going to grow old with.

"By my time, the world will have more than 50,000 nuclear warheads with more than a million times the destructive power of the Hiroshima bomb. If we were to explode only one percent of our capability, the world would cease to exist as a habitable planet. I could give you the scenarios—nuclear winter, radiation poisoning, the whole horror show—but I'll spare you that. If the U.S. were to go to war with Russia, we'd be looking at 150 million American dead and 100 million Russian dead. And very likely the eventual death of everyone else on the planet. This is not horseshit, Max, this is real. In my time we live with that possibility, live with it every minute of every day. I'm not appealing to your better nature, I'm appealing to your intelligence, your head, your guts, your ass. Jesus, I don't know if there's any way out of it, but we've got to try. *I've* got to try."

"No people could live that way. With that threat."

Alex laughed flatly. "Yeah, well, we do. Most of us don't ever think about it. Most people are generally too stupid to understand it anyway. I've got to say, people aren't going to get appreciably smarter in the next fifty years, and that's the scary part. The locals are still writing 'Die Nigger Die' on the sidewalks and burning crosses, and hating anyone in the least bit different from themselves. And that sort of thinking extends all the way up to our national leaders, only with them it's 'Die Commie Die.' Same stupidity, different group to hate. These are the people who have the power over the missiles and the atomic bombs. It can't hold, Max, someday it's going to blow."

Surrey sat staring stubbornly at the back of the seat in front of him. "Max, what's the worst thing you've ever seen?" There was a long silence. When he spoke, Surrey's voice was rough. "One time, I saw a hospital ward full of soldiers, WWI veterans, who had been gassed. It . . ." He stopped and cleared his throat. "I've seen men die," he went on, "but this was even more horrible than that. These men should have been dead. I think most of them would have preferred it."

Alex nodded. "This bomb is worse. A thousand times worse."

"I can't imagine it."

"Trust me. I've seen films. Read descriptions. Believe me, Max. It *is* impossible to imagine. But it's going to happen."

18

at the huge Army cargo plane that had brought them from Hawaii.
He squinted and shaded his eyes against the intense glare reflecting
off the metal skin of the plane. The hot, humid air wrapped around
him like a wet wool blanket. Hawaii had been nothing more than a
change of airplanes, going from the relative comfort of the civilian
Clipper to the bare bones of the military air-transport system, where
the aesthetic was strictly utilitarian and the message clear: men are
cargo. Another seventeen hours in the air, this time strapped into web
seats strung along a cargo bay full of wooden crates.

He waited for Surrey to collect his gear and climb down the metal
ladder. He turned away from the plane and looked at the low hangars
and the rows of fighters, shimmering in the tropical heat. There was
a sign over the largest hangar. Henderson Field.

Guadalcanal.

"You know," Surrey said, coming up beside him, "I thought it was
hot in the belly of that monster." He gestured at the cargo plane. Work
crews were beginning to off-load the wooden crates. "I didn't know
anything, did I?" Alex shook his head, picked up his seabag and pack,
and began walking to the terminal. By the time they'd crossed the
hundred yards of runway to the building, his upper body was soaked
with sweat. Inside, a fat sergeant sat at a gray desk. A rickety floor
fan blew a stream of hot air at the man's face. Other than the sergeant,
the desk, and the fan, the bare cinder block room was empty. The
sergeant looked up at Alex and Surrey with no apparent interest.

"We'd like to see the CO," Alex said, putting his seabag on the floor.

"He's busy," growled the sergeant. He looked down at his desk and shuffled a few pieces of paper.

"When is he going to be not busy?" Alex asked. He could feel the sweat running down his back and spreading along his belt.

The man grunted and spread his hands. "The CO's always busy. There's a war on. Who the hell are you guys anyway?"

Surrey snorted. Alex glanced at him in annoyance and pulled a set of orders from his pack. "We have business with the CO. Maybe you ought to tell him we're here and let him decide if he's too busy to see us."

"And whom should I say is calling?" the man said, with exaggerated politeness.

An officer stuck his head out of the only other doorway in the room. "Sergeant Simmons, just what the fuck is going on out there? If these men are here to see me, why don't you just send them on in?"

"Uh, yes sir." He composed his face into what he used for a pleasant expression. "The colonel will see you now."

"Colonel Bill Frazier," the officer said as they came through the door, leaning across the desk to shake hands. Alex swung his bag to the floor, shook, and sat on one of the metal chairs drawn up in front of the desk. They were green metal lawn chairs with tulip-shaped backs, the kind of chairs that rocked gently when you sat down in them. Perfect for any 1940s suburban garden party. Alex wondered how they had ended up on a tropical island in the middle of a war.

"Don't pay any attention to Gunny out there. He spent three months busting his nuts clearing the Japs off this island. Did a damn fine job. Two purple hearts and the bronze star. So we promoted him to a desk where he sits all day doing nothing, slowly going crazy. I think he picks fights hoping we'll bust him back to the field." Frazier stopped talking and looked them over for a minute. "You two are Balfour and Surrey, right?" They nodded. "I figured you'd be on today's transport. You made good time. Without beating around the bush, my orders are to move you on up the line. Your priority is high, not the highest, but it's up there. I can get you out of here tomorrow. I've got an LST going up to Rendova with supplies and troops. That all right with you?"

Alex nodded. "Can you give us an overview of your situation?"

Frazier pointed at the standard map of the Far East on the wall behind him. "This is us," he said, pointing at the silhouette of an airplane on an island. "We're presently running an operation against the Japs up on New Georgia." He tapped an island northeast of Guadalcanal. "This is the big island, the Japs have an airbase here on the western tip: Munda. There are hundreds of islands in the group; Rendova, Gizo, Kolombangara, Vella Lavella, Wana Wana. Those are just some of the larger ones. We've got GIs and Marines on New Georgia itself, fighting their way across to Munda. Our main effort right now is keeping the Japs from resupplying and reinforcing their defenses. They bring their supplies down the Slot from their big base on Raboul." Frazier stopped and listened as an airplane approached. The plane swept over the building, circled and came back for a landing. "Ours," Frazier said as the plane throttled back its engine. "A couple of weeks ago a planeload of Japs on a suicide mission got through our net and landed here. Sonsabitches jumped out and shot the shit out of us before we flattened them. I lost three fighters, a bomber, and twelve good men." He glanced out the window. "Anyway, I'll get you up to Rendova. From there on, how much closer to Japan you want to get is up to you. Questions?"

Alex looked at the map. The islands Frazier had pointed to stretched in a long northwest crescent that ended in the Japanese home islands. MacArthur's strategy was to advance up the line, bypassing areas of Japanese strength, cutting enemy troops off from resupply until they were starved out. Guadalcanal was at the lower end of the crescent. It had been the first of the great island campaigns and had taken six months to win. Some of the Japanese soldiers were still hidden in the hills around the airbase. It was said these holdouts would creep down at night to hide in the jungle at the edge of the base and watch the American outdoor movies. Occasionally, fired by some film-inspired rage, one of them would come crashing out of the jungle in a one-man banzai charge.

"How close are you to taking New Georgia?" Alex asked.

Frazier shrugged. "We send light cruisers up the Slot every night to bombard Shortland, take out shore batteries, look for barges with incoming troops. We've got our PTs out every night. The Aussie coastwatchers usually let us know when the Japs have got an Express coming down. Sometimes we intercept them, sometimes we miss them. It's real dark out there, never can be sure what's going to happen." He shrugged again. "That's about it."

"Tomorrow, then," Alex said, standing. From the window he could see a long line of smashed and burned airplanes. American airplanes. They'd been shoved up to the edge of the jungle behind the building. Vines, creepers, and small trees were growing through and around the aircraft.

"Be at the docks by 0800. LST 148. Someone will take you over to your billet, show you where to stow your stuff." He walked around his desk to the door. "Look, I don't know who you guys are, and I don't want to know. My job is to pass you up the line. But if I can give you a piece of advice, I'd come up with more of a story than you gave Gunny out there. Might save yourselves some trouble."

"Thanks," Alex said, holding out his hand. Frazier nodded and shook hands again with both of them.

Outside they stood in the meager shade of the building and waited for an enlisted man to stow their gear in a jeep. "You really added a lot in there," Alex said to Surrey.

Surrey laughed. "You were doing such a great job, starting with the sergeant, I hated to steal your thunder. Besides, you're the expert, I'm the bodyguard, or babysitter, or whatever I am."

"The partner. The assistant. We're a team, remember?"

"Oh yeah. Look, I had seventeen hours of discomfort to think over what you said on the way to Hawaii. About what things are going to be like in your time. It has sunk in, much as it pains me to admit it, that your time will eventually be my time. So I'm on board, as of now. I'll watch your back, do whatever needs to be done. It's a worthwhile cause. Doomed, probably, but I guess that's not worth dwelling on. Now, though, let's get out of the heat and try to work up a plausible story. The next officer we come up against may not be as obliging as Frazier."

THE MILITARY BAR on Guadalcanal was one large room with no exterior walls and a canvas tent for a roof. It looked out over a spectacular coral reef harbor ringed with white sand beaches and feathery green palms. The ten-foot-long bar and all the rest of the rickety furniture had been fashioned from discarded packing cases and ammo boxes. The contents designations and destination stencils remained visible on the bare wood. Care had to be exercised to avoid splinters. There were five tables with assorted chairs. Most of the six men present were support personnel. The vast majority of fighting men were being loaded into LSTs to be moved out the next day.

Alex and Surrey walked into the bar tent and sat on high wobbly stools at the bar. Several men nodded to them. Alex ordered a beer. The bartender brought him a beer glass full of green liquid. "What the hell is that?" Alex asked. He looked around the room. Everyone was drinking green.

"St. Patrick's Day came early this year, okay? We're not sure what the hell it is, but it's got alcohol in it," the bartender said. "Anyway, it's all we got. Cases of it. The usual Navy snafu."

Surrey picked up the glass and sniffed it. "Crème de menthe. I'll pass." The bartender shrugged. Alex took a sip. The cold sweet menthol coated his tongue. "Jesus Christ," he said, wondering how anyone could drink it without gagging. "What the hell." He took another sip. The second one went down a little easier.

"Listen up, assholes."

"Christ," the man on the next barstool muttered. He glanced at Alex. Alex was looking at the large Marine sergeant who had greeted them that morning in the colonel's office. The sergeant was sitting alone at one of the tables, two empty crème de menthe bottles lined up beside a partially filled third. "It's time for Gunny's 'Listen up, assholes' speech," the man beside him whispered. "We get it at least once a month. Gunny's brain ain't what it used to be. Not that it was much to begin with."

"Listen up, assholes!" Gunny thundered. The bar went dead silent. The sergeant sat perfectly still, bolt upright, hands resting lightly on the edge of the table. Ready to stand up and throw the table at any asshole who wasn't listening up.

"You motherfuckers are the biggest bunch of ass-wipe pussies that ever drew breath." His red-hazed eyes swept the men at the bar. His gaze fell on Alex. Alex felt his blood run cold. "Pukes, pussies, piddleshits, and rear-line turds." No one responded. Everyone stared down into their glasses of crème de menthe.

"Any Raiders here? No? Course not. Raiders is all fighting. Or dead. Dead so you pukes could sit here on your chicken-shit asses and drink this shit, whatever the hell it is." He raised his glass and drained it. "Let me tell you about the Raiders, pukes. Let me tell you about the Canal."

Outside, the sounds of men and vehicles had fallen away with the sunset. The bartender lighted two kerosene lanterns. Big lazy bugs immediately circled the lamps, plinking into the glass chimneys, flitting down into the flickering flames, crisping in small bursts of light.

The sergeant's uniform was taut on his massive frame, fresh and unwrinkled despite the heat. He no longer looked fat. Now he looked very big and very tough. His eyes were bright with drink, and memory.

"Let me tell you about the Canal, assholes."

19

HIS VOICE WAS A MATCH FOR HIS BODY; IT
was big and rough and filled the room. "We hit the beach on Tulagi.
That's the next island over, for all you pissants who just got here. It
was a breeze. Easy as pie. The Japs never knew we were coming. We
moved up off the beach into a plantation, and dug in. Marines. Edson's
Raiders. First Raider Battalion. The company commander was Captain
Lewis W. Walt and they don't come any finer. You think I'm big,
wait'll you see Lew Walt." He stopped and slowly and carefully filled
his glass to the top. The emerald liquid trembled at the lip as the air
shook from an airplane overhead. Someone said "Ours" and everyone
relaxed. Gunny didn't seem to notice. He sat staring at his glass, into
the past.

"Intelligence said the Nips were night fighters. We didn't know
much about them yet. This was our first fight since Pearl Harbor.
Most of the guys were as green as this shit." He held the glass at arm's
length. "Intelligence said we'd get it that night. Captain said to wire
in. Get ready. You got to picture it, pukes, it's the closest most of you
assholes are ever going to get to the real thing. Plantation palms laid
out in nice straight rows. Jungle all around us. Jungle noises. Can't
see a fucking thing. Lay there in your hole, can't see a thing but
imaginary Japs, shadows of Japs. After no time at all you've got it on
your brain: Jap birds, Jap crabs, could be Japs crawling toward you,
could be Japs in any direction. See, you can *hear* them. All around
you.

"Then there's this pop, a flare goin' off and I'll tell you the truth, even old Gunny's ticker skipped a beat when that shit hit the fan. Up out of the jungle comes a wave of crazy little brown fuckers, screaming their Jap gobbledegook, *'Banzai, Maline You Die,'* all that shit, officers waving samurai swords, and it's headed right at you. Tracer shells spraying everywhere. Grenades coming in, mortars blasting dirt in your face, and these insane fucking Japs who care no more about death than your average whore does about the Virgin Mary.

"You can't hardly kill them." He looked round the room, a look of mild astonishment on his face. "You've got to shoot them at least twice, bayonet them, sometimes go ahead and strangle them on top of everything before they lay down and die. I ain't shittin' you, men, those little bastards are tough. They got this code, called dushido or something. What that means is that it's an honor to die. As long as they kill your ass while they're doing it.

"Four times they came at us. Four fucking times we threw them back. Hand to hand. Right down in your hole with you. Swords, K-Bars, rifle butts, and bare hands. You'd kill one, throw him out of your hole, another one jumps over the body on top of you. One after another. Four times they came. Took all night."

He picked up his glass and drank all of it down. A small trickle of green ran down his neck as he swallowed.

"We walked the line in the morning. Lew and me. There was dead Japs everywhere. Piled up six high in some places. Hundreds of them.

"We came to one hole, had a big Marine laying in it. Near dead. Been shot twice, bayoneted at least three times as far as we could tell. Blood everywhere. PFC John Ahrens. An Able Company BAR man. Laid out around his foxhole was a Jap officer, a Jap sergeant, and thirteen Jap infantrymen. *Fifteen dead Japs.* All of them dead as shit. Ahrens could just hardly speak. 'Captain,' he says, 'they tried to come over me last night, but I don't think they made it.' Lew picked that boy up in his arms, just like a baby. That boy died right there. 'They didn't make it, Johnny,' Lew says. 'They didn't make it.' "

Gunny finished his glass, poured another, and looked around the room. No one spoke. Most of the men stared down at their drinks. In the jungle, a bird screamed, and Alex flinched. The small movement drew the sergeant's eye. He stared at Alex. Alex felt himself blush.

"But that wasn't shit." He shook his head. "That wasn't nothin'. They brought us over to the Canal. This is where we learned how to fight.

"The Navy dumped us off and turned tail. Admiral Fucking Frank J. Chickenshit Fletcher, the Gutless Wonder. Lost his fucking nerve and pulled out his carriers with his tail between his legs. Left us with a couple of days' rations and shit for supplies. Took our sandbags, howitzers, most of the ammo, all but eighteen rolls of barbed wire. Admiral Chickenliver heard that a big Jap fleet was on its way, so he farted twice, turned tail, and ran. Left us a few light cruisers. No air support. Then the Jap ships *did* come, and kicked what was left of the Navy's ass. Five of our cruisers. They sank four of them and crippled the fifth. More than a thousand American sailors in the water. More than a thousand drowned or eaten by sharks. Left us high and dry. Left us to sweat it out. The Navy never did really come back, not for four months. *Four months, assholes!*" His heavy fist slammed down on the rickety table. One of the empty bottles tipped over onto the floor and rolled away. "You understand? You understand what that means? We ate roots and weeds. The *only* food we had was Jap food. Red Mike Edson had the answer to the food problem. 'There's plenty of chow,' Red Mike said. 'The Japs have it. Take it away from them.' So we did.

"Most men were sick. Night blind. Malaria. Denge fever. Infected sores, skin falling off from jungle rot. The jungle holding us back. Best you could make in a day in a straight line was a hundred yards. Constant bombardment. Shells coming in all night long. You know what was in them shells? In the mornings, we'd find this scrap iron stamped 'Made in the U.S.A.' Nuts, screws, bolts. Bent nails. Door handles off of Ford automobiles. Scrap iron we'd been selling the Japs for years.

"There wasn't a safe spot anywhere. I was down at the command post, getting my ass chewed out by Shepherd Banta. General Vandegrift was there. All of a sudden this Jap officer with a samurai sword screams *Banzai* and rips through the tent swinging that fucking sword. One swipe and he opens up a sergeant. There was guts and blood flying everywhere. Banta pulls out his side arm and shoots the motherfucker through the head. Just glanced over and did it, never even stopped chewing me out. Now there's blood, guts, and *brains* all over the place.

Banta finishes up with me and kicks me out. Never mentions the Jap. There was a man, assholes, there was a man.

"Then there was the ridge." Gunny fell silent for a moment. "Bloody Ridge." He lifted his glass out of a pool of sticky green liquid, poured in the last of the third bottle, and drank it down. "Red Mike said we were going up to the ridge for a rest." He laughed quietly. "We Raiders was spread out along that hogback, up there in the Kunai grass, looking down the hill into the ravines and the jungle. Our line was all there was between the Japs and the airfield. They had to take the airfield or we'd beat them. That was where we made our stand. Bloody Ridge.

"That night twenty-five Jap Bettys flew up on us and dropped five hundred pounders. Shit was flying everywhere. 'Hold,' Red Mike said. 'If we don't hold, we lose the Canal.' We left a platoon down the hill as a listening post. We could hear the Japs hit them, cut them up. Fuckers were chanting, 'U.S. Maline, you be dead tomorrow.' One of our guys shouts, 'Hirohito eats shit.' They shout back, 'Eleanor eats shit.'

"Then they came. Flares. A wave of Japs out of the jungle. Bayonets. Swords. Screaming. Every fucking mortar we've got is pounding, machine guns mowing them down. BARs are working. Our guys are screaming." The sergeant suddenly stood up. One arm in the air, he bellowed, "Raiders to me! Raiders, rally to me!"

There was not a breath of sound in the bar. Slowly Gunny's arm lowered. "Morning comes," he said roughly. "Mike pulls us back to new positions." He sat down.

"Nine o'clock the next night, pitch black, a Betty comes over and drops a flare. Two thousand Japs boil out of the jungle. Running. Up the hill. Straight at us. Mike calls in our Long Toms, shells start dropping into those fuckers like hail. They come on, Mike calls the Toms in closer, marches those shells straight up the hill with the Japs. They were going nuts, jumping in our holes to hide. We'd throw the fuckers back out. Guys were breaking, falling back. Red Mike was standing there like a goddamn rock, turning our boys around, sending them back. Mike's got a voice like a gravel pit. 'The only thing that they got that you don't is guts.' Shaming them, see? They go back and fight. Christ, those boys fought like the damned. All fucking night.

"First light, p-38s from Henderson Field come in and strafed what was left of the fuckers. That was it, they turned. Left more'n a thousand behind. By midmorning the bodies were starting to swell. We'd licked them."

He looked around the room, as if just waking. "Listen up, assholes," he said, his voice so quiet you could barely hear him.

"Let me tell you about the Canal."

20

THE SHARP HULL OF THE SHIP SPLIT THE
surface of the slate gray ocean, curling away a high, creamy bow wave.
Alex leaned over the rail of the LST and gagged. As the ship wallowed
in a trough and heeled to port, Alex felt a clammy wave of nausea
wash over him. He considered throwing himself into the choppy sea,
to struggle and drown, to be done with this horrible sickness. Beside
him at the rail, Surrey laughed.

"This reminds me of my favorite part of your performance last
evening," Max said. "When you and your pal Gunny were hanging
over the ditch. Actually you were over the ditch, Gunny was holding
you by your belt."

"Please," Alex said, straightening up and fixing his eyes on the
horizon. The ships in their convoy were spread out around them. Two
destroyers and a submarine tender churned along in the near distance.
The convoy had been under way for more than an hour. Most of which
time Alex had spent at the rail.

"But this is the best part," Surrey went on. "Picture this. Gunny
is holding you up by your belt. You're dangling over the ditch, throwing
up everything you'd eaten and drunk in the last week or so, and Gunny,
solicitous, avuncular Gunny, is reassuring you. It was really a heart-
warming scene. 'Go ahead, son,' Gunny says. 'Puke it up, puke it all
up, you'll feel the better for it in the morning. Keep on puking until
something round and hairy comes up. That's your asshole, son,' he
says, 'swallow that, you'll need it. It's going to be a long war.'" Surrey
laughed again.

Alex swallowed rapidly to fight down his rising gorge. He remembered the scene, barely. He remembered he and Gunny finishing off a major portion of the bar's stock of crème de menthe. He gagged as he thought the name. *Crème de menthe.* Jesus, how could he have done that to himself? The ship wallowed in another trough. Alex's stomach followed suit. He looked up at the overcast lead gray sky to steady himself. It didn't work.

They were heading northwest up the Slot, also known as Iron Bottom Sound because of all the ships, Allied and Japanese, that had been sunk there.

"I'm going below," Alex said. "I've got to get some rest." He knew that as bad as it was up here, it was going to be worse down below. Close and hot, unbearably hot. Tiny canvas bunks slung one over the other in stacks four men high. *So be it.* He had to get away from Surrey. Having the world's worst hangover was bad enough—having it replayed was beyond bearing.

Surrey nodded. He had been in much better humor over the last few days. "Probably a good idea. Going to rain soon anyway. I'll stay up here. It's not much cooler, but at least the air is moving. I'll come get you if anything exciting happens."

Alex shook his head. The pain of his brain sloshing around in his head almost brought him to his knees. He turned and began edging away along the rail. "Don't come get me for anything. If we take a hit, forget about me. I'll go down with the ship. It'll be a relief."

SOMEHOW HE SLEPT. When he woke, he took a shower in tepid seawater and dressed in fresh clothes. He went up on deck and leaned on the rail of the ship and felt the cool spray arcing up from the bow. There was a fresh breeze, moving in from the east. Overhead, the cloud cover was breaking up, blue sky appearing quiltlike in ragged patches. He had slept for four hours, and it had rained, breaking the back, at least for the moment, of the oppressive heat and humidity. Four aspirin and the sleep had likewise broken the back of his hangover.

He glanced back at the ship. The crew had moved into battle stations while he'd been below. There was an air of, if not exactly tension, at least expectation. A watchful anticipation. Surrey came out on deck, glanced up at the sky, and walked over to him.

"What's up," Alex asked, "besides my stomach." Surrey didn't smile. "We're on Condition Red. Air attack expected." He nodded in the direction of the nearest neighboring ship. That ship, a destroyer, abruptly zigged into a right-hand turn. Their ship followed. Alex held on to the rail as they plunged through a series of cross-waves. The convoy was tightening up, ships had appeared closer around them, bows down as they raced through the chop.

He and Surrey strapped on kapok-filled life vests. Other men joined them at the rail. Alex felt his stomach tighten and his breathing speed up as he pulled taut the straps of the vest.

Without warning, the gun emplacement right above them opened up. Alex crouched down and covered his ears. The deck shook with each blast. "Bettys," a man beside him shouted, pointing into the sky. Alex could see a flight of twin-engine planes, still high, approaching in a ragged-V formation. As he watched, the planes began to peel off and dive toward the convoy. Guns all along the ship opened fire. The stink of gunpowder laced the air, spurts of blue smoke burst from the guns. Other ships began firing, guns spewing jets of flame and smoke. The heavy destroyers crossed the wakes of the lighter LSTs. Transports and supply ships lumbered steadfastly on, making minimal attempts to maneuver. The faster ships zigged and zagged around them in complicated designs. Stubby P-40 Wildcats from distant carriers began appearing in the sky, diving among the Bettys.

Alex felt the pace of the fire increase and shift toward the front of the ship. Ahead, one of the Japanese planes seemed to lower itself out of the sky, dropping down as if suspended by wires, directly in front of them. The forward guns fired almost in unison. Puffs of black smoke blossomed around the oncoming bomber. A long thin torpedo issued from the plane, dropping free, a malevolent egg, born in mid-flight. The torpedo nosed down and splashed into the water. "Long Lance," the man beside him shouted, "bad fucking news!" The enemy plane banked left and was immediately hit by gunfire. Smoke spewed from the fuselage and orange flame flickered briefly as the plane nosed down and cartwheeled into the ocean. No one cheered. Hardly anyone noticed. Even the guns had stopped firing as everyone along the rail searched for the incoming wake of the torpedo. And there it was, death made visible, driving toward them, perfectly configured, geometrically on-course. The whole ship seemed to hold its breath. "Turn," the man beside Alex muttered. "Turn, goddamnit, turn." The thin V-shaped wake arrowed toward them just under the surface of the gray sea. At the last possible minute, the LST turned to port and the torpedo raced by ten feet behind the stern of the ship. Now the ship's company cheered.

When Alex looked up, the air battle was over. The other ships were no longer firing and the only planes in sight were the Wildcats rolling in lazy turns overhead. Men removed their helmets and life vests and stretched and walked around the ship. The loudspeaker ordered the company to stand down. The ships around them shifted back into more orderly files and ranks.

Surrey gestured out over the water. One of the destroyers was burning, black smoke billowing from amidships as other ships hovered around her. "So fast," he said. "Everything goes so fast. So many dead. So many dead."

The ship's loudspeaker interrupted him, announcing that there was a Jap pilot down and the ship would attempt a rescue. The deck trembled lightly as the ship slowed and changed course.

There was wreckage spread out on the water around them. The ship inched its way through what remained of the downed plane. Men appeared from all over the ship to crowd the rail around Alex. "Anyone see the bastard?" someone asked.

"There he is," a man shouted, pointing. Fifty yards away, clinging to a piece of wreckage, was a helmeted man, frantically attempting to swim away from the ship. As they crept forward, the man stopped splashing and turned toward them, treading water. "Ready a line," an officer shouted. The floating pilot seemed perfectly calm, only his head showing above the water, looking like some strange brown fruit bobbing in the ocean swell. Suddenly his hand, holding an automatic pistol, appeared above the waves and a shot cracked across the water. The men along the rail shouted and ducked down as the pilot fired again.

It was an impossible shot under the circumstances, and the Japanese seemed to know it. The differing wave patterns shifted the boat and the man, throwing off his aim. He fired three more shots, as if making a statement rather than trying to hit anything. A Marine guard carrying a rifle appeared at the rail. He was greeted with a small cheer from the crowd. The Marine aimed and began firing. Catcalls and whistles accompanied each shot as bullets pocked into the ocean around the pilot. Alex watched with horror as the Japanese pilot calmly turned his pistol to his head and pulled the trigger. A spray of red puffed into the air. The body eased forward and floated facedown, bobbing and turning among the waves. There was another cheer and laughter from the ranks of watching sailors. Alex turned and looked at Surrey. Surrey shook his head. "How the hell can you win a war against people like that?" he asked.

Alex shook his head. "I don't know." A sailor at the rail beside them overheard Surrey's question. He turned to them and answered. "You want to know how we're going to win? We do what we just did. To every Jap we can find. It's simple, you just kill them all. When they're all dead, you know you've won. You guys must be new out here." The sailor shook his head and turned to contemplate the Japanese pilot's body, turning slowly in the waves.

RENDOVA, a mile wide and two miles long, is one of the larger islands in the mid-northern sector of the Solomons. Rendova Harbor is surrounded by a series of smaller islands. The LST from Guadalcanal steamed up the channel, entered the beautiful tropical harbor, and anchored. Launches from various landings in the harbor, looking like baby ducks come to cadge a meal from Mother, came, off-loaded men and supplies, and went. Alex and Surrey climbed down a rope ladder into the launch bound for Lumberi, an island five hundred yards long with a fringe of swaying palm trees and a picturesque screen of varu trees dotted with sprays of small yellow flowers. In the launch with them were three men headed for PT duty, and a rolled canvas bag with the dead Jap flyer inside. No one knew who had decided that the dead Jap should go to Lumberi, or why, but here he was.

The launch motored toward the dock. In the water around them were fifteen to twenty anchored PT boats, moored in nests of three. One of the sleek gray boats was at the dock, loading large barrels of fuel and supplies. The coxswain of the launch cut the motor and drifted neatly to the dock. A couple of PT boaters caught the lines and tied them up. They good-naturedly began helping unload the men's seabags and other gear. The Jap was handed up last. The canvas stitching, only loosely run, tore open and the bloody, water-logged body slid out onto the dock. It lay there, glistening like a freshly beached tuna as the men silently stared.

"Which one of y'all's carrying a dead Jap as part of his gear?" one of the PT boaters asked.

"None," the coxswain answered, preparing to cast off. "Had us a fight this morning. We shot this one down, just after he dropped a fish on us. Blew his brains out in the water. Must a been ashamed that he missed us."

"Yeah, well, that's great. But what the hell are *we* supposed to do with him?"

The coxswain shrugged. "Bury him, I guess." They all stood looking down at the pilot. He was wearing a leather jacket, brown putees, and what was left of his flying helmet. He seemed about fourteen years old. "Kind of hard to hate them when they're so little," Surrey said. The PT man looked at him. "You go out with us in the boat a couple of nights, you'll change your mind about that." He nudged the body with his foot. Then he bent down and rolled the body off the dock. It hit with a muted, almost apologetic splash and floated arms outstretched, facedown. *Why do they always float facedown?* Alex thought.

"Put a rope on his foot, drag him back out in the harbor, and cut him loose. Sharks'll take care of him in no time." The PT boater spit into the water.

The coxswain studied the body for a minute then nodded. Everyone else began picking up their gear. The sailor who had pushed the body off the dock turned to Alex. "You guys brass, or what?" he asked. He had curly blond hair and a boyish smile. "No insignia," he explained, pointing to Alex's shoulder.

"We need to see your CO," Alex said, sidestepping the question. The man nodded toward a group of rough huts up on the beach. "No problem. He's in the bunker behind those shacks." They all turned to watch as the launch started up and began moving away from the dock. In the water behind the boat the dead Jap trolled spread-eagled. A wide wake appeared behind the body as the launch picked up speed. The Jap appeared to be performing a complicated water-skiing maneuver. Backward. On his face.

"Welcome," the smiling sailor said to Alex. He stuck out his hand. "I'm Woodley." He gestured to the PT boat. "I'm the motormac on the 109. That collection of shacks is Todd City. Also known as the Asshole of the Pacific." Alex and Surrey shook Woodley's hand, shouldered their bags, and walked down the dock.

Out in the harbor the coxswain throttled back the engine and cut the tow rope on the Jap. The body bobbed and turned as the boat raced away.

21

It was as if Alex were viewing two photographic slides, one clipped from the movie version of *South Pacific*, the other from life. His mind kept attempting to overlay the slides into a coherent mental picture. But it wasn't working. First of all, there was the smell, a peculiar stench that emanated from the piles of rotting palm fronds and old coconut husks. As they crunched over a walkway made of pulverized coral, the odor seemed to creep in from the surrounding jungle and envelop them in a moist effluvia of equal parts rot and death.

No happy jungle here, no South Pacific swabbies singing and dancing across a soundstage of sand and sea. No indigenous bare-breasted hula girls. They walked through a makeshift town of thatched huts and jerry-built shacks. The row of jungle trees and vines and creepers opened up onto a small clearing where four Royal palms formed the corner trees of the headquarters bunker. Half underground, shorn up by sandbags, it was constructed of scrap wood, screen, and thatch. The crooked screen door swung open with a rusted-spring screech and slammed shut behind them.

"Don't slam the goddamn, motherfucking, ass-sucking door," roared a fat sergeant from behind a large black typewriter. Alex wondered if the Army issued these sergeants the same way they issued helmets and underwear, from some great depot in the Midwest, stocked with all the clichés, curses, and indispensables of Army life.

"What do you assholes want?" the sergeant asked. Surrey looked at Alex and smiled away any responsibility. Woodley, their sailor/

escort, grinned at the sergeant. "This here is brass, Sergeant," he said in a loud voice.

"Speak up, asshole!" the sergeant shouted.

"I said this here is brass," Woodley shouted back. "At least I think it is, so watch out who you're calling an asshole."

"Why the hell didn't you say so?" the sergeant said. "Sorry, sir," the sergeant said to Alex, in a more reasonable tone. "Since I saw you with Woodley, I thought you were just another asshole. The CO's waiting for you. Colonel Blair Morgan, United States Marine Corps, Commander PT Squadron 84. And he don't want to see you, Woodley." Woodley flashed his smile and held out a hand. "Glad to be of service," he said, "whoever you are. If you guys want to see some action, ask for the 109. Patch Woodley, Chief Motormac. At your service." He waved at the sergeant and went out the creaky screen door, letting it slam behind him.

The sergeant glowered at the door then nodded toward the office partition. "Colonel will see you now."

A tall Marine officer sat at a cluttered desk, studying a stack of papers. He looked up as they entered. The room was the same size as the outer office, the square bunker having been divided down the center. The upper-exterior walls were made of screen and looked out on the small clearing and the jungle beyond. The officer motioned to two chairs. He was wearing almost the same uniform they were, but with Marine insignias displayed on the collar. He had sandy red hair cropped to a short burr, a craggy face with skin that looked as if it didn't take the tropical sun well. It was a no-bullshit face, but the expression was carefully neutral, the look of a professional military officer.

"I received a communication on you men yesterday," Morgan began. "I'm not going to pull any punches. What you're going to see around here is exactly the way things are. We haven't the time nor the resources to put on window dressing for inspection teams."

"We don't expect it," Surrey said, surprising Alex by taking the lead. "Our instructions are to put together a reasonable assessment of your area and its problems. And any future problems."

Morgan sat back in his chair. "Fine," he said, and nodded. He studied them. Alex wondered if he saw them as that particularly odious form of bureaucracy: the Inspectors. Sent out from on high to assess a situation and make recommendations after a whirlwind, hit-or-miss tour. He and Surrey had decided against concocting any bogus cover stories. For those high enough to be in the know, like Morgan here, instructions always seemed to precede them. *Where do these communiqués come from? Who is controlling us?* For the lower ranks they were beginning to find that an air of mystery was most effective; it assumed they were of high rank, probably on a secret mission. Rather than encouraging questions, it seemed to discourage them.

"You men have clearance all the way from the top," Morgan said, glancing at a paper on his desk. "And I mean the top. But if you're going to understand what we're doing, you're going to have to participate. I can give you the Big Picture, explain the strategy, but if you're going to get a gut feel for it, you're going to have to see it up close."

Alex looked at Surrey, remembering his earlier assessment of their situation: *they're going to put our asses on the line every chance they get.*

"Our orders are simple," Surrey said. "We are to study your situation with particular reference to Allied end-of-war strategy. That may seem premature to you, but—"

Morgan cut him off with a wave of a hand. "Good strategy always includes final-phase operations. In point of fact, that is *our* purpose here. That is what the PT squadrons are about."

Alex looked at Surrey to see if he understood what Morgan was talking about. Surrey didn't appear to be particularly perplexed. Alex suddenly felt a chill of loneliness, as if he were the only one in the group who was not In The Know, hadn't been considered sound enough to have all the facts.

Morgan stood and pulled a map down. *Standard Army-issue map of the Pacific,* Alex thought, *probably sent out along with the sergeants and the underwear.* Alex forced himself to pay attention. Suddenly things didn't seem quite so simple as they had before. He couldn't help glancing out the screened-in walls, imagining a lurking Jap with paper and pencil, about to steal secret Allied strategy and battle plans. Morgan followed his glance and guessed his thought.

"We have sentries all around this bunker. You can't see them, you're not supposed to. Neither can the Japs. No one is allowed close enough to hear what goes on in here. That includes Sergeant Tragg out in the other room. He was on the beach back on the Canal when a 500-pound bomb took out most of his squad. Except for his hearing, it left him pretty much intact. So don't worry about my security, I can assure you that it is adequate." He turned to the map. "By now you're familiar with the overall plan." His hand swept over the Solomons and up the chain of islands that led to Japan.

"We move up the islands, skipping big bases, with the exception of airfields, cutting off their supplies and reinforcements, keeping the element of surprise on our side. Hit 'em where they ain't, as the man said. Once we take back Manila, we can kick them off Okinawa. From there we bomb Tokyo at will. We starve them, bomb the shit out of them, then we invade. There'll be one hell of a lot of dead Americans before it's over, but it will work."

"If there were a way," Alex said, trying to be careful, but at the same time taking a chance, "to shorten the procedure, at the expense of the Japanese civilian population, would you take it?" Both Morgan and Surrey stared at him as if he were crazy, both for different reasons.

"Hell yes," Morgan said. "What the hell do I care about Jap civilians? They're trying to kill us just as hard as any of those soldiers out there in the jungle. I said we were going to starve them and bomb the shit out of them. Don't believe any of that malarkey you hear about strategic bombing. With the normal cloud cover over Japan we can barely tell when we're over land, much less where the strictly military targets are. It's a hell of a long way to Japan, we drop whatever we've got on anything we can get. We'll kill whatever's there. Because in the end, it's the civilians we're going to have to fight. All indications point to it. They'll arm the surviving men, women, and children with sticks, guns, pitchforks, whatever they've got left, and send them down to the beaches to meet us." He looked from Surrey to Alex. "But first we're going to have to *get* to the beaches, which is what PT boats are all about."

Alex was lost. "I thought that the job of the PTs was to harass Japanese supply ships as they came down the Slot. That's what we've been told."

"That is the battle plan, yes. But that isn't the end purpose. That is not our reason for being." He hesitated. "I don't have to remind you that everything I say here is secret. In fact, I want no record of you even being here. You'll be living with the men, but as far as the real world is concerned, you don't exist. From now on, it's first names only when you introduce yourselves. Don't make a big deal of it, the men aren't going to pay much attention to you anyway, they're too busy, and when they're not, they're too tired. Understood?" They both nodded.

"All right," Morgan went on. "The end goal of Allied strategy in the Pacific is the invasion of Japan. Japan's warrior code, *Bushido*, requires all Japanese to fight to the death. Men, women, and children. We fully expect an armed populace to meet us on the beaches. And more to the point, as far as we're concerned, we expect to meet an armed populace *before* we get to the beaches. Japan is an island: we can jump out of airplanes onto it, and we can mount amphibious attacks. That's the extent of our options. By far the most practical of these choices is the amphibious attack. Imagine for a moment an invasion fleet of landing craft going in against the main island of Japan. The waters will be full of Jap suicide and fighting craft; civilian boats committed to battle in every possible way. The primary tactic will be the simplest, to ram our craft. We will be forced to sink these opposing forces before they get into range of our relatively slow, relatively defenseless LCs. What we'll need is one hell of a lot of extremely fast, maneuverable strike boats, with well-trained crews who understand that in all probability they won't be coming back from this last battle."

"PT boats," Alex said.

Morgan nodded. "Bingo. They'll stage in Okinawa. They can carry enough fuel to get there, not enough to get back. They'll go in first. They'll be hit first. If they're lucky, any survivors will be picked up by our support ships. If not, well, PTs are considered expendable. We're talking casualty rates of 100 percent. But without them, it will be a lot worse.

"So what they're doing now is—"

"Training." Morgan finished Alex's sentence. "Only they don't know it. What the men do is useful, but any serious enemy damage is beyond their capability. We had initially envisioned PTs as being able to take out ships all the way up to destroyer class, but it hasn't worked out." A look of annoyance crossed Morgan's face. "Not that it's their fault. These are very brave men. They go out every night in a goddamn boat made of thin sheets of stressed plywood with virtually no armor. They rely on speed, wits, and guts to get them out of trouble. The original design was based on the use of torpedoes. Great, except we've got shitty torpedoes. They get stuck in the tubes, catch on fire, and when we do get one off, it's more than likely to be a dud. They just bounce off the ships we're shooting at, or go around in circles and come back at us. I sometimes think that if we listened hard enough we could hear the Japs laughing. But they don't laugh. You know why?

Because they're scared shitless of our PTs. They call them Devil Boats. Because the guys that take them out have more guts than good sense. They'll attack anything that floats." He leaned forward. "These fellows move in so close you could hit the Japs with a goddamn potato. They slug it out with destroyers, even though they don't have a snowball's chance in hell." He shook his head. "They do okay against supply barges, troop barges, but what they want is the big stuff. And we encourage them. Give them medals, send them out every night against anything that comes down the Slot. You know why? The reason we send them out is so that in the end what we're left with are the best fighting units afloat. You know Darwin's work? Survival of the fittest? That's what we want. The fittest, meanest, gutsiest fighting bastards the world has ever seen in a goddamn speedboat. And when the time comes, we're going to throw them into battle with an insane enemy. I don't expect much in the way of survivors on either side. And that's what this squadron and this island and this part of the war are all about. Questions?"

Alex looked up at the map. *Yeah, I got a million of them. Most of them you can't answer.* "Why don't we wait until we look things over. Then we'll know better what to ask."

Morgan nodded. "Good idea. I'll assign you a crew. You already seem to know Woodley so you might as well go on the 109. Start tomorrow night. The 109's skipper is Lieutenant John Kennedy. He's young, but he's gung ho."

Alex stood up and held out his hand. "That sounds fine. Lieutenant Kennedy it is."

ALEX AND MAX sat on the dock watching the PTs loading up to go out on patrol. Alex waved to Woodley, sitting on the prow of the 109, nested at a buoy with two other boats. It was 6 P.M. and the sun was going down. Rapidly. Huge and red, it settled perceptibly behind the hills of Rendova. The PTs started their engines, a low rumbling that rolled across the bay, sounding like a teenager's wet dream of automobile glory. Glass packs, low riders. Power.

The boats began to maneuver into position. "What do you think they'd do if we told them that the military considers them expendable?" Surrey asked in a loud voice.

Alex glanced around. There was no one near enough to hear. *Does he check first, or does he just not give a shit?*

"Don't look at *me* that way," Surrey said, accurately reading his mind. "I'm not the one giving away state secrets. Why didn't you just go ahead and tell the colonel about the atomic bomb? You were already halfway there."

"I wanted to see what he'd say. We need to know how locked in these people are on this thing."

"This thing? You mean the invasion of Japan? It sounds as if they're pretty goddamned committed if you ask me. It seems obvious. Why do you think that any of them are going to have second thoughts? For them, there's no alternative. I think," Surrey went on, "that if you told these guys what Morgan told us in there, everything, even the 100 percent casualty prediction, that they'd just shrug and get on with the job."

The sun dipped lower. The boats were lining up and heading out. Alex could read the numbers as they went by: 168, 109, 207.

A breeze wafted over them, keeping the mosquitos at bay. The sun dropped behind Rendova. For a brief moment the sky flamed bright red, then deepened into purple, then black. A huge sky-wide swath of stars appeared, as if by magic. In the jungle behind them, birds, bugs, frogs, and assorted unknown creatures began to squeak, croak, sing, and scream. "Think about it," Surrey said. "All those guys who just went by. They'll all be dead."

"Maybe," Alex said, "maybe not. Here's the way I see it. If we drop the bomb on Japan, we kill hundreds of thousands of Japanese. And give ourselves a legacy of nuclear guilt and deterrence by buildup. We set the standard for the world: it's all right to use the bomb. If we don't drop the bomb, we have enormous casualties of Americans and Japanese as we invade the home islands. If we convince them to set up a demonstration of the bomb, we run the risk of the Japanese saying so what, we've been bombed before, we can take it, and going right ahead with their defense of the islands."

"That's supposing the bomb works," Surrey said.

"It'll work," Alex said grimly. "I can promise you that. But think about that pilot who blew his brains out, Gunny's stories of Guadalcanal. These people fight to the death. Maybe just *seeing* what the bomb can do won't really be enough. Back in Princeton, with Einstein, it all seemed so logical. Here, well, things look different when you're standing right next to them."

"Ain't it the truth," Surrey responded. "So what's the answer?"

"That's the $64,000 question."

"Let's deal with the $64 question first."

Alex shook his head. "You know what I mean. I guess we'll just have to keep going. We were sent out here for information, so let's get it. And get out."

And then another truth clicked into place. The facts snapping in like so many cherries on a slot machine: PT boats. Lieutenant Kennedy. PT 109. *They'll all be dead.* And that included John F. Kennedy, future President of the United States of America.

If we don't drop the bomb, if we don't convince the Japanese to give it up, they'll drag in every PT boater who's any good for the invasion. And that will include Kennedy, hero of the 109. Good-bye, Camelot.

22

ALEX STOOD ON THE BRIDGE OF PT 109
and studied the simple instrument panel. He was trying to stay out of
the way of the men loading last-minute supplies onto the deck. He
moved from behind the wheel and leaned against the supports that
had once held a steel windshield provided as one of the few pieces of
armor on a PT boat. The windshields were routinely removed by crews.
Since it was impossible to see through steel, you had to stand up and
look over them, eliminating any protection provided.

The hatch cover behind the bridge was gray, smooth, and pock-
marked with a row of bullet holes. Alex stepped over and put his hand
on the cover. It was warm with the stored heat of the sun. He put
his finger in one of the bullet holes. The edges were jagged. Wood.
No metal armor here. Anywhere, in fact. The boat was a thin eggshell
of plywood—light, buoyant, and completely useless as protection from
anything more lethal than a stone thrown in anger.

"They let the air in," a thin, smiling officer said, stepping into the
wheelhouse with Alex. "The bullet holes. It gets hotter than an Irish
hell down below," the man went on. "They strafed us up by Mindanao.
Four Jap float planes. Didn't hit anyone, but it made a mess below.
On the way back we found that the holes let out some of the heat so
we just left them. Also it lends a bit of romance, don't you think? Kind
of like Popeye's eyepatch." The man held out his hand. "Lieutenant
Jack Kennedy. Welcome aboard."

Alex shook the offered hand and felt a shock of pleasure. Kennedy
was as boyish and as handsome as he'd expected him to be. In fact,

he was so youthful Alex wanted to put an arm around him and give him some fatherly advice: *stay away from the women*. And Dallas, he added, sobering.

"The CO let me in on a little of what you fellows are up to," Kennedy said, with his familiar broad Harvard accent. "We'll be on a routine patrol tonight, up the Slot to see what Tojo's trying to put over on us. If we're lucky, we'll find a troop barge or some supply craft. If we're very lucky, or not, depending on your point of view, we'll scare up a destroyer or a light cruiser. Preferably not at the same time. I've got to see to a few things here, so why don't you men sit up on the 37-millimeter ready box until we're under way." Kennedy tossed a small dufflebag into a wooden locker. Alex and Surrey went out on the prow and sat down on the ammunition box that had been pointed out to them. Alex felt out of place and in the way, the new man on a new job being shuffled around by professionals who were busy but polite. There was another row of bullet holes in the deck near his feet. Butterflies of apprehension began to stir in his gut.

"Seems like a nice guy," Surrey said. "Kennedy," he added, nodding toward where Kennedy stood checking a box of ammunition. "Let's hope he's as competent as he is pleasant. I don't imagine that many out here know it, but he's a historian of sorts. Published a book just out of Harvard. Not a bad book, a young man's book but not bad. His father's our ambassador to England, or at least he was. Joe Kennedy. Tough old bastard."

Alex almost smiled. From Surrey's viewpoint, the captain of PT 109 was just a lower-grade Navy man upstart historian not long out of college. One book and a famous father weren't enough to impress Max. Alex toyed with the idea of filling Surrey in on the young man's future résumé. But then he'd have to include Kennedy's war record, which consisted mainly of having his PT boat run down by a Japanese destroyer. Which was a fact that Alex had been putting off thinking about ever since the Marine colonel had told them that riding with Kennedy on the 109 would be a good place for them to start their evaluations. He tried to dredge up a date for the ramming of the 109, but drew a blank. He had a terrific memory, but the information had to be in his brain before he could call it up.

The sun was lowering toward the horizon. Their acquaintance of the day before, Woodley, the young sailor with the blond hair, came trotting down the dock carrying a wooden box. He leapt lightly on deck and put the box down. Looking up, he saw Alex and Surrey and waved. "Dinner," he called, pointing at the box. Alex could read the stencil on the side: SPAM. "Breakfast too," Woodley added. "And lunch." Kennedy waved Woodley and his case of Spam below and made a cranking motion with his forefinger. Almost immediately, the deck quivered with the rumbling of the engines. Their engines were answered by several more nearby. Two other boats, the 238 and the 167, were going out on patrol with them. Alex watched men on those boats casting off lines. The general uniform of the day seemed to be anything the men wanted, from ragged boxer shorts to fairly neat fatigues. Kennedy appeared on the bridge and motioned them in beside him.

"Time to do it," he said, twisting the wheel and easing on the power. The boat heeled slightly and turned to the left, moving slowly forward. A small breeze ruffled Kennedy's hair. He pushed it back off his forehead. He was smiling to himself.

"We've got three Packard engines," he said, "but we'll be only running one for a while. Theoretically we can make forty knots, but this kid hasn't seen speed like that since she came from the factory. Twenty is about average." He pushed the throttle down and the bow raised slightly. He had to speak loudly to be heard. Alex and Surrey moved closer. They were heading out into the bay, all three PTs in a line. "We've got ten boats in our group, but no more than four or five are operational at any one time. They break down because of the heat and the humidity. Parts are hard to come by. We have to cannibalize each other to keep running. We go out three or four nights in a row, sleep a couple of hours, work on the boats to keep them going. A lot of the men are sick—malaria, denge fever, and just plain exhaustion." He looked at them, no longer smiling. "I don't know what it is you fellows are interested in, but if you've got any pull with the brass at home, I hope you'll tell them about the conditions we're working under. The men don't deserve it." He pushed the throttle further and the engine noise rose to the point to make ordinary conversation impossible.

Night fell with tropical suddenness. A sky full of stars gave a dim silvery glow, but high thin clouds came in and cut off all natural illumination. The boats ran without lights, surprise being their primary weapon. The 109 maneuvered northwest on one engine. In the dark they lost contact with the other two PTs. This being usual, the plan was to keep radio silence and meet at a predetermined rendezvous before dawn. It was important that the PTs be back at base by first light as all American pilots had orders to shoot any boat in the water during daylight hours. PTs were night craft. Any day traffic was considered enemy.

The black night seemed impossibly long. Alex checked his watch every half an hour to find that only five minutes had passed. All personnel on deck were assigned specific areas to watch. They stood at the low rail trying to separate one patch of shadow from another, trying to identify any movement in the darkness, anything that might be construed as a ship, boat, submarine, or barge. Taking a coffee break in the tiny galley down below, Woodley told Alex that one night in a driving rainstorm they had crept so close to a Japanese troop barge that the barge had actually run into the PT before seeing them. They had been so close that the guns on the PT could not be depressed far enough to shoot down into the barge. Using tommy guns, they had killed fifty Japanese soldiers in a matter of minutes without taking a single casualty.

The acid of constant watchfulness and anticipation began to eat at the men. Alex found himself jumping whenever anyone passed close by. He and Max stood at opposite sides of the boat. Kennedy stood at the wheel, conferring softly with another officer. Alex strained to see something, anything, and found himself seeing strange ghostlike forms that he imagined were Jap ships, looming out of the darkness to ram them. A rain squall opened up, soaking them instantly, cooling the night, leaving them shivering in thin wet uniforms. And for Alex there was always the enemy destroyer, bearing down on a collision course. When? Maybe tonight. Maybe now.

He wanted to warn Kennedy about the dangers of nighttime collisions, but realized that his contribution would be neither appreciated nor helpful. Kennedy would probably turn away from what he was doing to listen to Alex's warning and that's when they'd be rammed. What could he say? *This is the way it's going to be, Jack. See, this Jap destroyer is going to come along and cut this pitiful little PT boat damn near in half and men are going to die and we'll have to swim for it. So keep your eyes peeled, okay?*

It was the longest, most boring, most acutely terrifying night of his life. And they didn't see one goddamn thing all night long.

They maneuvered on instruments to the rendezvous point, a lonely lagoon beside a small, uninhabited flat coral island. Both boats were there before them. With bad news.

PT 238 had spent the night drifting and searching just like the 109. But the other ship, 167, had had a more eventful time. Shortly after midnight she had gone in close to an island to investigate a possible submarine sighting, but a floating mangrove stump had ripped a trash-can-sized hole in her hull. The crew then spent the rest of the night bailing. After they stuffed a bunk mattress patch into the hole, the water stayed mostly on the ocean side, but the boat was now virtually useless. They could make it back to base, but it was going to take a hell of a long time.

The three boats bobbed in the short swell while the skippers made their decision. The 167 was outfitted as a gun boat: plenty of topside armament at the expense of torpedoes. It was the only one of the three equipped to fight on the way home. The danger came mostly from Jap float planes prowling the Slot, looking for targets foolish enough to be out in broad daylight. Both skippers of the other boats offered to stay with their wounded sister, but John Stokes, the captain of the 167, rejected the offer. No sense endangering all three boats. The other two should head back to base at top speed and call up some aircraft to provide cover as soon as it was safe to break daylight radio silence. The 167 would limp in by herself. He did have one request. The entire 167 crew was exhausted after bailing all night long. They needed help if they were going to stay afloat and keep all the guns operational. Any volunteers would be gratefully accepted.

"Shit," Surrey said. He turned to Alex. "We're about to volunteer, aren't we?"

Alex shrugged. He was tired from simply staying up and staring into the night. He could imagine how the men on the crippled boat felt. Even now that crew was strewn around the deck, trying to catch a few minutes' sleep. "It'll give us a chance to see what things look like in the daylight. Besides—"

Surrey waved him into silence. "I agree. I feel like a fifth wheel just standing around here with my thumb up my butt while everyone else does their job. At least we'll have something to do on the way back. Let's go."

Alex, Max, and two other sailors, including Patch Woodley, known for his legendary ability, despite his youth, to repair just about anything broken on a PT boat, jumped from the 109 to the deck of the 167. The other two boats quickly cast off and pulled away into the now rapidly approaching dawn.

The crippled PT moved about as fast as a healthy man could run. At that speed, the captain announced, it would take at least six hours to make it back. One third of the crew was to man the bailing line, one third the guns, and one third would rest.

Alex worked the first shift, standing in the bilge shifting buckets of seawater. It was dark, but a lantern showed the mass of mattress stuffed into the hole and strapped to the hull. Water soaked the feather ticking and leaked into the boat. The men scooped the water up, passed it along, and threw it back overboard. Whereupon it leaked back in again. There were no pumps, powered or otherwise. All pumps had been sacrificed by the boats' designers to keep weight down. The general thinking was that the boats were so fragile that any sort of damage was likely to sink them anyway. The phrase "They were ex-pendable" began to take on new meaning for Alex.

After two hours below, he was sent topside to stumble blinking into the blazing sunlight of morning. He was looking forward to his two-hour reprieve where the most strenuous thing expected of him was finding somewhere to stretch out and catch about ten winks. Surrey was manning a twin .50 caliber machine gun, and Alex found the sight of the middle-aged history professor decked out in Mae West and combat helmet an almost amusing sight.

"You look pretty warlike, Pop," Alex said, walking toward him.

The bluejackets on the boat had nicknamed Surrey Pop. Surrey couldn't decide if he liked it or hated it.

"I don't feel very warlike. Mostly I feel tired, but I guess if some Japanese airman is foolish enough to try to kill me, I can bring myself to try and stop him. They say all I have to do is aim and pull the triggers. That's as far as my formal instruction has gone." Alex re-membered his own baptism by fire. And the death and destruction that went along with it. Fatigue had almost succeeded in crowding out fear, but this memory now brought back a solid dose of stomach-tightening fright. He glanced up into the bright cloudless sky, wondering if he was going to have to face that demon once again. "Point and squeeze, and don't hold on too tight or you'll break your wrists," Alex said, remembering advice passed along to him in his first encounter. Surrey nodded and went back to squinting into the sky. Alex wandered back to the stern and found a patch of shade beside a torpedo. He folded his Mae West and put it under his head as he stretched out on the hard deck. He had a moment's qualm, lying there staring up at the greasy underside of the torpedo, visions of being crushed flitting through his head. But then he dismissed them as unlikely in the extreme, and fell asleep.

IT WAS NOT the airplane that woke him, but the reaction of the men around him. And it was not any specific noise they were making, but rather an immediate tension, an electric alarm that seemed to jump from man to man as the ship's company all turned toward the dot in the sky that had been sighted by the stern gunner. Every hand went up to every brow as men shaded their eyes and strained to identify the airplane. Alex crawled out from under the torpedo and joined them, trying to make out any markings, all the while knowing that he would be one of the last aboard to know what he was looking at, but looking anyway, trying just as hard as the rest. As if his life depended on it. Which it very well might.

"Corsair," Alex said, surprising himself. A sailor next to him glanced over at him. "Corsair?" the man asked. Without waiting for an answer he turned toward the bridge and shouted "Corsair! Ours!"

Alex cringed as the man shouted. The airplane was still not much more than a suggestion in the sky, but Alex recognized the gull-wing configuration. As a boy he'd spent hours putting together plastic models of World War II aircraft. They were strung up all over his ceiling: Spitfires, Messerchmitts, Zeros, Corsairs, and that Cadillac of the sky, the North American P51 Mustang. Inhaling all that glue hadn't hurt his memory, by God, it *was* a Corsair. As the plane flew closer, it was obvious. The skipper turned the PT boat in a sharp right-hand turn, the standard recognition signal. The boat answered the helm sluggishly, proscribing a slow arc. The plane dropped lower and the men on deck relaxed and turned away, back to their work.

"Must be our escort," the sailor beside him said. "The other boats made good time getting back." Alex nodded and glanced up at the plane just in time to see the wing guns spit flame. A row of bullets slammed into the deck, sending up a storm of wood chips. The blasts ripped the length of the boat, scattering sailors across the deck. In the sudden silence as the plane flashed overhead everyone stood stunned, unable to assimilate what had happened. *They were being strafed by their own plane.*

"Holy shit!" the man beside Alex shouted, crouching down. "He doesn't recognize us!" The plane banked and came around. The skipper jammed the throttle forward and the boat began to pick up speed.

Men were jumping up and down, waving their hats, shouting at the plane. The captain yanked the rudder over and the boat heeled to the right. The plane began firing again and men dived as the shells chewed their way into the deck. Alex waited for the gasoline to take a hit and blow them all to hell. Men were still shouting as they hid under torpedoes and behind ammunition boxes.

"You stupid asshole!" a sailor shouted, running to the bow .50 caliber machine gun. The plane turned in the sky and dropped down into position. Everyone was shouting and running. The .50 caliber opened up. The plane fired back. Alex squatted on the deck and watched as Surrey, still standing at his gun, spun around and crumpled to the deck. Alex stood up and ran.

"You stupid motherfucker! You dumbshit!" the bow gunner shouted as he sent a line of tracers into the belly of the airplane. Alex glanced up as he reached Surrey, flinching away from the blast in the sky as the Corsair exploded into pieces that tumbled smoking into the ocean.

He turned Surrey over and his hand came up wet with blood.

"Help!" Alex shouted. "Get a medic!" He scanned the length of Surrey's body. There was a ragged hole at the shoulder and another in his upper leg. Surrey's face was blank with shock, his eyes staring upward.

Don't die! Don't be dead! I need you! Now! Later! Don't die! Don't die!

Bright blood welled from the two wounds, soaking the khaki uniform, smearing onto the deck. A pair of hands pushed Alex aside. A sailor knelt beside Surrey. "Okay, okay, I got him. Give me some room." The sailor tore open a pack and pushed a white wad of gauze onto the shoulder wound. "Hold that," he said to Alex. "Press down on it. Christ, he's bleeding like a pig." Alex leaned onto the bandage as the sailor ripped open another pack and began strapping it around the leg wound. Surrey's eyes seemed to focus and he turned his head toward Alex.

Surrey licked his lips and tried to speak. Alex leaned close. "Just lie still, Max, don't try to talk." Surrey made a rasping noise and swallowed. He shook his head from side to side. Alex leaned even closer. Men were gathering around them.

"I . . . must . . ." Surrey's voice was a cracked whisper. Alex strained to hear. "Bomb . . . atom bomb . . ." Surrey's eyes rolled back showing only the whites.

"Max! Goddamnit! Max!"

23

his eyes bright with fever and pain. "Take a painkiller," Alex said. "For God's sake, Max, knock off the heroics."

"No dope," Surrey said. "Not yet."

The damaged PT had crawled back to base. Surrey had regained consciousness while they were working on him. The doctors had finished up and left the tent.

"I'm sorry," Alex said, "all of this is my fault. If it weren't for me, you wouldn't be here."

Surrey shook his head. "Now *you* knock it off. It doesn't matter." His voice registered halfway between a whisper and a croak. Alex gave him a sip of water. Surrey was wrapped mummylike at the shoulder and leg, unable to move. "There's no one in here, is there?" he asked. Alex looked around. The tent was empty and would remain so until the orderly came back to check on them. "We're alone."

Surrey nodded. "Listen closely," he said. "I don't think I can get through this more than once. Shit." He stiffened and lay with eyes squeezed shut. He let out his held breath in a long hiss.

"It's not your fault. It's mine as well. Roosevelt's. Hell, the war's. Einstein's. You can't lay the blame that easily. You don't know what's going on."

Surrey was looking up at the canvas ceiling. Alex pulled his chair closer to the bed. *You don't know what's going on? What the hell was that supposed to mean?*

"I'm going to try and explain this to you." Max continued. "I don't understand all of it either. But here it is." He paused for a moment to wait out a wave of pain. He swallowed and went on. "We're out here because of the atom bomb all right, but not our atom bomb. We're here because of the one the Japs are putting together." Alex stared at Surrey, trying to understand.

"What the hell are you talking about? I never heard of any Japanese atom bomb. Einstein said they didn't have the capability. The Germans, yes, but not the Japanese."

"There's a lot that Einstein doesn't know," Surrey grimaced. "But I'm telling this, so just believe it. They're going to pull me out of here and you'll be on your own. You've got to go on. It's important. There's no one else out here to take over."

Alex felt a flush of exasperation. "Surrey, what the hell is this?" He looked closer at his friend, wondering if he was delirious. "Look, Max," he went on, "Roosevelt wants us to study the area. We want to stop them from dropping the bomb. That's the reason we're here. Or at least it was. I don't know what the hell it is now."

Surrey shook his head and managed a weak smile. "Jesus, for a guy who's supposed to know everything, you don't know anything. But that's not your fault. I tried to warn you about Roosevelt. Nothing is ever what it seems with him. He never sends you on a job and tells you the whole story. Here it is." Surrey tried to sit up straighter. Alex snagged another pillow off the next bunk and stuffed it behind Surrey. "We've captured a Jap, a scientist. One of their subs sank, coming up from the Philippines. The Jap survivors, there were only two of them, made it to one of the islands in this chain. An Aussie coastwatcher and some natives picked them up. The Aussie was an engineer out here, before the war. When the Jap scientist started babbling about a nuclear project, the coastwatcher knew he had something important. He got a message through, thank God, the right channels, and it ended up back in Washington. You happened to stumble along at the right moment. 'Serendipitous,' as Roosevelt is always saying. If it hadn't been you, it would have been someone else. And me."

"Why you?" Alex gave him another drink of water. Surrey was running down, like a balloon slowly deflating.

"Because I'm Einstein's keeper. The government doesn't trust him. All they see is that he's a German, so that means he might be a spy. Christ, it's laughable, but they're idiots. So they assigned me to keep an eye on him. I did some work for the government when Roosevelt first came in, so they assume I'm loyal. Albert and I were already friends. See the way it works?"

"I'm beginning to, yes. Are you loyal?"

Surrey looked at him and flushed, anger seeming to refuel him. "Hell, yes. I'm loyal to the government, but I'm also loyal to Albert. Jesus, the man denounced his German citizenship years ago. There's a death warrant out on him straight from Adolf Hitler. Since I was already involved in all of this, when you stumbled in they saw an opportunity and took it. That's why I'm here. I would have been here no matter what. We've got to get the Jap scientist out, get him back where Groves and the atom bomb eggheads can find out how far along they are. I'm supposed to talk to him in case something happens before we get him out."

"I thought you didn't know anything about the bomb."

"I'm no goddamn physicist, but I understand the concept. I know the basic procedures, enough to tell how far along the Japs are."

And how do I feel about this? Mildly betrayed? Tricked? Totally betrayed? At least foolish. Used. "So all that initial reluctance was an act?" He couldn't keep the anger out of the question.

Surrey sighed. "Yeah, I'm terrific, aren't I? What else could I do? You and Albert were cooking up your own scheme. Roosevelt had his. All I could do was to try and go along and keep everybody happy."

"You don't look too happy, Max."

"I didn't think I'd get shot up. I guess one never does." Max stopped. His breathing began to slow. He was looking up at the ceiling again.

"Max! Wait a minute, don't pass out on me now. What am I supposed to do now? I don't even know who I'm working for."

Surrey turned his head toward Alex. Alex could see him attempt to focus his attention. "Get the Jap out. He's on New Georgia, not far from here. The Aussie's name is Billy Gillam. Question the Jap. If they get the bomb, we're in serious trouble. We've got to stop them. *You've* got to stop them." Max's eyes closed. His breathing was slow and ragged. Alex watched him for a minute, somehow hoping that Max's eyes would open and he'd smile and say April Fool, or gotcha, or something, it was all a joke. But Max didn't open his eyes. Alex left the tent and found the corpsman.

Alex stood outside, having been assured by the corpsman that Max was not going to die. Evening had crept in. Out on the bay he could hear the rumble of PT engines as the men prepared to head out for another night. *Get the Jap out. And just how in the hell am I supposed to do that?*

He went back into the tent. The corpsman was wiping off a hypodermic syringe. "I gave him enough to knock him out until he gets on the ship out of here. He'll be all right. He'll sleep."

"Yeah. Great." Max's breathing seemed easier. *He'll be all right.* He didn't want to say it, but a little voice inside, the little voice of fear added it. *But what about me?*

The next afternoon, Alex lay on his bunk in the empty four-man tent wishing he were not alone. They had shipped Surrey out that morning, still sleeping, leaving Alex behind, feeling resentful, betrayed, and abandoned. A useless stupid feeling, he knew, but there it was. Surrey's exit, flat on his back with two bullet holes in him, was hardly the return home anyone would have wished. Alex knew that too. But still, he was alone, and in the geography of fear his own ever-present mental hill of apprehension was now building, transforming itself into a mountain with crags and cliffs and bottomless rifts. He was alone, facing his mountain, with no one to rope himself to, no one to help him over the difficult parts.

So far he'd been lucky. But one of the characteristics of luck is that eventually it runs out. Sooner or later. Sooner or later.

Jesus, the heat and humidity are killing me. My mental equipment is beginning to rust, my nerves are shot. He swung his feet over the edge of the bunk and stood up. It was another steaming hot afternoon. It had rained earlier, but it had not cooled down. He went to the front of the tent, where a Lister bag hung from the main roof support. He drew himself a tin cup full of water, took a sip, and swallowed an Army-issue Atabrine, an antimalarial tablet. He knew his skin would eventually turn yellow from taking the tablets, like everyone else on the base. But being yellow was better than having malaria. Most of the enlisted men hated the pills, saying that they were the Army equivalent of saltpeter, handed out to kill the sex drive in the troops to keep them in line. Which led Alex to thoughts of Molly and a wash of loneliness and self-pity that was so painful he almost laughed at the depth of it.

Holy shit, I'm turning into a mental case. If I keep this up, I'll be reduced to lying in my bunk, curled up in the fetal position with my thumb in my mouth. He took the cupful of water and dumped it over his head. The small shock brought him a measure of relief. *To hell with it.* He wiped the water over his face. *I'll go on because there's nowhere else to go. Einstein expects it, and no matter what Surrey says, the two holes in him are somehow my fault. And the goal is worth the risk of my sorry hide.* He remembered Einstein watching them walk away, remembered their purpose, remembered the future, remembered what the bomb would bring to the world. But the farther away he got from the world of morality and abstract thinking, the harder it was to think logically. The closer he came to the war, the less he remembered of what he had been, and what he was supposed to do. High-level philosophical positions quickly began to erode under the continuing stream of war. Seeing men shot, wounded, killed, being bombed, shelled, and strafed, all of it tended to promote the short view. Staying alive and protecting the men closest to you became the only real considerations. The future of the world was hard to hold on to in the middle of the jungle.

COLONEL MORGAN tapped a large island on the map. "New Georgia. The Japs have an important airbase at Munda, right here." He put his finger on the silhouette of an airplane on the southern tip of the island. "A few of the harbor areas are heavily defended, but a lot of the coastline is only lightly manned. Too many reefs for much in the way of concerted amphibious landings. We can get a PT in, though. Bitch of a mission, but we've done it before." He sat down at his desk. Alex leaned forward and looked at the map.

"That's where the coastwatcher, Billy Gillam, is?" Alex asked.

"Yes. He and his Fuzzy Wuzzies are up there in the mountains. The natives have a lot more freedom than Billy, of course. They keep watch and get him the dope. He sends it along to us. He's been up there for three years now. Good man.

"We've put men ashore there twice. We're going to have to take the island sooner or later. Sooner, I'd guess. We needed solid information, that's why we went in. Billy gets a lot out, but we wanted a firsthand look. You said you had to get a PT up there. All right, we can do it. Now, what's it all about?"

Alex crossed his arms over his chest. "I've got to get a Japanese prisoner, maybe two, out of there. This is top secret. All the way up the line. No records, nothing. I want everyone involved to have that impressed upon them most forcibly." Morgan nodded. If he was surprised, he didn't show it, at least as far as Alex could see. "You've got the clearance," Morgan said. "I'll go along with it. We'll send Kennedy up the Slot tonight to radio Billy his instructions so he knows what he's supposed to do. We'll go back for the pickup in three days. Will that do it?"

"Yes. I'm more interested in getting everyone out safely than I am in speed. I don't want anyone to get hurt."

Morgan grunted. "I guess having your partner evacuated out makes it rough on you. But we're in a war here. We're not running a spare-parts factory. People get hurt, people get killed, but you just keep on with the job. You don't have to go out there tonight. Kennedy can handle it. There's nothing you can do to help."

The offer to stay home lay there between them, bright and shiny. Nothing prevented him from picking it up. *Except self-respect, goddamnit. What am I going to do, lie in my bunk and drink Coca-Cola?* "I'll go along."

Morgan nodded. "These coastwatchers," he went on, changing the subject, "are doing a hell of a job for us. Most of them have been up in the hills for years. When it was clear the Japs were going to take all of these islands, most of the Aussies had time to get off, get back home. But they understood that this chain of islands leads not just to Japan, but also right to their own country. Taking Australia was, and is, very high on the list of Jap priorities. Guadalcanal changed all of that, but for a while it was a near thing. They bombed the shit out of Port Mosbey and a lot of the cities on the Australian coast. If it hadn't been for the steady stream of information from these men, we wouldn't have been able to stop one tenth of the ships that have tried to come down. And Billy Gillam's one of the best. He was out here on one of the plantations doing engineering when the shoe dropped. Gathered up all of the gear he could scrounge and headed for the hills. The Fuzzy Wuzzies love him. He's always treated them well. If anyone can get your Japs out, it's Billy."

Alex stood. "I hope so. It's important." Morgan stood and shook Alex's hand. "Be careful," he said. "Kennedy's good. Do what he says. He's young, but most of them are young. They're a lot older than they look."

. . .

THE NIGHT was pitch black. No stars, no moon. The boat bobbed on a light swell. The engine was barely turning over, barely holding their position. Alex could just make out the outline of Kennedy's face, leaning over in the green light of the crude radar set. "Go," Kennedy whispered to the radioman next to him.

Alex watched the radioman's lips move as he muttered their message into his set. Somewhere out in the dark, Billy Gillam and his natives would be huddled over their receiver. At least Alex hoped they were. He also hoped that no Japanese radiomen were listening, sitting at their consoles, twiddling the dials, finding the gift of their signal, leading straight to their small boat in the dark night.

The radioman finished up and switched off his set. He nodded to Kennedy, who straightened up, signaled to start engines, and grinned at Alex. Alex breathed his relief and moved to the rail. Kennedy joined him. "That's it," Kennedy said. "We can get the hell out of here." Alex looked up and saw, thirty yards away, the towering cliff of a destroyer as the Japanese ship rushed toward them.

Jesus! Here it comes!

Kennedy stood frozen, staring at the oncoming ship. Without thinking, Alex picked him up and threw him overboard, vaulted over the rail, and dove deep into the water. The destroyer rammed into the 109, tearing the small boat in half. Ruptured fuel tanks exploded in an orange ball of flame, spewing blazing fuel and oil across the surface. Beneath the water, Alex could see a flickering ceiling of fire above him, could hear the muffled roar of the flames and the churning of the destroyer's propellers. He swam away, toward the darkness.

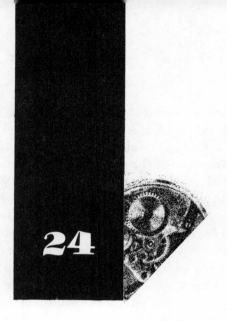

24

Alex burst through the surface of the water, sucking air into his lungs. His eyes and throat burned from the gasoline fumes and smoke hovering over the oil-slick surface. He swam farther away from the burning fuel and debris. He could see in the light of the fires that the forward section of the PT was still afloat, shorn in half through the cockpit. The front half was listing to port, but relatively intact and as yet unburned. Alex swam in a circle, looking for other survivors. Kennedy was twenty feet away, treading water. "See anyone else?" Kennedy called to him.

Alex turned around in the water, trying to spot heads. "No one," he said.

"I'm going to get closer," Kennedy said. "The fire's dying out." He began breaststroking toward what was left of the boat. Alex swam along behind him. Flaming chunks of plywood floated in the water around them. The stern, with the gasoline and the engines, had exploded and gone straight to the bottom. As they approached the remains of the PT, the flames in the water began to flicker and die out. In the ensuing blackness the chunk of hull appeared as a dark tilted boulder, rising up against the night sky. The clouds overhead began to break up and the emerging stars gave off a thin silvery light. Closer to the boat, the fumes were even heavier. Alex could taste the gasoline. He felt his gorge rise. He vomited seawater and fuel.

"Oh Jesus, is anyone there?" a frightened voice called from the boat.

Kennedy answered and kept on swimming. For the first time since seeing the ship bearing down on them, Alex slowed down and checked himself for damage. Aside from nausea he didn't seem to be injured. The shock of hitting the water and the necessity of getting away from the fire had delayed the worst of the fear. Now that he had realized he was alive, panic, like a disease rising up out of remission, flooded back in a chest-thumping surge. He tried to slow his breathing. A tumble of horrors, like terrified children, began to pluck and yammer at him: *Sharks! We're lost! The Japs will come back and finish us off! I'll drown! They'll leave me!* He closed his eyes and concentrated. *No . . . Stop . . . I am alive. I am not hurt. I am in trouble, but I am alive.* He repeated this mantra several times until he had subdued the worst of the panic. The water was warm, and he was a strong swimmer. The fire was out, and he heard voices in the water around him, proving that at least some of the crew had survived. In a small way, there was a feeling of relief. He had known that the destroyer would appear out of the night. At least the waiting was over. "Up here, everybody. Swim to the boat," Kennedy called from the forward section. "If you can't make it, sing out and I'll come get you."

A weak cry for help came from Alex's left. "I've got him," Alex yelled, and began swimming in the direction of the voice. In a minute he found the man, Evans, one of the motormen, held upright by a kapok life vest. "Burned," the man said. "Can't move my legs."

"It's going to be all right." Alex said, searching in the water for the belt on the back of the man's life vest. He located the belt and began towing Evans toward the boat. As he approached, he could see other men swimming in the same direction. Several men bobbed in the water beside the fragmented hull. Kennedy and Patch Woodley hauled the worst of the injured aboard. One by one the men were dragged or climbed up until all of them were sitting or lying braced against the slope of the deck. Kennedy called the crew's names. All but two answered. Jimmy Holt and Don Borkin were missing. For a few minutes all of the survivors shouted the names of the missing men into the dark, but there was no answer. Jimmy had been trying to sleep on the deck next to the cockpit. Borkin had been below in the tiny galley. Both in direct line with the destroyer's sharp hull, both probably smashed and sucked under, both almost certainly dead.

Two officers and seven enlisted men had made it. And Alex. Three were hurt. The man Alex had hauled in, motorman Arnold Evans, was badly burned, the other two had deep cuts. All of them lay on the deck, resting, waiting, and looking forward to the warmth of daylight. Until they realized that although the coming day would undoubtedly aid in their rescue, it would also expose them to every Jap ship and plane in these Japanese-dominated waters.

"Sitting ducks," torpedoman Willy Deal announced. "Japs'll fly over and knock us down like clay pigeons. We won't have the chance of a fart in a hurricane." He shook his head. Willy was a small man with a pencil-thin Don Ameche mustache.

"Where the hell are we gonna go?" asked Tony Arcosa. Arcosa, a motor machinist second class, spoke in a matter-of-fact tone, as if he were on a streetcorner with a couple of friends. "We can't swim back to Rendova. And if we leave the 109 they'll have a hell of a time locating us. I say we stay right here and wait for a PBY."

Kennedy scanned the sky around them. The PBYs were the patrol planes sent out to locate lost boats. The sky was still too dark for rescue planes to find them. They were floating in the center of Blackett Straight. Rendova Peak was thirty-eighty miles to the south. The island of Wana Wana was to the east. Kolombabngara and Gizo lay to the west. All of these islands were occupied by the Japanese. A series of smaller uninhabited islands stretched between the larger ones. "We've got three choices," Kennedy said. "Fight, surrender, or abandon the boat and try to hide until they find us. The first thing to remember is that we don't have to fight unless the Japs spot us." He glanced up into the progressively brighter sky. "Which is growing more and more likely."

"What the hell are we going to fight with?" Dan Koestler asked. Koestler was another motorman, big, with curly black hair. Even in the short time he'd been on board, Alex could see the man had the affable, easygoing, almost simple-minded good nature that many big men possess. "Good question," Kennedy said. "Let's take inventory."

Between them they came up with six .45s, one .38, and a Thompson submachine gun they found in the ruined charthouse. No one could say for sure that the water-soaked guns and ammunition would actually work. Three knives and a battle lantern made up the rest of the usable items.

Oscar Blume, the radioman, sat on the deck testing the edge of one of the knives. "I ain't going to surrender," he said, shaking his head. "We all know what the Japs do to prisoners."

"Yeah, well, you're a single man. I've got a wife and three kids," Pop Little said. Little was the old man of the boat. Old at thirty-two.

"Just because you got a wife and kids don't mean the Japs are going to let you live," Blume responded. "They ain't known for their compassion."

"I just don't see where we got much of a chance sitting here on this busted hunk of plywood. If we surrender, they probably won't shoot us outright. I ain't saying this 'cause I'm yellow. Just that I got kids." Pop glanced around at the others.

"Hold up," Kennedy said. "It doesn't matter to me, I don't have much to lose." He looked at Pop. "But I think we ought to try and get out of this by ourselves."

J. P. Smith, Kennedy's executive officer, a short, stocky man with a quick brain and a calm manner, sat up. He'd been lying on his back watching the men argue. "I think the skipper's right," he said. "Anyway, we don't have to decide whether to surrender or fight until we have something to surrender to or fight against. That decision is best put off until we're faced with it. Then we'll know the odds. Right now we've got to get off this boat. There's a chance a PBY will be looking for us, we're overdue, but there's a better chance that the Japs will be coming by. They own this piece of water, at least in the daytime. Let's get somewhere where we can hole up until our side comes looking."

Nods all around indicated agreement. Kennedy climbed down over the jagged plywood into the charthouse and brought up a map. He was studying it when Willy Deal spoke up. "I got a question. Been bothering some of us," he said to Kennedy. He nodded at Alex. "Just who the hell is he and what's he doing here anyway? It's bad luck to have visitors on a boat." Deal spit over the side. "I guess we proved that old myth, didn't we?"

Most of the men stared carefully at the deck. Alex felt himself blush and marveled that a lightweight emotion like embarrassment could still arise under such extreme circumstances.

"Here's the way it is," Kennedy said. "As far as we're concerned, this man doesn't exist. He's on a job, one that we're not supposed to know anything about. When we get out of this, no one will ever mention that he had any part in it. Understand?" Heads nodded. Deal, the man who had asked the question, looked mildly defiant but he didn't disagree. "Something else," Kennedy went on. "Right before we got hit, I was standing on deck with my mouth hanging open and my thumb up my ass, watching the Jap ship come at us. This man"—he nodded at Alex—"picked me up and threw me overboard. I was standing right about there." He gestured at the ragged edge of plywood. "If he hadn't dumped me over the side, I would more than likely be dead." Everyone stared at Alex.

Alex cleared his throat. "I may not exist," he said, "at least not officially, but I'm in this with the rest of you. I don't need any special considerations. You want me to do something, help out some way, just ask. As far as I'm concerned, I'm under Lieutenant Kennedy, just like everyone else."

Evans, the burned sailor, coughed and tried to sit up. Everyone turned and looked at him as Smith eased him back down to the deck. "He brought me in," Evans said in a rough voice. "He's all right. Lay off him."

There was another block of silence until Kennedy folded the oilskin map and pointed at the horizon. "Sugarloaf Island," he said. "Supposed to be uninhabited. Three miles away, take us about four hours to swim." He looked back at the men. "Get that long plank the deck gun was lashed to and get it into the water. I'll take Evans." He supervised the prying loose of the plank and shepherded everybody into the water. Evans cried out when the saltwater washed over his burns. They all wore life vests, and tied their shoes to the plank. The three who couldn't swim were put at the center, the others ranged at either end. Alex paddled over to where Kennedy was cutting one end of the strap at the back of Evan's life vest. "I'll help with Evans," Alex said. "Your back isn't going to take a three-mile swim hauling an injured man."

Kennedy looked sharply at Alex. "What about my back? What do you know about my back?"

Alex's mental alarm bell was ringing furiously. *Too late, as usual.* "I didn't mean anything. I just meant that it's a long haul, I'll help." He remembered photographs of JFK as President, strapped to various boards as his back problems recurred to the point of incapacitation. All the world knew that President Kennedy had back trouble, variously attributed to old football injuries and the PT incident, though it was in actuality a congenital weakness, present from birth. The young Kennedy had been commissioned into the Navy through influence directed by his powerful father. He'd never even attended basic training. But Alex shouldn't know that now.

"There's nothing wrong with my back, I can handle Evans. You take the fellows on the plank. That board won't hold them up, but it will keep them together. I'm going to go ahead."

"Don't worry, J.P. and I can get them there."

Kennedy nodded. "Sorry about what Deal was going on about up there. Sailors are superstitious. Visitors are supposed to be bad luck."

"It doesn't matter."

"Yes it does. I had orders from the CO about keeping you as quiet as possible. I intend to follow those orders to the letter, even though the circumstances have changed. Something else, thanks again for throwing my sorry ass overboard. I couldn't believe what I was seeing. That damn destroyer was not supposed to be there. It would have run right over top of me, I should have reacted faster. It was a mistake on my part. Not my first either," Kennedy added bitterly.

"It took everyone by surprise."

Kennedy shook his head. "You saw it, and you did something. I didn't. It's that simple."

"Forget it. Your job is to get us out of the mess we're in now." *To live and go on to be the President of the United States.*

"Right. Let's get to it before the Japs find us and finish us off before we even start." He swam over to the men on the plank and checked everyone's life vest. He tied the battle lantern to J.P.'s vest and swam back to Evans. "Let's go," he said. He took the strap from Evans's life vest, put it between his teeth, and began swimming the breast stroke, towing the injured man behind him, toward the distant island. Alex turned to the men, who were all watching Kennedy. "He'll make it," Alex said quietly. "Let's get this damn board moving."

THREE MILES is a long swim by any standards. Seven men on a board, three of them nonswimmers, all of them floundering and kicking, did not make for smooth progress. Even Kennedy, towing another man, made better time. Alex tried to organize the effort, but there were too many variables. After a while he let them go at their own pace while he swam from end to end, helping out where needed. He had no idea how long they took to traverse the three miles, it seemed like several days, but it gave him plenty of time to think over what had happened and what would happen. The water was warm, the surface calm, and he had the life vest to hold him up when he stopped swimming to rest.

As long as he remained pointed in the correct direction there was little he had to think about beyond keeping his arms and legs moving.

The thing to remember, he told himself, *is that Kennedy and the rest of them get out of this alive*. That was history, documented in myth, political lore, the book *PT 109*, and the movie of the same name. Alex could remember seeing part of the movie on late-night television. He had found it so bad, Cliff Robertson as a particularly wooden Kennedy, that he had eventually turned it off. Now he wished he had followed it to the end.

The basic storyline, as he remembered it, was that Kennedy would lead them to several islands, and eventually some natives would find them. The natives would report them to a coastwatcher and help would soon be on the way. *And just where do I fit in this?* Alex paddled along and tried to work it out. After Surrey had been wounded, Alex had reached a conclusion on one of his ever-present questions: did his presence affect events? And now he thought the answer had to be yes. The Maxwell Surrey he had known in the present had no major scars. Now he would have two of them, and very probably a limp as well. So things *could* be changed; Max certainly was. That meant he could be hurt as well, could die. And it followed that if he could affect Max's future, he could affect the world's future. Which is what he was supposed to be doing out here all along, what Einstein believed him to be doing. But what he, Alex, never really thought was possible, not deep down, not where it counted. Until now. But first he had to get himself out of his present predicament.

Jesus Christ!

He stopped swimming and began to tread water. In front of him was a huge jellyfish, three feet across with who knows how many feet of dangling, stinging, poisonous tentacles. He had been so caught up in his thoughts he'd almost swum into it. He carefully sidestroked around the milky white creature. He'd just about conquered his fears of sharks, now he'd have to add jellyfish to the list of seaborne dangers.

As the island grew larger, the men settled down and worked together. Alex varied his strokes and kept himself pointed in the right direction. Just how much should he be doing to ensure their survival? And would his participation be noticed, would it become part of history? The event, the ramming of Kennedy's PT boat, was in itself extremely important. The young Kennedy would use the exploit to launch his political career. And continue to use it whenever expedient. Alex remembered pictures of Kennedy's inaugural parade, in particular a shot of a PT 109 float with all the surviving members back aboard, smiling and waving to the crowd. *And I sure as hell wasn't on that float.* No Alex there to produce a major glitch in the seam of history.

Alex jammed his foot on a chunk of rough coral. They were still well away from the island, but a wide reef ran all the way out to where they were now standing. They could walk the rest of the way, treading carefully over the sharp coral. They untied their shoes, put them on, and began wading tiredly through the water.

Would it be just like the movie? Or is it something that I do? Please, let it be just like the movie.

25

KENNEDY WAS LYING ON THE NARROW strip of beach, half out of the water. Evans was tugging at him with his burned hands, trying to drag him into the underbrush. Alex stumbled up and put his hand on Evans's shoulder. "I'll help him," Alex said. He leaned down and pulled the exhausted Kennedy to his feet, finding once he had him up, he wasn't sure he had the strength to carry him. The three of them dragged themselves into the bushes and dropped to the sandy ground. Alex held back a branch and watched the rest of the men stagger out of the water, hauling the plank with them. Alex called to them and they made their way up the beach to the small clearing. The men collapsed around the base of a large palm tree, slipping into unconsciousness within seconds. Alex wondered briefly if they shouldn't put someone on watch, but then, afraid he might be taken up on the suggestion and assigned the job, he rolled over and went to sleep.

He awoke to a steady thumping—the sound of offshore shelling, bombs exploding, heads being crushed beneath the rifle butts of evil Japanese soldiers. He opened his eyes and saw it was Smith pounding one coconut against another. The coconut split open and Smith stared at the pieces. "Green," he said, looking at Alex. Alex pushed himself up against the base of the tree. Smith stirred the pieces with his finger. "No milk in them, can't eat the meat. We're not going to be living off these things." He sat back on his haunches and watched the other men beginning to wake and sit up. Kennedy walked out of the underbrush into their small clearing. His uniform was torn and dirty and flapped around his skinny frame.

"Nothing here. No water, nothing to eat," he said, sitting down.

"No Japs?" Smith asked.

Kennedy shook his head. "That's the good news. I walked the perimeter. The island's about a hundred yards in each direction. Not much good to anyone. It'll hide us for a while, but that's about it."

Kennedy stood back up and moved to where Evans was lying. Pop Little was kneeling beside the injured man. "He's hurting pretty bad, Skipper," Pop said. Kennedy crouched down and looked at the burns. "Take some of those green coconuts and see if you can get any oil out of the meat. Drip it on the burns, it might help." He came back to Alex and Smith.

"I'm going back out there," Kennedy said, gesturing toward the strait.

Smith looked confused. "What?" he asked.

"I'll swim out. They'll be sending boats on patrol from Rendova tonight. I'll stay out in the strait and flag one down. I'll take the lantern and a pistol."

"Jesus, Jack, that's a screwy idea. You'll never make it. It's too far. It'll be too dark. And I'm not so sure that there'll be any boats coming up. There's no way of knowing."

Kennedy shook his head. "There's a chance. We've got to do something. I'll entertain any better ideas." He looked around at the rest of the men who were listening to the discussion. "Anybody got a better plan?" No one spoke for a moment.

"I don't have a better one, but I got to agree with Mr. Smith that the one you got ain't so hot," Tony Arcosa said. "You go out there and start blinking your light and shooting off your gun, well, you're either going to catch the attention of any Japs in the vicinity or get your butt shot off by our boys. You know how antsy everybody gets out there."

Kennedy looked down at the ground. "Maybe, Arcosa, but I still haven't heard anything better."

"How about we just sit right here and wait for our guys to find us?" Willy Deal suggested. "It ain't too fancy, but it's a hell of a lot safer than what you got in mind."

Kennedy picked up a stick and scratched at the sand. "You know, when I was a boy, I used to read a series of books. By an Irish writer. Irish books for Irish boys, my mother used to say. Anyway, they were about this gang of boys who were always headed off on some adventure. Whenever they came to a stone wall that seemed like it was going to stop them, because it was too high or too hard to climb, these boys would throw their hats over that wall." He looked around at the men. "There was nothing they could do except figure out a way to go on so they could get their hats. That's all I'm doing, throwing my hat over the wall. You fellows with me?"

Alex was surprised to see most of the men looking ashamed. He wondered how such men would have looked, say, in Vietnam if some commander told that story under similar circumstances.

"Didn't mean we weren't with you, Skipper," Deal said. "Just sounds kind of dangerous."

Kennedy stood up and brushed off his pants. "I'll get started now. I can walk along the line of reefs pretty far. I'll be in position when it gets dark. J.P., you organize things here, scout the island again, and put a watch out on our blind side. Try to make Evans as comfortable as possible." He smiled his wide grin. "Don't worry about me, I'll just be floating around out there enjoying myself. Don't forget, if I get picked up, I'll get the first cup of hot coffee."

Smith set about organizing the men. Kennedy clipped his .38 to a piece of rope and slung it around his neck. He picked up the lantern, a large, floatable gray Navy lamp, and walked down to the beach alone. Most of the men went about their tasks, but Alex could see they were watching Kennedy. He waded out into the water. His hair stuck up in the back, as if he'd slept on it wrong. His wet pants clung to his thin legs. He stumbled on the sharp coral and splashed forward. He began to dog-paddle away from the island. Soon all they could see was his head, bobbing among the shallow waves. And then he was gone.

TEN HOURS LATER he still hadn't come back. During the night thousands of birds had flown in and roosted in the trees and bushes, keeping them awake with their screeching and constant defecation. Alex had finally quit trying to sleep and crawled to the edge of the undergrowth. He sat beneath a bush looking out over the strait. Dawn was just beginning to color the dark sky. The rest of the men were asleep, he could hear them muttering and groaning. Thirst was beginning to become a real concern. There was no water anywhere on the island, and the accidental ingestion of seawater over the last day and night had dehydrated all of them. Alex sat watching for Kennedy, trying to think of other things besides tall cool glasses of springwater. Or even muddy warm puddles of rainwater. Anything that was wet and salt-free.

The men had willingly gone about their assigned tasks, even though it was obvious that most of the jobs were simply make-work, designed to keep them busy rather than to accomplish anything of real value. They cleaned all the pistols, made beds out of leaves, squeezed drops of oil from green coconut meat onto Evans's burns, and set up watches on both sides of the island.

They discussed Kennedy's swim back out into the strait. The general consensus was that it was a harebrained scheme, but all of them admired him for it. They also all agreed that Kennedy was a good skipper and that they'd do whatever he asked of them. They might bellyache a little, but they would follow orders.

And so Alex sat in the brush waiting for the twenty-six-year-old Lieutenant John F. Kennedy to climb back out of the water, as he hoped to God he would do, and mused on the curious phenomena of leadership and trust and men. And what seemed to be the lack of it in his own time.

Alex had not gone to Vietnam, had in fact done everything he could to stay out of it. Not because he feared it, though he certainly feared going there, but because he believed it was wrong. As did many of the men who actually went. And most of the tales that came back, at least to those who fought against the war, were of dope-smoking rebellious young soldiers, most of them black and poor, who had no faith in their leaders and who believed the war purposeless and unwinnable. In the short time he'd been in the Pacific, Alex had seen nothing like those attitudes, even though part of him had been looking for them, searching for confirmation of his own antiwar philosophy.

These men, boys actually, the average age was nineteen, had a list of beliefs that they all agreed on. They believed that this war was something that had to be fought, that America was the bastion of the free world, that the American way was the envy and model of the rest of the world, that the Japs and the Germans had to be licked or they would take over America, that our leaders might be at fault at times, but that they were to be obeyed, and that the good ones would be obeyed at the expense of their own lives. They hated the war, were afraid of combat, would do most anything to get back home. But when called upon, these men would fight. Against any odds, if properly led. Because they *believed*. And Alex, whose cynicism was the equal of any man's, found their attitudes to be, in some fundamental way, moving.

In the face of this trust, the more aware, intelligent perceptions of men and women of his own time seemed lesser things, the people actually poorer for their loss of innocence. It would have been easy to make fun of these men, to poke intellectual holes in their convictions, to explain to them that they were being used and manipulated by the same government they saw as essentially blameless, to point out the corruption and moral failings of their leaders. But he knew they would have responded to him with disbelief and sadness, and would have pitied him for his notions. And while they may have been naive in their attitudes and opinions, he could see that their world, at least spiritually, was a better place than his.

Kennedy appeared, splashing toward the island. He dragged himself out of the water. Alex stood and ran down to the beach and caught him in his arms as he fell. He helped him back to the clearing as the men hovered.

"No luck," Kennedy said in a hoarse voice. "Didn't see a thing. The current carried me way down, had to swim back, walk the reefs. Cut me up pretty bad. Anything happen here?"

"Nothing, Skipper," Smith said. "The men are pretty thirsty, but we can hold out a little longer."

Kennedy nodded and swallowed. "Okay. Everybody get back to sleep, if you can, get as much rest as possible. Keep the watch out, we could get a Jap barge anytime. They may check these smaller islands on some sort of a schedule." He looked at the circle of worried faces surrounding him. His smile was a pale reflection of his old self. His cheeks were flushed, but his skin was gray. "Knock it off, fellows, I'll be all right. I almost got that first cup of coffee." The sailors smiled back and turned away. "Pull me under a bush, Alex," Kennedy whispered. "I've got to get some sleep." Alex helped him away from the center of the clearing. He settled him under a low bush and turned to go when Kennedy caught his arm. "Wait a minute. Don't go yet. I have to tell you something." Alex stopped and sat back down. Kennedy shook his head, as if trying to clear it. Alex felt his forehead, it was hot with fever. The coral cuts were probably already infected. Kennedy must have been exhausted. He'd been in the water over the last two days for more than thirty hours. His lips were cracked, his face peeling from exposure.

"I've got to tell you," he whispered. "You're the only one. You don't exist." The feverish light in Kennedy's eyes, the wide-open, imploring stare gave him an intense crazy look. Alex wondered if he should call one of the other men.

"I told you back at the boat this wasn't my first mistake." He laughed. More a rattle than a laugh. "Not by a long shot. Pearl Harbor." He looked at Alex as if expecting a response. Alex shook his head. "Pearl Harbor," Kennedy went on. "It was my fault. Somebody's got to know, in case I die."

Alex looked around for help. "Take it easy . . ."

"No, goddamnit, I'm not crazy. This is the straight dope." His raspy whisper was harsh with urgency. "I was with ONI, Office of Naval Intelligence. We were the ones who were supposed to figure out what all the intelligence meant, we were the clearinghouse, the brains. We were getting some high-level stuff, really high-level . . ."

"The Magic codes, I know." Alex knew, though few others in this time did, that the Americans had broken the Japanese code and had listened in on their secret transmissions for the last four years. The code name was Magic. The ONI was the unit responsible for putting those decoded transmissions into order and drawing conclusions from the data.

"You know about Magic?" Kennedy whispered. Alex nodded. "I knew you were different, there's something about you that isn't right. You know a lot more than you let on." Kennedy licked his dry lips. "Anyway, it's my fault. I should have guessed. We had all the pieces, we just didn't know where they were going to hit. Pearl was our last choice. We weren't even close." He rose up on his elbows. "*I should have known!*" he whispered urgently. "My father would have known. Joe Jr. would have known. Don't you see? It was my fault. And now this. I should have never left the cockpit. I should have gotten us out of there. I should have seen that ship." Alex eased Kennedy down. The man wasn't even looking at him anymore. His eyes were focused somewhere else, talking to his father, confessing to his older brother. "I'm sorry, Dad, I let you down." His face assumed a look of sadness. And then his eyes closed. Alex waited for a few minutes and then turned to crawl away. He jumped as he felt a hand grasp his wrist. The grip was strong, the skin hot against his own. "Wait." Kennedy was turned toward him. "You go out there tonight. You try it. They'll send someone, you hear me?" Alex nodded. "You'll go?" His eyes held Alex's, would not let him escape. "Yes," Alex said. Kennedy's eyes closed. His grip loosened and fell away from Alex's wrist. He was asleep, or unconscious. Alex crawled out from under the bush to the clearing. The sun was up now, and the heat was rising. It would be a long dry day on the island.

ALEX WAS retying the laces of his shoes, making sure they would stay on for the walk over the coral reef. "You don't have to do this, Alex," J.P. Smith said, watching as Alex went over his gear one last time. "It's not going to do any more good tonight than it did last night. Jack's out of his head, or at least he was this morning. He'll probably be all right when he wakes up, he probably wouldn't want you to go." Alex stood up and slipped the lanyard with Kennedy's .38 around his neck. He was moving on autopilot, sure that if he stopped to consider what he was doing, he would chicken out. His gut was tight with fear.

"He said for me to go. It was an order. I said earlier that I would do what needed to be done." *Who the hell do I think I am with this John Wayne shit?*

"This is crazy. It was crazy when he did it," Smith said, shaking his head. "Surely you can see that."

Alex looked at Smith. *Yes, I can see it. No, I don't want to go. Yes, I'm scared shitless. No, I don't see any way out of it. Any honorable way.* "It doesn't matter. He said to go. If he told you to do it, would you?" Smith lowered his head, and nodded. "So, now it's my turn." He managed a weak smile. "Tomorrow it may be yours." He turned away and walked down to the beach. It was approaching evening. He could see the men watching him. Smith caught up with him at water's edge. "Go down the reef line," he said in a low voice. "There are other small islands, get your butt up on one and spend the night. No one will know the difference."

Alex glanced at the man as he tightened the straps of the life vest. He waded into the water.

"I'll know," he said. "I'll know the difference."

. . .

THE SALTY WATER stung as it worked on the old coral cuts and sand-burr wounds. For a minute the cool water had felt good on his sunburn, but that had only lasted a moment. Now his face and hands and any other sun-exposed skin began to burn. He waded forward, chest high, along the coral reef, carefully balancing on the sharp, slippery out-croppings, acutely aware that every time he slipped, he risked a serious cut somewhere on his body. He used his arms for balance and to push himself forward. Night had come with its usual suddenness. High clouds curtained any light that would have come from the sliver of new moon.

He waded and swam for two hours. At one point he thought he heard a boat in the distance, but he hadn't chanced firing a shot. The likelihood that it would be Japanese was as high or higher than that of it being American. He decided that he would not give himself away until he was sure that any passing boat was friendly. And that meant waiting to hear if those aboard were speaking English or Japanese. And the probability of his getting that close was extremely slim.

He reached the southernmost point of the reefs. The dark outline of the last small island was on his right. This was where he was supposed to kick off into the channel. Or turn back and climb up on an island and wait out the night. He cursed himself for a fool and pushed off into deep water.

In another hour he decided he must be in the center of the chan-nel. He stopped swimming and let himself drift. He was bone tired already. No food and yesterday's swim had depleted him. The water was warm. A few stars began to show between the clouds. He fell asleep. He jerked awake, amazed that he could doze off. He ought to be too afraid. He had sharks and jellyfish to worry about, even if he forgot the Japanese. There was a good chance that his life vest would become waterlogged and no longer support him. He could easily get lost and swim in the wrong direction. He could get run over by a boat. Jesus, how could he sleep?

How did I get myself into this? Well, he reasoned, he was where he was because a half-deranged twenty-six-year-old kid who just happened to be a lieutenant, junior grade, in the United States Navy, told him to do what he was doing. He had obeyed because it was what any of the others would have done.

More stars began to show. He spent a half an hour staring at the sky, orienting himself. He knew his constellations, had spent hours as a boy lying on his back, all over the world, studying the sky. The Southern Cross gave him his direction. He decided to lay off the questions and just drift. He dozed and swam, alternating between the two. The only sound was a faint whisper of the wind and the occasional lap of a wave. The only sights were the broad starry sky and the phosphorescent blaze that accompanied any movement on his part. He could lift his arm and watch the water, jewellike, tiny drops of light, drip from his fingers. It was very beautiful.

THE GENTLE TOUCH against his thigh woke him. A long stroking movement. He smiled. And saw the phosphorescent glow in the wake of a fin protruding above the surface of the water and came instantly, heart-poundingly awake as the shark circled and came back. Alex stifled a scream. He could see its long body, four feet long, five feet, ten feet, *oh Jesus he couldn't tell how long it was, long enough to kill him*, he made a moaning noise as the shark nudged him with its blunt snout. And nudged him again.

Think! Shark lore. His brain raced as he tried to remember what he should be doing. Playing dead was for bears, snakes, and maybe sharks. Thrashing the water just aroused their interest. Smacking them on the nose sometimes worked. Dye packets and shark repellent did and did not work, depending on who you listened to. He slowly and carefully unhooked the .38 from the lanyard. He wished for the tommy gun, but that had fallen apart on the swim from the boat. He moved carefully in a circle, looking for the fin. *Put the gun to its head and blow its fucking brains out.* If he could get it to hold still and cooperate. *Where was it?* He thought of the scene in *Jaws* where Quint describes being aboard the *Indianapolis* at the end of World War II when she was torpedoed and went down and a thousand men met their end in the warm tropical water, not by drowning, no, but by shark, the bloody water a mass of flailing screaming men. Alex imagined his shark rising from below, building up speed until it hit him, hard enough to lift him out of the water, midriff firmly planted in the fearsome mouth as the great fish began to shake him, tear him . . .

Fuck this.

He clipped the pistol back to the lanyard and began to swim. It might be the wrong thing to do, but he had to get away from where he was. He kept swimming until he could no longer lift his arms. His body ached. He began to doze, snap awake, swim, then doze again.

DAWN. His eyes opened. He had made it through the night. He hadn't exactly covered himself in glory, but he was alive. He felt the comforting jolt of coral underfoot. It would be hours before he made it back to the island, but somehow having something to stand on was a comfort. Not exactly dry land, but close enough. The walk was long and slow, but he made it. This time it was Kennedy who came to water's edge to help him up the beach to the clearing.

26

THEY LET ALEX SLEEP UNTIL NOON, AND
then it was back into the water. Thirst was driving them to try another
island. The drill was essentially the same: Kennedy hauling Evans,
the rest of the sailors clinging to the plank, Alex swimming around
the long board, helping out where needed. It took three hours. The
island was marked Olasana on Kennedy's maps, and when they made
it, they found that the coconuts were plentiful and ripe. They hacked
open the coconuts and greedily drank the water and ate the meat.

After the coconut orgy, Alex sat on the beach with Kennedy, studying the islands around them. Kennedy had the oilcloth map spread out
beside him, the corners held down with chunks of coconut shell. Both
of them chewed on pieces of coconut meat.

"What is it you do, Alex?" Kennedy asked offhandedly, fiddling
with his map, "Back in the States. When you're not a secret agent,
or whatever it is you're doing out here."

"I teach history."

Kennedy looked at him. "Really? That's probably what I'll end up
doing when this is all over. That or journalism. I like to write. Maybe
I can combine the two."

Alex smiled. "I'm sure you could. You've got Harvard and a well-
received book under your belt. I'm sure you could find a job somewhere.
Somehow, though, you don't strike me as the professorial type." *History
professors don't get much opportunity to sleep with Marilyn Monroe. You'd
be bored, it's too tame for you, Jack.*

"You're smiling. What do you think I'd be good at?"

"Well, I think you'd be good at anything you put your hand to. Ever thought about politics?"

Kennedy laughed. "Not much chance of that. That's Joe Jr.'s department. Dad's been grooming him for the presidency since he was a little kid. I'm the second son, which means I'm not meant for such lofty heights. My brother is the good-looking one, the one with all the charm and the terrific grades. And a brain to match. I couldn't beat out Joe Jr. No one can."

Alex picked up a chunk of coconut shell and threw it into the water. "Don't sell yourself short, Lieutenant. You never know what's going to happen. Life plays some pretty strange tricks."

"True, but this is preordained. My father has decreed it, so that's the way it is."

Alex was listening for some hint of bitterness, but he couldn't hear it. "That doesn't bother you?"

Kennedy shook his head. "Nope. My father is a smart man. A lot of people think he's a son of a bitch, but most of that is jealousy. He's advised me on every major decision I've ever made, just as he has with Joe and the other kids. I wouldn't go against what he wants, and he wants Joe to be President of the United States. And he will be. My father gets pretty much everything that he wants. It doesn't mean that he loves Joe more than he loves me, just that Joe's got a better chance. I agree. Joe will make a hell of a President."

They sat quietly for a few minutes. "You're probably right," Alex said. "But let me give you some advice. There's two things about advice. First of all, it's free, and second, you don't have to take it. Anyway, if the opportunity ever comes to run for office, grab it. I think you'd be damn good at it."

Kennedy folded up his map. "Thanks, Alex, I'll remember that. I appreciate the vote of confidence. But so far on this expedition, I've struck out." He looked uncomfortable for a moment. "Look, uh, yesterday, when I came back in, I was out of my head. I think I spouted some pretty crazy stuff at you." He stopped, but Alex didn't say anything. "Anyway, I'd appreciate it if you forgot anything I was going on about. I know you've got a high clearance level, but I shouldn't have been talking."

About how you caused Pearl Harbor? Or at least how you failed to warn your government in time? "Don't worry. Like you said, you were off your head."

Kennedy stood, picked up the broken coconut shells, and hurled them into the ocean. He pointed out into the strait. "There's the next objective. Naru. I'm going to take Smith and swim over there. We can't live on coconuts forever, and this is a lousy way to win a war. There might be something there we can use to get out of this mess. It's only a quarter of a mile away. If we find anything interesting, we might have to spend the night. Otherwise we'll be back this evening."

"You're leaving now?"

"Yes. It's another wall to throw my hat over. Got to go get my hat." He stooped and picked up the map, turned and waved, and walked back up the beach.

Alex sat alone, suddenly feeling exposed, vulnerable to any Japanese sailor or pilot who happened to train his binoculars in this direction. He stood and brushed off the sand, realizing as he was doing it that his sun-bleached, tattered clothing was hardly the worse for a little sand. He walked up the beach and sat back down again in the shade of a tall bush. There were small yellow flowers on the bush and Alex found himself wondering idly if they were edible.

He felt a mantle of gloom fall over him. The day was bright and hot, the sky a dazzling blue, the pristine beach blindingly white. All it needed was a couple of good-looking blondes lying on blankets. No, he was in the middle of a war, there would be no blondes, only a barge full of Japanese whose greatest pleasure would be to mow him down with their Nambu machine guns. He was trapped here, and he had no idea what was supposed to happen, or what would happen. He watched as Kennedy and Smith walked down to the edge of the beach and splashed into the water.

So Jack Kennedy thought his brother Joe was destined to be the President of the United States. But Brother Joe was slated for another destiny. In slightly more than a year, young Joe would volunteer for Project Aphrodite, a British scheme to destroy Nazi submarine pens on the coast of France. Kennedy would pilot a B24 that had been packed with explosives. His job was to fly the plane into the general area of the submarine pens, then bail out while another pilot in another airplane guided the flying bomb, via remote control, to the target. There were so many explosives in the plane there was no room for a co-pilot. Even the pilot's seat had been removed to shoehorn in more explosives. Kennedy flew the plane standing up. It was to be the largest single conventional explosion of the war. When he flipped the switch to arm the explosives, the plane blew up in midair, ending both Project Aphrodite and Joe Kennedy Sr.'s dreams of installing Joe Jr. in the White House.

John F. would become the thirty-fifth President and die three years later under the bullet of a young ex-Marine defector who was very probably a Mafia stooge working under the indirect manipulation of Fidel Castro. A very pissed-off Castro, angry because the same Mafia guys had arranged six attempted hits on the Cuban dictator's life with the cooperation of the CIA.

Alex scooped up a handful of sand and let it trickle through his fingers. Had he saved Kennedy's life for this end? If it hadn't been for him, Kennedy's boat probably wouldn't have been sitting where it was when it was run down by the Jap destroyer. No PT 109 legend to jump-start a young man's political career. Maybe no President Kennedy.

Alex lay flat on his back, staring up through the thick leaves of the yellow-flowered bush. Was all of this his fault, of his making? Or was he a bystander swept up in the rush of history? He was back to his original question: could he make a difference to the future? He sat up, pushing away the frustration. He had long ago learned that there was no answer to this question. All he could do was just go along, trying to do his best in whatever situation he found himself in. But that didn't make it any easier. He pulled off a yellow flower and ate it. It tasted awful.

He fell asleep under the warm blanket of the afternoon sun.

He opened his eyes. He had been dreaming of Molly. Down at the water's edge, two natives were dragging a dugout canoe up on the beach.

By the time Kennedy made it back from the other island, night had fallen and the men were all sitting around a campfire, eating C-rations, smoking cigarettes, and singing "What a Friend We Have in Jesus" with Biuku and Eroni, their two new native friends. Kennedy walked into the clearing, looking from the fire to the natives to the men sprawled on the ground. Willie Deal lifted a crude cup Eroni had fashioned from a coconut shell. "How about a cup of Java, Skipper?" he asked. Kennedy looked around again.

"I'll be goddamned," he said, shaking his head. "Good news, boys, I found us a one-man canoe. Got some Jap crackers too. Found them over on the island."

"Great, Skipper," Willie went on. "I'll try some just as soon as I finish my can of peaches. And eat my piece of cheese. Our friends here brought dinner along in their canoe."

"Tell you what, Deal," Kennedy said. "You can have all my crackers for one of your peaches. I'll even throw in my canoe. As long as your two friends are willing to carry a message back to Rendova."

Willie threw Kennedy a small C-ration can of sliced peaches. "You can keep the canoe, Skipper. Meet Eroni and Biuku. They've got their own transportation. And they're quite willing to take out a message, as soon as we figure out something to write it on. You got any suggestions?"

Kennedy looked around the clearing. He pulled out the large knife he wore strapped to his waist. "I want two coconuts," he said. "One to drink coffee out of, and one to write on. Move over boys, we're going home."

ALEX WATCHED them go. From his bush on the beach. Watched the PT boat that came for them slowly back away, turn, and head down Blacket Strait. He watched the prow lift as she picked up speed, watched the spray arc up behind her in a rooster-tail wake. Watched her take away everyone but him. Leaving him alone. It hadn't sounded too bad when Kennedy gave him the news. Back in the clearing while they watched the rest of the men file down to the beach and swim out to the PT. It hadn't sounded too bad then. But it felt like hell now.

He had ten gallons of fresh water, a case of Spam, and a box of Jap crackers. Not exactly a balanced diet.

Everything had moved quickly after the natives found them. Time that had seemed to drag before then, now, at least in retrospect, was moving at the speed of light.

KENNEDY HAD given him the news as they stood in the clearing and watched the men climb aboard the PT. "The word from the CO is to leave you here for a day or two. You're not supposed to exist, remember? They're going to send another boat to pick you up. It's my fault in a way. They've got a photographer on this PT, waiting to snap some pictures of the ex-ambassador's son as he's rescued off a lonely island in the South Pacific. I didn't ask for it, Alex, you understand that?"

Alex nodded. "They're going to make this into a hero thing," he said bitterly. "I lose my goddamn boat, get two men killed, hurt some others, swim around in the strait until two natives sent by a coastwatcher find us. Some hero. And to top it all off, I've got to leave behind the fellow that saved my hide. How the hell do you figure it?" he asked.

Alex had a large hollow feeling in the pit of his stomach. It made sense. If he went back with the others, he was sure to get written up. This was PT 109. Legend. But it scared him. *What if they never come back? What if they forget I'm out here?* Dumb, cowardly questions, but tell that to the little voice that lives inside all men and thinks only of itself. *So I'll sit here another two days. I've got plenty to eat and drink. I'll be fine, as long as the Japs don't decide to see what all the commotion is about.*

"Don't worry about it, Lieutenant." Alex made himself smile. "This is going to make great copy for you. Never can tell when you're going to need a good war record."

"Yeah, well, we'll see about that. Anyway, I got something for you. A souvenir." He handed Alex a coconut. It was the one with the message carved on the side. Alex ran his fingers over the incised message.

NARU ISL
NATIVE KNOWS POSIT
HE CAN PILOT
11 ALIVE
NEED SMALL BOAT
KENNEDY

"You keep it," Kennedy said. "You carved it."

Alex remembered newsreels of Kennedy sitting in the oval office. The coconut was always on the President's desk. Alex handed him back the shell. "Yeah, but you dictated it. Doesn't mean anything but that I'm a better wood-carver than you are."

Kennedy tucked the coconut under his arm. "I'll keep it with me, Alex. I won't forget what you did."

. . .

ALEX WAVED GOOD-BYE as the boat sped away. He couldn't tell if anyone saw him. He thought maybe one man waved back. A tall skinny young man, maybe. The boat was too far away to tell. The sound of the engines faded away. And he was alone.

27

ALEX SWEPT THE WHITE BEACH WITH A
palm frond, erasing the marks of American Navy–issue shoes. Then
he hid himself and his supplies in the undergrowth. As he expected,
a Japanese patrol barge circled the island, but didn't bother to land.
Alex lay in the brush watching the low barge as it chugged along. A
squad of soldiers lounged in the boat, chattering and laughing. They
were so confident and carefree he felt like running out on the beach
and lobbing a coconut at them, just to show that he was putting one
over on them. But an indefinite stay in a Japanese POW camp didn't
really appeal to him. So he lay low and wished them Godspeed as they
motored away into the shimmering heat of another day in the South
Pacific.

The rest of the first day wasn't bad. He studied the behavior of
seagulls and other shorebirds, pretending he was an ornithologist on
a field trip. He ate a couple of cans of Spam and drank some water.
The wind blew, romantically rustling the palm fronds. The sugary
white sand of the beach beckoned, and the calm ocean curled onto the
shore with comforting regularity. He was surprised how quiet it all
was, without the rest of the crew. He missed them. He missed everybody.

The next day he roamed the small island. He found a nest of turtle
eggs and decided not to eat them. The Navy had left him a heavy,
battleship gray Zippo lighter, but he thought a fire might draw a return
trip from the Japanese. Besides, the turtles lived on the island, or at

least nested there. He was a guest. He wasn't hungry enough to eat his unwitting hosts.

The morning of the third day found him down on the beach scanning the horizon. *Okay. One or two days, we'll pick you up. Day number three. I'm a patient man, let's go out there. Time to get me the hell out.*

The PT crew had donated a fresh set of clothes, but they weren't so fresh after three days. He was unwilling to use his supply of water for anything but drinking, and you can't take a decent bath in coconut milk. He washed in the ocean, which left him refreshed for a few minutes until the warm breeze dried him. Then he was left with a thin crust of sea salt that didn't brush off, but worked itself into the folds and crevices of his body and the myriad cuts and scratches he had accumulated. The lovely fine sand was everywhere. Every mouthful of Spam was spiced with beach sand. It was a permanent condition: sand in his underwear, sand in his food, sand in his water. He stood on the beach searching the calm sea and felt the sting of sand as it peppered his body and blew into his eyes.

After four days he decided he'd better ration his food and water. He piled up a pyramid of coconuts, and forced himself to eat the meat and drink the milk. He vowed, once he returned to civilization, never to eat another macaroon as long as he lived. The water was stale by now, tepid and flat. The Spam remained only Spam, more odious with every mouthful.

On the fifth day he began to entertain serious doubts. He was in bad shape and sliding rapidly downhill. His diet of canned Spam, Jap crackers, and coconuts was worse than just salty and boring. Nutritionally, it would eventually kill him. He began to dream of vegetables, crisp fresh vegetables.

On the sixth day he found himself weeping with frustration. He wiped the encrusted sand and tears from his eyes and lay on his back, cursing the United States Navy, Franklin Delano Roosevelt, and whoever it was who had invented Spam.

After one week, he tried to come up with ways to kill himself. When the water ran out, he would be reduced to a steady diet of coconuts. In time even the coconut supply would be exhausted. By then he would be insane. He tried to busy himself with Robinson Crusoe activities, but the climate was so mild there was no need for cleverly crafted huts. There were no parrots to catch and tame, or natives to befriend. There was only himself, and he was sick to death of his own company. At night he dreamed of Molly and New York, and his bed, and food. But mostly of Molly. His dreams of her were a cool sanity in his world of heat and increasing instability.

The days began to meld together, and he was no longer sure where one ended and the next commenced. Mostly he slept, in his little camp beneath the waving tousled head of a Royal Palm, his supplies gathered around him, water cans, coconuts, Spam, and crackers, everything at arm's length.

He ate when he could remember, and forced himself to do so. It was a constant struggle to keep from gulping down the rest of his dwindling supply of water. Mostly, he slept.

He was lying on his back, staring up at the shifting palm fronds, when a voice found him. "Well now," the voice drawled. "This is surely a sad state of affairs."

Alex didn't even need to sit up and look. He recognized the voice, knew that it would eventually come to this. He pushed himself up anyway.

There, perched on a downed palm tree, sat Mark Twain. In a past time, Alex had spent a month with Twain, and come to know him well. Twain was wearing a bottle green smoking jacket and alligator skin slippers. He was smoking a large cigar. Alex shook his head. "You're not here. I'm imagining you."

"You are, are you? Then why don't you imagine me away from here. It's damned hot, and damned dry."

"Don't remind me. What do you want?"

Twain puffed on the cigar. "I thought you could use a little company. A man in your pitiful condition deserves a measure of compassion. What the hell are you doing here anyway?"

Alex brushed sand off his shirtfront. He hated for Twain to see him like this. "There's a war on, didn't you know?" Twain grunted and looked around. "Doesn't look like much of a war to me. But what do I know? The only war I ever came in contact with scared me so bad I retreated all the way cross-country to the Nevada Territory." Twain stood up and stretched. "What's it all about, anyway?"

"Actually," Alex began, "it's several wars." He tried to get it straight in his own head. He knew that when you talked to Twain, you'd better have all your ducks in order. Before Twain started shooting them down. "See, the British, the U.S., the French, and some other countries are fighting the Germans and the Italians." Twain bent down and pretended to look under a bush.

"Not here," Alex said. "Out here we're fighting the Japanese."

"The Japanese! Why on earth are we fighting them? They're small and they have poor eyesight. It hardly seems fair."

"We're fighting them because they've decided to try and take over the entire Eastern hemisphere. Besides which, they attacked our main navel base in Hawaii."

"You mean the Sandwich Islands."

"Right. And that business about their eyesight is just a myth. They can see just fine."

Twain set his cigar on the log and did several deep knee bends. "Doesn't that just beat all. The Japanese. Are we whipping them?"

"Not yet." Alex stood up. He swayed dizzily. "We will, but it's going to take a while and cost a lot of lives."

Twain nodded, and picked up his dead cigar. "Got a match?" he asked. Alex found his Zippo and struck it. "Good God, what's that? An automatic match!"

Alex shook his head. "Not again, Twain, forget it. Maybe you'd just better go back to wherever you came from. I've got enough problems."

Twain looked mildly aggrieved and then nodded. "Well, maybe you have. How'd you get yourself into this mess anyway?" He sat back down on the log, and removed his slippers, one at a time, and dumped sand out.

Alex sighed. "That's a long story. See, you know how I move around in time . . ." He paused for a minute. Twain looked up and waved the cigar. "Anyway, I found myself back in 1943, actually first I was at Pearl Harbor, but now it's 1943, and I linked up with an old friend of mine, and he took me to see a friend of his, who happens to be a world-famous physicist, and there's going to be an atomic bomb, so we decided to try and stop it. You used to tell me that it was a man's duty to try and make things better, to try and change what he could, to save lives." Twain was sitting patiently, nodding his head. "Go on, it all makes absolute sense."

"All right. Then we went to see the President, that's Franklin Delano Roosevelt, and he sent us out here because the Japanese may be making their own bomb, but I wasn't supposed to know that . . ." He looked closely. Twain's eyes were closed. "Are you listening?"

Twain opened his eyes and smiled. "Of course I am. What's an atomic bomb?"

"It's a weapon that may end up destroying the world. We're going to drop it on the Japanese."

"Do they deserve it?"

"Nobody deserves this. This is larger than retribution or revenge. This is as big and terrible as it gets. Except for the hydrogen bomb, but don't ask me about that."

Twain appeared to mull it over for a moment. Alex sat back down. He opened up the can of water, tipped it up, and drank. He offered it to Twain, who shook his head. "You wouldn't have any whiskey, would you?" he asked hopefully.

"No. Sorry. Want some Spam?"

Twain looked at the blue can Alex was pointing to. "No, thank you. A man in my condition doesn't need to eat." He sighed. "I could use a drink, though. All right, let me tell you a story. Back in my day, we had a super weapon as well. The Gatling gun. Everyone said that it meant the end of civilized warfare. Which in a way, it was. A very effective weapon, as our Indians and other assorted natives were to find. The man who invented it, Richard Gatling, lived almost as long as I did. Toward the end of his life he became a man of some mystery. Each day Gatling would rise, dress, and leave his house. At night he would show back up, have his dinner, and go off to bed. No one knew where he went, no on knew what he was doing. Men everywhere expected he was working on a new weapon that would once again revolutionize modern warfare. Finally, someone decided to follow him, see what was going on. It seems Gatling had rented himself an apartment. Every day he went to the apartment and sat in a darkened window, looking out onto a busy street. He had a pea shooter. A long brass tube. He spent all day, every day, shooting peas at people passing on the street." Twain buried his cigar in the sand. He stood up and brushed off his smoking jacket. Alex thought the white-haired Twain was beginning to look a bit insubstantial. He could see a palm tree through the man.

"Wait a minute. Don't just disappear on me. What the hell is the point of the story?"

Twain appeared distracted. "Point? What's the point? I don't know, you figure it out."

"But wait! What am I supposed to do?"

Twain was almost gone. His voice was now very faint. "Do? Why, you should do your best, of course. What other choice is there?"

28

TWAIN WAS THE TURNING POINT. AS THE
old man faded away, Alex decided that if he was going to survive, he
had better seize the situation while he was still at least mildly rational.
He knew that his discourse with Twain had been imaginary, but he
also knew that it had been real enough to scare him. The next time
Twain might decide to stay.

He set aside his earlier scruples and dug up the turtle's eggs.
Unfortunately, they had formed themselves into little turtles by now,
inedible no matter how desperate he was. He found a gull's nest and
several eggs. Then he set a trap with an empty water can and some
Spam for bait and caught himself a gull. He defeathered the bird and
boiled it and the eggs in the water can and ate the entire mess. The
tough stringy meat tasted of dead fish, but he got it down and immediately felt better. He found some very young palm trees and stripped
away the bark from the hearts and ate them raw. By the time an LST
hove to offshore and dropped a Higgins boat to collect him, he felt
pretty good. He had been on the island a total of thirteen days.

The man who stepped out of the boat onto the beach was Colonel
Bill Frazier, the Marine colonel who had briefed them back on Guadalcanal when he and Surrey had first arrived. Alex remembered Frazier as friendly and helpful and wondered if the officer had brought
his green lawn chairs with him.

"I imagine you're surprised to see me," Frazier said, holding out
a hand. Alex shook it.

"Not really, Colonel. After thirteen days here, I wouldn't have been surprised if Franklin D. Roosevelt himself had come off that boat." Alex allowed the first tendrils of relief to enter his being. He was damned glad to see Frazier, but he wasn't going to show it. There was a point of honor involved, and as long as he could keep his knees from buckling out of sheer gratitude, he was going to be as calm and collected as was expected of him.

Frazier looked closely at him then nodded his head. "Well, I'm sorry it took so long to collect you. The snafu didn't originate with the PT boys on Rendova," Frazier explained. "They were champing at the bit to send someone out for you. I had orders on you anyway, so it seemed reasonable for me to organize your pickup. We're moving on up the line, and that seemed to fit into your overall plan, at least as I understand it, so I elected to let you sit it out a few days. I wanted to collect you without including anyone else. The 109 fellows are all heroes now. You'd never have escaped the newshounds. We just enlisted you in a more anonymous branch of the service. You're a Marine now. You're coming with us."

They walked down to the boat, where the coxswain waited patiently. Alex looked around at the island, wondering for a moment if he had anything he should be taking with him. Nothing. Coconuts and Spam were his only possessions, and he could live the rest of his life without either of them. They climbed in and the boat backed off the beach into the light surf.

"Your friend Surrey is doing all right. He should be stateside by now. We got him patched up pretty good and on a plane. I spoke to him before he left. He passed along what you boys were working on. He was extremely reluctant about including me, but as I'd had orders from the top to look into it, he decided my bona fides were in order." Frazier looked away from Alex, watching the LST as they moved closer. A stiff breeze off the water, kicked up by the bow, created a cool dampness that was a welcome change from the dry, still heat on the island.

"The coastwatcher?" Alex said carefully.

Frazier nodded. "That's right. I know he's got something, or someone for you. Something important. I'm supposed to help you out, within reason."

"Can't I just work it out with the PT people. That's what we were doing when we got hit by the Japanese."

Frazier looked at him. "That's out of the question now. What we're involved in takes precedence. The PTs won't have the time nor the opportunity to be taking anyone off New Georgia."

"Give it to me, Colonel. What are you getting at?"

"Well, son, we're going to get you your Aussie. Trouble is, we may have to kill about ten thousand Japs to do it. Your man's on an island up ahead, and he's got whatever it is you're supposed to get. We're going ashore to help you, me and the First Marines. We're going to take that island, and when we've got it, you'll link up with your man. But as I said, first we've got to take it away from the Japs."

"And I'm going in with you?" A new fear began to dawn.

"Yes, you are. I can't leave you behind. I'm the only one who knows what you're after. You can't stay on the LST. It'll be leaving as soon as it drops us off. You can't go back, you'll get lost in the shuffle for sure. The only direction to move during a war is forward. That's where we're headed. That's where you need to go. Stick with me, you'll be all right. I'm handing you over to one of our best men. He'll take you under his wing." Frazier smiled at him. Alex supposed it was meant to be friendly, but it was a hard, distracted smile, the polite smile of a man who had other things, bigger things, to think about than another's particular well-being, fears, and comfort. "I'll turn you over when we get on board. You can pick up a uniform and gear, a weapon if you want it. You've got about a day to get ready. We go in at dawn, day after tomorrow."

They reached the LST and climbed up a ladder lowered over the side. Once on deck they were met by Frazier's staff. Frazier turned to Alex. "I believe you know Sergeant Simmons?" he said. Alex looked at Gunny. The taste of crème de menthe came to mind.

"Hello, asshole," the sergeant said. "Time to make a man out of you."

AND THERE WAS only one day to do it. Gunny lectured him from sunup to sundown. During meals and in their bunks at night. Alex could see that these lectures were a way to pass the time for all of the men, time that hung heavy in the holds of the troopship, heavy with fear. So they gathered around and watched Gunny give it to Alex, their eyes following every movement of the old sergeant's hands as he fondled whatever weapon he was demonstrating at the moment. He passed along survival lore, and the men took it all in, knowing that some small piece of advice might mean the difference between life or bleeding to death on a warm tropical beach.

"M1 Carbine," Gunny said, slapping the weapon into Alex's hands. "Thirty-five point six inches long, five and one-half pounds unloaded. Standard magazines are fifteen and thirty rounds. This weapon was invented by Marsh Williams, known as Carbine Williams, while a convicted felon in a South Carolina prison. He drew the plans on stolen scrap paper and built the prototype out of metal scrounged from the prison machine shop. It is a superb weapon; it is lightweight, it is reliable, and it is simple enough for even you assholes to operate. Some say it is too light, that it is not a mankiller. Tell that to the Japs back on the Canal." He took the gun out of Alex's hands and inserted a magazine. "It is now ready to fire. Treat it with respect and it may save your life." Alex laid the carbine on his bunk, afraid that if he screwed around with it he might accidently pull the trigger. And then Gunny would kill him.

Gunny handed him a .45 automatic and a belt. Alex handed it back. "I don't need this, Gunny," Alex said. "I'll have enough to do keeping track of the M1."

Gunny ignored him. "This is your Colt .45 M1911 A1. This here's a real gutbuster. Do any of you shitbrains have any idea why this weapon was developed?" A man on the opposite bunk spoke up. "Because the old Springfields didn't have enough stopping power."

"Very good, Goldberg. At least one of you was paying attention back in basic. Actually, they didn't tell you the whole story back there. This weapon was developed during the Philippine Insurrection, one of our more minor wars. But the Philippinos were tough, like the Japs. Their chief weapon of war was the machete, and when a wave of these half-naked yellow fuckers with their pig stickers came up out of the jungle at you, you wanted something that would drop them like a bad habit. See, these little fuckers had a secret weapon. Before they went into battle, they strapped up their balls with leather thongs. When the time came to go over the top, they cinched those belts tight and the pain was enough to overcome any lesser annoyances, like a plain old rifle bullet. This .45"—he showed the pistol around—"will put a man down, and the shock can even kill him if you so much as hit him in the hand. Pound for pound, this is the most effective weapon ever made." Gunny slipped a magazine into the butt of the automatic and eared back the hammer. "It'll stop a Jap. They don't tie up their balls, but they don't need to—they're mean enough as it is."

He looked at Alex sitting on the bunk beside him. He continued, his tone almost kind. "You don't need to take this weapon right now. You'll want one later, I guarantee that, but there'll be plenty of them available." He looked up at the men crowded around. "When you hit that beach, you'll find all the firepower you need. M1s, Thompsons, BARs, .45s. Feel free to use whatever weapon fits the situation. Most of the guys on the beach'll already be dead, go ahead and take whatever's there, they won't mind. Just get the right ammo, and don't forget to pull the bolt back on the Thompson. It won't fire unless you do."

Late that night the division was assigned to waves. Alex was relieved to hear that the group he was going in with would be in the third wave. The idea of hitting the beach first was too much to think about. Until Gunny straightened him out.

"Third wave's the worst," Gunny said calmly. He said it quietly, so the others around them couldn't hear. "By then the Japs will have the range. Zero right in. Blast those landing boats out of the water just as easy as finding your dick in the dark."

Alex lay in his bunk listening to the men around him not sleeping. A few of the old-timers, like Gunny, could be heard snoring away. But even Gunny was up long before first light. Checking his arsenal. Alex could hear the slide on the M1 as Gunny worked it, wiping the rifle down with a soft cloth. Alex could smell the gun oil. He could hear Gunny muttering to himself as he clipped grenades onto his webbing. *Telling stories, getting ready, making sure, and what about me? This time I am in real trouble.* He tried to lick his lips and found his mouth was too dry. He sat up on his bunk. In the dim light of the hold, he could see the others lying on their bunks, eyes wide open. Waiting.

THEY FILED INTO the amphibious tractors, down on the amtrac deck, jamming in until Alex was pressed against the pack of the man in front, as someone, he couldn't turn around to see who, was pressed in behind him. Gunny was somewhere in front. Alex kept scanning the packs and helmets, trying to find the Sergeant, as if even the sight of what passed as a friend would give him strength. The air was full of blue carbon monoxide exhaust as the amtrac raced its engines. The deck trembled beneath them. In a few moments the big bay doors at the front of the LST would open up and the amtracs would lumber down the ramp into the water. Alex was more afraid than he had ever been in his life.

All of them were afraid. You could feel it in the bodies around you, the attitudes the men assumed: stiff and unyielding, some trembling. Faces pale, bloodless; eyes empty and staring. Someone threw up. The man behind Alex was making little whimpering noises. The ship rattled as the doors opened. The amtrac lurched forward and stopped, throwing the riflemen behind onto the men in front. Alex fought to stay upright, fought to keep from fainting. The amtrac rumbled forward again, down the ramp, and splashed into the water.

Dawn had arrived while they were being loaded. Men shuffled against each other, blinking in the light. Guns from the ships shelled the beach. The air was full of the noise of war. Alex lifted his head to the railing. "Keep your fucking head down!" Gunny roared at him. Swearing, Gunny squirmed back beside him. "Listen," he said, his voice strung as tight as fence wire. "When we hit the beach, pile over the side of this thing and get the hell away from it. The Japs'll be using the amtracs for targets. Don't try to hide behind it. Got it?" Alex managed to nod. His helmet tilted forward. He pushed it back with his rifle barrel. Gunny winced, mumbled something about blowing his fucking head off, and began to work his way up to the front of the trac. The machine gunner on the prow of their vehicle opened up. The air above them was filled with the hum and whiz of bullets as small arms fire flew overhead. The shelling from the ships behind them was constant, planes roared and dove and fired rockets onto the beach. Alex peeked over the gunwhales, unable to ride blind.

The beach was wreathed in smoke. Amtracs stretched in a long line on either side of them in the water, heading in. A wave of carriers in front showed briefly as they topped the surf. As Alex watched, the amtrac to their left took a direct hit and water plumed into the air. The stricken boat wallowed stupidly, out of control, turning sideways. A fire was burning at the front of the boat. Someone near him was muttering, "Oh my God, oh my God," over and over. Alex watched as men tumbled over the sides of the boat that had been hit, insects pouring from a flaming nest. Alex ducked as a mortar shell landed close behind them, throwing water into the boat. Small arms fire smacked against the side of the amtrac. Their driver suddenly stood up and screamed, clutched his chest, and tumbled down from his seat, into the clot of men below. Another sailor climbed up and grabbed the wheel. The trac lurched as the treads caught the sandy bottom then lost it. "I'm dropping the ramp!" the new driver cried.

"You drop the ramp, I'll blow your fucking head off," Gunny shouted, pushing his way forward. "It's still too deep. Get the fuck up on the beach!"

"I can't! I can't! They'll hit us sure. They're hitting all the boats!" Gunny cursed. Alex leaned his head against the metal side of the boat. He could feel the pounding of bullets smacking into the other side. He tried not to moan. Up front a man began hollering that he was hit. The noise of shelling and bombing was continual, a ripping shriek-ing thunder that shook the water. Alex heard the rattle of chains as the back ramp slapped down in the water. The treads caught the sandy bottom and lurched forward, knocking the men off-balance.

"Get off, get off," Gunny shouted, turning men around and pushing them toward the back. Alex saw a man step off the ramp and disappear into the water. Gunny was punching and kicking at the herd of men. All of them had the look of wild-eyed animals being forced down the ramp to the slaughterhouse. Alex was breathing so hard he thought he might faint. Sweat stung his eyes. He followed the man ahead, stepped out on the ramp, and jumped. He hit the water heavily and tipped over, pulled down by the weight of his gear. He struggled to get his feet underneath him, touched bottom, and pushed back up. His helmet tilted forward over his eyes. He spluttered above water and turned himself toward the beach. *Get away from the boat, get up on the beach.* Gunny's words clamored for his attention. *Get away from the boat, get some sand underneath you. Don't bunch up.* He splashed forward, holding his rifle across his chest, breathing heavily, trying to keep his helmet back. He sensed men around him, headed in the same direction, but he saw only a small patch of sand, fixed on it, directly in front of him. He sloshed up out of the water and threw himself down. The hum of bullets overhead was louder here. Smoke roiled along the beach. He pressed his face into the sand, trying to catch his breath. Someone kicked him.

"Get up! Get up! Move up! Get off the goddamn beach, get into the trees." He looked up and saw men crawling forward. He squirmed ahead on his belly. The beach around him was strewn with wounded men and various pieces of equipment. Alex understood what Gunny had been going on about—there were weapons scattered everywhere.

He crawled over the lip of a huge shellhole and slid down to the bottom, ending faceup against a pair of boots. He rolled away and sat back against the side, gasping, looking at a man who had had his guts blown out, cut in half by some terrible explosion. The man's face was unmarked, almost serene. He was the first man Alex had seen that day who didn't look terrified. Just dead.

He inched his head out of the shellhole until he could see the line of trees thirty yards in front of him. A mortar slammed into the ground to his left. Alex waited, eyes squeezed shut as sand and dirt showered down. *Over the top, thirty yards to safety, keep your ass down, your asshole puckered, move it, move it, move it . . .*

He crawled out of the hole. Toward the trees. Gunny was up there somewhere. Gunny would save him. A line of mortars marched along the beach toward him, blowing debris into the air. He got up into a crouch and ran for his life.

29

ALEX FOUND GUNNY SITTING WITH COLO-
nel Frazier on the edge of a swamp ten yards beyond the trees that
bordered the beach. Alex stumbled in, crouched over and still running,
suddenly realizing that a zone of relative safety had been reached. He
stopped and slowly straightened, like a man with a bad back, aware
that disaster lurks in even the simplest movements. He was panting,
out of breath from fear more than exertion. He stared uncompre-
hendingly at Gunny and Frazier, as if now that he had found them,
he didn't know what to do with them.

"Jesus Fucking Christ," Alex said, his voice shaking.

Frazier took a cigar from his mouth. "Glad to see you made it,"
he said. "I trust you found the trip exciting?"

Alex slowly unsnapped his helmet and tilted it back. He stared at
his hands. They were trembling. He could think of nothing to say.
"Jesus Fucking Christ," he said again.

Gunny laughed. "Come over here and sit down. You'll be all right.
The first few minutes are the worst. Shit, you didn't even get hit."

Alex walked over to the two men. He was acutely aware that there
was a steady stream of gunfire snapping through the palm trees overhead. But it was high, obviously aimed at men and boats in the water,
and he had already learned if it wasn't aimed at you, ignore it. Leaves
and branches from the palms sprinkled down on them. Frazier and
Gunny went back to a map they were studying. Frazier motioned to
several other soldiers who were standing nearby.

"Here's the problem," Frazier said, as the men gathered around.

He took the cigar out of his mouth and pointed it to an area on their right. "We got a pillbox in there that's pinning down Red Beach. There's a heavy machine gun and an assortment of lighter stuff. Shelling didn't dent it. If we're going to get that company off the beach, we're going to have to take that box out." He held the map up so the others could see. "I sent a scout over and he came back with some good news. The shelling knocked down a big tree that's covered up the firing port on the right side. That's how we were able to get up this far. They've only got access to a field of fire in front of them and to the left. I want a demolition man and a flamethrower, Gunny will take you in." He looked at the circle of men.

"That's me, Colonel, I'm your demo man," a Marine said. He had a huge pack on his back. A white skull and crossbones was painted on the green canvas. No one stood very close to him. Another Marine, tall and husky with two large tanks on his back, raised a hose with a long nozzle on the end. The flamethrower. "Let's go," he said.

Gunny nodded and stood. "You can tag along," he said to Alex, smiling, "but I want you to stay back where you won't get hurt. You can help cover us."

Alex felt sick to his stomach. The last thing in the world he wanted to do was go anywhere. Even with the heavy fire in the trees above, he had begun to feel safe in this little clearing. In a very short time it had begun to feel like home. Everyone was looking at him. He nodded and stood up.

Gunny recruited two more men, formed them up, and moved out.

The route through the swamp was a winding game trail. In low spots, water oozed over their jungle boots. On the map the whole area was marked "Damp Area." "Damp up to your asshole," Gunny pronounced it.

As they approached, the sound of firing grew louder. Measured clusters of heavy machine gun fire were interspersed with the lighter crack of rifles. Gunny stepped off the trail and led them through a knee-deep, leg-sucking bog to a screen of vines that trailed down from several of the tall palms. Gunny crouched down and pulled away the vines.

Thirty feet in front of them, facing to the right, was a cement pillbox. Wet earth had been piled high on top and around the sides. "There's a ventilator on top," Gunny said in a low voice. "I don't think it's big enough to get a grenade through. You're gonna have to put your charge through the front slot," he said to the demolition man. "You know the drill." The man nodded. "You hold off until he blows it," Gunny said to the Marine with the flamethrower. "Then cook 'em. The rest of us will spread out on the right and fire into the gun port to put their heads down. Give us some time to get into position." They all stared at the pillbox for a moment. "All right," Gunny said, dropping the screen of vines. "Let's do it."

Gunny, Alex, and the two riflemen moved off to the right, Gunny leading. They worked their way through the underbrush. Gunny positioned each of them ten yards apart. He pressed Alex down behind a large palm tree. "Shoot if you got the guts, but *keep your ass down. Understand?*" Alex nodded, trying to swallow. Gunny moved a short distance away and crouched down.

Alex was on his knees. Swamp water seeped up his thighs and into his crotch. He watched the pillbox. The rate of fire was steady, unrelenting. Alex thought of the Marines on the beach, a lethal canopy of bullets whirring inches overhead, cutting into the men still splashing ashore.

Gunny began firing. The other riflemen followed. Alex flinched at the sound. Gunny was using a Thompson machine gun, firing in even bursts. Bits of concrete blasted off the pillbox around the firing port. The machine gun inside fell silent. Alex braced his gun against the tree trunk and lined the front sights up with the dark oblong slit. He squeezed the trigger. The gun bucked against his cheek. The smell of gunpowder was sharp. He lowered the gun and peered around the trunk for a better look. In the dark port he could see something moving. The muzzle of the Japanese machine gun flashed and bullets ripped into the jungle around him. The box was like a great armored beast, they hadn't hurt it, just drawn its attention. Chunks of palm tree flew as the tree shuddered under the hammering. Alex tried to make himself invisible, scrunching up into a ball at the base of the tree. Gunny opened up again. *Don't do it, Gunny, you're just letting them know where we are.* His brain supplied the answer Gunny would have doubtless offered.

That's the idea, asshole.

Alex peeked around the base of the tree. Everyone except him was firing at the pillbox. Alex could see the demolition man creeping up the dirt-topped box. Suddenly everyone stopped firing except the Japanese. The demo man trotted forward, leaned down, and jammed a square packet through the hole. He dove to his right, rolling down the embankment. A muffled boom shook the ground. Smoke spurted out the two firing ports and the ventilator on top. Immediately the Marine with the flamethrower was running at the pillbox. He jammed the nozzle into the front port and squeezed the trigger. Flames roared inside. The man held it for five seconds then stopped. The guns had fallen silent. The Marine stood up, still staring at the port. He turned to where they lay in the swamp and raised his hand, waving them in.

On top of the pillbox a camouflaged trapdoor popped open like a jack-in-the-box. A flaming figure rolled out, stood up, and staggered to the front. Alex watched in horror as the black, smoking Japanese lifted a machine gun and squeezed off a burst that cut the Marine down like scythed wheat. Alex heard Gunny shout and saw him run forward, firing from the hip. The burning man spun around once and dropped. Gunny reached the pillbox, leapt to the top, kicked the smoldering man out of the way and poured gunfire down the opened trapdoor. He turned and put another burst into the smoking body.

The two other Marines were at the flamethrower's side before Alex could get to his feet. Gunny dropped a grenade down the trap and slammed the door shut. No one even looked up at the dull thud. Alex slowly walked to the kneeling figures, keeping his rifle pointed at the pillbox. He felt useless and foolish and sickened all at the same time; a pretend soldier, a tin soldier, a little boy in a man's world. The two Marines glanced at him as he came up. "Dead," one of them said. Gunny joined them. "We should have been quicker," he said angrily. "We got no excuse for that one." His face was grim. "You can't never forget how hard it is to kill a Jap. They're like snapping turtles. Catfish. You got to kill 'em two or three times. Fuckers ain't human." They all stood, looking down at the bloody form of the flamethrower. "Get his tanks off him," Gunny said. "Take him back."

FRAZIER SET UP his command post beside the burned-out pillbox. The company that had been pinned down on the beach joined them. Alex took one end of a stretcher and carried the dead Marine flamethrower back to the beach, where the casualties were being laid out for transfer to the ships.

The beach was still under heavy artillery and small arms fire. They were forced to move along in a crouch, trying to keep the stretcher from dragging on the sand. Masses of sweating men worked to unload supplies from the Higgens boats that made it through the Japanese shelling. Since the pillbox had been eliminated, the steady stream of bullets had slowed, though it was still common to see men unexpectedly clutch themselves and fall to the ground, dead or wounded.

Alex squatted in a shell hole after delivering the body. The man who had carried the rear of the stretcher climbed in with him. His face was vaguely familiar to Alex. "Goldberg," the man said, offering a hand and a pack of cigarettes. "Kenny Goldberg." Alex remembered, as he unconsciously accepted a cigarette, that Goldberg had been the man on the LST who had answered Gunny's question on the origins of the .45. Alex lit the cigarette and realized after a few puffs that he had just reentered the ranks of smokers after seven years of cold turkey.

"Where you from?" Goldberg asked.

"New York," Alex said, drawing smoke deep into his lungs.

"Hey, me too. Brooklyn."

"West Village," Alex said. For a moment he thought of New York. Even the New York of this time seemed far away, in more than just geography. His short stint as a dishwasher at Longchamps seemed almost a dream. His life as a teacher, with Molly, was lost in a haze of battle smoke.

"I guess we ought to get back," Goldberg said doubtfully. "Maybe we should eat first?"

"Sure," Alex said.

Goldberg took off his pack and emptied out a pile of cans and cardboard boxes. He took a small knife-type opener, sawed the tops off two cans, and handed one to Alex. It was some sort of meat. Alex scooped it out with his fingers and ate it. He didn't know what it was, but he was hungry. They ate a box of crackers and a piece of cheese apiece. Water from their canteens finished off the meal. Goldberg held a packet of instant coffee in his hand. "What I wouldn't give for a cup of hot Joe," he sighed. He tore open the paper packet and sprinkled a few of the grains on his tongue. He grimaced. He threw the accumulated trash over the lip of the shell hole and leaned back. "You know," he said. "It's goddamn strange that a meal of C-rats and a deep hole can make a man feel pretty good."

"Yeah," Alex said. He understood. *It was weird, but it was true.* The *carrump* of a mortar hitting nearby chased away any feelings of safety. Sand spattered down on them. Alex got up on his knees and peered over the edge.

"What the hell are you anyway?" Goldberg asked. "You a Marine?"

Alex glanced back at him. "I'm an observer. At least that's what I thought I was. Gunny seems to have other ideas."

"Yeah, that's the way Gunny is. He wants everyone to participate. He knows what he's doing, though. Fought in Haiti, China. I'm sticking close to him. He'll get you through."

"Yeah, well, I guess we'd better get back to him, otherwise he'll kick our ass worse than the Japs." They gathered up their gear, said a silent prayer, and climbed out of the hole.

The swamp led to a series of low hills that had been fortified by the Japanese. The Marines were penned up in the swamp by the heavy volume of fire from the hills. Late afternoon found them digging in, looking out on the enemy positions through a screen of palm trees and hanging vines. Alex dug a foxhole with Goldberg. The ground was soft and easy to dig, but as they finished, they watched water begin to seep in at the bottom. "What the hell did we expect?" Goldberg said. "We're digging a hole in a swamp."

"Throw some branches in it," Gunny said as he walked by. "Get your asses in gear, I want you guys wired in by sundown."

The Marines had extended their beachhead perimeter through the swamp. Supplies were now coming in at a reasonable rate. Fresh men were promised but not due until sometime the next day. For a classic amphibious attack against fortified positions, one needed a three-to-one advantage in men and material. No one knew how many Japanese were in the hills, but so far there weren't enough Marines to take them.

An explosion a hundred yards down the line blasted mud and swamp into the air. Machine gun fire erupted in the enemy hills, raking along the Marine line. More explosions announced a mortar attack. Goldberg looked up miserably as a near hit showered him with wet muck. "Get the hell in here!" Alex shouted from the bottom of the foxhole. Goldberg climbed down and huddled against the side. Explosions shook the ground. Pieces of vegetation sprinkled down from the trees. "Oh, sweet mother of God," Goldberg moaned. "Save me save me save me."

"Are we supposed to be shooting back?" Alex asked, not wanting to hear the answer. Without warning he was smashed down by a great weight, knocking the breath out of him. *I'm hit! I'm hit!* his brain screamed.

"Jesus H. Christ," Gunny said, rolling off Alex. "Couldn't you assholes make this hole a decent size? Get your heads up and start shooting. You guys want to live forever?" He peered over the edge and got ready to climb out. He had belts of machine gun ammunition bandoleered over his chest. "Oh yeah, we're expecting a night counterattack, so don't both of you go to sleep at the same time. Keep on your toes. Fire at the muzzle flashes. There's no one friendly in front of us, so you've got a free field of fire. Whatever you do, stay in your hole. Don't stand up, don't get out, don't run. We got barbed wire strung with cans and shrapnel on it. You hear anything clank, shoot the shit out of it. And don't even think about moving back to the beach. This is where we make our stand. Got it?" He didn't wait for an answer. He rolled over the lip of the hole and squirmed off into the dusk.

Goldberg leaned up over the edge and snapped off a few shots. "Nothing out there to shoot at," he said. "They're just softening us up for later." He and Alex sat back and smoked and watched the last of the evening light fade away into darkness. Alex was grateful for the dark, knowing that he couldn't keep the tension and fear off his face forever. He was beginning to understand that it was all right to be afraid. You'd have to be insane to not be afraid, but you weren't supposed to show it. Flashes from incoming mortars lit the scene with brief violent light. Tracers glowing red and green laced from the swamp to the hills and back again. Alex could see Goldberg's sad face in the sickly green light of a Jap flare. They were both soaked to the waist from the water leaching into their hole.

"It can't get any worse than this," Goldberg said. And then it began to rain.

THE RAIN SPARKLED like jewels in the light of the green flares. The Marines huddled in their foxholes, wrapped in ponchos as the rain began to inch up from ankle to calf. "What do you suppose is worse," Goldberg said seriously. "Death by drowning or bullet wound?"

Alex shifted his position, trying to stay up out of the rising water. "This," he said. "This is worse. All of it." They stared out into the dark, trying to see anything in the dancing light of the flares.

"Hey Joe!" an amplified voice shouted. "Hey Joe, you die!" The voice seemed to come in out of the dark from a distance of about ten feet. Alex realized that was impossible. Hoped that was impossible.

"Hey Joe! You die tonight. You bastards die pretty soon."

"Eat shit!" an American shouted.

"Franklin eats shit," the Jap came back.

"Hirohito eats shit!"

"Eleanor eats shit!"

"Tojo eats shit!"

"Babe Ruth eats shit!"

"You guys shut the fuck up!" Gunny hollered. "It's a trick. They're getting a fix on our position by hearing where you are." The night was silent again.

"Malines eat shit!" The guy was farther over on the left. No one responded.

ALEX WAS DOZING when the man in the next foxhole began to scream. Alex woke up with a start, heart pounding. "Oh my God!" the man screamed and then fell silent. "What the fuck's going on?" Alex whispered. "I don't know," Goldberg whispered back.

"They're here!" Gunny shouted, and opened up with his BAR. In the flashes of muzzle light Alex could see shadows flitting around in the darkness. A grenade exploded, flashing quick light, revealing running figures. A flare popped. There were Japs everywhere. Guns began firing. A man reared up in front of their hole and Alex shot him without thinking. The man tumbled down directly in front of them. A screaming man ran at them, rifle held in classic bayonet-drill fashion. Goldberg grunted and grabbed the rifle and pulled the man down, tearing out his K-bar knife and stabbing it into the struggling soldier. Alex tried to watch Goldberg, tried to stay out of range of the kicking dying man and look for other incoming Japs at the same time. Grenades were exploding all around them. The noise was terrifying. Alex squeezed off two shots at a shadow. A grenade rolled down into their pit. "Get out! Get out!" Goldberg shouted. They scrambled up the rain-slick dirt. The grenade blew the contents of the foxhole skyward. Alex lay dazed for a moment, his ears ringing as chunks of dead Jap and tree branches rained down on him.

He got to his knees just as a panting figure loomed up and stabbed down with his bayonet. The man slipped clumsily in the mud, skidded, and went down. Alex jumped on him, trying to get his hands from under the tangle of his poncho. He squirmed on top of the mud-soaked soldier, tearing at the man's face. He got his hands around his throat. The man reared and bucked beneath him. In the pale green flare light Alex could see the man's face, eyes squinting with pain. The man's hands were locked around Alex's wrists. Alex shouted against the night, against the deafening thud and roar of chaos, he shouted and squeezed, his voice lost in the barrage. He bore down, putting his body weight behind his hands. He felt the crackle and snap of the larynx as the man stiffened and trembled and arched under him. He shook the now-limp body and thumped the head in the dirt. He let loose and rolled away, feeling the ground for his rifle, trying to see into the dark. Gunny was still firing the automatic rifle. He could hear the curses and grunts of fighting men around him. Grenade duels splattered mud and shrapnel. Men were howling, wounded men were screaming for corpsmen. The Japanese were jabbering and shouting to each other. An American tank ground out of the swamp and began firing point-blank into the Japanese.

Alex found his rifle and slithered backward into his hole, now made larger by the grenade. He lay for a moment on the edge, frantically searching the dark for targets. The firing and explosions were tapering off. Alex glanced at Goldberg. "You okay?" he whispered. No answer.

In the darkness he reached over and shook Goldberg. He didn't move. Alex's hand found the shaft of a bayonet with rifle still attached. The bayonet was buried to the hilt in Goldberg's chest, pinning him to the back of the foxhole. Alex eased his rifle down and moved to Goldberg's side. He searched for a pulse. No pulse, no breath. He sat back, wiping his hands on his trousers. He picked up his rifle and climbed up the side of the hole. "Gunny," he whispered. "Gunny. Goldberg's dead."

Gunny's voice came out of the night. "Keep it down." His voice was patient but firm. The voice of the instructor. "A lot of guys are dead. You Boots stay in your holes. If you got a Jap near you, use your K-bar on him. Make sure they're all dead. Good and dead. Two or three times dead."

Alex waited and listened. Through the darkness around him came the rustle and chunk of knives working. He pulled out his own knife and reached for the Jap he had strangled.

30

IN TWO WEEKS OF FIGHTING, ALEX HAD earned the look of a veteran. He was dirty, unshaven, and his eyes had the thousand-yard stare that marked a front-line Marine after weeks of combat. He had stuck with Gunny and Gunny had kept him alive and taught him to fight.

He learned to make a cup of coffee in the middle of a battle, starting the fire with Composition C, an explosive, lifting the hot metal cup with his knife. He learned to keep his ass down, and to regulate his automatic fire in short controlled bursts. He learned to remember to pull the bolt back on a Tommy gun and how to change the red-hot barrel of a BAR. He learned to tell incoming fire from outgoing and to recognize different Japanese weapons by their distinctive sounds. He learned *not* to salute an officer at the front because it marked them for snipers. He learned to rip open sulfa packs with his teeth, to battle dress a wound, to quickly choose between a man who would live and a man who would die, and to help the living and comfort the dying. He learned how to sleep through a bombardment, and to come awake at the snapping of a twig. He learned to throw a grenade: pull the pin, you got four seconds to get rid of it. He learned how to kill a Japanese soldier from far away and close up. He learned to call them Japs. He learned to hate them, individually and collectively, and to wish them all dead, man, woman, and child. He learned to almost die, time and time again, and still go back on the line, not knowing why he was doing it, but doing it anyway. He learned all of this and more. When his education was complete, he was no longer the man he had once been, but something else, some other species, more animal than man. And it was a terrible thing to have become, but he was alive. Many men had not learned. Many men were not alive.

In any other circumstances, in any civilized condition, he would have understood that he was ill. In spirit and in body. All of the men had contracted tropical fevers. The constant wetness, the heat of the days, and the damp chill at night had left his clothing rotting off his exhausted body, and sapped what little strength remained after days and nights of no-sleep, no-rest, only constant anxiety punctuated by periods of terror. He had contracted the combat soldier's sickness of soul. He was attacked by the bacteria of killing and guilt and most of all hate, until his moral organs were infected, and he was kept alive only by the fast-fading memory of a better past, and the dim prospect of any future at all. He was afflicted by war, wounded in ways that would never heal, damaged by the constant, brutish bloodshed, the carnage, the loss of pity, the banishment of hope. He might not die of this disease, but he would never again be well. He was changed, altered, for the worse certainly, and there was no better here. There was only this dark shade of life.

HE WAS SITTING in front of the command post smoking a cigarette, wondering if he could trade the Jap flag he'd taken off a body for something decent to eat. A fresh shipment of Doggies, Army men, had arrived that morning, and they hadn't yet learned the value of an orange or an apple.

"Are you the one they call Alex, mate?" a small Aussie dressed in bush clothes asked him. The man was wearing a hat with the brim tied up on one side, khaki shorts, and ragged knee socks.

Alex looked at the man without interest. "That's me," he said. "Who the fuck are you, Crocodile Dundee?"

The man frowned and said, "No. Who's he?"

Alex shook his head. "Nobody. At least not yet. What do you want me for?"

"Well," the man said, brightening, "I think I've got something you've been looking for. I'm the coastwatcher who's been living, if you can call it that, on this bloody island for the last year. We were to meet on the 109, but that ended in a bit of a shambles, wouldn't you say? You were supposed to collect the two Japs I've been keeping for you."

Alex ground the cigarette out and shredded the paper. He studied the Australian. It was as if he'd arrived from another planet, another time, walked in and said, hello, remember me, I'm your past, or your future. G'day, mate, let's have a chat. Alex worked it over in his mind, but it was hard. He'd narrowed his existence down to a set of rules and habits that were designed, first, to keep him alive, and second, to kill Japanese. He didn't have room for loftier ambitions or plans. What he'd been was gone, lost in a two-week past of death. He hadn't the slightest idea if he could get it back, whatever it was he'd been.

He rubbed his leg. He'd been peppered with shrapnel when a grenade had landed a few feet away during a night *Banzai* charge. The mud had absorbed most of the blast, necessitating only a short stay in a medical station, under the forceps of a doctor who plucked the shards of metal from his leg and pronounced him lucky. Lying in the medical tent he'd been reminded of bee stings, a memory of the past that slipped away leaving only the taste of memory, the sting of some time past.

"Well, I'm the runner here," Alex said. "I've got to wait in case they need me." He gestured vaguely to the command post tent behind him. Gunny and Frazier had decided to use him as the company runner, which was supposed to be less dangerous than being a rifleman. As indeed it was, rifleman being the worst job on earth. But it had had its share of dangers. "They may need me," he said again.

Alex could see the concern in the Australian's eyes, and he understood it stemmed from his ragged-ass condition, but he didn't want any sympathy, didn't know what to do with it. It didn't fit into his life. Mostly he wanted the man to go away so he could smoke another cigarette and not think.

"It's over, mate. Your Army just pushed what was left of the Japs onto the beach and finished them off. Actually, most of the Japs finished themselves off. Very obliging. Got to mop up, but that won't be your job. Plenty of Army for that."

Alex lit another cigarette and thought it over. *No more Japs? Couldn't be, there were always more Japs. Always more hills, and caves and holes, homes to Japs, breeding grounds for Japs. Got to dig them out, burn them out, blow them out, seal them up. Nope, this man was crazy.*

Alex felt a hand on his shoulder. Gunny stood beside him. Somehow

Gunny had managed to stay fairly clean and reasonably healthy. Alex didn't know how he did it, some advanced skill that he had yet to learn. "He's right, Alex," Gunny said. "It's over." He looked out at the jungle, in the direction of the beach. They had come from one beach to another, crossed the center of the island, from beginning to end. "It's over. At least for now."

In the last few weeks Alex had learned a strange brand of humor. Men would declare themselves cowards, then charge machine gun nests into certain death. Dying men would joke about their wounds. The squad comedian could draw a laugh in the middle of an artillery barrage. Probably this was just another example of combat humor. An elaborate joke.

"Sure, Gunny," Alex said. "If you say so." He looked up and smiled and tried to believe that it was true.

31

SHOWTIME.

Alex sat in the fourth row of one thousand Marines assembled on a hillside in front of a makeshift stage. A large white placard announced: MOVIE STARS, COMEDIANS, SINGERS, DANCERS AND BEAUTIFUL WOMEN. It was the USO Show Tour, the serviceman's reward for successfully securing one more island on the khaki brick road to the end of the rainbow. The night was agreeably cool, and the men were in good humor, patiently waiting, more than willing to forget the last weeks of killing and dying. For a few hours they would join the world back home, at least as it was represented here, the world of movies and jokes, entertainment and women.

The island had been secured for three days. Every Jap that could be rooted out was dead. The few that had been taken prisoner, usually by accident more than design, had been sent off to be questioned and locked up for the duration.

Those Japanese left alive after the intense shelling and the battles had killed themselves on the beach in a variety of ways: blowing themselves up with hand grenades, shooting themselves, or kneeling on the sandy beach to commit ritual *seppuku*, all of them sure they were then off to join their honored ancestors. They would not surrender. Their code rejected the concept. When they had finished, the beach was littered with bodies and soaked with blood. The incoming tide was tinged pink as the crabs marched in to feed. Marines had stood at the treeline at the edge of the beach and watched the self-slaughter.

And now they were waiting for a show of another sort. They had washed, eaten their first hot meal in weeks, and carefully dressed in their cleanest clothing, as if each of them had a date with one of the USO's Beautiful Girls.

Three men filed onstage: a drummer, a trumpet player, and a guitarist. The three men sat down and began softly tuning the instruments and warming up.

The stage abutted a large khaki-colored canvas tent that was in turn connected to a military truck. As the sun dipped below the horizon, a generator clattered to life and after a minute of steady chugging, large lights flickered on, washing the stage in white light. Some of the men cringed as they waited for Jap artillery to home in on the lights. But the night was quiet, save for the generator. After another minute, the three-man band thumped into a jazzy rendition of "Happy Days Are Here Again," and through the gold curtain at the back of the stage stepped Phil Silvers.

Alex was amazed. Silvers was so young, in his early thirties, and he still had hair. To Alex, Phil Silvers was Sergeant Bilko and bald. Phil, wearing a dark suit and tie and looking as out of place as an Arctic penguin, walked to a microphone at the front of the stage and began to sing. He waved to the audience, who applauded, beckoning them to sing along. As the Marines sang and shouted "Happy Days," Phil danced around the stage in a sort of rhythmic song-and-dance shuffle.

Phil finished the song and held up both hands in a V for Victory while the drums beat out a snappy tattoo and finished up with a cymbal crash. The Marines applauded themselves, Silvers, and the fact that not one Jap plane had dropped a bomb on the gathering.

"Alllll righttttt!!!" Phil shouted. "Okay, Marines, wadda ya wanta see?"

"Girls!"

"Wadda we got for ya?"

"Girls!"

"Wadda ya gonna get!"

"Not what we really want," shouted a lone voice. The Marines laughed and shouted as the band cranked up "Boogie Woogie Bugle Boy," and out trooped a line of women dressed in slit-skirt WAC uniforms. They tramped to the front of the stage and formed a line, marching in place, saluted the Marines, and then began a modified cancan. The men roared approval as long legs were lifted high, exposing abbreviated, khaki-colored boxer shorts. Alex found himself up on his feet right along with everyone else. The line of ten women seemed to be a chorus line of hundreds. Phil Silvers stood to the side, clapping along and grinning. The band was cooking, trumpeter wailing into the upper registers, and Alex felt himself transported, lifted on wings of exhilaration as the men clapped in time to the tune and hollered at the women who were the embodiment of sex, delight, and life, all of which had been long absent, left behind at home, far away.

The band finished the song with a flourish as the girls spun around and hiked skirts to form the words GO MARINES! on their rear ends and then ran offstage to thunderous applause and rebel cheers.

Phil was back centerstage with both hands raised for quiet. The Marines talked excitedly as they sat back down.

"We're gonna . . ." Phil stopped while the PA system whined for a moment. "We're gonna show you a lot *more* of the girls," he said, and winked broadly, "in just a few minutes. But first, did you fellows hear the one about the general and the colonel walking down the street? Every time a private would walk by and salute, the colonel would salute back and mutter, 'The same to you.' After a while, the general's curiosity gets the better of him and he asks why the colonel always says 'The same to you' under his breath. 'I can't help it,' the colonel says. 'I was a private once myself, and believe me, I know what they're thinking.' Phil waited out the wave of laughter.

"But seriously, fellows, before we continue the show, I want to thank each and every one of you from all of us back home for the really marvelous job you boys have been doing out here." The crowd grew quiet. "I know that sometimes it must seem like you've been forgotten by your loved ones, but just let me assure you that there's not one of us back in the States who doesn't think of you guys with terrific respect at least once a day." The drummer began to quietly tap out a military cadence as Phil continued. "You know, back in the States, things have been pretty rough. I know it doesn't compare to what you boys have seen . . ."

"Damn right," a man near Alex muttered. Several other men shushed him.

". . . long lines, hard work, and plenty of heartache worrying about you fellows. There are a lot of moms, a lot of wives, and a lot of sweethearts that read the evening newspaper with their hearts in their mouths, looking for news of loved ones, longing for just a word, and at the same time dreading what they might find." The guitar came in softly, playing the melody to "America the Beautiful."

"We just want you to realize, all of us up here on this little stage and those at home, that we're behind you every inch of the way, that our thoughts and our prayers are never far from our lips, and that we love you, America loves you . . ." Then Phil broke into the song, "Oh beautiful, for spacious skies . . ." as the instruments took up the melody behind him.

The song seemed to swell on the small breeze. The three-man band became an orchestra, and what should have been stupid and manipulative somehow was not. The men got to their feet with a sighing rustle of one thousand uniforms. The music worked to a climax, and as Phil's voice faded away, the trumpeter began the first notes of taps. "This is for all the guys who won't be coming home," Phil said.

A spotlight snapped on from the low hill behind them, lighting up a flagpole to the left of the stage. The American flag began to slowly rise. The trumpeter sounded taps as the Marines stood at attention. There was complete silence as the last notes floated into the night sky. Alex looked up at the broad swath of stars above him and at the snapping flag. He could hear some of the men around him sniffing. Everyone stared at the flag, even after the trumpet had stopped playing. And Alex found that his hard cynical modern heart was unaccountably full of pride and he understood some of the reason those around him had fought. If it were true that there were no atheists in foxholes in this war, then it was equally true that there were damn few cynics. At least when it came to patriotism. These men believed. They believed that their war, though terrible, really *was* just. The entire time he'd been on the island, he'd never heard anyone say that they shouldn't be fighting the Japs. No one wanted to be there, but everyone believed there had to be a fight. All they wanted to do was get it over with, and get back home. And to them the flag was the embodiment of home.

They stood at attention. The light on the flagpole snapped off and the stage lights came up and there centerstage was a man holding a guitar and wearing a cowboy hat. Three women dressed in cowgirl garb stood by his side. They swung into "Deep in the Heart of Texas." From the side of the stage, into his mike, Phil shouted, "Cowboy Steve and his three Golden West Girls!" and the men applauded and hollered and sat back down on the sandy ground as they sang along.

The show went on for another hour and a half. Cowboy Steve was back with the girls, followed by the team of McHugh and Jenkins, introduced by Phil as "The Daffiness Twins . . . Their act is strictly not from hunger!" They swapped jokes and executed a goofy song-and-dance routine. These variety acts were interspersed with dancing from the ten-girl chorus line, whose each appearance was met with thunderous applause, more for the skimpy costumes than their dancing ability.

The last of the dancers disappeared through the curtain. Phil moved the microphone back into centerstage. "Yeah," he said, "things are pretty tough at home. Did you know it's damn near impossible to get a room in a hotel?" There were mock groans of sympathy from the Marines. He held up a hand. "I know, it doesn't sound like anything to you, but it can be a real pain in the keister. A Marine on leave goes into a hotel and asks for a room. The clerk says they're full up, but since he's a Marine he'll let him have a cot in the ballroom of the hotel. 'There's a lady in there, in the opposite corner,' the clerk says, 'but if you don't make any noise she'll never know you're there.' 'Fine,' says the Marine, and into the ballroom he goes. Five minutes later he comes running out to the clerk. "Say,' he hollers, 'that woman in there is dead!' '*I* know it,' says the clerk, 'but how did *you* find out?' More laughter and groans from the Marines. Someone in the crowd shouted, "A real Marine wouldn't give a shit that the broad was dead!" which brought more laughter. Phil held up both hands until the crowd had quieted. Then he said simply, "Gentlemen. Betty Grable."

The stage lights went dark and a spotlight cast a sharp round circle on the empty stage. The curtain opened briefly and a pale blond woman dressed in a white evening gown entered the pool of light. She seemed to glow, white and clean, beautiful, the bright light sparkling from her sequined dress. She smiled and began to sing, "My Dreams Are Getting Better All the Time," and the men were quiet, listening to the words of the song and watching the beautiful woman. She followed with "I'll Get By," a song she introduced, in a slightly husky voice, as being a hit by her man, Harry James. Each song was met with applause, but no yells. She sang several more, ended with "Sentimental Journey," and walked offstage to a standing ovation that went on until she came back on and did "I've Heard That Song Before," "Pistol Packin' Momma, and "Boogie Woogie Bugle Boy," which brought out Phil Silvers and the rest of the cast to dance around the stage as everyone sang and the Marines roared.

When the lights went out and the stage was empty, the men looked around as if confused, suddenly back on the island, alone, left behind, as the real world disappeared back into its magic trunk. They stood for a few moments in the dark, looking at the empty stage, and then filed back to the rows of pup tents and empty blankets and the long night, listening to the rush of the surf, remembering the songs and the Beautiful Girls.

THE FLASHLIGHT glared into his eyes. For a moment he dreamed he was onstage. "Hey," a man's voice said. "You Balfour?"

Alex sat up, shading his eyes. "Yeah, who wants to know."

The man grunted. "About time. Jesus Christ, you're the fifth guy I've waked up. The other four almost killed me. On your feet, you're wanted."

Alex crawled out of his tent and stood up. The sky was still bright with stars. "What time is it?" His watch had succumbed weeks ago.

"Midnight. Why the hell can't you guys put your tents out in some kind of order?"

Alex could see the man's MP armband. "Who wants me?" he asked again.

"You'll find out." The MP looked him up and down. "Though for the life of me I can't see why."

Alex followed the silhouette of the MP as they made their way through the tangle of tents scattered on the sand. Sounds of snoring rose from the small one-man canvas tents. Legs, most still wearing boots, projected out the ends. Small fires silhouetted late-night coffee drinkers who had lost the knack of sleeping. Alex had seen men who could sleep in the middle of combat and then stay awake for days after the danger had passed.

The amphitheater that had held the Marines for the earlier show was empty. Alex thought he saw the shadowy forms of guards along the top of the natural bowl-shaped formation. A series of large tents stood alongside the big Army truck that had been connected to the stage. Alex was led to a tent pitched to one side of the others. "Good luck, buddy," the MP said, and stood back as Alex pushed back the flap and entered.

The tent was tall enough to stand up in. A small kerosene lantern cast a feeble yellow light onto the canvas walls. Betty Grable sat at a low table with a folding mirror propped up in front of her. She was wearing a white terrycloth robe. She still had on her makeup. "Sit down, soldier," she said, nodding to the cot, the only other piece of furniture that was visible.

Alex sank down on the cot, stunned. The two of them sat looking at each other for a few minutes. "Usually," she said, "the guys that get invited to this tent look like they've died and gone to heaven." She had a lopsided smile on her face. "You, on the other hand, are a frowner. What's the problem? Rather be back there on your own?"

Alex shook his head, feeling stupid. Normally he wasn't easily starstruck, but he'd been away from home for a long time. Now he didn't even know what to do with his hands. He crossed his arms over his chest. "No, this is fine. I'm just surprised. Anyone would be."

She gave him a nice smile. "It never ceases to surprise me either. The reaction I get from you guys. Anyway, this is a business call. We can socialize later. The Boss wants to know what you have to report. You can either tell me, or you can write it up, and I'll take it back."

"The Boss," Alex said, to take up time. *Who the hell is she talking about? Has she got the wrong Balfour?* He hoped not. Now that he was here, he wanted to stay. To bask in the glow of a fresh, clean, attractive woman whose face and figure were so familiar. *Welcome to the late show.*

"I'm not sure who you mean."

"The Boss. Franklin. The Prez. You don't have to play dumb with me, I'm in on the ground floor. Like I said, you can tell me what you want to tell him. If it's something you don't want me to hear, write it down, I won't peek, cross my heart and hope to die. I'm the message girl, you can trust me, honest." She crossed her legs.

Alex tried to concentrate. Roosevelt. The Oval Office. The President, smiling at him, saying, "I've got a rather remarkable string of free-lance people working for me. They'll keep us in touch." *Remarkable. Yes, I should say so.*

"I don't have anything to report. Sorry," he said. "I've been too busy trying to stay alive." He hadn't thought about what he was supposed to be doing for weeks. And lately, after he wasn't so worried about dying, it seemed like he was already a little dead. Nothing was worth trying to plan. He remembered the Australian and his two prisoners. Alex had sent him back to the hills to wait. *To wait for what?* To wait until the whole thing just went away? Now she was frowning at him.

"Look," she said, "no one doesn't have a message. He's the Boss. He wants something from you. I can't go back and tell him you're not interested enough to respond."

Alex tried to engage his mental gears. He pulled out his Luckies, offered her one, took one himself, and lit both of them with his khaki Zippo. He blew smoke out his nose and tried to put it together.

The last he remembered was Max telling him that they hadn't really been sent out to do what they had been told they were being sent out to do. Confusing enough. Besides, he, Max, and Einstein had their own agenda, trying to avert the atomic bomb. Then it turned out that there were a couple of Japs who had been captured or defected or something and he was supposed to collect them. All of it was tied up with the A-bomb, and the possibility that the Japs were building a bomb as well. He had never really considered that proposition seriously. But by now he should have talked to the Japs, and had something to report. Only he hadn't, and he didn't. The only thing he'd done with Japs was to kill them.

"Tell them I'm working on it," he said.

She raised her eyebrows. "You're working on it? That's it? You're a pretty cool customer. I don't think I'd have the nerve to tell that to the President."

"I guess you're going to have to, if you're going to tell him anything at all."

"Can I tell him that there's more coming, that you'll send more later?"

"Sure," Alex said. "I don't want to put you in a tough spot."

She shrugged and stubbed out her cigarette. "I guess it's your problem, not mine. I've got to say, this is the easiest one I've ever been sent out on. I don't even have to take notes."

He wondered if he was supposed to leave now.

"You want a drink?" she asked, answering his unvoiced question. "Now that we got the business part out of the way." He nodded. She reached under the table and brought up a bottle of Scotch and handed it to him. "No glasses," she said. "We'll just have to make do."

He unscrewed the bottle top and drank. The liquor hit his throat like a blast from a flamethrower. His eyes watered as he lowered the bottle.

"Hits you hard when you haven't had any in a while," she said, taking the bottle and tipping it up. Her eyes didn't water. "You want to spend the night? What's left of it."

That hit him as hard as the whiskey. He tried to put together a moral position, but it was too difficult under the circumstances. He tried to remember what he was, and where he was, and what he was supposed to be doing, but all that was a fog. The past. His future. She leaned over and blew out the small lantern. In the sudden dark her voice was as smooth as warm silk. "Cat got your tongue?"

He swallowed. He still didn't know what to say. His eyes grew used to the darkness and he could make out her white robe, her blond hair. She stood up and walked the few steps to the front of the tent and threw back the flap. The moon was up. A silvery patch of moonlight spilled into the tent. He could see quite clearly. She went back to the chair, sat down, and shrugged the robe back down to her waist. Her breasts were large and round. Her nipples hardened into small upright buttons. He could see that she was smiling. "I can't stand to sleep alone, Alex. I'm a sleepwalker. You wouldn't want me wandering around out there all by myself, would you? Could be dangerous. I'd like you to stay."

He tried to conjure up an image of Molly to give him strength, knew that's what he should be doing. All he could see were Betty Grable's breasts.

She stood up.

"Tell you what, let's give you a good look. All the guys ask me to do this." She walked to the tentflap into the moonlight. She dropped her robe to the floor and turned away from him. She peeked back over her shoulder, hand on her hip, smiling, eyebrows raised. It was the great Betty Grable pinup. Every Marine and GI in the Pacific had seen it a thousand times. Many of them carried it in their wallets. They'd even found Japs with the picture. Grable in her backless white bathing suit, high-heeled, white-satin, baby doll pumps, thin gold ankle chain, a gift from George Raft, smiling coyly back over her shoulder. And here it was, only this time it was real, and she was naked. Alex wondered how the average GI would handle this situation. He felt his breath quicken. *Probably just about like I am.*

"I'll tell you a secret," she said, turning around to face him. She smiled at the expression on his face. She put her hands on her hips and stood with her legs slightly parted. "That picture almost never got shot. I don't want to put you off or nothin' but it's an interesting story. Kinda shows what show business is really all about. I showed up at the photo studio, got into my suit, and my period started. I put on a Kotex, but it showed under that tight bathing suit. I went in and told the photographer, Frank Powolney, and he said not to worry, he'd just shoot me from the back. And he did. That was three years ago. The rest is history." She moved closer to him. Her voice was not so smooth now. "Pretty funny, huh?"

He couldn't take his eyes off her. She spread her legs farther apart. She leaned against him. Her breasts were soft against his cheek, against his mouth. "I know what you guys like," she whispered. Her voice caught as he took her nipple into his mouth. "I've got more tricks than a Chinese whore," she whispered, rubbing her body against him. "I can make you forget."

She could, and she did.

32

HE LEFT HER IN THE HOUR BEFORE DAWN
and walked back to his own small tent through the jumble of sleeping
soldiers. He felt the dawn breeze against his skin. His body seemed
newly awakened from a long, debilitating, soul-draining coma.

He had once read an account of patients who suffered from sleeping
sickness, *encephalitis lethargica*, men and women frozen for decades
into living statues—standing, sitting, lying, mute and immobile, for
years at a time. These patients had been suddenly awakened with the
application of a new medicine, L-dopa, and it seemed the disease fell
from them as if it had never existed, as if the intervening years had
never been. Some of the patients began speaking in the middle of the
sentences left off years before. Some walked away, midstride in steps
begun long ago in the past. Alex felt a touch of that release, that
freedom. He stood in the dark and lifted his hands toward the strip
of rose light beginning to dawn on the horizon and stretched, feeling
the pull and give of muscle and bone. He touched his face and smelled
the fragrance of her, and knew that she had returned him to the living.
He looked at the small tents scattered around him, scuffed and worn
boots projecting from the open ends, and hoped that these men who
had fought to the point of death would receive some balm, some magic
that would release them as he had been released.

He slept for an hour, and woke to the full morning sun. He lay in
his tent, thinking of the night before. He searched around for some
remorse, and found very little. Mostly it made him miss Molly. But
she was so far away. And there was no place for her here. He sighed

and kicked off his blanket. He made a quick inventory of all his major physical and mental systems and found, in general, he felt pretty damn good. He climbed out of the tent and stood up. He looked into the bright blue sky and knew that it was time to pick up his life, rejoin the stream of history, continue on, to wherever he was being sent, for whatever ends. He was alive. It was enough.

ALEX ASKED GUNNY where the coastwatcher might be found. Gunny rustled up one of the Fuzzy Wuzzies, the island natives, who promised to track down the Australian and bring him in.

"Gonna ship our asses out of here in a day or two," Gunny said. They were sitting on a downed palm tree near the Operations Tent, which had grown into the Operations Building, courtesy of a detachment of Seabees who were digging, grading, and shaping the island into a functioning link in the Pacific campaign. "Captain says you ain't goin' along."

Alex took a drag off his Lucky. "You know, Gunny, I can't say that I'm going to miss it."

The sergeant spit on the ground near his own boot. "And I can't say as I blame you. Fighting these fucking monkeys is getting to me, too. I think the plan is to send us back to Australia before they make us hit the beach again. Lot of women in Australia. Supposed to relax us, or something. Okay with me." He paused for a moment. "What the hell are you anyway, Balfour? I never have figured it out."

Damn good question. I am not what I was, and I will never be the same. "I'm not exactly sure myself. Couldn't say even if I knew."

"Gimme a Lucky," Gunny said, holding out his hand. Alex fished a bent cigarette out of the crumpled, red-and-white pack and handed it over.

"Know why they changed the color?" Gunny asked.

"Color of what?" Alex said. He'd been thinking about just who or what he was supposed to be, not paying attention to Gunny.

"The color of the Luckies pack, asshole. Don't ya remember? It used to be green and white. Green ink's got metal in it. We need that metal to kill Japs with. So they changed it to red. Jesus, if you don't want to talk, I'll just shut up."

Gunny lit his cigarette and took a few puffs, staring up at the tangle of wrecked palm trees that stretched along the beach. The whole area had been bombed and shelled and burned until there was not a standing piece of live vegetation in sight. A bulldozer worked nearby, pushing trees out of the way, making room for the road-making machines that would be following along soon after. "I'll tell you something," Gunny went on, staring straight ahead. "You're pretty much a Marine now. There's a world of shit you ain't got the slightest fucking idea about, but somewhere up on the line you learned how to fight. You did okay. Once you figured out which was your ass and which was your weapon."

Alex flushed, feeling a balloon of pride swell inside him. Back in his own time he might be horrified by what he had done, but he was not back in his own time. He hadn't the luxury of perspective, the safety of distance. There was a moment, he supposed, when he could have refused to participate, stood up and said no. But he couldn't remember when that might have been. He'd stepped onto this road too far back, had traveled it far too long to do anything but keep on marching, moving ahead, following the path. The Roman emperors, returning victorious to receptions of great triumph, had with them in their chariots men whose sole job was to whisper into their ears as they rode through the cheering crowds, "You are only a man. You are only a man." Yes, well, he was only too aware that he was only a man. But the praise touched him in surprising ways, and he was grateful for it.

"Thanks, Gunny." Alex knew that if he said one more word Gunny would probably punch him in the nose out of sheer embarrassment. Praise and gratitude, either giving or receiving, came hard to the sergeant.

Gunny spit again, ground the cigarette out against his boot, and ripped the butt into tiny pieces. He stood up. "Yeah, well, maybe I'll see you around. Here comes your Aussie, and he's got a couple of Japs with him. Get me out of here before I strangle them." Gunny smiled to show that he was joking. Perhaps it was a smile. Perhaps it was a joke.

"Take care of yourself," Alex said, standing. Gunny waved a hand. "Yeah, shit," he said, walking away.

■ ■ ■

THE JAPS were manacled at wrist and ankle. The Aussie pushed them into a sitting position some yards away and walked up to Alex. The two men shook hands.

"I need to apologize for the way I acted the last time we met," Alex said. He remembered all too well the mind-deadening result of weeks of combat, and his curt dismissal of the Australian. The other man waved a hand.

"No matter. I understood perfectly. You Yanks had a job to do. Work like that takes something out of you. Needs a few days to get it back. Quite all right."

Alex nodded. The Australian's name was Billy Gillam, and he'd been holding on to the Japs for weeks now, patiently waiting for someone to take them off his hands. Alex motioned to the Japs. "Looks like you've got those boys under control. Did they give you any trouble?"

"On the contrary, they've been quite docile. At least the one on the left, Tomishiro, the one with the glasses, has been. The other one, Mashita, is a different story, I'm afraid. Doesn't actually do anything that I can put my finger on, but he definitely bears watching."

Alex sat down on the log and Gillam followed. They watched the Japs for a few minutes. The prisoners' hands were fastened behind their backs. "Wash Tubbs and Captain Easy," Gillam said.

"What's that?" Alex asked, wondering if he'd heard the man correctly.

"Wash Tubbs and Captain Easy," Gillam said. "That's what one of your chaps named them. After two of your more famous cartoon characters. Showed me one of those color comic strip books. Wash Tubbs is the short, foolish-looking one, Captain Easy is the tough one. I must say, the resemblance is quite accurate. The names have stuck. Those two are now Tubbs and Easy as far as our lot are concerned."

"Don't they mind being named after a couple of comic book characters?" Alex asked. Gillam laughed. "Can't say as I've inquired, actually. Wouldn't matter much if they did, would it?" Alex studied the two Japanese. One was indeed short and pudgy, with large round wire-rim glasses that kept slipping down his nose. The other man was lean, hard-looking. Hair cropped short, muscular torso. Neither of them was wearing a shirt. Their ragged pants were torn off just below the knee. They were barefoot and their clothes were filthy.

"Why don't you just give me the whole story," Alex said. "Start at the beginning. That way I'll know what questions to ask."

Gillam pulled a small bag of tobacco and a pack of rolling papers out of his pocket. He deftly rolled a cigarette with one hand and lit up, regarding the two prisoners through a puff of bluish smoke. "Right. Theirs is an odd story, one that I can't say I believe in all respects. Of course I'm not privy to the level of information that you blokes seem to be working on, that might make a bit of difference, might not, I couldn't say. But to me, something smells a bit rotten about their little fairy tale.

"Anyway, I'll let you chaps decide that. I'd been on New Georgia for a year or so when the Japs took over. I'm an engineer by trade, worked on one of the big rubber plantations. I should have gotten out, gone home, I suppose, but there was nothing back there for me, really. I'm single, parents deceased, not much in the way of family. So I decided to stick it and see if I couldn't be useful. Spent my time on a few of these islands, watching what comes down the Slot and reporting in, helping with any downed aviators, sailors off ships. Seen a fair share of action. So when my boys told me that there was a raft with two men floating in on the east side of the island, I went up straight away. I've got good boys, the lot of them are as brave and loyal as any soldier in the King's army. So I went and, sure enough, there were these Japs coming in with the tide. We paddled out and took them in tow, and we've had them ever since."

Gillam stretched out his legs in front of him. The expanse of leg between his bush shorts and his socks was tanned and muscular. The man looked to Alex to be in his early thirties and in extremely good condition. His canvas boots, in contrast, were worn at the heel and split at the seams. "We could issue you a new pair of those if you want," Alex offered.

"I'd be obliged," Gillam said. "Bloody weather rots them out in no time." He sighed.

"So we round up the Nips and take them back to camp. Figured we'd see if they had any information they'd part with. Lost cause, usually. But we were pretty far up in the hills and the main concentration of Japs was several miles north of our camp. I wasn't much worried about being seen, or heard. Seemed worth the effort. The two of them came right along, no trouble at all. When we got to camp, we fed them and let them sleep. Next day they began to talk. Actually, only one of them talks, the one with the glasses. Tubbs. And wait till you hear this lad. Speaks the mother tongue like a gentleman. Educated at Cambridge, don't you know. And bloody well sounds it, the monkey's a regular toff. Gives you the willies, listening to it coming out of that fat yellow face. The other one speaks no English at all, or at least they say he doesn't. Sometimes the blighter has a way of looking at you, though, makes your skin crawl. Like he understands, even if he doesn't know the words. So I wouldn't say anything you don't want known in front of him. Just to be on the safe side.

"When young Tubbs found I was an engineer, he really opened up. He says they're part of a survey team sent out from Japan to look for various metals crucial to their war effort. Tubbs is a physicist and the other one, Captain Easy, is a metals man. Both of them know their subject as far as I can tell. Supposedly they were in the Philippines where they had finished up their work and were being taken off by a submarine. The submarine ran afoul of a roving PBY and after a quick argy-bargy our lot sent the sub to the bottom. Some of the crew escaped, these two in their own life raft. They became separated from the others in a storm, and drifted down here after a week or so at sea. They had some rations and some water. They weren't in terribly bad shape when we got them. Didn't look to me to have been in a raft for a week, but who can tell with a Jap? Tough little effers, the old wear and tear doesn't show much on them."

"How come he told you all of this?" Alex asked.

"Well, naturally, the same question occurred to me. Tubbs claims he doesn't go along with the military men who are ruling Japan at the moment. Says he's for peace with the West. He's not Army, says he was a university professor. Captain Easy *is* Army, but supposedly he doesn't go along with the established power structure either. I suspect his motives are somewhat different than Tubb's, but they're not very forthcoming on that score. It's the talk of experimental weapons that, shall we say, triggered all of this. Normally we might have just shot them to save everyone the bother, but one hears rumors and talk, so I decided it might be best to have them looked over by someone in the know."

Alex studied the two manacled men. Tubbs was pushing up his glasses with his shoulder. The one called Easy was staring at the short length of chain that bound his ankles together. Tubbs was sweating, eyes skipping anxiously from sight to sight, looking for any hint of approaching danger. Captain Easy was just that: easy. With himself, with his surroundings. He seemed drawn inward, resting lightly on another plane where there were no manacles, no enemies. Some sort of Zen meditation technique, Alex decided, probably part of his *Bushido* training. Tubbs would break, had already broken, but Easy was another matter. The Captain would bear watching. Men like him who follow the code are dangerous, forever and always.

"All right," Alex said, standing. "I'll take them off your hands. You did right to keep them alive." He felt for the holstered .45 at his side, made sure the strap was firmly snapped over the butt. Gillam stood up and nodded.

"I'm glad to be rid of them. My orders are to move along up the chain. Bougainville is next. The boys and I are off to a new home. Perhaps we'll meet again." He held out a hand and Alex took it.

"Perhaps. These things have a way of coming around, don't they? Would you like to say good-bye to your two friends?"

Gillam shook his head. "They're no friends of mine. Nor yours." He turned to Alex. His face was serious. "Watch them. I've got a bad feeling about them. Captain Easy is a right bastard, I'm sure of that. Eyes in the back of the head and all that. Yes?"

Alex nodded. The Australian turned and walked off, toward the line of fallen trees and piled vegetation. He waved at a bulldozer operator and disappeared behind a mound of smashed Japanese block-house. *Your boots*, Alex thought. *I forgot to get you some new boots.* Too late. Alex turned around. Standing directly behind him was the one called Captain Easy. Tubbs was still sitting on the ground where he'd been left. Easy stood silently, staring at him, still chained but completely relaxed. The man had moved as silently as a cat.

I could be dead. He could have killed me. Somehow. Chains or no chains.

THE SEABEES built him a cage. Alex set up his tent on the beach just at the tree line, away from the main concentration of soldiers. Gunny and the Marines had shipped out. The Army had moved in, taking over the organization and operation of the island. Awareness of Alex's status had been passed along to the new commander in some way that Alex was not privy to, but he found that he had only to ask, and if the request was not immoderate, he usually got what he wanted.

A young soldier was detailed to guard Alex's small camp and the two prisoners.

The first thing Alex did was to separate the prisoners. A wire wall ran down the center of the cage, dividing it into two sections. He had the Japanese manacled hands-in-front, and the leg chains removed entirely. The cage was made of heavy-gauge wire that extended several feet down into the sand to prevent digging under. There was a wooden roof for shade. The prisoners were fed twice a day, and let out twice a day to relieve themselves and wash in the nearby ocean. Blankets were placed on low wooden platforms for sleeping.

Alex decided that his job was to interrogate the prisoners, or rather simply talk to them to learn what he could. If he was part of Roosevelt's information apparatus, then he would extract information and send it along when the opportunity presented itself. He hadn't any idea how long his present task would take, but he was in no hurry. The idea of going into battle again was virtually unthinkable. No sane man put himself into that situation voluntarily. The miracle of this war was that men actually did what they were ordered to do, climbed into the boats, stormed the beaches, fought their way through deadly Japanese defenses simply because they thought that it was what they were supposed to do, and that it needed to be done. Alex knew there were a myriad of complicated reasons why the men did what was expected, he had learned them all in his training to be a historian. But he had never understood the simplest reason. They did it because it was expected of them.

He supposed that he could hurry up the questioning process if he were to use more extreme methods, but he was incapable of them. Besides, Tubbs was quite willing to talk, and with Easy it wouldn't have worked.

They fell into a routine that passed the days in orderly fashion. A curious Swiss Family Robinson sort of mentality settled over them, with Alex as the father, leader, and organizer. His young soldier guard, Billy Tanner, a blond-haired baby-faced eighteen-year-old from North Dakota, was a kind of surrogate son, and the two prisoners were visiting relatives that bore watching lest they make off with the silverware. Or worse. It was a testimony to something in the human spirit that Alex soon forgot to hate the two Japanese. He would always be wary around the silent Captain Easy, but Tubbs was so unthreatening and anxious and incapable of inflicting harm it was difficult to remember that he was the enemy. That he professed to be a friend made it more difficult still.

In the morning Billy would build a fire and start water for coffee. His job as guard quickly evolved into guard cum general handyman and helper, as it became apparent that the Japanese had nowhere to hide even if they could escape from their stout wire cage. Alex would roll out of his tent when he smelled the coffee, and cook breakfast for all of them. The Japanese were fed in their cages, after which Billy cleaned the dishes while Alex took the prisoners down to the ocean to bathe. Alex would then gather his writing materials and sit on a wooden chair built by Billy out of an ammo box and question Tubbs about Japan's weapons research.

Tubbs was always willing to discuss whatever topics Alex suggested. His knowledge of the wide scope of Japanese research showed that he had had access to a variety of materials. Those areas that Alex supposed would be top secret to the Japanese were shown by Tubbs to be as shot full of security holes as the American's own atomic bomb project.

"We know of your efforts," Tubbs said, leaning forward toward the wire fence that separated him and Alex. As Billy Gillam said, Tubbs spoke almost perfect English.

"We have spies, in particular a Spaniard, who has given us quite a bit of information. We know that your research is situated in your southwest, not far from the Mexican border."

"But how do *you* know this? How is it that you are privy to all this information?" Alex's chief concern was that Tubbs was a Trojan Horse, set among them for disinformation purposes.

"We who are working on the atom project are aware of these things. We are a family in many respects. We have all the scientific journals from before the war, and the Germans have kept us supplied with those published since. It was not difficult to notice your studied silence on matters atomic. Our organization is housed in a scientific complex, the Nichi, with other scientific teams. The men talk, like members of any family." Alex was struck by the similarity of this description to Einstein's depiction of the world's scientific community as a family.

"Where is this Nichi? And what other scientific areas are being studied there?"

"It is in Hiroshima. There are many teams. We study jet airplanes, suicide squadrons, lethal gases, there is the death ray, germ weapons, explosives testing, biological testing, and probably others that I am not aware of."

Alex contemplated Tubbs. The Japanese had lost his original, faintly comical appearance of anxiety and ineptitude. Alex wasn't sure if this was because he had simply grown accustomed to the man, or that it was something that Tubbs put on and off when he felt the need for some protective coloring. Tubbs was extremely intelligent and obviously no fool. He could slip into such topics as death rays as casually as another man might discuss foreign affairs or football teams. "Tell me about some of these areas," Alex said, writing in his notebook.

Tubbs shrugged. "I know little of the technical details, Alex-san. The suicide squadrons are being planned because we have not much left in the way of airplanes. Jet aircraft, rocket planes, we have acquired from the Germans. They attempted to send us a prototype on a cargo submarine, but it was sunk. We have the plans, though, and have built several test craft. Gasses, germ testing, that work is obvious. It is simply a matter of finding an effective delivery system."

"I thought that work was being done in Manchuria," Alex said. He thought of Molly.

Tubbs eyed him with interest. "You know of our work in Manchuria? And elsewhere?"

"Maybe," Alex said. "Go on about the laboratory work." He checked his notes. "At the Nichi."

"The death ray is quite interesting. The purpose is to debilitate your aircraft, to stop the engines in midair. We are using microwaves. You understand the term?" Alex nodded. "The system itself works, but we are unable to boost the power to effective levels. We can disable an engine, but only when it is unshielded and at close range."

Alex was tempted to explore this area further, the image of Japanese microwave beam shooters aimed at high-flying B-29s was compelling, but as far as he had ever heard, never came to fruition. But then he had never heard of any atomic bomb effort by the Japanese either.

"Tell me more about the atom research. What are your areas of responsibility? How far along is the general effort? What do you know about any American research? Details, Tubbs, details."

The Japanese took off his glasses and polished them on his shirt. Alex had procured American uniforms for both of the prisoners. "The

Australian," Tubbs said, "he was an engineer. He understood a little of these matters. You are not a technician, are you?"

Alex shook his head. "Don't worry about that, just answer the questions."

"I meant no disrespect," the Japanese said, closing his eyes in a way that was almost an apologetic bow. "I am the pupil of a scientist, Bunsaku Arakatsu, who was, in turn, a colleague of some of your greatest scientists. He is a personal friend of Professor Einstein and has studied with Neils Bohr. He has worked in Cambridge and at the Cavendish with Rutherford. It is through his personal intercession that I, too, was fortunate enough to work in England at the Cavendish. That, in brief, is my history. Perhaps you might tell me something of yourself. For example, how extensive is your knowledge of nuclear fission? It would be helpful to know on what level we are conversing."

"Jesus. You just talk, let me worry about what I can understand."

"No offense intended, old boy. Our project is under the Navy department. It is code-named F-go. We have been working on it for several years. One of our first concerns was the accumulation of uranium reserves. We have procured a stock from the Germans, confiscated from the laboratories of the Curies, as well as pitchblend from Czechoslovakia. We also have supplies arriving from Korea. That was my original area of responsibility, to ascertain where we might prospect for the raw materials. Which is why I was in the Philippines, looking into a report from one of our scouts of a promising mine. Lately, though, I've been working on a separation process. Something that, no doubt, you in your country have been laboring over. We have been successful, but it is an exceedingly tedious process." Tubbs pushed his glasses up and paused expectantly. Alex waited patiently. He wasn't sure he knew enough about atom bomb research to actually give away any useful secrets, but Tubb's continual, openly obvious attempts to get him to do so were beginning to annoy him. He did know that the separation process the Japanese was referring to was extremely difficult. The U-235 isotope, which is needed for the fission reaction necessary to atomic reactors and bombs, must be refined from naturally occurring uranium utilizing extremely delicate and expensive procedures.

"And what methods are you employing for the separation," Alex asked.

"Thermal. I say, do you suppose we might dispense with the wrist chains?"

"No. Why are you telling me all of this?"

Tubb's usually unperturbed face showed mild surprise at Alex's gearshifting. "I thought I had explained that. The militarists have taken over my country and they are determined to continue this war even though it is clear that we cannot win. It is quite possible that we will construct a bomb in time for use when you invade our homeland. This does not mean we will win the war, even if we have these bombs. It is too late to think of winning. But consider what will happen. We will use our bombs against your invading craft, your airplanes, your landing troops. You will then use your bombs on our people. The destruction will be far beyond anything the world has ever experienced. We cannot allow this to happen."

Alex agreed with him on that. The destruction would be, indeed, horrendous. The fanatic Japanese military armed with A-bombs could very well mean the end of the world.

"All right, Tubbs. What's the answer? What is it you want? How do you propose to stop this from happening?"

"You, Alex-san, must inform your leaders, Franklin Delano Roosevelt and his war ministers, that we are aware that you are working on a bomb, and that we are as well. Surely they will see that there is a great danger. I do not expect them to quit the fight, but to allow us to negotiate a peace when the end is near. We will eventually lose this war, but we are still strong. It will take you years to defeat us. The end may be inevitable, but it is not immutable. We can avert this atomic slaughter on the beaches through diplomatic means. You must allow our people this chance to save our civilians."

"They'll never believe me back in Washington. They think you don't have a prayer of building a bomb. Why should they allow you to negotiate from strength when as far as they are concerned you must be totally defeated? The terms are unconditional surrender. Nothing less."

"I would not expect them to believe you simply on my word. We will give them more proof. An eyewitness account from one they trust. A top-drawer, unimpeachable source."

Alex tried to imagine *any* Japanese that would be considered trustworthy by the administration. "And who might that be?" he asked.

"Why, you, my dear Alex-san. *You* will be the messenger. You will be the bringer of truth. You will stop the massacre. You will come with me to Japan."

In the corner of the wire cage, beyond the center skein of wire, the Japanese called Captain Easy sat on his wooden sleeping platform with his legs folded into the traditional lotus posture. He was looking at Alex. He was smiling.

"You're crazy," Alex said. "You're out of your fucking mind."

33

ALEX COULDN'T HELP IT. HE WAS PRAYING
for Betty Grable, but what he got was something else entirely. In the
end, it was Orson Welles and his Mercury Wonder Show, Direct from
Hollywood in a Surprise Super-Secret (Don't Let the Japs Know!)
Performance. Joseph Cotten was Jo-Jo the Clown, and Rita Hayworth
was the Beautiful Assistant in the skimpy outfit. But in this show and
in real life, she was Orson Welles's new wife and what he did with
her was to put her in a box and saw her in half in front of several
thousand cheering GIs. Princess Nephrotite Cut to Ribbons yet She
Lives! Joseph the Great Escapes Alive! Doctor Welles, All Nature
Freezes at His Glance!

The troops loved it.

After the show, Alex went back to his camp and built a fire. He
told Billy, the young guard, to turn in; he'd watch the Japs. He sat
on a log drinking coffee. When Orson Welles walked out of the night
into the circle of warm firelight, Alex wasn't really surprised. He'd
come to expect celebrity messengers from FDR. He remembered his
brief glimpse of Welles several months before when he and Surrey had
gone to see the President. It was interesting to see Welles here on the
island, Alex thought, but he would rather have dealt with Betty Grable.

"You're Balfour, right?" the tall, lanky Welles said in his deep
sonorous voice. Alex nodded and motioned to a log on the other side
of the fire.

"Yep. There's coffee if you want it." Alex reviewed what he knew
of Welles circa 1943. *Citizen Kane* had been released a few years before

to critical success and box office failure. *The Magnificent Ambersons* was a recent flop. Several other movies had died before birth, and he vaguely remembered some sort of Broadway show that was a disaster. Welles would be divorced from Rita Hayworth in 1947, which was a crying shame for Welles in view of what Alex had seen of the lady this evening. The moviemaker was now entering his Failed Boy Wonder period. And Alex wasn't sure if the man ever really came out of it. *We will sell no wine before its time.* Later on, he'd be a big fat guy flacking cheap wine. Fortunately, he would always have the greatness of *Citizen Kane* to fall back on. Alive or dead.

"Fabulous, just fabulous," Welles said. He was wearing a white linen suit, white shirt, open at the collar. The pants were worn high on his stomach. Alex could never get used to seeing pants worn so high, though it was the fashion of the time. Welles was so baby-faced it was almost a shock, as if the face of a child had been superimposed on the body of a grown man. Welles would have been in his late twenties, Alex supposed. His face looked about twelve years old.

"What?" Alex asked. "What's so fabulous?"

"This place, this island," Welles answered, gesturing expansively around him. Alex glanced out into the dark.

"What the hell are you talking about?"

"The trees all thrust to the ground, the landscape prostrate, the destruction." Welles sighed and put his hands on his hips. "Jesus, what a great place to shoot *Macbeth*. There's something so Shakespearian about the devastation. I love it."

Macbeth? Where are the Scottish castles, the wind-swept moors? "I don't get it."

Welles frowned at him. "They never do, they never do," he muttered. "Think about it," he said in a loud voice. He waved his arms around as he spoke. "The witches gather around a fire just such as this, bagpipers marching out of the jungle, flares popping in the sky, they float slowly to the ground, shadows dancing . . ." He stopped talking and looked over the fire at Alex. "Sounds crazy, huh?" he asked. Alex nodded. Welles sighed. "I guess I get a little carried away. I have a lot on my mind these days. I don't know, projects just seem to pop into my head. I lose a lot of money on this kind of stuff." He sighed again and sat down. He stared moodily into the fire. They sat in silence for a few minutes. Alex waited for Welles to get to the point. Welles sat unmoving.

"Mr. Welles," Alex said, "I'm sure you didn't come all this way just to discuss film locations with me . . ."

"What's that?" Welles said, looking up at Alex and then around at the dark. "Jesus." He ran his hand through his thick black hair. "You wouldn't happen to have a drink, would you?" Alex shook his head. "Sometimes I think I'm going nuts," Welles went on. "Yeah, well, the Boss sent me. I don't know what it's all about, and believe me, I don't want to know. I've got enough problems of my own. I've got more people suing me than a dog has fleas, but you don't want to hear about that." He waved a hand in dismissal. "Anyway, The Boss knows you've got some Japs. He wants to know what the score is. You're supposed to write him up something, and I take it back. Say, did you like the show tonight?"

Alex nodded absentmindedly. *Write it up?*

"I love doing magic," Welles said. "Rita's not too crazy about the box, though."

He supposed he could put it in a way that Roosevelt would understand, but would still be suitably murky to the casual snoop. He had been hoping that Welles had come all the way out here to tell him that it was time to go home. Turn the Japs and their crazy ideas over to someone else and just go back. The problem was, as usual, he was in too deep for that. The Japanese scientist, Tubbs, had given him too much in the way of solid information on the possibility of a Japanese bomb to just walk away and say the hell with it. If the Japanese really *did* have the capability to make a bomb, that changed the complexion of everything. If they could make it, they would use it. There was no question of that. And Alex didn't think they'd restrict its use to invading forces. They'd got as far as Pearl Harbor without too much trouble. They had already halfheartedly bombed the Northwest, and shelled California. If they could make a bomb, they could get it across the Pacific. What would an A-bomb dropped on Seattle do? Not only to the city and the country, but to history? The possibility that he could never discount was that the reason he came to be in the positions he found himself in was to stop incidents just like this from occurring. History, his present, this world's future, demanded that he be a factor. Not that the world would be different if he *did* something, but that the world would be different if he *didn't* do something. *No, wait a minute, the Japs don't have a bomb. I never heard of it, the future never heard of it, the goddamn thing doesn't exist. But I still should report it, turn over what Tubbs has given me.*

"All right," Alex said. "I'll write it up." *I'll write it all up, including Tubbs's last insane plan. Somebody else can decide what to do.* "It's going to take me a couple of hours. How long will it take you to get the message back to Washington?"

"Three days, at least. Don't worry about me, I'll just sit here and think."

Alex went to his tent and collected his writing materials. He sat by the fire and wrote a summary of everything the Japanese had told him, leaving out the more scientific details. The important part was that Roosevelt understood that the Japanese had some sort of atomic project. What would be done about it was Roosevelt's problem. High-level bombing, sabotage, whatever, it was out of Alex's hands. At least he hoped it was. He'd spent his season in hell, now he wanted to go home. If he was going to influence the use of the bomb, steer the government away from dropping it on a Japanese city, he could best do that from Washington or Princeton, couldn't he? Not some forsaken island in the middle of the Pacific Ocean. He'd fulfilled everyone's intentions, Einstein's and Roosevelt's. That part of the job was over.

He shook Welles awake. Welles was stretched out on the sand, head on the log, snoring. He sat up and rubbed his eyes like a small child. *This is a spy? I'm entrusting this man with a secret of national importance?* Alex handed him a square of paper, several sheets folded twice. "Here it is. I wouldn't read it if I were you." Welles got to his feet and brushed off his pants.

"Don't worry about that. This spy stuff is starting to wear a bit thin. Rita wouldn't stand for another trip out here, that's for sure. I'm patriotic, but there are limits. I'll pass this along, after that I'm out of it." He looked around the campsite and shook his head. "You really think a tropical *Macbeth* is a bad idea?" he asked.

Alex smiled. "It's a terrible idea."

"Yeah, okay," Welles said, walking into the dark. "Maybe *Othello*." After a moment, out of the dark a spectral voice boomed, "I've got it! *Henry V!* Picture it. The Japanese substitute for the French in the Battle of Agincourt scene." There was a disembodied laugh and then silence.

Alex sat back down and tossed a few broken coconut husks onto the fire. A stream of sparks shot into the sky. For some reason, now that Welles was gone, he was lonelier than he had been in months. Welles and his goofy ideas had reminded him there was more to life than sand, sun, and secrets.

Three days to get the word to Washington. How long to get back here? And who's the next show business spy? Bob Hope? And how long before I get out? How long? How long? Othello? Henry V? Jesus Christ.

34

THE WEATHER NEVER VARIED—BLUE SKIES,
shimmering heat, cool nights. Perfect. Alex began to loathe the sameness. His tropical island existence, like sand in one's underwear, had begun to chafe, and as the days wore on, to seriously abrade. He was tired of eating warmed-up C-rations and chow scrounged from the GI mess tents. He was getting tired of Billy Tanner's constant good nature and smiling blond blandness. And while the fascination of Tubbs's scientific recitations still held him with their frightening possibilities, he knew that even that would soon wear as thin as the Army-issue bologna they ate for lunch every day.

The thrill of simply being alive had been leached away by time, boredom, and the human mind's capacity to adopt itself to almost any set of conditions. Even the memory of Betty Grable failed to rouse him. He was restless, distracted, and wanted to go home. Although he wasn't sure where home was. Princeton, he supposed. Returning to New York and Molly was a possibility that he did not allow himself to dwell upon. He had found, in the past, that it did no good to give in to bouts of self-pity and useless wishing. He was here, and would be here until whatever or whoever held the strings of his existence decided to pull him forward to the present. His purpose in this time, he felt, had not been achieved. Or at least he had achieved little that he and Einstein could work with. Geographical distance from the pacifist professor and an overwhelming closeness to the enemy had colored whatever good and noble intentions he had carried with him as he exited Princeton, those few short weeks ago. Now he was simply riding the flow of history, the little tin soldier in his paper boat, down the sewer, over the waterfall, trying to stay alive, and waiting to see what new peril would rise up midstream before him, what new variety of fish would swallow him whole. *Hang on. Ride it out. Keep your head above water. Don't give up the ship. And as Gunny used to say, keep that asshole puckered.* Words to the wise.

WHEN THE messenger arrived, he appeared out of the dark. No Mercury with winged ankles, no Hermes wielding a wand twined with snakes. Not even Bob Hope with a golf putter. This messenger was a mild-looking, gray-haired, stocky man wearing officer's tans with no insignias. He resembled a cross between Herbert Hoover and W. C. Fields. He stood, deferentially, hands in pockets, waiting at the edge of the circle of light from the campfire until Alex nodded and motioned to the guest-log position across the fire. The man surveyed the area for a moment, as if checking for any hidden danger, visually inspecting Alex's tent and the wire cage before walking to the log and sitting down.

"Maxwell Surrey sends his regards," the man said. "He says for me to tell you to remember the Czar."

It took Alex by surprise, like a quick right-hand jab, a bucket of water in the face. No warning. *This is some serious shit. This man is the real thing. No show business trouper moonlighting on the side. This is not just a messenger, this is the avatar.* In another time, he and Max had been in Russia, during the revolution, and done something that could never be told to the rest of the world. And now Max had let out a tiny piece of it. Max would never have mentioned the Czar to this man unless he wanted to establish his absolute trustworthiness. Alex told himself to relax, whoever the guy was, he wouldn't think that Max's reference to the Czar was anything more than a private code-word. Max was too smart to even hint at Alex's capability.

"I never met the Russian Czar," the man went on, offhandedly. "I was in Siberia at the end of their civil war. Traveled in from Vladivostok on the train, a diplomatic mission. The Japs were there in force even then. Christ, everybody was there. We had American troops guarding the railroad, the Japs had 120,000 soldiers in Manchuria, the Czech Legion was trying to fight its way East, the British were backing the Kolchak government. It was a real mess."

"I know," Alex said. He'd fought his way East as well, along those same tracks.

The other man regarded him with interest. "I found the Russians appalling in their behavior," he went on. "The Bolsheviks were recruiting soldiers by gun and whip, murdering all the educated people. The Whites were raiding the villages near the tracks, corraling the villagers and demanding money and supplies. When they didn't get what they wanted, they strung the people up by their ears to the fronts of their houses." He stopped and shook his head. "It was fifty degrees below zero, middle of the goddamn winter. They'd take the village leaders, the elders, out to a river, hack a hole in the ice and dip these poor devils in, over and over, like candles, until they were covered with a thick, clear coat of ice. Stand them up in the village square like some sort of crazy statue. They'd stay there until the spring thaw. Then there were the Cossacks. Animals. Totally uncivilized. Seize a train full of people and kill every living soul aboard. Men, women, and children. Machine-gun them, rape them, bash the babies' heads in."

"Throw them over cliffs," Alex said distantly. And then he was back, in his mind, back on the train listening to the screams of men and women, the long-drawn-out screams as they were thrown over the cliffs, down the rocky gorge into the stream far below, the sounds of pistols, machine guns, drunken laughter and shouting . . .

"You okay?" A hand on his shoulder. He looked into the man's eyes and saw not death and Russia, but concern, kindness. He realized that he was standing. His hands were shaking and he was cold.

"I shouldn't be telling those old war stories," the man said, moving back to his log. "You fellows have been through enough on your own."

Alex rubbed his hands together and held them out to the fire. He wondered if the night were suddenly especially cool, or if the chill had crept in on the memory of that past time. "It's all right. You brought back something that I thought was safely stored away."

There was a moment of silence. "Well, that's not why I'm here. Max and I worked together in the past. He was worried about you so he contacted me and put me in the picture. I spoke to Roosevelt, he filled me in on your mission and what you've pieced together. I read the paper you sent back with Welles."

"Excuse me," Alex said, "but who the hell are you?"

The other man smiled. "I won't bullshit you. Donovan, OSS. And

I could ask you the same question. There was no time to vet you, but I was coming in this direction anyway, so here I am."

Donovan of the Office of Strategic Services. Wild Bill Donovan, master spy, architect of America's wartime intelligence network, and the founding father of the CIA. Alex had read that the first thing one saw when entering CIA headquarters in Langley was a life-size portrait of Wild Bill Donovan, the legendary spymaster.

"You're a long way from home, Mr. Donovan."

The man shrugged. "Got to check up on my people. It's a big war."

"And am I part of your people now?" Alex said, giving his words an edge of sarcasm. He could see Roosevelt's hand, moving him around on the chessboard.

Donovan sat up straight. "Mr. Balfour, as I said before, I don't know who you are. I don't know if you're good enough to be one of my people. When this war started, America didn't have shit in the way of intelligence gathering. Outside of Hoover and his boys. I put my outfit together based on personal knowledge of the individuals involved. And so far they've done a hell of a job. Now, you come recommended by Max Surrey, who is a friend of mine, a damn good friend, which is a damn good thing because otherwise I wouldn't be sitting on this goddamn log on a beach not more than two degrees off dead-center of the asshole of the Pacific. From all I can tell, you seem to have a problem here. I can help you with that problem. Or I can get up, walk back to my C-54, and fly on out and leave *your* ass sitting on *your* log with two Japs and a world of trouble for company."

Alex was glad it was night. His ears were burning. It would have been humiliating for Donovan to see that his lecture had struck home. "I wasn't being cynical, Mr. Donovan." *I was, but you didn't have to take it to heart, you crusty bastard.* "Sometimes the President's method of passing me around makes me feel a bit like a favored whore."

"Son, at least you're favored. When Roosevelt decides he's through with you, things can get pretty tough. Think of it as gaining a new friend who might be useful another time."

Alex nodded. "All right, Mr. Donovan. Now just what is it you have in mind?"

"First I want to see the Japs." They stood up and Alex led him the fifty feet to the wire cage. It was situated far enough away from the campfire so the Japanese couldn't hear what was being said, but close enough to derive at least some visual comfort from the flames.

Tubbs was lying on his pallet, seemingly asleep. Easy was in his usual lotus position, calmly watching them. Alex could see the reflected glitter of the fire in the man's eyes. Donovan stood silent for a few minutes then led the way back to the fire.

"Have they told you anything new since you sent your report in?"

Alex shrugged. "Nothing of substance. Just more of the scientific details. Just how much do *you* know about the subject under discussion?"

"That's what I like to see, a man who's careful about what he says. You don't need to worry about me, I've been aware of our Manhattan Project for several years. Once again, Mr. Balfour, it would be more appropriate for me to ask the question of you."

Alex nodded. "Maybe. As you've figured out by now, I know a hell of a lot about the project myself. And I'm not the only one."

"If General Groves knew what you just said, you'd be guaranteed a warm berth in federal prison or worse. And what do you mean you aren't the only one?"

"The Manhattan Project security is shot full of holes. I keep running into people who know bits and pieces of the whole picture. So far nobody who'd be dangerous, except the Japanese. And that's one hell of an exception. Tubbs told me that they have a Spanish spy who's done some work on it. Supposedly the Germans ferried this man to Mexico, where he interviewed some Indian boys who live on the reservation near Los Alamos. The Indians brought samples of dirt, and tests were done on the two boys. Sound like a security problem to you?"

Donovan frowned. "Hell, yes, but there's not much I can do about it. Groves has got security under Army jurisdiction. He won't farm any of it out. This is a huge project. We've got facilities all over the United States. Hundreds of thousands of workers, most of whom haven't the slightest idea what they're working on, and every one of whom would have to be Jesus Christ incarnate to never gossip about what they're doing. We know about the Spaniard. We keep an eye on him. But I didn't know about the trip to Mexico. Mexico's as bad as Portugal. There are so many spies we can't keep track of them, and they can't keep track of us. At least I hope they can't." Alex tossed some coconut husks onto the fire and both men watched as the loose hairs on the hulls glowed bright and burst into flames.

"Let me see if I've got this straight," Donovan said. "The two Japs here want us to believe that they're on their way to building the same bomb that we're working on. These two know they're going to lose eventually, and that trading atomic bombs is going to destroy what's left of their country. But they're patriots, opposed to the ruling militarists. The militarists will go down to glorious death leading every man, woman, and child to stop us on the beaches, throwing every weapon they've got at us, from atomic bombs to wooden spears. These two want you to tell Roosevelt that they have atomic capability so when the time comes they'll be able to negotiate a better peace."

"That's about it."

"Pretty goddamn sophisticated for a low-level scientist and his bodyguard. Do you believe it?"

Alex shook his head. "You've got me, Mr. Donovan. I'd never heard of any Japanese bomb research, but Tubbs has a pretty convincing line of argument. If they are capable of it, if he's right, it would be the biggest bargaining chip that they could bring to the table. If it's true. But I don't believe it."

"The truth. That's what it all comes down to, right? Do we believe them, or don't we?"

Alex nodded. "That's it. Which is where you boys come in, and I step out. You decide."

Donovan stared into the fire for a moment before going on, as if he hadn't heard Alex. "He says this place, the lab, is in Hiroshima?" Alex nodded. "Well, it looks like he might be telling the truth about that much of it. We've got a man in place in Japan. We've got listening posts in China that monitor his frequency twenty-four hours a day." Donovan shook his head. "One man in the entire godforsaken country. He gets out weather reports, troop movements, mostly incidental stuff, but he did mention a concentration of scientific types in Hiroshima. Our boys read that as a possible weapons lab. If we knew for sure what was going on, it would mean a hell of a lot to our side. If your two Japs are telling the truth, well, the world is hip deep in shit and about to hit the skids." Donovan stared moodily into the fire.

"So what's the bottom line?" Alex prompted.

"Bottom line?" Donovan asked.

"Where's that leave us? What's the plan?"

"It's a classic situation. You've got two basic choices: You take the Japs back to home base and put them on the rack, squeeze everything they've got out of them, and work with that. Or you set them up and turn them loose, but keep them on a string. You use them. The first method is the safest, but the rewards are limited. The second is dangerous, but the possibilities are much greater. You get a constant stream of ongoing information. You use your assets to create situations that exploit your own aims. For instance, we could use these two to get one of our own men in to verify what we already suspect." He looked directly at Alex. Alex felt a new chill creep up his backbone.

"No, Mr. Donovan."

"That's General Donovan, son."

"And I'm not in your goddam Army, so don't try that rank shit on me."

"I wouldn't think of it. I know you can't order a man into a situation like this. He's got to want to go. He's got to go willingly if he's going to be any good to me."

"Yeah, well, you can forget it as far as I'm concerned. Find someone else."

Donovan pursed his lips for a moment. "Yes, but that's the problem, isn't it? The Japs have offered to take you back with them. You're just about the only one around who has knowledge of the atomic process, you'd know what to look for. You've got guts, I asked around about you and they tell me you held your own in the fight for this island. And if you're interested, I know a way we can get you out. I'll have to have a talk with the one you call Tubbs, but it can be done."

"I'm not interested," Alex said flatly. They sat in silence for a few minutes while his mind turned it over, even though he didn't want it to. *Are you crazy? It would be damn near certain death to go in there. Besides, there is no Jap bomb. If there were, I would have heard about it.* "Just as a matter of curiosity, how *would* you get someone out of Japan? Accepting for the moment that that someone would still be alive. You're talking about sending a Caucasian in to spy on a race of Orientals. Such a spy wouldn't exactly blend in with the crowd. Just for the sake of argument, how would you get him out of there?"

"In broad daylight with the approval of the Jap government," Donovan said. "You're right, there'd be no way to do it without proper authorization. Here's the way it is. Soon, within a month, we're going to be bringing out our embassy people who've been trapped there since the war began. We're going to make a trade, their people for ours. This has been in the works for a long time, there's no question that it's going to happen. We've been holding their people down in White

Sulphur Springs. We can get you into the country with the two you've got here. You check it out, see what they've got. Then we'll take you out with the others. I'll have a talk with your man Tubbs. If he has any pull, and it sounds like he does, he can get you transferred to the embassy people. It's simple."

"Simple." Alex laughed. "Oh yeah, simple. What kind of story are we going to use to get me in?"

"We'll use the same story *they* used to get in *here*. They can say that they captured you, that they were on their way home when their ship or sub was sunk under them. Who's to say they're lying? We'll put you out in a lifeboat and let the Japs rescue you this time. The story worked pretty well for them once, why won't it work again?"

"Because the Japanese are crazy," Alex said. "Or haven't you noticed? Spend a month clearing out an island full of them, you'll begin to see certain signs of unbalance. They'll take one look at me and kill me on the spot."

"Not if they think you'll be useful to them. They may appear crazy to us, but that doesn't mean they're stupid. You'll get in, get word out through our people where the lab is, if it really is in Hiroshima, and we'll take care of the rest. You'll be traded out of there. The bomb plant, if there is a bomb plant, won't be a threat anymore, not once we get through with it, and the world will be one hell of a lot safer place. I can't think of a thing we could do that would be more important than taking out that lab. Think what it would mean to the future if the Japanese had the power of the atom bomb."

"General . . ."

"Just shut up for a minute and think about it."

Alex closed his mouth and looked out into the darkness. *All right, I'll sit here and look like I'm thinking about it.* He sat regarding his fingernails, and soon found it was as if someone said, Don't think about elephants. In no time at all, all he could think about was elephants. Atomic elephants.

Donovan was right about one thing, the world would be a lot worse off if the Japanese had a bomb and used it. Even if they didn't win the war. *We* were going to use the bomb, that was bad enough. If both sides threw them at each other, the result would be horrendous. For now and forever. There was a slim chance that he, working through Einstein, could get America to use the bomb as a demonstration rather than dropping it on civilians. But there was no way in hell he could stop the Japanese once they were ready. But what if it were all bullshit? It *had* to be bullshit. What if the whole story was a red herring, thought up by the Japs to make us think they had a bomb and would use it? Just to force us into a bargaining posture more advantageous to them. What if Tubbs and Easy never expected anyone to be crazy enough to take them up on their offer to actually go and see the evidence?

Throughout his time here, people had been asking him to volunteer for things that scared the piss out of him. And he kept finding himself saying yes, sure, I'll go. Like he was some sort of superman, which he was damn sure he wasn't. He was as mortal as the next man, and the last several weeks had proved just how mortal that was. He'd seen a lot of men die, and he'd killed a lot of men himself. *For what? Why?* And that was the strange part. He didn't really know why. Part of it was to keep from being killed, that was for sure, but he could have gone somewhere else and hid and been a lot safer. He thought back on the long list of men he'd met since he'd left New York. Gunny; Spiegle, the sailor who'd been killed back on the *Nevada*; all the men at Pearl Harbor; Goldberg, the boy who'd shared a foxhole with him and died; Billy Gillam, the Australian; all the kids who squatted in landing boats waiting to run down the ramp into a wall of bullets, all of them doing what they were told to do. And the reason they did so, he'd heard them say over and over again, offhandedly, sheepishly, and proudly, was *because they thought it was their duty*. To their country, to their families, to their buddies, to themselves. They might have been bashful and tongue-tied when it came to putting it into words, but they weren't ashamed. They said it and felt it until the idea seemed to be part of the atmosphere, part of the air they all breathed, a shared thing that was simply taken for granted. Like loving your wife, or your kids. These people loved their country. They were willing to die for the United States of America. They believed.

In his old life, back in New York, he would have just smiled to hear such childish talk. No one would have said such things, not seriously. People were too smart, too hip, too knowing, too wise to the ways of governments and the world. *Maybe they were. But what if they weren't? What if this way was better? Just what was so great about being ironic and cynical and hip. Was the way he lived better than the way these people lived? Were his ideals superior, his morality higher? What did he believe in that was more important?* He thought about it. He thought about it as hard as he could, because his life depended on it. But he kept coming up with the same answer.

Nothing. Our morality doesn't even come close to theirs. Most of us don't believe in anything. Besides, and this was the real question, what if the Japs really did have the capability to build a bomb?

If anyone would have a chance to pull something like this off, it was him. When you got right down to essentials, he was the only one who knew what would happen in the future. This knowledge might not be enough to save him, but it had to be an advantage. And after all, wasn't this *his* duty?

"All right," he said, his voice shaking. *Oh Lord, I am afraid.*

"I'll go."

"TOMORROW MORNING?" Alex asked incredulously. "We leave tomorrow morning?"

They were in the commanding officer's operations tent, commandeered by Donovan. The OSS man shrugged. "Why not? The sooner the better. Now let me fill you in on this radio."

Alex looked at the radio. He was sick to his stomach, so afraid that he kept checking his hands to see if they were trembling. "Look," Donovan said, not unkindly, "the worst part is the waiting. Once you shove off you won't be nearly so scared. Now look at the radio, and *think* about the radio."

Alex looked at the radio again. It was two by three feet, covered with switches and dials. It looked like it weighed three hundred pounds. "Don't you have anything smaller?" he asked.

"No. You're not taking it with you," Donovan said patiently. "I just want you to be able to operate one if you need to. They're pretty much all the same, Jap radios, our radios, if you can work one, you can work the other. These are your power switches, this is your tuner, it's calibrated in frequencies. The writing may be in Japanese, but the numbers, as you can see, are the same. Here's where you want to be." He pointed at a spot near the left end of the dial. "Right down here on the lower end of the scale, around 35 megahertz. Nail it right on 35 and we'll catch any drift on our end." Alex memorized the numbers and configuration of the dial.

"That's the channel that the listening post in Chungking stays

tuned to. We've got a woman operative there who's never far from the
set. When you want to raise her, set the channel and repeat her call
sign until she answers. We'll try it in a minute. Her call sign is *Bon
Appetit.* That's French for Good Appetite."

"I know what it means. What's her name?"

"You don't need to know her name, just repeat that until she
answers. Give her time, she's usually in the kitchen, which is only
five feet from the radio, but sometimes she's so busy eating and cooking
she doesn't get to the radio right away." Donovan switched on the
radio, fiddled with the dial, repeated the code word several times, and
waited. A rush of static filled the tent. He repeated the code words
again. This time the static was broken by a faint voice, almost lost in
the scratchy sea of radio noise. "There she is," Donovan said. He
announced a test, repeated his words twice more, and signed off. "I'm
going there tomorrow, so I can tell her to listen for you. The signal
will be stronger where you are, don't worry about her hearing you.
What you want to do is simply say the threat is real and give the name
of the city, or the location as near as possible, of the laboratory."

Alex sat staring at the huge khaki-colored metal radio. "Where the
hell am I going to find a radio? And why would the Japanese let me
anywhere near one?"

"They probably won't, but you've got to know how to do it if you
need to. We'll be banking on our man in Japan getting to you. You'll
give him the information, he'll get it out to us."

"Who is he? How will I know him?"

"The thing you want to do is get in touch with the local Catholic
church. The Vatican is neutral territory in this war so all the belligerents are letting the Church officials stay in country. If they want
to. Our man is a priest, his responsibility is any foreign souls that
need tending, any non-Asiatics. Tell whoever you get in contact with,
you want to speak with Cardinal Montini, that's not our man's name
but that will get the message across. Once again, you don't need to
know our man's name. That way if you get caught and tortured, you
won't have any local information to divulge."

"Thanks, that does a lot for my peace of mind. But how will I
know when I've got the right guy?"

"Just trust in the Lord, son. Besides, how many priests are going
to be telling you that they're your contact? You'll know." Donovan took
a small tin box from his pocket. "Next order of business, your L pill.

I think you're going to be okay, but if you have to pull the plug on the operation, you might want this. In fact, I'm going to have to order you to take it along." He handed Alex a clear pill with white powder inside.

"Well, Jesus Christ," Alex said, holding the pill up to the light. "Is this my suicide pill?"

Donovan nodded. "We all carry them. If you get into trouble, put it in your mouth. If you can't get out of trouble, bite down. It will break. It's fast."

"Cyanide, right? I've read about these things. Fast it isn't. Two minutes probably. Supposed to be extremely painful." He shook his head, "No thanks." Donovan flushed.

"If this operation goes wrong, two minutes of pain might seem a godsend. You know too much for your, or our, own good. Put it in your pocket and take it with you. That's an order."

Alex put the pill in his shirt pocket. He'd never take it. *Hell, Francis Gary Powers didn't take his, and he got out in the end.* There was always the chance that no matter what trouble he was in, he might revert back to his own time before he was killed.

"Weapons," Donovan said, opening a leather case.

"Forget the weapons," Alex said. "They aren't going to let me keep anything once they pick us up. And I won't have any use for a gun before that. Keep your toys." Suddenly he was very tired. All the pills and guns seemed like so much chickenshit. If he actually made it out of this alive, it wouldn't be because he was cleverly armed.

"You're right," Donovan said. "One gets into habits. You won't need anything but your own wits to pull this off. You go back and get a few hours' sleep. I'll radio the sub. They're standing by offshore. You'll leave at first light."

"Wait a minute. The sub is standing by? It was here all along? And you came in by air? In other words, you knew I was going out on this thing when you came in. What made you so goddamned sure of yourself?"

Donovan smiled. "I wasn't sure of myself, I was sure of you. Surrey said you'd do it. He said you were that kind of guy." He held out his hand.

Alex stood up, looked at the offered hand, then shook it. He sighed. He was exhausted, and at the same time his heart was racing. "Tell Max I said thanks. Thanks a lot."

"You can tell him yourself next time you see him. You'll be out of there inside of two months."

"Yeah," Alex said, wishing that he'd never said he'd do it, feeling the mild nausea of fear down in his gut, knowing it would be there until he got out of this. "I'll tell him next time I see him."

ALEX STOOD on the bridge beside the captain and the executive officer of the submarine. He could feel the trembling of the engines in the deck beneath his feet. The two Japanese, a folding liferaft, and supplies were stowed below. Donovan stood on the dock, watching the submarine. Alex reached into his pocket and took out the suicide pill. He shivered in the cool morning air. He started to flip the pill into the water so Donovan could see him do it. Then he put the pill into his pocket. *You never know.*

"Good luck," Donovan called.

"Yeah, right," Alex answered. He had to raise his voice to be heard over the engines. "Bon voyage and bon appetit!" he shouted as the sub began to inch away from the dock. Donovan frowned. The captain of the sub and the other officer looked from Alex to Donovan. Alex smiled as he remembered how it had come to him during his few hours of sleep. *Had to be. It all fits.* "The radio operator," he shouted, "Her name is Julia Child." Even from the bridge of the submarine he could see Donovan blanch.

35

THE WAVES LAPPED GENTLY AGAINST THE side of the inflatable yellow canvas raft. Alex lay in the back of the raft, staring at the rubber-coated canvas tubing, wondering just how advanced Japanese inflatable life-boat technology was in 1943. So far it looked pretty good. He brushed at a sore spot on his arm and watched a two-inch patch of skin flake off. He was shedding like a snake, his body scoured by sunburn, saltwater, and the constant abrasion of the rough canvas. He rolled onto his back and put his feet up on the side, trying to get comfortable in a small inflated world where there was no comfort. For a moment he tried to remember what soft felt like: Molly's skin fresh from the bath, Molly's silk nightgown as he slipped it over her head, the inside of her thighs . . . *Oh, Jesus, don't do this, stop, it only makes it worse.*

The two Japanese former prisoners sat at the other end of the raft. Captain Easy was paddling, Tubbs was staring intently at the horizon, attempting to conjure up a ship, or land. In the center of the boat, stored in a waterproof bag, were their supplies: ten days' worth of food and water. They'd eaten and drunk their way through four days' worth. Alex had thought that his experiences as a castaway with Kennedy would have helped him endure this particular raft ride. But they didn't. Pain remembered does little to relieve fresh, up-to-the-minute pain.

The boat and supplies were all authentic Japanese Navy, supplied courtesy of Wild Bill Donovan. The equipment had been on the submarine when they boarded, the final piece of evidence, as if he needed it, that Alex's participation was a foregone conclusion. Donovan had expected Alex to be right where he was, in the raft, on his way to Japan, even before Donovan had walked into the circle of firelight five nights ago.

All right, Alex could accept that, he was used to being pushed around the board. It was necessary to remind himself, on occasion, but that was why he was here. He expected to be used. But knowing it did little to relieve the core of resentment. He wondered if other OSS men, parachuting behind Nazi lines, creeping through impenetrable jungles with ragtag bands of native insurgents, swimming onto enemy beaches in the dead of night, felt the same way. No matter how strong the patriotic urge, no matter how gung ho a man might be, there still had to be that little voice of sanity that asked, why me? In Alex's case the resentment was not against the job he was doing, but that it had been a foregone conclusion that he would do it. That he would go so willingly. He also wondered if the other men were as afraid as he was. The big fear had worn off, leaving behind a permanent lump of dread, a kind of sickness that surged over him every time he thought of what was in his future. Or what might be in his future. Or whether he was going to have any future at all.

The sub had dropped them a hundred and fifty miles south of the bottommost tip of Japan. They were directly west of the Bonin Islands, Alex realized. If they floated around for another year or so, they might meet George Bush on *his* life raft after being shot down by the Japanese.

Right now there wasn't another man-made artifact in sight. Either they would be picked up, or Easy would paddle them to safety. The seemingly indefatigable Japanese had been paddling all day, every day, for four days now. He ate very little, drank less, and worked harder than anyone else. Alex watched the smooth muscles of the man's back as he shifted the oar from one side to the other, and wondered just how the hell these people ended up losing the war. If they had all been as dedicated and tough as Captain Easy, the end of the story might have been different.

The colonel, Alex reminded himself. After a day in the raft, Tubbs had explained that the other man was in fact a colonel in the Japanese Army. Alex found it difficult to think of him as anything but Captain

Easy, but he was making the effort. He seldom had any reason to speak to the colonel, but when he did he made sure he used the man's proper rank. It might make a difference in Alex's future. Tubbs had been content to remain Tubbs. Either he didn't know it was the name of a comic strip character, or he simply didn't care. He said that Alex wouldn't be able to pronounce his Japanese name correctly anyway, so Tubbs would do. There was an obvious assumption of superiority in Tubbs's notion that Alex was too dumb to pronounce his name correctly, a clear indication that the balance of power had shifted between them. Alex was treated as an almost-equal, but there was none of the deference Tubbs had shown while he was living in his wire cage. Alex had expected it, but it still made him uneasy. He found it difficult to shift roles, at least it was difficult to go from a position of power to one of subservience. Probably not difficult at all for the Japanese to assume their higher positions. The colonel seemed above such considerations. He'd never acted like a prisoner while he was one, and he didn't act like a master now. Alex had formed a grudging respect for the man. Tubbs was something he still hadn't figured out. Yet. The chubby scientist seemed to shift from role to role, but Colonel Easy was simply whatever he was. Warrior, Alex decided. Samurai

"Plane," Tubbs said, sitting up straighter. He said something in Japanese to Easy, who answered. Alex sat up and scanned the blue sky. The weather had been kind to them, blue skies, gentle winds, low seas. Now Alex could hear the faint buzz of an airplane engine. His stomach tightened. This would mean rescue. Rescue for the Japanese. What for him?

"The colonel says that he has been hearing the aircraft for some minutes," Tubbs said.

The airplane engine grew louder. Easy spoke and Tubbs looked to the south, shading his eyes against the bright sun.

"I see it. Too far away to see whose it is," Tubbs said.

It has to be Japanese, Alex thought. They were too far North for any Allied planes. He sat up and found the pinpoint of light in the sky. The colonel kept paddling, his back to the approaching airplane. They all waited.

The colonel took the oar out of the water and turned around. He carefully stowed the paddle and stood up, accommodating himself to the rocking of the waves. He stared with narrowed eyes at the approaching airplane and said something to Tubbs. Tubbs responded, seeming to argue. The colonel barked what was obviously an order.

"He says we must get out of the boat," Tubbs said to Alex. "He says that it is an American plane. We must get out and swim as far away as we can, but we must keep the raft in sight."

Alex looked at the colonel and knew that he had better do as he was told. The man's face was impassive. The colonel bent and rolled up his pantleg. He unstrapped a pistol from his calf.

Alex was astounded. How the hell had the man gotten a gun? He knew he didn't have it on the island. He'd been strip-searched several times. He must have stolen it on the submarine.

The colonel barked at them again and pointed the pistol in their direction. "He says we must go. Now!" Tubbs got up on his knees and flopped awkwardly over the side. Alex rolled off into the cool sea. He hung on to the side of the boat for a moment, feeling the sting of saltwater, and then swam away. He sidestroked, keeping his eyes on the Japanese still standing in the boat, gun at his side.

Alex eased over and swam on his back. The water seemed much choppier now that he was down in it. The plane was actually discernable as an airplane now, though Alex didn't know how the colonel could have identified it. He looked around but couldn't spot Tubbs. When he was fifty yards away from the raft, he stopped to rest, treading water. The plane began to descend.

Alex could now see the two engines and the stubby nose of a B-25 Mitchell bomber. Maybe out of China, surely on some reconnaissance mission to be so far from home. Alex felt a surge of hope which he instantly squashed. Absurd. He was not here to be rescued. He was trying to *reach* Japan, not be taken back to his own side. The plane dipped even lower and began a run at the raft. Alex began to swim farther away. The American crew would check out the passenger on the slim chance that it might be a downed American flyer or sailor. As the bomber roared over the raft, the colonel lifted the pistol and emptied it into the airplane, thus ensuring a proper identification.

Alex understood what the man was doing.

"**SON OF A BITCH!** Captain, that monkey in the raft just shot three holes in our aircraft!" Sam Walton, the pilot, nodded and thumbed on his intercom. "Jimmy, the Jap Navy down there wants to make a fight of it. I'm going to go around again. Finish him off, will you? We're not supposed to be seen, and he's seen us. He's game, but he's got to go."

Walton listen to the bellygunner okay the order and hung up the mike. He pulled the big plane around in a tight turn, leveled out, and aimed straight for the small yellow raft and the little man.

"Good-bye, Jap."

ALEX UNDERSTOOD what the colonel was doing. He felt a mixture of admiration and horror as he watched the man in his last few seconds before certain death. The colonel was decoying the plane away from Tubbs and himself, sacrificing his own life to save theirs. As the plane rushed upon him, the colonel dove over the side and disappeared beneath the waves.

"GODDAMNIT!" Jimmy Unger, the bellygunner, clicked on the intercom. "Captain, I've lost him. He went in the drink before I could get him. Come around again, come around again. Do you read?"

"Roger." The plane banked, turning in a tight arc. The sunlight flashed from the wings as she came around and dropped level. "He's back up, swimming away from the raft," the co-pilot said, pointing down through the clear nose of the airplane. The pilot spoke into the intercom. "Target in sight, northeast of raft. Do you copy?"

"Roger. Sighted. Bring her in on deck," Jimmy Unger said. He aimed the twin-barreled gun straight ahead, centering on the head and splash of the swimming figure. He squeezed the triggers.

ALEX SAW THE muzzle flash from the ball-turret gun. He was too far away to see where the Japanese must be, but he could imagine the colonel, swimming away from the raft, caught in a storm of bullets churning the water, being hit, his body torn apart in an explosion of blood and flesh, too sudden, too powerful for pain or knowledge, only the quick curtain of darkness and then he was no more. The plane came around one more time, swept low over the place of death, rose up into the sky, and flew away.

Alex swam slowly back to the raft. He pulled himself over the side and lay in the bottom, looking up into the sky. Tubbs's hands appeared. "Help me up." Alex got on his knees and hauled the other man aboard. The two of them sat dripping, breathing heavily. Alex looked out over the water, but there was no indication of where the colonel had been.

"I thought he would get away," Tubbs said, following Alex's gaze. "When he dove overboard."

Alex glanced at Tubbs and leaned back against the round tubing of the raft. "He wasn't trying to escape," Alex said tiredly. "He was drawing them away from us. And the raft. He knew we wouldn't have a chance if they sunk the raft. Which they would have done if he'd stayed in it."

Tubbs nodded. "Bloody good thing he got far enough away before they shot him. I don't feature us swimming the rest of the way." He pulled over the pack of supplies. "This will give us more food and water."

Alex felt a rush of anger. "Jesus Christ, don't you feel anything? I thought that man was your friend."

Tubbs looked at him incredulously. "My dear Alex, control yourself. What I feel is respect and gratification. The colonel was just doing his job. He died well, that is enough. He would not want my sorrow, and he doesn't need yours. Now I suggest you pick up the paddle and get to work. It's a long way home."

Alex thought about punching Tubbs in his face and flinging him overboard, but as gratifying as that might be, it would serve no good end. His job was to get to Japan, stay alive, and make his report. And then get out.

He crawled to the front of the raft, retrieved the paddle from where the colonel had carefully stowed it, and began to paddle. *All the way to fucking Japan. And back, if need be.*

AFTER FOUR MORE days they were picked up by the *Osaka Maru*, a Japanese cargo ship en route from China. The rusty old steamer had been pushed south by a storm and was making her way back to Japan, the big island of Honshu. Evidently the American sub had dropped Alex and the two Japanese off much farther south than any of them had supposed. If the storm hadn't forced the steamer in their direction, they probably would never have made it. After a week's slow and uneventful journey, they docked on the southwest tip of the island. The problem was how to get him ashore and to Tubbs's laboratory without attracting undue attention. The solution was simple and direct, and for Alex, extremely uncomfortable.

36

"I'm fat," Tommy Fellows said to the airline boarding agent. TWA, Flight 101, Washington to L.A. to Japan. He smiled pleasantly to the man behind the counter. "I'm real fat. We want an aisle seat and a window seat. You put someone between us and they'll suffocate before we reach Cleveland."

The ticket man smiled back. He was tall and dark, with a Tom Selleck mustache. "We don't land in Cleveland, sir. And I can see that you're quite large. I'll assign you folks the aisle and window and try to keep the middle seat open, but I can't promise anything. If we're full, someone goes in. You'll have to do your best to keep them alive."

Molly glanced around, vaguely embarrassed. No one else in line seemed to be paying any attention. Harry, her editor, had booked them on a flight out of Dulles so they had had to fly from New York to Washington, D.C. Tommy said it was some sort of obscure Harry punishment for blackmailing him into giving them the trip. Their tickets were stamped and handed back to them. They walked over and stood at the huge floor-to-ceiling window looking out over the broad expanse of Dulles Airport. In the distance she could see a Concorde being fueled. Farther on were the low rolling hills of Virginia.

"I'm sorry if I embarrassed you," Tommy said. "Sometimes that works, sometimes it doesn't. It's not the first time that guy's had it tried on him. There are a lot of fat people in this world. Twenty years of being sardined into seats designed for economy rather than comfort have inured me to embarrassment." The loudspeaker announced the boarding of their flight. They lined up and thumped along the covered walkway to the airplane. Molly had checked through a large suitcase and carried on an overnighter. Tommy had a black duffle-type bag that he squashed beneath his seat. Molly wondered how a man so large could get enough clothing for a trans-Pacific trip of unlimited length into one small bag.

The middle seat between them remained empty, which allowed Tommy, on the aisle, to overflow in only mild discomfort. After takeoff, he ordered a Bloody Mary, which Molly declined. Tommy settled his bulk as far back as the seat would allow. As he sipped his drink, he gave Molly her first lesson in the uses of chemical and biological warfare in the services of terrorism.

"Muammar Kaddafi. Did you know there are thirty-six ways to correctly spell his name? Even the Mummer himself can't make up his mind. Anyway, link that name, however you care to spell it, with poison gas and you've got a guaranteed nightmare. Irrational, incomprehensible evil wielding the ultimate invisible horror." Tommy took a sip of his drink and placed it carefully on the seat-back table. "The specter of Libya spraying Sarin on downtown Tel Aviv at the height of rush hour is indeed a chilling one. Do you know Sarin?" Molly shook her head. "Also known as GB. It's the basis of our gas armaments. Nerve gas. One third of our shells are mustard gas left over from World War II. The rest are Sarin. Scientific name, ready for this? Isopopyl methylphonofluoridate. And just as deadly as it sounds. Nerve gas inhibits the action of a specific body chemical: cholinesterase. Once ingested, inhaled, or injected, the body poisons itself. All your muscles, including those controlling respiration and defecation, go into a state of violent vibration. You suffocate. In fairly short order. Or your heart stops. Same thing, in the end. Very nasty stuff. The effect is the same as bug spray on a bug. The Nazis came up with it. Tested it on prisoners in concentration camps. It's still in use today. Michael Townley, the man who assassinated Orlando Letelier, smuggled a bottle in for his work. Carried it through customs in a Chanel No. 5 atomizer. Townley went with a car bomb in the end. Much easier to deploy. There's the problem, or one of the problems—deployment."

Tommy attempted to swivel his bulk so that he was facing her. Molly wondered what the man in the seat in front of them thought about this recitation. Tommy's voice was not overly loud, but it had a gravelly edge. It caught the ear.

"See, even if Mad-Man Muammar keeps his chemical plant operational, he's still got to be able to deliver the goods. Large-scale spraying is pretty much out of the question. He hasn't got planes with enough range. Which leaves the terrorist market. And that's what's got our government in such a sweat. But I think they're missing the boat by concentrating on Libya." He stopped talking and frowned. "You want to hear all this, Molly? One of my special joys is showing off my intelligence to pretty young ladies. If you like, I'll shut up and let you read or sleep or whatever."

Molly shook her head. "I need to hear anything that will help me. I can sleep later, and anything I would have brought along to read would seem pretty tame by comparison. Go ahead, don't worry about me."

Tommy nodded. "Not that it's a particularly uplifting subject. Fascinating, though. Anyway, there are a number of reasons why chemical and biological weapons are attractive to terrorist groups. They're cheap and relatively easy to make. If you've had high school chemistry and have access to some basic, easily obtained equipment, you can whip up a batch of lethal agents in your bathtub. Formulas for nerve agents, mustard gas, and herbicides are easily obtainable. In 1971 the Department of Defense declassified its formula for VX gas. You only need small quantities to make big problems. You can introduce some form of toxins almost anywhere, be it the White House or the Pentagon. Or the Kremlin, for that matter. It's a lot cheaper, easier, and more possible to build than a nuclear weapon. And a hell of a lot more reliable.

"But *your* area my dear, is biological weapons. That's what the Japanese were really interested in. Once again our government is focusing on third world countries like Libya and ignoring serious dangers right here in our own country. You won't see much of this in the newspapers. They're afraid that if they publish anything in detail some crazy is going to read up on it and try it out. Biologicals are really frightening. Eight ounces of botulinus toxin, if properly dispersed, could wipe out the entire world population." Tommy upended his Bloody Mary and finished it. The ice rattled in the glass as he set it back down. "Eight ounces. Just about enough to fill up this glass."

"If all this is so easy to do, why don't we hear about people doing it?" Molly glanced out the window. Great reaches of woodland stretched beneath them. Small puffy clouds drifted along over the trees.

"Just because you don't hear about it doesn't mean it ain't happening, sweetheart. In 1972 two kids were arrested trying to put typhoid into the city of Chicago's water supply. The same year the FBI uncovered a terrorist plot to use chemicals in an attack on a nuclear storage site in Europe. Then there was the Alphabet Bomber out in L.A. in 1974. He mailed toxic material to a Justice of the U.S. Supreme Court and threatened to kill the President with a homemade nerve agent weapon. He was very knowledgeable, had the damn thing near built when they nailed him. Some people say it was ready to go, but the police hushed it up. A chemical engineer in Vienna made a batch of Sarin and offered it for sale to some bank robbers. In '78 unknown Arabs injected Israeli oranges with mercury." He stopped and smiled.

"Still think nobody's using it? Also in '78 the Russians assassinated a Bulgarian with an umbrella weapon that delivers Ricin pellets."

"I know about Ricin," Molly said. "Extremely powerful, made from castor beans."

Tommy nodded. "That's right. I've got an issue of *Soldier of Fortune* magazine back in my desk that's got an advertisement for a book that tells you how to brew up a batch at home. Easy as making beer. Actually, it's easier. The FBI has confiscated homemade Ricin on a number of occasions. Incidentally, that umbrella number has been used a lot. The Russians are crazy about it. It's their weapon of choice for deep-sixing defectors. Mimics a heart attack. Anyway, the roll continues. In 1979 four hundred kilograms of nerve agent compounds were discovered in a terrorist safe house in Germany. Ditto a bathtub full of botulin toxin cooked up by the Red Army Faction in Paris. In '85 someone slipped the nerve agent carbamate in coffee being served to Israeli soldiers. I could go on with this, but I'm sure you're getting the idea. And I don't know the half of it. This is the stuff I'm able to ferret out. What's *really* going on is a lot worse. They're just keeping it quiet."

"They?"

"The government, the police, the CIA, the Department of Defense, any one of a number of government agencies. They figure if the ordinary criminal knew how easy it was to do this stuff, we'd have a lot more of it. They still haven't caught the people who were putting arsenic in the Tylenol. Easy crime to perpetrate, easy crime to get away with. But deadly. Damn deadly. Virtually any type of bacillus can be ordered from labs listed in the American Type Culture Collection in Rockville, Maryland. You can get your *Bacillus anthracis*, that's anthrax, and your botulism bacillus. I saw an ad in one of the supply magazines that offered five toxins, including T2, that's the infamous Yellow Rain used in Afghanistan, all for the low low price of a hundred dollars. What a deal, folks, get 'em while they last." He shook his head. "Sometimes even old Tommy is amazed. Of course if you don't want to spring for the cultures, lots of toxins occur naturally. Corn is an excellent source of tricothecene mycotoxin. Very deadly. Aflatoxin can be produced from peanuts. And don't forget every year more than a few people croak from botulism poisoning in poorly prepared foods."

"Excuse me."

They looked up at a stewardess, smiling down at them. "My name is Suzi, and I'd like to welcome you aboard. Are you ready for your lunch?"

37

THREE NUNS IN FULL REGALIA STROLLED by, followed by a young woman on roller skates. The woman on skates was eating an ice cream cone and wearing very tight short shorts. Molly watched her coast by and felt pale, dumpy, and old. They were sitting in the L.A. airport waiting for the Japan Airlines flight to Tokyo. Molly was sipping coffee out of a Styrofoam container. Tommy was still talking.

Discourse seemed to give him strength. In many ways, he appeared even fresher than he had when they boarded the plane that morning. For a big heavy guy, he didn't seem to wrinkle much. Tommy stopped talking as a line of schoolchildren filed by, strung out like a row of baby ducks trailing after their mother.

"If you research this thing in any depth," Tommy said, "you eventually run across a photograph of soldiers who have been gassed in the First World War. They're being led away from front-line aid stations to hospitals in the rear. They're in single file, just like those kids, and they've all got one hand on the shoulder of the guy in front. At first you think they're prisoners, that they're blindfolded. And then you realize that they're all blind. Mustard gas. It's a powerful photograph. Somehow I visualize these men for the rest of their lives, dependent on others, being led around by Seeing Eye dogs, sitting on park benches. It's a picture that strikes terror into the heart of any soldier who sees it. To them, gas is the ultimate, most hated weapon. One sniff, one drop anywhere on your body, and you're blind, disfigured, or dead. In that respect, the First World War was the ultimate horror.

"After the first attacks, after both sides developed and perfected chemical weapons, the soldiers in the trenches became so sensitized to this type of warfare that just the *possibility* of a gas attack was enough to destroy the fighting ability of whole units. I once read an account of a group of British soldiers who had been under attack for days. This was after a brutal winter campaign. Trench warfare itself was horrible. Thousands of men froze to death, died of disease, malnutrition, neglect. There was a lull in the fighting and the men were resting. Then someone noticed the odor of violets. Phosgene gas smells a bit like violets, so word sped down the line. Gas. The odor became stronger and the entire line broke and ran. A thousand men panicked, threw down their weapons, abandoned their positions, and ran for their lives. Later, when the Germans didn't follow up on the attack, one of the officers went back. He crawled out of the trench and made his way up a rise to the brow of a low hill. There, on the other side, was a large field of purple violets."

Molly put her empty coffee cup on the floor beside her chair. A Spanish guy wearing earphones and pushing a broom danced by, sweeping up her empty cup. He smiled and winked at her. She managed a halfhearted, tired smile in return. They heard their flight called over the PA system. She gathered up her bag and her purse. "Thank God," she said, "nobody used gas in World War II. Despite what the Japanese were doing. Maybe the world learned something from World War I."

"That's an interesting point," Tommy said as they walked down the long hall toward their gate. "No one is quite sure why gas *wasn't* used in World War II. The only major wartime leader who was really against it was Franklin Delano Roosevelt. A lot of people on the American side wanted to use it against Japan, especially in the last days of the war. The Combined Chiefs of Staff approved a plan to soak the island of Iwo Jima with poison gas. Roosevelt vetoed it. Churchill pressed for gas warfare throughout the war. Even after the English were demonstrably winning, he wanted to use it. His commanders wouldn't go along with him." Tommy stopped and put his suitcase on the floor as they joined a line at the check-in counter. "The Russians thought the Nazis would use gas on the Eastern front. Ribbentrop threatened the Italians with gas attacks if they abandoned the Axis cause. After the war, Goering said they didn't use gas to stop the D-Day landings because they were afraid it would backfire and kill all their horses, which were the backbone of the Nazi transportation system. By the time it was over, the Japanese had stockpiled 7,500 tons of gas, and we had 135,000 tons. From 1941 right through 1945 all nations regularly shipped gas shells, bombs, and rockets to the various fighting fronts. The reason it wasn't used was probably that, strategically, conventional weapons were more effective. Even in the First World War, after the surprise of the first few attacks, the services learned to escape the worst effects. Only about one in thirty-six injuries was due to gas."

"Oh my, you a very fat man," the young Japanese woman behind the counter giggled. Molly and Tommy looked at each other. "I put you two with seat in between, okay?" Tommy nodded.

"I'm going to like Japan," Tommy said as they sat down to wait. "At least I *think* I'm going to like it."

"I'm not sure I'm going to be able to divorce myself from all of the things I've learned in the last week. The terrible things they did to their prisoners."

Tommy nodded. "True enough, but they weren't alone. You have to remember that this kind of warfare is very old. In ancient times armies would poison enemy wells with dead bodies. The Tartars catapulted plague victims into walled towns in the fourteenth century. The British and the Americans used smallpox-infected blankets to wipe out whole Indian tribes. During World War Two the Russians used germ warfare on the borderland between Russia and Mongolia. They bred a really aggressive strain of rat, put them in cages with glass containers of plague germs, and parachuted them out of airplanes. The cage would hit the ground, the glass would break and soak the rats, the doors would pop open, and out would go the rats.

"The Russians screamed the loudest after the war about the Japanese experiments, but in 1941 they were using Japanese POWs for testing. They had this tent with cages of plague-infected rats. The prisoners were chained there until they were all infected. One of the prisoners escaped and spread plague all through the region before the Russian Air Force finally killed enough Mongolians to stop the contagion."

Molly put her hands over her ears. "Jesus, Tommy, isn't anyone clean? Wasn't there a country who didn't do these things?"

Tommy thought for a moment. "No," he said, shaking his head. "No major country. We used Seventh-Day Adventist conscientious objectors for testing during the Vietnam War. The English used terminal cancer patients to test deadly viruses. The CIA used drug addicts to test drugs. Molly, America didn't even sign the Geneva Protocal condemning the use of gas until 1975, fifty years after it had been drawn up. There aren't any good guys here, not with this type of warfare."

She looked away, out the window. "How can you stand knowing all of this? There's so much, and it's all so terrible."

"Yes. But I just know it, I didn't do it. There's no one, no government or people occupying the moral high ground, no matter what George Bush and the administration says. I don't condone it, I just learn about it and write stories for the newspaper. It's what we do. It's our job."

"Are we the good guys, Tommy?"

Tommy laughed. "No, not particularly. Sometimes I'm afraid I take too much joy in what I do to be a good guy. Our job is to sell newspapers. I guess if we do good along the way, then that makes us better than a lot of people. I've been looking under rocks for twenty-five years now and I still don't know whether people are basically good or fundamentally evil. I just do my job."

"You do more than that, Tommy."

"Yeah. I sell a lot of newspapers."

"Oh," she said, smiling, "the tough, cynical, world-weary reporter. Cut it out, Tommy, I've been around newsrooms too long to believe that one. Reporters really believe they're saving the world, exposing crime and corruption. The reason you turn rocks over is to let in the light. That's the reason we're making this trip, isn't it?"

"The reason I'm making the trip is to see if there's a link between what the Japanese did in World War II to terrorists today. Also I'm going along to protect you. Pretty young girls need the protection of fat old men."

Molly laughed. The PA system called for boarding and the two of them joined the line shuffling into the airplane. A kimonoed stewardess met them at the door and pointed them to their seats.

Hours later, over the Pacific, in the darkened cabin, Molly sat staring at the blackness outside the window. She could see only a reflection of herself, looking even more ragged and tired, and Tommy, stretched out in his seat, staring at the ceiling of the airplane. Time, wear, and several drinks had finally slowed him down. The cabin was quiet, only the muffled rumble of the planes engines and the occasional brush of a passing stewardess broke the fatigued quiet.

Molly smiled at the reflection of Tommy's bulk, squeezed into the airline seat.

"What's so funny," he asked her. "I fail to see any humor in our present situation. Unless you find body- and mind-numbing air travel amusing."

"No," she said, shaking her head. "Just something you said earlier. About how you were coming along to protect me. I was just thinking that now I've got two steadfast tin soldiers to take care of me. One very large one."

Tommy grunted. "And who's the other?"

"Alex." Tommy and Alex had met at several office functions. Both had liked each other, having a mutual passion for history.

"Alex has always seen it as his role in our life. The tin soldier guarding the ballerina. It was his favorite fairy tale as a child. *The Steadfast Tin Soldier.* Only then I think the ballerina needing his protection was his mother."

"That's a role that most boys play," Tommy said. "I myself remember guarding my mother from several extremely fierce dragons. Only in my older years I never replaced her with my own fair damsel."

"He used to recite it to me. Other girls get Shakespeare. I got Hans Christian Andersen. "The little ballerina was standing at the open door of the castle. She was cut out of cardboard, but she had a skirt of the finest gauze. Over her shoulders, like a scarf, she wore a narrow blue ribbon. And in the middle of the ribbon was a tinsel rose." Molly glanced at herself in the window. "That's me, Tommy, cut out of cardboard wearing a tinsel rose." She looked at Tommy. He was asleep, cheeks puffing in a gentle snore. She whispered the next line to herself. "That would be the wife for me, thought the little tin soldier, but she is much too grand and lives in a castle." *I've changed my mind, Alex. Wherever you are. I'm tired of living in this castle. It's too much work building the walls and repelling the invaders. I surrender. When we get home. When we get home . . .*

38

THEY WHEELED HIM DOWN THE GANGPLANK
in a box. A large wooden crate that had once contained food for the
ship's crew, and now contained Alex, a few stray cracks of light and
air, and a musty heavy odor emanating from the wet wood of the crate.

The ship's captain and carpenter had gone along with the ruse
without a murmur. Tubbs told them Alex was a German saboteur who
needed to enter Japan under conditions of the greatest secrecy. On a
mission for the Emperor himself.

They rolled him down the gangplank, the box bouncing over the
crossbraces as Alex held himself upright against the inside walls. There
was only room to sit, legs up, with a few inches between his head and
the top. They left him on the dock. The box grew unbearably hot in
the sun, the day stretching on and on in an agony of heat, thirst, and
aching discomfort. After hours of sitting scrunched up, he longed to
straighten out his legs. He passed the time imagining Donovan of the
OSS trapped in a box on a wharf in Japan. The only thing wrong with
the image was the probability that the crusty bastard would find some
way to enjoy it. Hatch his plans, play with his suicide pill. Night came
and the cold and loneliness seemed worse than the heat of the day.
Alex sat in his box and listened to the rats gnawing on the wood, trying
to chew their way inside to reach the old food ground into the floor of
the crate. Perhaps they smelled the two rice balls he had been given
to sustain him. He nibbled on the rice and finally, unable to withstand
the call of nature any longer, he wriggled himself around and urinated
in the corner nearest the sound of scratching rats.

Long before light began to appear at the cracks of his box, the dock area began to stir with life. He listened to the rapid-fire shouting and chattering of Japanese and Korean laborers, the sliding thudding sounds of men shifting freight. He held his breath as his box was picked up and carried a short distance and dropped. The box was skidded and rocked into a new position. He prayed that the wood would hold together. He envisioned the sides falling apart, leaving him cast down amid the rubble with a gang of Japanese laborers staring open-mouthed at the white devil-spy. Police. Haul him away to the city's darkest dungeons. Put him to death.

"Alex-san!" A harsh stage whisper outside the box. "Are you all right, old boy?"

Tubbs had returned. Alex thought about remaining silent, perhaps giving the delinquent Tubbs something to worry about, but it didn't seem worth it. He made a small noise.

"Ah, good. I must make this short, I cannot be seen conversing with a wooden box. Ha ha. You will be picked up soon and transported to the Nichi. I have hired a driver. Please remain quiet. Do you understand?" Alex answered with a grunt. *Just get me out of this god-damned box.*

HE WAS LOADED onto some sort of vehicle. He tried to keep track of time and distance, but the constant stop and go made it impossible. He hadn't the slightest idea where he was, had been, or was headed. The sounds of a city were all around him, muffled by the box, but still evident. Finally the truck stopped and he was unloaded and moved into some sort of shelter. After the box unloaders left, it was as quiet as a tomb. He had no idea how long he waited, hours certainly, perhaps years. The creak of a door. The sound of a light switch.

He cringed as a loud hammering commenced at the top of the box. He peered up and could see a crowbar inching through above him. With a nerve-jangling screech the top was pried back and light poured in. For a moment he was too stunned by the light to move. Tubbs peered in at him. "There you are," Tubbs said. "Rise and shine."

Alex pulled himself up by the sides of the crate. His legs unfolded with all the ease of a rusty jacknife.

"Welcome to the Nichi, Alex-san." Alex looked around. They were in some sort of storage shed, walls lined with crates and barrels. The interior was lit by a row of unshaded bare bulbs. "We have made it," Tubbs went on. "We are here. I have brought you clothing of a foreign type. You will put it on, and you will become a German, just as we planned." Tubbs handed him a pile of clothing.

New clothes, yes, a disguise. The visiting German scientist. Herr Balfour. First, get out of the goddamn box.

He climbed out, shrugged, and stripped off his old tan pants and shirt. The clothing was reasonably clean, and almost fit. Wool pants, white cotton shirt, incredibly ugly necktie, and a suitcoat. It was hot and itchy. "Very fine clothing," Tubbs said. "Top drawer. They were the property of an Englishman who was here when war was declared. He had to leave very quickly. I kept them against his return, but you may have them. What we do is more important."

Alex walked around the box and stretched. His muscles and joints were beginning to loosen up. "All right, Tubbs. What time is it? Where the hell are we? Can I get something to eat? And where's the nearest bathroom? We'll start with the last first."

"Follow me," Tubbs said.

TUBBS SHOWED HIM an outhouse behind the shed. Tubbs went away to find him something to eat, and brought back a small black tray with rice balls and pickled radishes. The rice was studded with small flecks of fish. They sat on packing crates in the shed while Alex wolfed down the rice. He ate with his fingers. Tubbs watched in silence. There was a covered cup of tea which Alex found hot and spiritually soothing after his days in the crate. He held the warm cup between both hands and inhaled the smoky vapor from the pale green tea. While he drank, he felt as if the hot liquid were seeping into every cell of his body. He finished the tea and set the cup on the wooden tray. "All right. I'll live. I'm not even going to ask you what the hell took so long back there on the wharf."

"Alex-san . . ." Tubbs began. Alex waved him into silence. "I know, it wasn't easy. You had to fill out forms, clear it with someone, whatever. I'll forget it until someday I've got you in a box. Ever try to take a piss while you're sitting in a wooden box?"

"No, Alex. Actually I have never—"

"Forget it, Tubbs, it was a rhetorical question." He stood up and walked in a circle, easing the kinks out of his muscles. "Let's get on with it. Your job is to show me what you've got and then get me in with the embassy personnel that are being shipped back. I'm going to want to talk to someone from the Catholic church pretty soon, but we'll get to that later."

Tubbs looked confused. "Are you a religious man, Alex?"

"Extremely. Every day I pray." *To get my ass home as quickly as possible. Contact the local Catholic church, Donovan had said.* "Don't worry about it. Like I said, we'll take care of it later. Right now I want the grand tour. I want to get outside this building where I can get some air into my lungs."

Tubbs nodded and stood up. "But now we must speak in German. No more English. And you must remember that there are many here who also speak German. We have studied in Germany under the great physicists. Most of whom are now in America, I am sorry to say."

Alex pressed his hands to his lower back and stretched. "I'm not sorry to say it," he said. He rolled his shoulders and rubbed his neck. "If the Nazis hadn't been so stupid, they wouldn't have chased them all out. And killed the ones that didn't leave. Their theories of the master race did away with the one group of people who could have won the war for them. The Jews. Do you understand how odious your allies are, Tubbs?"

The Japanese narrowed his eyes. "I understand some things, Alex-san. Some things I simply do not care about. The German war in Europe matters little to me. You say the Germans are stupid, that they have lost the war. You might try to tell that to those Germans here in Japan, I'm sure they would be interested. We are not stupid. We realize that their concept of race does not include Orientals any more than it includes Jews. The Germans are our allies because they have need of supplies that we can provide. And we are allied to them for the same reason. We are not interested in Europe. We are concerned with Asia. We are attempting to remove the white man from Asian lands. Forever. The Dutch, the English, the Russians, the Americans, and even the Germans. You will all go. If not now, in this war, then eventually. Asia will not be the colony of the West. Make no mistake, I am your enemy. I am a Japanese. If I, and others in the scientific community, are aware that we are no longer winning this war, this does not mean I would have wished this to be so." He bowed to Alex. "You are here to see that any victory you might eventually attain will be at great cost. Greater than your country will be willing to pay, I believe." He looked Alex in the eye and Alex could see that the man was neither foolish nor afraid. "We Japanese do one thing better than you Americans. It is a thing that cannot be equaled by bombs or technology, by force or size. We die well, Alex. We are prepared to die. Are you?"

Not if I can help it. Alex bowed back. "Allow me to suggest, Tubbs, that if the willingness to die is your greatest strength, then it is also your greatest weakness."

Tubbs smiled and nodded. "Perhaps. But it entails serious consequences for your side. I do not wish my people to die. That is why I have brought you here. I will show you that it is *your* people who will die on our beaches. As well as ours."

They stared at each other for a long moment. "Then show me," Alex said.

39

ALEX STOOD IN THE BRIGHT AFTERNOON sunlight. Somehow, he had expected it to be night. He squinted his eyes against the sun and searched for the source of the sound he had been hearing since he'd climbed out of his box, a half-recognized background memory, louder now. Children playing. He shaded his eyes and scanned the field in front of him. At the far end of the dry brown field he could make out a gang of small boys. They were chasing each other around a series of stakes set in concentric circles, laughing and shouting. He turned to Tubbs.

"I thought this was a research facility."

Tubbs gestured around them. "It is. But we have a boys' school. Some of us teach there when we can. It is for those who have been orphaned by the war."

Alex looked behind him. They were in a cluster of ten or twelve low wooden buildings. There was a high wall that extended around the buildings and the large field in front of them. Beyond the wall, Alex could see the tops of other buildings, a city, and in the distance a series of green hills. Then a rush of fear hit him: the city was full of Japanese, the same people he'd just spent weeks trying his damndest to kill. *Does it show? Is there a mark on me, a scarlet K, a stigmata, some identifying characteristic?* He wondered if he was responsible for any of the young boys being out there on the playground. He watched the children and felt the fear begin to fade. It seemed that the longer he was under constant threat, the shorter the flashes of near-panic. It was as if his body could sustain severe anxiety for only a limited amount of time. His adrenaline-response was weakening. It wasn't a matter of bravery, but physiology. *If they knew what I had done, what I am doing, they would tear me apart. Do the job, get out, go home.*

"Where do we start?" Alex asked, looking around.

"That is a surprise, Herr Balfour. Remember, only *Deutsch* from now on. And please, no more Tubbs. I am Saburo Tomishiro. You may call me Tomishiro, and you will be Alex or Herr Balfour. We must be very careful. There are many who would kill us in a moment if they knew what we were doing. They would not understand that we are involved in negotiation rather than treachery." He paused for a moment. "This is very important, please pay close attention. The laboratory is not completely under the control of the scientists. The military maintains the prisoners of war who are interned here. It is a very small contingent, but they are closely watched. The commander of this unit is Colonel Udo. He is a very dangerous man. To your Western eyes he may appear ridiculous, but do not mistake his loud voice for bluster. He and I have opposed one another many times. Until now I have been able to contain his efforts and excesses to his own unit. Do not give him the excuse he is searching for to extend his control over the scientific areas of the Nichi. Now, if that is clear, please follow me, I think you will be interested in our laboratories."

BOTH THE EXTERIOR and the interior of the two-story office building appeared very ordinary.

The ground floor and above were administrative offices. There were bowing, smiling secretaries, and nods and handshakes from various officials.

Alex was issued a pass. They clipped it onto his shirt. At the stairway that led downward they encountered a tough-looking Army sergeant in leggings who scrutinized Alex's pass for several unending moments, *he can see, he knows*, and then motioned them abruptly on.

Down.

THEY ENTERED a long hallway through a steel door at the bottom of three steep flights of concrete steps. The wide hallway was well lit, the cement walls painted a soft gray. At twenty-foot intervals young Japanese soldiers were stationed beside a series of doors. These guards stood at attention, rifles at their sides. Alex and Tubbs walked by the guards without a flicker or twitch from the Japanese. Alex looked straight ahead and concentrated on the incongruity between the soldiers, the gray steel doors they guarded, and the softly lit hallway. In another world or time, minus the guards, he would have expected the soft blur of Muzak, maybe an employees' cafeteria with ranks of vending machines and tables of chatting workers. "Where are we, and what are these rooms we are passing?" Alex asked as they passed the last of the guards, remembering to speak German.

"We are thirty feet underground and these rooms belong to various units attached to the Nichi. This particular section is the realm of Colonel Udo, and you would be wise to ignore it. As you will be studying only one phase of our scientific endeavors, there is no reason for you to concern yourself with the other areas." The hallway abutted in an L. They passed through an unguarded metal gate with bars and continued down the hallway to the left. There were other Japanese, men and women, walking and talking in this area. Some of these white-coated workers glanced at him, but most paid no attention.

Alex was just beginning to appreciate the size of the underground complex when Tubbs stopped before a door, opened it, and went through. Inside, Alex stared at the room that spread out around them. His grudging admiration at the scope of this underground engineering achievement now turned to awe. The room was huge. Long tables with chemical and electrical equipment ran in four rows down the center of the room. Along one wall was a row of desks and offices. At the far end was an open space where several large machines sat in various states of fabrication. A twenty-foot-high tubular machine, looking like a small silo set down in a shallow well, swarmed with workers. On his left, stretching the length of the room, was an elongated doughnut-shaped metal machine that Alex recognized as a cyclotron. The air smelled of electricity, hot insulation, soldering irons, and freshly welded metal.

Tubbs was greeted with "*Konnichi wa*," and "*Ogenki desu ka?*" which Alex assumed meant "Hello" and "How are you?" Tubbs bowed but retained a serious expression as he led Alex to one of the offices. These were three-sided cubicles with a half wall looking out on the workroom. Tubbs's window was glassed in, but the other offices were open to the large room.

"Aren't they curious about me? Isn't someone going to ask questions about a mysterious white man?" Alex asked. Tubbs sat behind a West-ern-style desk. Alex sat on a wooden office chair.

"They may be curious, but they will not show it. In our work we have learned to accept the unusual without comment. We exist within a closed web of secrecy and at the same time there is the need to consult with others, to share our discoveries. It is difficult to know who to trust, and equally difficult to know who to question. We are scientists. We answer to the military, but they allow us to administer our own affairs. The sight of a Westerner is rare, but not unique. There are Italians in Japan, many Germans. There are even Americans who are married to Japanese. Most of us have studied in Europe. Do not expect to be accepted, but you will also not be rejected because of your skin. Later, when we eat, you will meet some of the people who work here. Until then simply nod. As a German you have little need to show your emotions."

"That's fine with me. I'm not here to fraternize. Let's get on with it."

Tubbs nodded and stood. "Let us begin, Herr Balfour."

THE TALL SILO-SHAPED machine at the far end of the room was a thermal separator, one of the several methods used to refine U-235 from the heavier U-238. "The raw ore is mined in Korea," Tubbs said, standing before the silo with his hands clasped behind him. "It is refined there and shipped to us. We create crystals of uranium hexa-fluoride, which is turned into a gas and separated here. There are some difficulties, to be sure, but the process is sound. We are also exploring the possibility of using our mass spectrometer as a method of isotope separation, but I believe the thermal method will be the avenue we pursue. On a larger scale, of course."

"Where is your reactor?" Alex asked. He was already in trouble. His threadbare knowledge of nuclear physics was beginning to wear through at the elbows. He understood that his primary job was simply to observe, and remember what he had seen, and stay alive to report back. But faced with the tables of fantastic equipment and the obvious complexity of the technology, he began to doubt his ability to keep it all straight. One thing he *did* know was that you needed a reactor to teach you the basics of the fission process if you were going to put all the other parts of the bomb puzzle together. He had seen pictures of the original American reactor, assembled by Enrico Fermi, a huge Rubik's Cube of graphite blocks in a squash court at the University of Chicago. He knew that a reactor was big and black, a square temple to the atomic gods, and there wasn't anything in this room that resembled it.

"Ah, yes, the reactor. We are working on that. We have several models that we will utilize. We are using the heavy water technique. The deuterium is rare, but we have obtained an adequate supply from our fellow scientists in your country, Herr Balfour, and from Korea. I hear the Americans are using graphite for theirs, a workable method, but not as efficient as the heavy water."

Tubbs stared up at the separator and bounced on the balls of his feet, an attitude that Alex thought he must have learned at Cambridge. *How does he know that we're using graphite? The whole Manhattan Project is beginning to look like a piece of Swiss cheese.* "Show me more, Tomishiro," he said, trying to look as if he were scanning the room through a monacle. Tubbs nodded approvingly and began a tour of the room that took the rest of the day and left Alex's head spinning with terminology that he knew he would never remember. Remember what things look like, Donovan had said. Forget the words, we've got guys who will pry the words out of you. *Cold comfort,* Alex thought.

Alex was assigned a room in an outside, ground-level dormitory, situated near the building that led to the underground complex. The room was small, no more than five feet wide and eight feet long, and had a rolled futon for sleeping, a small chest for his clothing, and a low writing desk with paper and pen. There were many other sleeping rooms and a communal dining room. Most of the Nichi workers lived in this building, though Tubbs did not. He had shown Alex to this small room and departed, promising to come back for him in an hour to take him to dinner.

Alex sat crosslegged on the woven straw tatami mat in his room and contemplated his future. It was the sort of monk's room that encouraged contemplation. So far, he was unscathed. His journey and arrival had been conspicuously uneventful, if floating in the ocean for a week, being machine-gunned by your own side, and sitting in a box for more than a day and a night surrounded by an entire nation of enemies could be thought of as uneventful. *Anything short of death or torture is uneventful.*

He wanted to try and get a look at some of the other facilities at the Nichi. What he had seen of the nuclear physics lab had been impressive, at least to his novice's eyes. Then he needed to get in touch with whatever emissary of the Catholic Church was resident here. Then he had to get his ass out of Japan and back to America so he could report in and attempt to sort out everything that he had learned. The evidence, on the face of it, seemed persuasive. The Japanese were undertaking a large-scale atomic bomb project. But Japan would never get the bomb in time to use it. They would in fact hide the possibility that they had ever even attempted such a thing, just as they hid the fact that Hirohito was an active participant in Japan's war plans. But was it his, Alex's, place in history to be the man who brought about that particular outcome? Was he here to ensure the time line that contained an atomic bomb that was indeed dropped on the Japanese? And how could he live with such a possibility?

Apparently, it had not occurred to Tubbs that if Alex reported on Japan's attempts to build a bomb, this would surely spur the Americans on to an increased effort. Alex thought that Tubbs was operating from a cultural position that contributed to this belief. The Japanese really felt that their natural superiority would see them through no matter what, even if they lost the war. They also assumed thirty feet of dirt and concrete overhead was enough to protect them from bombs of any variety. The natural superiority was bullshit, but the concrete was probably enough protection for the lab against conventional weapons. And probably against the early atomic bombs. So maybe Tubbs and his superiors *did* think it possible that the Americans could get an atomic bomb first and drop it on Hiroshima. If they could accept the loss of life above, they were probably right in thinking that the lab could keep right on working.

Alex shifted on his mat. It crinkled under him. He liked the way it felt, and how it made the room smell of freshly mown hay. He also liked the austere cleanliness of his room. It wasn't home, but it sure beat the hell out of a wooden box.

By the time Tubbs returned, Alex was so deep in contemplation that he was snoring.

THE COMMUNAL DINING ROOM reminded Alex of college. Most of the faces were fairly young, and being Japanese, everyone seemed even younger than they probably were. The great majority of workers ate at long low tables. Alex and Tubbs ate at one of the few small individual tables which seemed to be reserved for senior personnel. As Alex squeezed his legs under the table, he thought that this was probably a Japanized version of the Cambridge-style method of dining.

The room was filled with the chatter of men and women. The ubiquitous lab coats were gone, replaced by Western-style clothes for the men, and a sort of pants and jacket uniform for the women. The dining room was decorated in the same Zen-minimalist manner as his sleeping room. The dark wooden tables were spotlessly clean, buffed to a high sheen. The floor was covered with tatami mats. Shoes were parked near the doorway. Serving women collected trays of food at one end of the hall and delivered them to the tables. A young girl handed Alex and Tubbs their food, bowed, and went away. Alex ate silently. Along with the usual rice ball and pink pickled radish, he was given a bowl of clear hot soup. A slice of daikon, a large white Japanese radish, floated in the broth. Alex drank the soup straight from the bowl and watched the other tables. The mood was dignified but still lively. The men and women segregated themselves as to sex, but looks were passed between the two groups. All of which tended to reinforce Alex's first impression of the group as college-oriented.

His gaze stopped at the table farthest from him. At the end, with a group of other woman, sat a Caucasian woman with short brown hair. She was dressed in the same dark blue uniform as many of the others, but her height and hair color gave her away.

"My wife was very grateful to see me, Herr Balfour," Tubbs said conversationally. "I must say she rather thought I would not return." He gave Alex a small smile. "I am like the bad penny, am I not. Always dropping in?"

Jesus. Japanese small talk. "As you say, Tomishiro. By the way, who's the European woman at the far table?" Tubbs's eyes flickered to the table and back to his tray of food.

"I do not know. She is not in my section." He looked up at Alex. "My children were very happy to see me. Do you have children?"

Alex felt himself flush. "No. I am married, but we have no children." He was surprised at how the lie slipped out. *What am I going to do, explain how modern couples live together?* "My wife's name is Molly." He found he liked saying it. Wife. But saying it opened up the gulf of feelings that surrounded her name: home, safety. Love.

Tubbs nodded. "I am sure you must miss her. When this war is over, there will be no need for such separations. A man's duty is to his family. After his duty to the state, of course."

"She has red hair," Alex went on. "And she works for the New York *Times.*"

Tubbs looked sharply at him. "Your wife works?" he said very carefully. "You, ah, Germans are curious people. But that is probably the reason you have no children. And surely you mean that she *used* to work for a foreign newspaper."

Alex suddenly realized that he was digging his own grave with his mouth. He casually looked around the room. No one was listening, or at least no one seemed to be listening. But a German national announcing that his wife worked for an enemy newspaper was the sort of stupid error that would land him in a prison cell, or worse. There were surely members of the Kempeitai, the Japanese secret police, in the room. Or at least people who would report to them. No group of workers so important to the war effort would be exempt from police spying. Tubbs seemed to wield a certain amount of power. He might be able to shield Alex from close examination for a time, but there were limits. Alex stared at his rice bowl until he had control of himself, amazed at how a wash of homesickness could unhinge one's brain. And then it came to him. Out of nowhere, the answer slid home. He looked at the end of the long table at the thin, pretty woman with the short brown hair and a picture formed, a memory of a newspaper photograph, the woman in another time and place, standing on the wing of an airplane, smiling, waving to an unseen crowd.

Amelia Earhart.

40

THE LAST RAYS OF THE EVENING SUN
flamed orange across the bottoms of a drifting range of high billowy
clouds. The air was warm. Alex walked across the wide field toward
the boys' school, toward the setting sun. He stopped at the edge of the
playground, examining the concentric rows of seven-foot-high posts,
trying to imagine what Japanese boys' game was played in and among
the trunks of this man-made forest. He touched one of the thick posts.
Large chunks had been chewed away. Sharp slivers of wood pricked
his fingers. He heard footsteps behind him, felt the hair on the back
of his neck begin to stand. He held himself very still. "Good evening,"
he said in German, turning around slowly. It was Earhart.

"I don't speak German," she said mildly. Her voice was flat, Midwestern, but not harsh. Up close she didn't look as determined as she
always had in the pictures he'd seen of her. The kid-sister spunkiness
was gone, replaced by wariness, a narrowing of the eyes, caution. And
of age, and strain. She went on, still speaking quietly. "You don't need
to pretend with me. Are you English or American?"

"Why aren't I a German?" he asked in English.

"German men walk like they've got a riding crop up their ass. Even
when they're taking the evening air. You walk like a normal person.
Don't worry, the Japs don't notice things like that."

Alex turned away from her, uncertain. Was she a friend? This
was Amelia Earhart, for Christ's sake. Girl hero, friend of the President, model for American Womanhood. "Looks like beavers have been
at these things," he said, running his hand along the side of a post,

giving himself time to think. He had no idea whose side she was on. As far as the rest of the world knew, she was dead. Gone down in the Pacific on the last leg of her around-the-world flying attempt. He thought for a moment. Nineteen thirty-seven. Six years ago. She would be forty-three years old now. Here she was, seemingly working with the Japanese. But then so was he. He picked at the rough wood. "Maybe termites. Something's been gnawing at these poles. Be tough on the kids if they run into them."

She made a small noise. "It's a lot tougher on the poor bastards they tie up here." She pointed at the center of the circle. The soft earth appeared recently plowed and then smoothed. Tamped down by hundreds of small feet.

"They explode their bombs in the center. The experiments are to measure the destructive capability of whatever poisons they've infected the bombs with. As a matter of fact I wouldn't touch anything. If you pick up a splinter it could kill you." Alex jerked his hand from the post. She walked away, and he followed.

"But the kids . . ." he began.

"Notice how there's no grass here? The guy who mowed the grass died of some strange disease. Nice old guy. So they dug up the grass. They keep the kids inside. They keep everyone inside, while it's going on and for a week after. Until they get it cleaned up. I've seen it, though. Terrible. They all eventually die. Americans, Brits, Aussies. Koreans and Chinese. They do a lot of tests out here." She led the way up a low mound of earth against the wall. At the top they could just see over. The wall was studded with broken glass and strung with razor-edged wire. The spidery wire trembled in the light breeze. The sun was now a deep rose suggestion on the horizon. Earhart looked at the sun as if she were studying it, calculating distances. Alex was surprised to see water, a bay or wide river. The gray buildings of a city were evident in the distance. A high bright dome caught the last rays of sun. The dome was familiar, but he could not quite place it. "Where are we?" he asked.

"Hiroshima. What's your name?"

"Alex Balfour." He couldn't think of any reason to lie. She'd seen through his German disguise easily enough. And then it came to him. The domed building would be one of the few left standing after the atomic bomb. It would become known as the Peace Dome.

"I used to know a Harry Balfour. A radio operator. Good friend of mine. I wanted him to come with me on the flight, but he wouldn't do it. Stuck me with that drunk Fred Noonan. Poor Fred. The Japs chopped off his head for dumping a bowl of soup on them. He might have been a drunk, but he was a brave man." Earhart rested her arms on the top of the wall. If the pieces of glass bothered her, she didn't show it. "Who are you, Balfour?"

"Nobody. You don't want to know." He glanced back at the playground. Only now it wasn't a playground. He couldn't shake the image of men tied to the posts, bombs exploding. Biological warfare. For a moment he thought of Molly.

"They tie them up and cover their bodies with a kind of chain mail armor," she said, seeing where he was looking. Her voice was still perfectly matter-of-fact. "They leave their buttocks exposed to the blast. Sometimes I think the Japanese are insane. All of them." She turned to face him. Her eyes were light blue, her expression still guarded. While time had taken away her little-girl prettiness, it had left her with a kind of calm that seemed in this time and place to be beauty. In the evening light her skin was still smooth, unlined. "What you mean is you're not going to tell me who you are," she said.

The new image, men bound and draped in chain mail, was worse than the one he'd first imagined. Much worse. He concentrated on her. "You'd just get in trouble if you knew," he said.

She smiled thinly. "Just get in trouble?" She turned back away. "What do you think I've been in for the last six years? I saw you at dinner tonight with Tomishiro. Heard you pretending to be a German. Are you a double agent?"

"I could ask you the same question." He remembered Donovan saying the same thing to him. This business of being a spy seemed to always reduce itself to two suspicious strangers asking each other who the hell they were and whose side they were on.

"Jesus Christ." She shook her head in exasperation. "Okay, to hell with it. I think we're on the same side, Alex. Let's knock off the twenty questions and operate on that premise. I don't know what your pal Tomishiro's up to, but you don't seem slick enough to be a traitor or a German. If I were you I'd be damn careful around Colonel Udo. Have you come across the colonel yet?" Alex shook his head. "He's the head honcho in the prison unit. Works real tight with the germ warfare people. Not exactly a security officer but he'd like to be. He can't stand the scientists and the feeling is mutual. He acts like a character out of central casting but stay away from him. He's dangerous." She stopped and then sighed. "It's damn good to have someone to talk English to, Balfour. Let's get inside before the guards start their rounds. We're not allowed out here at night."

HER ROOM was twice as large as his. There were shelves for books and a chest of drawers for her clothing. A black lacquer screen stood in one corner of the room. Carved ivory warriors in bas-relief dueled across the face of the screen.

The sleeping arrangements were the same, as were the inevitable tatami mats on the floor. There was an ink brush painting on the wall: Mount Fuji with a bird flying high over the snowy crest. Earhart knelt on the floor Japanese-style, and poured tea from a large earthen teapot. "One of the girls brings me tea every night," she said. "I've come to depend on it."

"How long have you been here?"

"I've been a prisoner in Japan for six years. Here for the last two. This isn't bad. I've seen a hell of a lot worse."

"No one knows you're alive." He sipped at the tea. It was hot and grassy-tasting. "The official verdict is that you and your navigator ran out of fuel and crashed somewhere in the Pacific."

"And the unofficial verdict?" she asked.

"That's the subject of controversy. Some people evidently have it right; they say you're a prisoner of the Japanese. That you were on a spy mission for Roosevelt and got shot down over the Marshall Islands. That the Japs were doing a lot of military work on the islands and couldn't let you go once you'd seen it. There are other theories."

Earhart was smiling to herself, as if the idea of being the subject of controversy was pleasing. "They've got the part about being a prisoner right enough. But I'm not dead yet." She smiled at Alex. "The next time the world sees me they're never going to forget it. And not just because I've returned from the grave." She stood up and put her cup on the shelf. "I'm going to change my clothes, Alex. Help yourself to more tea." She was wearing the same black cotton pants that most of the other women wore. She went behind the screen. Alex could hear her humming tunelessly to herself, hear the soft rustling of clothing. When she came back she was dressed in a kimono worn as a robe. It was slippery blue silk with orange maple leaves cascading from the shoulders. The silk fell in planes, angled over her thin body. She'd brushed her soft shoulder-length hair.

"Tell me about this place," Alex said. "It's not exactly a prison, is it?"

She shrugged and sat back down. "For the workers it's better than living on the outside, in the city. It's safe; there's still plenty of food as long as you like rice. But for the prisoners it's worse than a POW camp. There they keep you in a cage, beat you, work you. Here they use the men for experiments. They kill them in terrible ways. Not me, I'm in no danger. They need me." She picked up a pack of German cigarettes from the bookshelf and handed him one. They smoked for a minute. The cigarette tasted like sawdust to Alex.

"Is this allowed, me being in here?" he asked. He couldn't figure this woman at all. Was she a prisoner or wasn't she?

"It's allowed if I say it is. They let me do what I want, at least within the limits of the grounds. There are guards out at night. There's the wall. And where would you go if you could get out? We're on an island. The Japs have a funny notion of security. Once you're inside, they figure you belong. Like I said, where would you go? What would you do? There's no escape, I decided that long ago. There's only one way for me to get out of here, and I'll get to that in a minute. Jesus, it feels so good to just talk. It's been six long years, and you're the first American I've talked to in all that time."

She handed him a pillow to lean against. She was still kneeling, sitting back on her ankles without apparent effort. Her eyes were fixed on the brush painting of Mt. Fuji on the wall behind him. She lit another cigarette with quick nervous movements. The air was thick with smoke, hanging in blue-gray veils. For the first time Alex noticed that there were no windows in the room.

"I don't know who you are, or what you are," she began, "but you're here. That's going to have to be enough. I've been careful for six years. Planned every detail for the last two years. Now I'm taking a chance on a guy who shows up pretending to be a Nazi, playing pals with the head of the unit." She shook her head. She looked at him and sighed. "I've never been known for not taking a chance. What the hell." Her eyes returned to the brush painting.

"I should have studied up on radio techniques, but I thought that Fred knew all we had to know. He was the navigator, so let him worry about the radio. Turns out that Fred didn't know much more than I did. He was a seat-of-the-pants navigator. Best in the world at one time. It had gone pretty well. We were on the last leg of the trip. Across the Pacific to San Francisco and we were home. It was going to be my last piece of stunt flying." She smiled. "I guess it was. No, not the last." The smile went away. "There's one more. Anyway, we took off from New Guinea headed for Howland Island. Once we made it there it was clear flying to the States. Trouble is, we never found Howland. Fred was so hung over we had to carry him to the plane. By the time he came around we were already lost. I've flown it a thousand times in my mind and I'm still not sure what happened. I think we were off-course to the northwest. We hit some weather. I couldn't raise anyone on the radio, at least not long enough to get a fix on the direction finder. Finally I decided to turn around and fly back to the Gilberts, but by then we were too far north. We flew straight back to the Marshalls, right into the arms of the Japanese." She stopped talking. Alex waited a minute.

"Then all the spy stuff was wrong?"

She laughed without humor. "No, at least not exactly. Franklin asked me to fly over the Marshalls and take pictures. I told him he was crazy, that it was too dangerous. I told him if something went wrong I might never get out. I couldn't carry enough fuel to fly that far out of the way. I was right, wasn't I? It's crazy how things work out, isn't it?" Alex nodded. In his mind he saw Franklin D. Roosevelt as a spider, sitting in his wheelchair in the center of a gigantic web. All of them, Earhart, Max, Einstein, himself, Welles, Donovan, all of them were little flies stuck in the web. Roosevelt held all the strands, plucking one, then another.

"So we ditched near this little coral atoll, Mili Mili. The Japs rounded us up in a matter of hours. Fred was hurt, he'd split his head open and cut his knee when we hit the water. They patched him up and hauled us away. Eventually we ended up at their big base on Saipan. That's where Fred bought it. They were starving us, feeding us one bowl of soup a day. We were getting weaker all the time. Fred couldn't take it, said he'd just as soon be dead as slowly dying."

THE GUARD CAME and handed Fred Noonan his bowl of thin soup. He stood absolutely still, staring at the bowl. They were both dressed in rags. Dirty. Starving. She took her bowl and began to sip at it, watching

Fred in the adjacent cell, feeling the tension in his thin body as he stood stock-still with just the faintest tremor in his hands. "Eat the soup, Fred," she said, trying to calm him. "It's the only thing that's going to keep us alive." He looked at her and she could see it in his eyes. He was already somewhere else. "It's no use, Amelia. I just can't take this shit any longer."

Fred moved to the bars and called the guard. Very calmly he told the guard that he was a piece of dog shit, and that his mother was dog shit, and that each of his ancestors was dog shit. When the guard, who spoke no English, didn't react, Fred threw the bowl of soup in his face. And then the Japanese went berserk. It was so fast. They were on him, kicking, screaming, beating him. In the blur of fists and feet she could see him twisting on the floor. His face was bloody and already swelling, but he was smiling. Grimly. For the first time in months he was smiling.

She stood at the bars of the window, holding herself upright, as they dragged him out into the dusty yard behind the cellblock. They made him kneel at the edge of a ditch. They lined up all the civilian workers and forced them to watch. Fred. Kneeling. Still smiling, eyes squeezed shut. She could smell the dust, feel the heat of the noonday sun outside baking the dirt of the prison yard. Her lips were dry, cracked. Her arms were trembling.

A short burly guard with a long sword stood behind Fred and with one terrible stroke took off his head. The head fell into the ditch. The body still knelt. Blood arced in a curving stream from the stump of his neck. The guard placed his foot in the center of Fred's back and kicked him into the ditch.

SHE STUBBED her cigarette out in a ceramic ashtray. "That's when I decided to live. I guess that was the difference between Fred and me, that might have been the difference all along. Fred gave up, first to the bottle, then to the sword. Not me. When I go, it's not going to be in a ditch. I'm going to give these bastards a run for it." She ran a hand through her hair. She seemed to shake off the story of her capture. "All right. Now you tell me what you want to know. I don't want to hear what your job is, I don't want to hear anything important. Just tell me what you need."

"As you said earlier, I need everything. I need to know exactly what this place is, what they're working on, various stages and progress on the work, what it is that you do here. All of it."

She sat back on the tatami mat and folded her legs under her, lotus-style. She moved the ashtray next to her and reached for another cigarette. "All right."

41

"THE NICHI IS THE MAIN CENTER FOR JAP war science. They do a little bit of everything here. Korea is where the heavy industry and the manufacturing take place, but the brain work originates down in the underground lab."

She seemed to settle into herself. She stared down at the ashtray. "In the two years I've been here, I've seen at least a little bit of almost everything that goes on. They're a strange bunch, these scientists, almost like children. They want to show you their toys, even when the toy is designed to kill men in the most awful ways. They're so puffed up and proud of themselves. They strut around, shouting and pointing, eager for you to pat them on the back. Especially me. For some reason they see me as someone who can bless their projects, provide dispensation. As if I'll understand that even though their work is killing my countrymen, I'll forgive them because they're so brilliant. I hate them and what they do. I can scarcely hide it, but they're so conceited they can't see it. They're so sure of their superiority that they're blind. They have blinded themselves." She looked up at Alex. "I work with them on jet propulsion. Do you know what that is?"

Alex nodded.

"We're building airplanes that will be powered by jet engines. They'll be faster than any craft now in existence. The Germans have sent us plans, which we are modifying. They even sent us a prototype, but it was shipped on a submarine that went to the bottom. We are building two airplanes, the Shusui and the Kikka. The fuel for the engines has been the most difficult part. I can't help them there, but the actual design and fabrication is something I *can* do. Something I *am* doing." She stared at him, her jaw forward. "You don't need to ask the obvious question. I'll ask it for you. Why am I helping if I hate them so much?" She leaned closer and lowered her voice.

"Because I'm going to build this goddamn airplane and then I'm going to steal it and fly myself out of here." Her pale skin was flushed. "These bastards have done unspeakable things to me. They killed Fred and until they decided I might be useful they were in the process of killing me. They have held me here against my will, and they have the audacity to think that I am helping them because they are the natural inheritors of this entire goddamn planet and no sane person, white or yellow, could ever doubt that for a moment. Think of it, Alex, picture the headlines. Amelia Earhart, in a stolen jet airplane, the first of its kind, flying out of here to an Allied air base, back from the dead. No man or woman has ever pulled off a stunt like this. And it'll be a real punch in the gut for the Japs. They'll look so bad they'll probably sue for peace out of sheer embarrassment.

"If they can just get the fuel right, I can give them the airplane. By the time we get everything worked out, the Allies ought to be plenty near enough for me to get to a friendly landing field. Even though there's a blackout here on real war news, I've heard that the Jap army is pulling back from some of the islands. All I've got to do is stay alive and in their good graces."

"How long will it take for the jets to become operational?"

"At least a year, maybe two."

He nodded. "We'll be well up the islands by then. If you can get one to fly, you'll make it out." For the first time since meeting her, she smiled her broad Amelia Earhart smile. "But what about the atomic research they're doing?" he asked.

"That's what the jets are for. They expect to make some sort of superbomb and deliver it on a suicide jet. The planes will get through because they'll be so fast. But you don't have to worry, I'll steal the prototype and they'll have to start over again." She crushed out her cigarette. "You believe me, don't you?"

He sat up. His bones ached from lying on the floor. To his mind, her plan was improbable. But this lady was already a hero, and he was beginning to find that things happen when you take chances. After all, here he was, sitting in the middle of the hornets' nest. Still alive. "I believe you. But I also need to know what else they're working on. And anything else you know about the atomic research."

"Well, I believe that jet propulsion will be the most important factor in the war. That and the death ray. They've got the ray set up in the lab beside ours. The ray project is run by Shunichi Yoshida, a smart guy."

"How big is the whole unit?"

She shook her head. "You wouldn't believe it. It's huge. They say it took ten years of digging to hollow it out. All on land that borders right on the water. Hundreds of men were killed building it. Besides the labs, they've got cells for a hundred prisoners. Anyway, besides the germ people, the death ray workers have the worst job. They're always complaining about headaches. They've got this machine that sends out electricity. I saw them kill a monkey with it."

"What are the prisoners used for?"

"Germ warfare. Nobody likes the germ people. Everyone stays away from them. They have to eat by themselves in the dining room. Sometimes Udo sits with them, but he's the only one. The prisoners are usually airman who've been shot down and picked up by the Navy. I stay away from the holding cells because that's where they expect me to go. Udo keeps his eye on me. If I'm going to get in that airplane, they've got to have absolute faith in Amelia Earhart." She stood up and listened at the door of her room.

"Anything?" Alex asked quietly as she sat back down.

"Nothing." It's really amazing how little eavesdropping there is here. The Japs have lived cheek to jowl for so many centuries that they've developed a privacy code that's damn near sacred. Even Udo doesn't hang around closed doors. I'm not so principled. I listen in when I can. I speak fluent Japanese. That's one of the things I worked on after I decided I was going to get out of here someday."

Alex shook his head when she offered him another cigarette. *How can she smoke those things? Sawdust and dog shit.* He was getting tired. His afternoon nap had helped, but he'd spent the last few days in a box. Talking to Earhart was turning surreal. Death rays, dead monkeys, germ warfare, atom bombs. All of it was beginning to flow into one vast sump of Japanese scientific madness. If everything that Earhart said they were working on came to fruition, the Japanese would have enough secret weapons to win this or any other war.

"Can you draw me a floor plan of this place?"

She shrugged. "I guess so, but you're never going to smuggle it out of here. How are you getting out anyway? Is your pal Tomishiro helping you?"

"Maybe," Alex said carefully. He watched as she found a set of brushes, inkstone, and rice paper. "Just what exactly does Tomishiro do here?" he asked.

She looked at him in surprise. "I thought you'd be the one to know that. He's the boss."

Alex sat for a moment, trying to assimilate this information. "How would you characterize his politics?"

She shrugged. "He's probably a Moderate. There's no such thing as a dissenter here. The secret police threw all of them in jail a long time ago, if they ever existed at all. The Japanese are strange." She laughed humorlessly. "Jesus, that's an understatement. Individually, most of the civilians will admit that they've probably already lost the war. No one thinks that Pearl Harbor was a good idea. The regular people hate the war, and hate the militarists who run the government. But no one will go against the leaders. A lot of that is their worship of the Emperor, but the whole society simply does as it's told. No one stands up for what he believes if he has to go against the government. At least no one I've ever met."

"It isn't because they don't have the guts," Alex said. "I've seen them in action, I can testify to their bravery."

"I know that," she said. "It's something else, some kind of craziness, or maybe some kind of weakness. I've been here six years and I don't understand it. I don't think any of us will ever understand it."

"I'm afraid you're right. And in the end they're going to pay for it."

ALEX STARED at Amelia's drawing of the underground lab. He was smoking another cigarette, hoping the harsh taste would wake him up. The L-shaped configuration of hallways was retained in the overall design. The holding cells for the prisoners were off the main hallway near the entrance where the heavy metal doors with the Jap guards were. He studied the map and rubbed his face, feeling the rough scratch of whiskers. He'd have to ask Tubbs to find him a razor. He'd only been one day in Japan, at least out of the box, and it felt like months. "What's this?" He pointed at the drawing of a small room with a lot of little diallike schematics.

"That's the radio room," she said, leaning close to him. He could smell her, the smell of soap. "Any guards there?" She shook her head. He felt a small thump of excitement. He remembered Donovan and his orders: *Get to a radio. Let them know if there really is a bomb lab in Hiroshima.*

"They only use it when one of the teams has to get in touch with some other scientists. Usually they're just calls to one of the universities. It's a shortwave. I've been in there when we've radioed Korea with instructions on our fuel project."

"Can I get into the room?"

She looked at him for a long moment before nodding. "Probably. If you look like you know what you're doing, you might get away with it. No one wants to offend our German friends. The door isn't locked; none of the doors here are locked. The only guards are in the hallway at the bottom of the steps."

Alex pushed the radio room to the back of his mind. He couldn't do anything right then. It would have to be during the day.

"If I can get you out of here, would you come with me? It might be dangerous."

She shook her head. "I'm not worried about the danger, but when I come out I'm doing it on my own. In the airplane that I helped build. I'm going to hurt these bastards and this is the only way I can do it."

"Maybe I can get some sort of help into you. If Roosevelt knows you're in here, he's sure to—"

She held up her hand. "No. No one is to know. It wouldn't do any good. In fact, they'd just foul up any chance I have of getting out with the jet. As far as the rest of the world is concerned, Amelia Earhart is dead. When I rise from the ashes it will be on my own wings. Either way I'll be flying, as an angel or as a hero. This idea is the only thing that's kept me going. I've got to see how it all works out." Her expression was stubborn, and at the same time he could see tears in her eyes. She looked away from him.

"About a month after they killed Fred," she said, her voice a flat, distant monotone, "before they brought me to the main island, the Japs decided to make me work for my keep. They started giving me more food, put me in a better cell." She was staring at the painting of Mt. Fuji again. Her next words were so quiet he could barely hear her. "They made me a whore. I serviced Jap fishermen. Jap Army men. Navy. Anyone who wanted me. Nothing I could do about it. At first, I wanted to die, then something turned in me, some part of me got cold and hard and cut my mind off from my body until I could lie there and let them do what they wanted while I planned my break. Eventually I talked a Navy man into letting me see a tech officer off one of the ships. I convinced him I could help out with their war effort. They agreed and brought me to the main island, Honshu. I've been helping them ever since." She looked at him and there were no tears in her eyes now. "Another year. Maybe two. When I take the plane up it's going to be loaded with as many bombs as it can carry. On my way out, people are going to die."

42

ALEX WALKED DOWN THE LONG HALLWAY
trying to look German. *Riding crop up the ass, riding crop up the ass . . .*
His ID card had taken him past the sergeant on the upper level, just
as it was supposed to do. The guards at the doorways to the prison
and germ section paid no attention to him.

He'd memorized Earhart's drawing, counting off doorways until
he came to the radio room. Without hesitating he opened the door,
stepped inside, and closed it behind him. He stood in blackness, leaned
against the door, and listened to the rasp of his own rapid breathing.
The unmoving air smelled of dust and vacuum tubes. He was surprised
by a sudden memory from his childhood; he was twelve or thirteen,
had been sent to Surrey's for the weekend. He'd found an ancient
radio in the attic and plugged it in, pressing his face against the
ventilation holes in the back, peering in to watch the old tubes come
glowing to life, and smelling the same smell that was in this room.
The memory of Surrey and another, less dangerous life seemed to calm
him. He reached to the side of the door for the light switch and could
not find it. He checked farther along the wall, stretching his arm.
Nothing.

He turned around and began to inch crablike along the wall. His
shin banged into a low bench. He stopped, holding his breath, wondering if the thump had been heard outside. He shuffled blindly on.
The room was so small he immediately found himself in a corner. He
ran his hands along the next wall and felt metal boxes with switches.
He pictured himself with his finger inadvertently jammed in an open

electrical outlet. He banged his shin again. *Try overhead, dumbshit. Look for a chain, a string, something* . . . He began waving his arms in the dark. As his eyes adjusted, he could make out light around the door. His waving hand knocked away a thin chain. He clutched at it, then forced himself to stand absolutely still, hand raised in the air, and wait while the chain returned to vertical. His fingers closed on the metal beads. He tugged it. Light flooded the room.

He stood looking stupidly up at the overhead light fixture. He looked around the radio room. It seemed more like a seldom-used storage closet. The walls were painted white. Wooden benches and tables ran around three sides. Pieces of electrical equipment lay scattered on the tables. Right in front of him, painted flat gray rather than U.S. Army khaki, was a shortwave radio almost exactly like the one Donovan had shown him. Alex pulled up a wheeled stool and sat in front of the console.

He studied the dials. A long band with numbers dominated the upper half of the face, just as Donovan had explained. Several dials and a row of switches were positioned on the lower part of the box. Alex found a switch with a small red dot painted below it. He flipped it upward. The radio began to hum; the dials lit up. He sat back for a minute, trying to slow the rapid beating of his heart. He listened carefully, but the sounds outside the door were muted, people walking and talking, barely heard. His luck was holding.

He turned a dial on the lower right and heard scratchy static coming from a speaker. He turned the volume low. The long dial at the top was the channel selector and he began moving the lighted bar to the far left of the dial. Small blips of spoken Japanese flicked out of the speaker as he passed over other transmissions. He set the dial on the 35 megahertz line and picked up the microphone. He nervously cleared his throat and squeezed the send button.

"Bon appetit, bon appetit," he whispered, feeling stupid. He waited a minute and then whispered it again. This time he remembered to take his finger off the send button while he waited for an answer. He fiddled with the selector dial, bringing in only static and a low power-hum.

"Bon appetit, bon appetit," he said softly. He had a mental image of a young Julia Child at the other end. Tall, aproned, goony-looking, humming to herself, whipping up a soufflé, a lentil soup, or a cloud of puff pastry. The kitchen noise drowning out his pleading whispers.

"Bon appetit, bon appetit, goddamnit," he said in a normal voice. He turned up the volume and inched the selector knob back and forth over the 35 on the dial. *Shit, shit, shit, answer goddamnit, I can't stay in here forever.*

"Bon appetit, for the love of Jesus, bon appetit, for Christ sake come in, come in." This time his voice was loud in the small room, frighteningly, imploringly loud in his own ears. To his amazement a thin reedy voice came out of the speaker. "Bon appetit, bon appetit, go ahead, go ahead." He stared at the speaker for a minute, trying to remember what he was supposed to do now that he'd gotten through. *Donovan: let us know if the lab exists and where it is. That's all.*

"The lab exists, repeat, the lab exists . . . Hiroshima, Hiroshima, Hiroshima . . ."

A hand knocked the microphone away and smacked the power switch to off. Alex spun around into the flushed, angry face of a small Japanese man in an Army officer's uniform. The Japanese slapped him in the face and shouted at him, "What you do? What you do? You speak French. You speak American. Who you call on radio?" He slapped Alex again.

Alex was stunned more from surprise than from the blows. The Japanese was the size of a young boy. His hair was cropped close to his bony head and his face was twisted in fury. The man stood with his right hand drawn up clawlike against his chest and his right leg held with only the toe touching the ground. Part of the fury on the face came from an ugly scar that twisted from the edge of his right eye down over his cheek and disappeared into his shirt collar. The man hit him again and Alex grabbed the man's hand and held it as he stood up.

Two soldiers with rifles appeared at the door and peered in. The small officer twisted out of Alex's grasp and stood back, shouting orders to the two soldiers. The men came into the room and grabbed Alex by the arms. He was so much taller than any of the Japanese he felt an urge to push them all down and make a run for it. But where would he go?

And then, curiously, he felt a strange sort of peace settle over him, as if a long-awaited shoe had finally hit the floor. He shook the Japanese hands off his arms. "Okay, okay, calm down," he said.

The small officer glared up at him. "You say calm? Okay, calm, take you to cell. We see calm." He jabbered at the soldiers and they began tugging at Alex. He went in the direction they were pulling him. They marched down the hallway, through the wire gate, and down the hall toward the steps that led up to the outside. They stopped at one of the metal doors, opened it, and pushed him inside. There was a line of barred cells along the left wall of the room. One of the soldiers took a ring of keys off a hook, opened a cell, and pushed Alex in. Alex turned around as the door clanged shut. The officer stood outside the bars, still breathing heavily. The scar pulled the corner of his eye down and twisted the side of his mouth up. The effect was grotesque. "Okay, you calm now, yes, now you be here while I find who you are. You think Colonel Udo not find out, you crazy. You sit, shitface American. You wait. I be back." The officer, Colonel Udo as Alex now knew, turned clumsily and limped back out the door to the hall.

ALEX SAT DOWN on the shelf that was bolted to the wall. It had all happened so fast that it seemed to be over before he really had a chance to react. Now the cold dread, the nausea of capture, began to come over him. He looked around the cell. The wooden shelf he was sitting on was the only furnishing. The cell itself was only eight feet square. The room outside was large, long, and dominated by a high, slanted, gleaming metal table. Against the far wall were sinks and cabinets. The walls and even the floors of the room were painted white. A row of bright lights along the ceiling added to Alex's first impression of the room as a medical facility. It called to mind laboratories in which animal experiments were performed. This was not a comforting thought. He jumped as a nearby voice said, " 'Ello, lad. And who might you be?"

In the next cell, a bundle of rags on a shelf stirred. Alex stood and walked to the bars separating the cells. A head at the end of the rags turned toward him. Alex swallowed rapidly as he stared at the head.

It was a man, or what was left of a man. The head itself was covered with large black welts, lumpy sacklike protuberances. The body was oddly truncated, too short to be a whole man. Alex realized that not only the legs, but also most of the arms were missing. "Is someone there," the head asked, "or am I dreaming? Are you real? Or am I off my bleedin' noggin again?" The head made a sort of snuffling sound. "Lord love a duck."

Alex looked down at the cement floor. "You're not crazy, I'm here. My name's Alex. I'm an American."

A sigh came from the other cell. "Bad luck for you, laddy. But it's nice to have someone to talk to. Besides the Nips. 'Bout all I can do, now, talk. Probably take that away from me next." The rags stirred around. "I can see you, yer know? See the way you're lookin'. Must be something to look at, old Johnny. That's my name, mate, Johnny Jump, though there's not much a' that left in me. There, I've said it first, save you the trouble. Johnny Jump, Johnny Jump, laying here, all in a lump." The snuffling sound came again and Alex realized it was a laugh. Supposed to be a laugh.

Alex sneaked another look at the face. Beneath a hank of dirty hair, in spite of the black welts, the man was smiling. "There you go, lad, not so bad after all, is it?"

Alex looked down at his hands. He'd never seen anything so dead as this man was and still be alive. He'd seen some terrible things in the jungle, but the men those things had happened to had at least been dead. Or were soon in that condition. Here was this man, afflicted with some horrid disease, missing his arms and legs, and he was smiling. Making jokes.

"You've gone and put Udo's back up, that's for certain. What have you done? And where have you come from? Never mind if it's none of Johnny's business, but Lord, it's good to see old Udo pissing down his pants leg. Dangerous, right enough, but there's not much left to be done to me. You're another story. You don't want to get that boy's wind up if you can help it. Udo's a nasty piece of work, I can attest to that. Don't be tricked by his Jap way of talking, he sounds a right fool, but he's not. Wounded in China, they say. Can't you talk? Alex, didn't you say? Is it the sight of old Johnny that's got your tongue?"

Alex shook his head. It was, of course, but he wasn't going to say so. Some absurd vestige of civilization kept him from hurting the man's feelings, about the only thing he had left to hurt. "No, it's just that I'm still in shock. He caught me using the radio. I'm supposed to be a German, it's . . . well, it's complicated."

"Umm. Using the radio without permission. Naughty, naughty."

Alex leaned back against the rough concrete block wall. He wondered when Udo would be back. And what would happen then. He doubted that Tomishiro was going to be able to get him out of this. "Why are *you* here?" he asked. Listening to Johnny Jump was better than sitting in silence and worrying. He looked over into Jump's cell. Jump had raised himself up on the stumps of his arms. Alex felt his stomach roll over. The man smiled again. Most of his teeth were missing.

"Where did Johnny spring from, you ask? Where indeed." He eased himself back down on the board and rolled over on his back. Alex could hear the man humming. "It's a Long Way from Tipperary."

"I was assigned as liaison to your lads back in the Philippines. Corrigedor, Corrigedor, look out mates, she's a fine old whore. Caught us there, they did. Marched us to Bataan. Plenty of the boys didn't finish that little stroll. I've been hither and yon since then, kicked around a few camps till they brought us up here. Did some time in a work camp down in Osaka. Not bad duty, that. Unloading ships, lots of food to steal, sweet duty, sweet duty. Not sure how long I've been here. Things have not gone well for Johnny since coming to the lab, nooo, nooo, not well at all." Alex sat and listened to Jump's labored breathing. How in hell the man had the strength to go on was more than Alex could figure. Insanity had to be one of the factors. Alex could forgive Johnny Jump his insanity. Perhaps it eased the pain.

" 'Ere's where they took my limbs." Jump was back up on his arm stumps staring at Alex. His eyes were bright with fever, or anger. " 'Ere in the lab. It was Udo what put the docs up to it. 'E hates old Johnny, Udo does. Can't understand why I don't just give it up and die. Doesn't understand that I stay alive just to drive the blighter crazy.

"First they froze me legs, see. Some sort of experiment. Try to see how long a man can 'ave his limbs froze and live to tell the tale. Did them one at a time, they did. Froze 'em stiff as a bloody fencepost. Course then they go rotten on you, got to have them off. After they did me that way, they tied me up and bombed me. Most of the other lads were done for in the bombing. Give you a disease for extra measure. Not enough to just blow you up, but the nasty shits have got to make you sick while they're at it." He shook his head and lay back down. "Hard to understand, in't it? How they can be so bad. Enough to make a man loose his faith in his fellow creatures. Something missing in the Japs. The whole bloody lot of them are bent."

They sat and lay in silence. The medical aspect of the room outside the cell door had taken on an even more ominous look.

■ ■ ■

THEY HAD several hours to contemplate the perfidy of the Japanese before Udo returned. Alex spent the time worrying. Johnny Jump seemed to be either unconscious or asleep. Udo arrived with his two soldiers, his scar, and his rage. Alex thought the rage, like the scar, was permanent.

"Okay, you talk now. No bullshit. Tomishiro tell me all about you. That fool think you German. You trick Tomishiro but not Udo. Who you call on radio? Talk now."

Alex was glad he had the bars between him and Udo. Under the circumstances, he hadn't the slightest idea of what to say. Donovan's one-night, short course in spying hadn't covered the finer points of withstanding interrogation. The thought of Donovan brought his hand up to press at his pocket. He still had the suicide pill. When he had changed into the clothes that Tubbs had given him, he'd carefully put it into the lining of the shirtpocket. By then he'd come to think of the pill as a sort of macabre good-luck piece. Its thin glass shell had resisted total immersion in salt water and a long raft voyage. The thought, now, that he might have to use it was chilling, but at the same time comforting. He wasn't going to let them turn him into Johnny Jump.

His tissue-thin cover story, though, was worthless. All Udo had to do was check with the Nazis to find out he wasn't one of them. He could say he was a Frenchman. He'd been caught jabbering in that language, but he couldn't see any usefulness there. The problem was, there just weren't any lies to explain his presence. So he decided to tell the truth. This was a tack that he had used before, and while it had never done much good, it had the advantage of being easy to remember.

"I'm an American, and I'm from the future. I'm here trying to avert the greatest disaster that Japan has ever faced. I am probably the only man alive who has the barest possibility of saving the lives of half a million of your people." *Especially now that I've got a message through saying the lab is here. I've got to get out and tell them it won't do any good to drop the bomb on this place. Even their A-bomb won't dent it.* "Let me out, Udo, it's the smartest thing you can do."

Udo smiled up at him. Or at least Alex thought he was smiling. The scar so distorted the face that it was difficult to tell, but a certain crinkling of the eyes had the look of a smile. Not a nice smile.

"Oh, good. Nice story. Now you here to save Japan. Thank you very much but Japanese going to save Japan. Only thing you do is die here. Smartest thing you can do is tell me truth. Maybe save you life."

"I already told you the truth."

"Then we show you how to tell truth better. We, ah, convince you better." He nodded at the cell where Jump was sleeping. "Ask Mistah Jump. He convinced very fine. Yes. I show you tomorrow what can happen to American who does not tell me what I wish to know. You sleep good." Udo nodded curtly, turned on his heel, and shuffled out, dragging his crippled leg behind him.

They let him out in the morning and escorted him to a lavatory at the other end of the room. The same two guards then carried Jump down for his turn. Alex had spent the night trying to sleep and trying not to think about Udo and his comic-book English and his dire threats. He had been unable to sleep, and unable to think about his prospects, none of which were particularly hopeful. Here there was no option but to wait and see what they would do. In the back of his mind there lived the possibility that he might shift out of this time and back to New York. But such a shift, he was well aware, had never happened under pressure. But it was a possibility. It was hope. Of course there was always the pill.

Two civilian men came in and began setting up chairs facing the raised metal table. Alex resisted thinking of it as an operating table, but that's what it appeared to be. Or a mortuary table, which was probably the same thing here. Sixteen chairs were arranged in a neat square. Then the men began setting out trays of operating tools, including scalpels and clamps. Bright chrome instruments that he could not, and did not wish to, identify.

"Going to be a show, eh lad," Jump said from his cell. He hadn't said anything all night or all morning long. Alex had watched the sheets around the man and had seen them moving with his breathing, but he still thought Jump was near death. He was relieved to see the man up on his stumps.

"Johnny's done his time on the table, Johnny's been the star of the show. It's not a pretty time, up there, all them Japs staring at you while they carve away. It's a terrible time, lad, pray to God it won't be one of us."

"Last night Udo seemed to indicate that it was going to be me.

Said I'd learn what happened to an American who didn't talk. I talked, but I didn't say anything that he wanted to hear."

"Well, it doesn't matter much what ye say, most still ends up on the table. Might not be you, though, might not even be Johnny. There's plenty of others next door in the cells: Yanks, Aussies, all manner of Orientals. I've seen the table in action many times, though mostly I don't look. Aim yer mince pies toward the skies. That's my advice, lad, turn your head. If it's you, of course, you can't help but look. Being right there and all."

Several Japanese men in white lab coats came into the room, hesitated, and then sat in the chairs.

"Come to the bars, lad, so I can talk to ye," Johnny whispered. Alex moved over and sat on the floor. "It's like a show, see," Johnny whispered. His voice was rough. This close Alex could smell the sweetish odor of rot and sweat that emanated from the swaths of sheeting that wrapped the man. "Most of them's doctors, but they bring in others as well. I think it's supposed to teach the Japs a lesson, the ones who don't go along with the military. They get an invite to one of these parties. I don't think they'll do ye, Alex. They want you to talk, once these docs get done with ye there's usually no more talking. Hold your ground and your tongue, that's the tickety-boo."

More civilians were coming into the room, chatting among themselves, as if about to attend a concert or a play. They took their seats and soon all sixteen chairs were full. Alex stood up and walked to the bars in front. With a small shock he saw Tomishiro sitting in the second row of onlookers. *Tubbs, here to see the show. Invited guest? Interested observer? Reluctant attendee?* Tubbs didn't look at him.

The door opened one more time and Udo limped in. His was the only military uniform among the onlookers. He took up a position near Alex's cell, but did not acknowledge him. From the other end of the room, a large steel door opened and two soldiers walked in holding a Caucasian man between them. They were half carrying the man, whose legs didn't seem to be working correctly. The prisoner looked like an American, short blond hair and a Midwestern face. Tall and extremely thin. The look on his face was one of terror.

A short Japanese wearing rimless glasses and a long white lab coat came in behind the two soldiers and the prisoner. He moved briskly to the side of the metal operating table and began to address the small audience in rapid-fire Japanese. At one point he stopped, turned to

the prisoner, and introduced himself in English as Professor Ishiyama
Fukujiro. The white-faced prisoner simply stared at the professor. The
two soldiers hustled the prisoner to the head of the table. The table
was tilted on an angle, the head, where they stood, higher than the
foot. At an order from Fukujiro, the soldiers stripped the shirt off the
prisoner.

The soldiers, who acted as if they had done this before, leaned the
prisoner against the head of the table. The table came up to the man's
chest. "I don't deserve this," the prisoner said in a shaky voice. "I
didn't do nothing to you all, I'm just a navigator. Don't do this to me,
please."

Fukujiro stepped to the man's side and patted him on the arm.
Two assistants moved to either side of the table. One, holding a tray
of instruments, positioned himself next to Fukujiro, the other stood
across the table holding a large surgical pan. The two soldiers moved
up close behind the prisoner, holding his arms behind his back and
supporting him. The prisoner's eyes scanned the room, searching for
help, hope, anything but what he saw. His gaze fixed on Alex.

"Hey, buddy," he shouted, struggling with the guards. "Can you
stop them? Can you do anything? Can you help me? For the love of
God!"

Alex didn't move, didn't speak. He felt literally frozen in place,
waves of horror flooding through him.

Fukujiro began chattering as if the situation were perfectly normal,
as if he were demonstrating a standard medical technique for the
edification of a group of students. He picked up a thick black grease
marker and drew two lines on the prisoner's chest. The lines ran in
a curve, starting at the throat, down the sternum and arching along
the rib cage on either side, ending up resembling a large upside-down
Y. The prisoner looked down at the lines and then back to Alex.

"Terry Neil. I'm from South Philly. Tell my mother you saw me.
Oh, Jesus." Fukujiro picked up a scalpel and made two rapid, deep
cuts along the lines he had previously marked. The prisoner screamed.
The soldiers thrust him forward over the table. Blood poured from the
cuts, onto the metal table, trailing down the steep incline in scores of
rivulets.

Working quickly, Fukujiro cut deeper into the two arcs along the
rib cage. Blood soaked his hands and ran down his sleeves. The prisoner's knees buckled and the guards forced him upright. His head was

back and he was groaning. The audience sat bolt upright in their seats. Alex stared, unable to turn away, dimly hearing Johnny Jump whispering over and over, "Don't look, don't look, don't look . . ."

Fukujiro put down his scalpel and placed both hands on the man's chest. He slid his fingers under the man's ribs and strained up and out, spreading apart the rib cage. His assistant inserted a jack in the opening and began turning a crank that levered the ribs open further. Alex could see into the chest cavity, could see the man's lungs, red and heaving.

"For the love of God!" the man screamed again, his voice a high, thin wail.

The other assistant lifted the surgical pan to the chest and Fukujiro reached into the cavity and carefully pulled the lungs out, flopping them into the pan with a wet slap. The man's head sagged forward. The soldiers were straining to keep the body upright.

Fukujiro began to jabber again, poking at the still attached lungs with a finger.

Alex slammed into the bars, shouting, "Jesus Christ! You fucking animals! You goddamned, mother-fucking animals!"

Everyone in the room except the unconscious prisoner turned to him, their faces registering various degrees of shock at his outburst. Fukujiro looked as if he were about to issue a stern reprimand.

Alex's hands were wrapped around the bars, his face was white with rage, his whole body trembled. "For Christ's sake, kill him! Put him out of his misery! You're all animals." He looked at the audience. Some of them were watching him, some had gone back to examining the prisoner. "How can you stand it? How can you put up with this? How can you go along with this evil?" He looked at Tomishiro, who was now staring at the floor. "You're not men! You don't deserve to live! I hope you all die! God damn all Japanese to eternal hell!" He turned away. In the silence he could hear Johnny Jump still chanting his mantra, don't look, don't look, don't look, and Alex did look, he looked at the prisoner who was now thankfully dead, and he looked at Udo and saw that Colonel Udo was observing him in a calm dispassionate manner. As if he were measuring him. Studying him.

43

THE UNSPEAKABLE SHOW HAD CONTINUED
for a time, Alex wasn't sure how long, fifteen minutes, a half an hour, not more than an hour. He no longer registered time in increments of minutes or hours, time had become instead a measureless piece of existence to be lived through, a monstrous event that could never be overcome, only endured.

He'd stayed on his bunk, facing the wall, sunk into a trance of anguish, his body and mind seized by the sights and sounds of the vivisection. Fukujiro prattled on. Alex could hear him cutting, explaining, lecturing, and then it was over. The audience departed, the chairs were taken away, the body was removed, the table was washed down. Alex stared at the wall, listening as buckets of water splashed down the bright surface of the operating table, washing away the blood, down the table and into the drain neatly positioned in the floor at the base, the concrete surface carefully sloped to catch the runoff. He heard the cleaners going about their business and imagined it all while they worked, picking each detail and identifying it by its characteristic sound and seeing it in his mind, the blood, especially the blood, pink and frothy in the hot soapy water. And then it was over and the cleaners left and they were alone, he and Johnny Jump, except they weren't. There was a shuffling, a dragging, limping scraping, then a harsh voice that shouted, and Alex felt his body jerk in fright, and Udo shouted through the bars, "You next, shitface! You remember this! You next!" And then the sliding scraping again and it was quiet. Only the tiny sound of water dripping. From the table, into the drain.

• • •

IT WAS JOHNNY who woke him with a whisper. "Alex? Can you hear something? A kind of thump?"

Alex lay for a moment while it all came back, surprised that he had slept. He listened. And then the door at the back of the room opened and there was a scraping, a dragging, and he was afraid to look.

"Alex-san?"

Alex rolled over. Tubbs. Standing by the bars of the cage, a small body at his feet. The body was inert. Tubbs had been dragging it.

"Get up, Alex-san, get up and help me."

"And who the bloody hell are you?" Johnny asked in an outraged voice. "We're trying to sleep, don't y'know?" Tubbs glanced into the adjoining cell. Alex sat up.

"It's all right, Johnny," Alex said. "At least I think it is. What are you doing here, Tubbs? The last I saw, you were watching a man being cut into pieces."

"They made me come. It is a test, to see if we can watch such things without speaking out. Udo is behind it. I have tried to stop him here at the Nichi, but if I complain too much, then I am suspect."

"Catch 22," Alex said.

"What? I do not understand."

"Forget it. Who the hell is that?" Alex pointed at the body on the floor. Tubbs bent and rolled the man over. It was Fukujiro, the professor who had so calmly performed his work on the American flyer. Alex heard Johnny Jump hiss when he saw who it was. Fukujiro's glasses were missing. There was a trickle of blood at the corner of his mouth.

"I hit him on the head," Tubbs said. "I called him from my laboratory, I woke him up and told him there was a problem here. He brought me in, past the guards outside. I could not be part of this terrible thing. They are going to use you next, Udo told me this. I must get you out of here. There is no other way."

Alex felt the twin pull of conflicting emotions—fear at the mention of Udo and his plan, and sudden hope. "Get the keys," Alex said, nodding at the ring hanging on the wall. Tubbs opened the cell door and Alex walked through, feeling a small weight lift from his shoulders.

He was a hell of a long way from safety, but he was out of his cage. Fukujiro moaned and opened his eyes.

"Sit on him," Alex said to Tubbs. Alex went to the cabinets that lined the opposite side of the room and began opening drawers. He found a box of small glass vials that contained surgical thread immersed in liquid. Alex snapped one of the vials open. The sharp cold scent of alcohol filled the air.

Tubbs rolled the weakly moving Fukujiro over on his stomach. Alex pulled the man's arms behind his back and wrapped the surgical thread around and around until his wrists were tightly tied. He broke open more vials and tied the man's ankles.

"Lord, that's a pretty sight," Johnny said from his bunk. He had pushed himself up on his stumps. "What's going on, lad? Are you getting out of here?"

"Maybe," Alex said. He rummaged through several more drawers and found a roll of gauze bandaging and wrapped it around Fukujiro's mouth until he had him firmly gagged. He turned the man on his back. Fukujiro stared up at them with wide-open eyes. "Okay," Alex said to Tubbs, "if you've got any bright ideas, let's hear them."

Tubbs ran a hand through his short black hair. The overhead lights reflected off his rimless glasses, giving him a frightened look. "No one knows who is involved. It is very early, 3 A.M. Unless Fukujiro told someone, no one will know it was me who called him. We must get you out, hide you, and when it is safe, send you away from Japan."

Alex laughed harshly. "Great. Now why don't you wave your magic wand and make all of that happen. Fukujiro obviously knows who called, and then there're the two guards outside. I assume they were there when you came in with him?" Tubbs nodded. "We've got to get past them and go somewhere that Udo isn't going to think to look. He'll tear this place apart when this shit hits the fan. Which will be the first cell check in the morning."

"I have thought of this. I can hide you, I know a place they will not look. We will dispose of Fukujiro and the two guards, and then no one will know it was I who freed you." They both looked down at the man at their feet.

"Ooohh, yes," Johnny Jump said. Both Alex and Tubbs started when he spoke. They had forgotten him. "Give him to me, lad, please, please, Johnny will take care of the doctor." His words came in a sort of croon. "The doctor's the one what did this to me. 'E's the one that sawed off Johnny's legs and arms, just as he did for that nice boy this afternoon. 'E's the one, and I want him." He rolled to his side so he could look up at Alex. His eyes were bright. "Do this for me, lad. I'm done for anyway. There's no use me trying to get out. Let me have the croaker." Fukujiro was looking wildly back and forth between Alex and Johnny's cell. Alex didn't know if the man understood English, but he seemed to be catching the drift of the conversation. "I can do it, I'm capable," Johnny said. "Just drag him in here and leave him. Let me have my payback, there's a good lad."

Alex looked at Tubbs, who had turned his head away. In a horrible way, the idea appealed to Alex. It had a certain symmetry. What had been done to the American flyer that afternoon had burned any compassion out of him.

"The guards," Alex said. "What do we do with them?"

"I will call them in. We will kill them. There is no other way," Tubbs answered.

"These are your countrymen, almost innocent bystanders," Alex said. "You're willing to just kill them?"

Tubbs turned to him. "You ask this of me? Did you not see what was done here this afternoon? They are a part of it. We are all a part of it. There are no innocent bystanders. What you and I are attempting is more important than these few lives." He lowered his voice. "You must escape. You must return to your country and tell them what you have learned. If either of our countries uses these new weapons, there will be hundreds of thousands of lives lost. What are these three against that possibility?"

"What are you two going on about?" Johnny asked. "No need to whisper in front of Johnny."

"First the guards," Tubbs said.

"Just a second," Alex said. He walked away from the others. He looked around for a weapon, but the real purpose was to give himself time to think. Time, he realized, that they didn't really have. If one of the guards decided to check on the two Japanese scientists, it was all over. At least for Tubbs, and by extension, himself.

The whole island is full of madmen. Fukujiro, Udo, Tubbs, none of them gives the slightest damn about killing. Johnny Jump is almost sane in comparison. The whole thing is crazy.

Now he was going to kill two unsuspecting Japanese guards. It was the unsuspecting part that got to him. He'd killed other Japanese, but they always had known what they were getting into. It wasn't a question of fairness, that quaint notion had disappeared from his consciousness months ago. What was fair about a bomb dropped from twenty-five thousand feet? An artillery shell fired a mile or more away? There was no fairness in this war, or probably any war. What it came down to was numbers and the individual's drive to survive. Tubbs was measuring the lives of three men against hundreds of thousands. The American leaders who would or would not eventually drop the bomb would measure tens of thousands against a possible half a million. But numbers were meaningless when it came to the moment of coldly holding a man down and cutting his throat. There were no numbers then, no abstract computations that excused your actions, no strategies or plans. There was only existence and the raw hope that you would live, at least for the moment, and if another had to die to ensure that, then so be it. Now the numbers were reduced to three against one, three men who had to die if he were to live.

He picked up a four-foot length of metal pipe that was leaning in a corner, part of another operating table under construction.

"Call them in one at a time. I'll wait behind the door."

AND THEN there was Fukujiro. When they had finished with the guards, Alex realized that all the hate that he held for Fukujiro, the hate that he had burned into him over the course of the long death of the American flyer, was gone, buried under the disgust he felt for himself. What was the difference between the two of them? Fukujiro had killed a man who was conscious, who had watched himself die. He had just killed two men who were unconscious. Fukujiro had killed a man for reasons that seemed deluded and mad to Alex. And yet the two *he* had just killed, for his own reasons of survival, were just as dead. Numbers. Reasons. Excuses. Delusions. And in the end, they were both just as guilty, but to measure that guilt, to compare the depths of guilt, was useless. Each of them was damned.

"Give him to me," Johnny pleaded. And they did.

ALEX LEFT Johnny a gift. He tore the suicide pill out of the lining of his pocket and left it on the man's bunk. It lay there, like some jewel of death, the promise of release. Alex did not look back. As he and Tubbs went through the door into the hall, he heard Johnny thump off the bunk and begin to drag himself across the floor of the cell, toward Fukujiro, who lay bound and fully conscious, waiting for Johnny Jump.

44

THEY WERE STANDING IN FRONT OF THE
massive uranium separator in Tubbs's laboratory. The large room was
silent and dark. A small bare worklight threw stark illumination onto
the lower half of the twenty-foot silo that thrust upward into the
darkness. A row of small red lights glowed on one of the machines,
the watchful eyes of predators in the night.

"You're going to put me in there?" Alex asked, incredulously. One
of the few things he knew about the process of uranium separation
was that the gas used, uranium hexafluoride, was perhaps the most
caustic substance ever discovered. Human flesh would last bare seconds
under a wash of this gas.

"There's nothing in the tank. You will be safe. Udo and his men
will never touch the tank. They think it is too dangerous."

"All right, so is it dangerous or not?"

"Not."

Alex felt the growing bubble of frustration and impotence, the lack
of control over the flow of events in his own life, burst in a wave of
anger. "What the hell are you talking about?" His whisper was harsh
in the dead silence. "Just what the hell is going on? All you've given
me for answers is one riddle after another since we began all of this.
You've been bullshitting me since we were back on the beach. We've
left a trail of dead men behind us, and I'm goddamn sick and tired of
not knowing what is going on. I want to know why those men died.
Now you tell me the truth, and you tell me now!"

Tubbs walked to the side of the silo, picked a wrench off a nearby bench, and began unscrewing a line of bolts that held a small door flush with the metal side. "You talk very big for a man who is dependent on others for his life, Alex-san. There is no gas in this tank. There is no uranium. There is no possibility of fashioning an atomic device. This is all . . . what would you say? A sham?"

"You mean bullshit."

Tubbs nodded. "Yes, I have heard you use this expression. All right. It is all bullshit."

Alex looked around the dark room at the lines of machinery, the huge particle accelerator.

"No," Tubbs said, seeing where he was looking. "The accelerator is quite real. But that is one of the few pieces of equipment that actually functions and has a purpose. This—" He tapped lightly on the side of the metal tank. It boomed hollowly. "—is a tank used for the underground storage of aviation fuel." He unscrewed the last bolt and lifted off the door. He leaned it against the tank and turned to Alex.

"Here is the truth. We know America is working on a bomb. We, the scientists of Japan, feel that you will succeed in your efforts. We have no hope of emulating you. Our country is too poor in resources and too depleted by the excesses of our military. Given time and other circumstances, we could also succeed, but we have too little time, and our circumstances are dire, or soon will be. We are not fools, the people of Japan, no matter what you may think. We know that the war is going badly for us. The newspapers tell us of strategic retreats from the islands of Guadalcanal and New Britain. I have now seen this for myself. The authorities attempt to put a good face on what are obviously defeats. We can see that what was begun so gloriously is now destined to end ignominiously. But we can face ignominity. It is complete destruction that we must prevent. And so we planned this." He gestured around the room. "We scientists who have studied and worked in the West. Our purpose was to contact someone we knew, someone of trust in England or America. We planned to convince them that we have the capability to produce a nuclear weapon, and that use of such weapons would mean unacceptable ruin for both sides."

"It's called mutual deterrence," Alex said.

"I did not know this term, but it is correct. The results would be mutual salvation, for all of us. Do you understand now?"

"Yes. Maybe." *Jesus, all the effort that went into it, all the planning. But it worked. At least up until now.* "And I just happened to be in the right place at the right time."

"Yes." Tubbs nodded. "The Australian was an intelligent man. We were lucky to have been captured by him. We were transported to the vicinity of his island by one of our submarines. We drifted ashore and were taken prisoner. We told him our story, and he contacted his superiors. But it worked better than we ever thought it would. We never thought we could actually have someone from the West to come here, that part was fortuitous."

"But why build the lab then? Why go to all that effort?"

"Our original intention was to show this facility to the man you referred to when you first arrived. The priest you said you wished to see." It hit Alex with a small jolt. *Donovan's priest, the only spy the Allies have in Japan.* "You know about him?" Alex asked.

"Yes, our intelligence facilities have been aware of this spy for some time. They do not feel he is dangerous. He sends out weather information and troop movements, movements that we arrange for him to be aware of. He is useful to us. We thought that after your government became aware of our existence they would contact this spy and work out arrangements for him to come here. We have already allowed him to discover us, to send information on the concentration of scientists here at the Nichi. That was the first step."

Alex shook his head. They had taken the bait, swallowed it whole, and sent him in for a closer look. If Udo hadn't caught him in the radio room, he would have probably been on his way back to American lines and safety by now. Carrying information that the Japanese also would one day have atomic weapons and that there was very little the Allies could do to prevent it. And what would have been the result? *Would America have accepted the Japanese surrender before risking the possibility of a nuclear exchange? Possibly. Very possibly. It's one thing to nuke an unsuspecting, undefended enemy. Quite another when retaliation is probable.*

"And what is it you want me to do now?" he asked. *What have you thought up next, you clever bastard?*

"Now you know the truth. We cannot bargain with you. I wish you to go back to your government and tell them this. Tell them that Japan is defeated. That the people, the civilians of Japan, do not want this war, that we are captives of the military. Tell them that our armies will fight on, but there will come a point when we are exhausted, and then we will ask for peace. Ask them to accept this peace. Ask them not to use this terrible weapon that they are building. There will be no reason, it will not be necessary. Many will die that should not die. Earlier I said there were no innocents. There are. The children who will die do not deserve this fate. Tell them there are children here. Tell them there are many who do not hate them. Tell them there are those who do not deserve to die."

And so now I know. It was all a trick. And perhaps it will work itself out and I can stop them. Perhaps.

"How are you going to get me out of here?"

A look of relief swept over the Japanese. "As I have said, Alex-san, you will hide in this tank. I will bring food and you will stay in here until it is safe. Several days."

"And then?"

Tubbs smiled. "And then your old friend, the box. You will be shipped out the same way you arrived. The *Osaka Maru* is still in port. The captain will do his duty without question once again. You will be taken to within the vicinity of your own troops and set adrift. With only a small amount of luck you should reach safety. And our message can be delivered."

It might work. And just what are the alternatives? None.

"Okay. But for God's sake, bring me some sort of a toilet to put in there." He walked over and touched the side of the tank. The metal was cool. For a moment he was seized with the notion that they were going to seal him in and perform some sort of perverse experiment on him, turn on the gas, or leave him until he starved, too afraid to bang on the side and ask for release. The image of Udo's twisted face came to mind. No, the tank, the box, anything was better than that.

"Lock me in."

SEVEN DAYS LATER the ship, the *Osaka Maru*, headed southwest on a detour before continuing on to China, steamed into the sights of the American submarine, *Silverfish*. The old rusty Japanese merchantman was torpedoed and sunk in a matter of minutes. The submarine surfaced and searched the water for survivors. There were none.

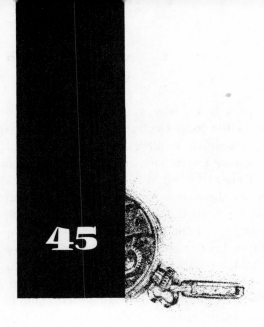

45

IT WAS COOL IN THE BAR. OUT OF THE SUN.
Out of the rush-hour throngs crowding the streets and being crammed into the subways. Tadashi Ishikawa sat in the back of the large, pink-walled, pink-ceilinged, pink-floored room and sneered at the ranks of giggling office workers seated around the circular center stage. *Modern Japan. Salarymen. Come in after work for a little fun, ogle the girls, drink till you can't walk, look at real live naked women.* Tadashi was bored.

He had been at the Hiroshima Deluxe for a half an hour, sipping at a warm glass of Santori beer, waiting for the old man to show up. They had never met face to face. Their previous negotiations had taken place over the telephone, but now they were to finalize their agreement and the old guy had chosen the Deluxe, one of the more disreputable striptease parlors in all Hiroshima, as their meeting place. Tadashi sensed the faint odor of irony in the old man's choice, but he wasn't sure. *You never know, maybe the fellow's just got an eye for the babes.*

The overhead loudspeaker cracked on and a man welcomed the audience and announced the first number. An old recording of "Strangers in the Night" began, the music nearly lost behind a smothering storm of crackles and scratches. Two warm pink spotlights snapped on and five smiling ladies in red polyester nighties sauntered onstage. Each girl carried a picnic basket covered by a bright red cloth. They squatted down, spread out the cloth, and lined up various pieces of equipment: condoms, dildos, and as Tadashi noted with a small jolt, several cucumbers of impressive size.

The girls were neither beautiful nor ugly, all rather average-looking

Japanese ladies who would seem perfectly at home on the assembly line of the local electronics factory. They smiled mechanically and began to shuffle in place as they slowly took off their nighties. Nervous jokes were tossed back and forth by the all-male audience.

Tadashi looked at his watch. Six o'clock. The old man had said anytime between five-thirty and seven-thirty. He groaned at the thought of another hour and a half of "Strangers in the Night." A *nopan* girl—a "no pants" waitress—sidled up and asked if he wanted another beer. He didn't, but he ordered one anyway. She bent over his table to write out his order and give him a good look at her breasts. He perfunctorily admired them and smiled and nodded to her. He sighed. It could have been worse. He could have been assigned a story on the plight of the crowded subways, or the downfall of the Japanese rice farmer, or the life story of any one of a number of empty-headed, vapid, talentless *talentos*, young performers who had seized, for the moment, the imagination of the idiot-adoring public. He settled back in his chair and watched the girls strip off the last of their clothing. *Yes, it could be worse.*

Tadashi Ishikawa was a lucky man. Hardworking, a graduate of prestigious Tokyo University, ambitious and mildly ruthless, he'd been assigned the job of shepherding his colleagues, the two New York *Times* reporters, over some of the ground that the Japanese press had already plowed. None of his colleagues on the Hiroshima *Journal* could decide if his assignment was a step up, down, or sideways. Neither could Tadashi, but after a period of intense speculation and self-examination he decided that he would do the job as well as he could, and keep an eye out for the nickel in the rice bowl while he was at it. After some long-distance bargaining and agreements, he'd settled down and begun working his list of experts and fellow journalists. A complicated series of phone calls and afterwork drinking sessions had led him down a labyrinthine, saki-soaked path to the man who was supposed to meet him here at the Deluxe. Old Mr. Udo, ex-Army, ex-scientific advisor, ex-who-knew-what, nevertheless a man who had been on the spot as far as Pacific War scientific and industrial work in Hiroshima was concerned. At least that's what the old guy said, and Tadashi's sources had agreed; Udo was the man if you were in-terested in Japanese technical and scientific advances circa 1943–45. He seemed to be untapped, a fresh source, untainted by the handling

of other fellow journalists. Tadashi was surprised when the old guy
said he would talk.

The girls on the stage had finally gotten around to their sex gear.
Tadashi leaned forward. He wished he'd brought his glasses. The girl
with the cucumbers went into action, and now he wished he'd taken
a seat a little closer to the stage. *No, it'll never work, it's too big. Look
at that!* The girl finally freed the cucumber and held it in the air to a
round of raucous applause and cheers.

The song ended and was clumsily restarted. The girls put away
their gear and began clapping their hands and motioning the audience
to come up and join them. Loud joking and taunting accompanied the
pushing and coercion of a group of young men onto the stage. They
stood blushing and giggling as the girls took their hands and began
slowly maneuvering them around in a sort of dance. They rubbed up
against the men and the banter from below grew louder. Two of the
girls unbuckled one man's pants and pushed them to the floor. Hands
reached into boxer shorts and began playful tweaking. Now the men
in the audience really began to shout and cheer. The girls pulled the
men close and tried to rub a little life into the various members, all
of which remained frightened and flaccid. Various company names—
Nippon Steel! Go Mitsubishi!—and patriotic homilies were shouted up
from the audience, but none of them was able to work up enough
stiffness to achieve even the slightest penetration. After a few minutes
of attempted insertion, the girls looked at each other and theatrically
shrugged and shook their heads at these sorry specimens of Japanese
manhood and began shoving them back off the stage to their seats amid
great shouts and hoots. Belt buckles clanked along the floor as the men
struggled to get down off the stage, find their seats, dodge the friendly
blows of their friends, and pull their pants up all at the same time.
Tadashi watched and scorned and was wholeheartedly grateful to the
sacred memory of his sainted mother who had prodded him through
the best high-pressure schools and bribed him to study hard. She had
succeeded in producing a son who would never have been forced into
the ranks of the lower-echelon salarymen who would allow themselves
to become part of such a sad show all in the name of good clean fun
and company solidarity.

A chair scraped and Tadashi looked up into the scarred face of an
old man, and his first thought was no, not a *hibakusha*, not a bomb

survivor. *We've told that story again and again.* Then it occurred to him that being a *hibakusha* might be an asset in this case, the instrument needed to pry information out of an unwilling subject. "Mr. Udo?" Tadashi said, standing and bowing. The older man nodded and lowered himself into the chair. The old man's face was twisted and bubbled on the right side with a white, wrinkled keloid formation, the clawlike scar typical to atom bomb survivors.

"Mr. Ishikawa," the old man said formally. "Forgive me for not standing, but my injuries are advanced by my age." He was interrupted by an announcement from the loudspeaker, heralding the next segment of the show. The music had stopped, and there was a sustained hiss as the needle traveled back and forth between the end of the track and the label. With a loud pop the needle was lifted and the master of ceremonies breathlessly announced the *Tokudashi*, the Big Special Event. The needle bounced down, and the opening notes of "Strangers in the Night" began again.

Both of the men watched as the girls crouched down at the edge of the stage and bent as far back as possible, legs spread wide in the faces of the avid audience.

"Forgive me for choosing such a situation for our meeting," Mr. Udo said. "I was looking for a refuge where I would be in no danger of being seen by certain individuals who would be unhappy with my decision to speak to a member of the press." He watched for a moment as the girls hunched closer and the men leaned in, scant centimeters away from the object of their fascination. "I believe I have found such a place."

Tadashi wondered if anyone had ever referred to the Deluxe as a refuge before. "Don't worry about it, Mr. Udo. In my line of work I see many unusual sights. This is just the *salarymen* out on the town for a night of fun. Harmless entertainment."

"Yes," Mr. Udo said, turning back to Tadashi. He maneuvered his chair around until his back was to the stage. "I feel that I must explain to you why I have decided to speak to the American press about our scientific efforts during the war."

"You don't have to justify anything to me, sir. Your reasons are your own. I'm interested, of course, but you are under no obligation to explain yourself."

Udo closed his eyes and nodded, accepting Tadashi's courtesy. Tadashi tried to keep his eyes off the stage, but the sight of the wiggling girls and the bobbing heads was mesmerizing. The girls inched crablike around the circle from one man to the next, giving each a long look at her sacred treasure.

"I have remained silent for almost fifty years because I felt our work would be misunderstood, that we would be condemned. As indeed recent events have borne out. But now I also sense a resurgence of pride in our homeland. A certain sector of our community is ready to cast off the mantle of defeat and stand again with pride. It has been effective in the past to be seen as the bearers of the atomic burden. This was especially useful during the occupation, but now we are strong again. The old East Asia Prosperity Sphere is no impotent boast. We have achieved victory over much of our world. It is time to reassert ourselves. We must stop being led by the ghost of the Occupation army. It is time to show our people that the Japanese were second to none in technology and science, even then."

Tadashi cleared his throat nervously. "Yes, *sensei*, you may be right, but may I humbly remind you that it is we who lost the war."

The old man leaned forward. One eye was bright, the other, Tadashi realized, was blind. "Did we?" the old man asked with a twisted smile. "Did we?"

Tadashi allowed no emotion to show on his face. He had interviewed these old military men before, and such sentiments were nothing new. In fact they were rather widespread. The latest textbook controversy had brought them out again. The official schoolbooks had begun referring to the Pacific war as a simple attempt of self-defense and various ministers had made speeches in the same vein. He himself was too young to remember the war or the bomb and didn't care much one way or the other. As far as he was concerned, it was a period of history best forgotten. "I see what you mean, Mr. Udo. But do you have new evidence of our superiority? Many books have been written on this period."

The smile remained on Udo's face. He nodded. "Yes, Mr. Ishikawa, as a matter of fact I do have new information. I have reports that were written at the time. I have photographs. I buried this material after the surrender when others were burning such incriminating evidence. It has remained in very good condition. The West has an interesting expression concerning their graveyards. I know where the bodies are buried and can lead you to them."

Tadashi didn't have the slightest idea what the man was referring to. He looked over at the stage at the crab women and their gawking slaves. One of the *nopan* girls was passing out magnifying glasses and small flashlights. He looked back at Udo. Udo was staring at him.

"Ama no Uzume," Udo said.

"What?" The old man was leaving him far behind.

"Ama no Uzume," Udo said again. The old man's eye was bright, almost fevered. Tadashi understood in that moment that the man was crazy. This was not unusual among the *hibakusha*, the survivors. "The Dread Female of Heaven. Those women on the stage are recreating her dance for the gods. The men are the gods. The Strong-handed Male will soon grab Amaterasu and drag her out of her cave. The world will be light again. It has been dark for so long."

46

THERE WAS NO SENSE OF RELIEF, NO FEEL-
ing of deliverance or rescue or liberation. His body was suddenly free
of the wooden box, out of the darkness, away from the rolling of the
sea and the constant rumble of the *Osaka Maru's* engines. But there
was no joy in it, no release. There was, instead, as soon as he understood where he was, the dull ache of failure. It closed over him as
he lay on his living room rug in his empty house. He stared up at the
ceiling. The air of the room smelled stale, dead.

He sat up. He was home. Back in the present. And now there was
no way he could deliver the message from Tubbs, no way to tell
Roosevelt that the Japanese would be beaten, were already beaten, no
way to convince the government that there would be no civilian army
of millions on the beaches, no atom bombs lashed to kamikaze planes.
The Japanese didn't have a bomb, weren't capable of producing a bomb.
There would be no need to destroy Hiroshima and Nagasaki. No need.

If he could get back . . . But he couldn't. A rush of anger flowed
over him. Anger at whatever force controlled him, pulled him away.
Anger at the randomness of it, if it was random, chance. Or the caprice
of some unknown god. And so, hundreds of thousands would die.

He tried to push it away; knowledge, judgment. It was too much,
too big, too terrible, too soon. He concentrated on controlling his limbs.
He stood, swaying, still adjusting to the ship's roll. His rickety body
protested as he moved. He walked haltingly to the kitchen and put
water on the stove to heat, having to think out every movement, having
to remember tasks that were now strange to him. He stood at the stove

and listened to the hiss of the gas burner. He reached out and touched the objects of this world, as if by touching their physical presence he would regain his memory of their usefulness. His fingers strayed over the control pad of his microwave oven. He flinched as it beeped to attention.

He looked for some indication of Molly. An unwashed teacup, some scrap or crumb, something that showed she had been there, that she would return. The kitchen was clean, empty. He would call her at work. He would see her soon. That thought helped. Soon.

He opened the freezer door and took out a can of Café Bustelo, inserted a paper filter into a Melitta funnel, and carefully poured in one heaping tablespoonful of the dark coffee. He stood and watched the summer sun warming a patch of wooden countertop. He thought of the *Osaka Maru* and wondered what the captain would say when the box was opened and he and the first mate found it empty. When the tea kettle began to whistle, he poured the water through the filter into a heavy gray and blue mug. He held the mug close as he inhaled the steam. He closed his eyes.

HE SAT ON THE edge of the tub and turned on the taps. Air in the pipes rattled and banged and knocked a brown flow of rust into the spluttering stream, which quickly warmed and cleared. He patiently waited as the last of the rusty water swirled down the drain, then inserted the old-fashioned black rubber plug. He filled the tub and turned off the water. He removed his clothing and stood looking in the full-length mirror on the back of the bathroom door. He had lost weight, twenty pounds at least. He was gaunt, still slightly bent from his two days in the box. He made an effort to stand up straight. His ribs showed against his pale skin. His face and arms were tanned dark in comparison. His jaw was rough with a week's stubble, scabbed where Tubbs's borrowed razor had refused to cut beard but had easily sliced away flesh. His eyes were dark, sunken, somehow lost. They stared back from another time, understanding the awful failure that hung around his neck. It had never occurred to him that he would come back, at least not while he was so caught up, so part of the skein. He had come so close. He had been taking it one step at a time, never thinking beyond the next move, holding the threads together, trying to do what was right, trying to get home. And not the home of New

York, the present, but back to Surrey, and Einstein, because that was where he could have made a difference. He had been trying to deliver his message, to halt the bomb, the nightmare of the future. He had been hoping to change the world, and whoever or whatever controlled him had laughed at his puny attempt and drawn him back. And as far as they knew in the past, he was dead, his last words being the affirmation of what Donovan and Roosevelt believed, that the Japanese were building a bomb and would succeed. He was sure that Julia Child had faithfully passed along his message. *It exists. Hiroshima. Hiroshima.* And the past would not be changed. The future would remain the same. *Bon appetit.*

He climbed into the tub and eased down into the hot water. *And there's not a goddamned thing I can do about it. The war did continue, and the United States of America did drop atomic bombs on Hiroshima and Nagasaki. And the world never knew that we did it to keep them from dropping one on us. The world will never know because the government quickly learned that there was no threat in Japan. And what could they say then? Sorry, we made a mistake? No, we'll say nothing, cover it all up, scratch the litter over the truth, and hope that no one ever discovers the lie.*

He leaned back. The hot water began to leach the ache from his joints. This was the first bath he had had in months and the pleasure was almost overwhelming. *Not a goddamn thing I can do about it.* He felt himself drifting off. He sat up and splashed water on his face. *Not yet. First I find Molly. Then I can sleep. Then I'll let go.*

He dressed in a clean pair of blue jeans and fresh polo shirt. He dialed Molly's office and waited as he was switched from one desk to another. He ran a hand through his wet hair, and wished he had a cigarette, wondering if he was now a smoker again.

"Yes, what is it?"

Harry Watkins, Molly's asshole editor. "Harry, this is Alex Balfour. I've been out of town for a while, just got back. I wonder if you could tell me where I could find Molly."

There was a moment of silence. "Well, she's in Japan. She's been there for a week. Didn't she tell you?"

One week. In this time I've only been gone a week. "I knew she was going, I just didn't know when or exactly where. Have you got a number?"

Sounds of rustling on the other end. "As a matter of fact, I don't." Alex could almost hear the other man frowning. "They left Tokyo yesterday, supposed to be in Hiroshima today. She should have called in with a number, but she's there with Tommy Fellows and he doesn't go by the book any more than she does. They'll probably call this afternoon. If they don't, I'll cut off their expense accounts. I'll tell her you're looking for her."

"What's she doing in Hiroshima, Harry?" A small throb of apprehension. *Not Hiroshima. It's dangerous there.* He frowned at his reaction. *No, this is not then, this is now.*

"Christ, who knows? She started out on this germ warfare thing. Then she got tied up with Tommy, and once he gets his fat feet on the trail there's no telling where the two of them will end up. I'm the editor, for Chrissake, I'm supposed to be directing the operation . . ."

"Hiroshima, Harry? What's the significance? What's it got to do with the story?" *No, it's so far in the past, so far away . . .*

". . . some atom bomb thing, I don't know. It's the anniversary, they got some sort of lead, so off they went—"

"What anniversary? What's the date today, Harry? Tell me the date!"

"Jesus. Take it easy. It's August the fourth. It's Tuesday. What are you, crazy?"

He tried to think it through, but the pieces wouldn't fit. "Yeah, maybe. Look, Harry, have her call me right away, as soon as she checks in. You got that?"

"Yeah, sure. Hell, I'm just the—"

Alex hung up.

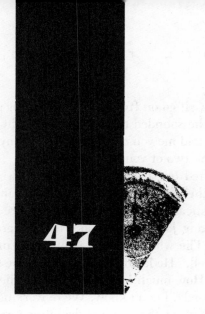

47

MOLLY SAT ON HER BED IN THE HOTEL AND
waited for the connection to go through. A succession of electronic
clicks and clatter testified to the progress and difficulty of the call.
And then he answered.

"You're alive," she said. Her voice seemed to echo down the line.
She could hear her own excitement. *He is alive.*

"Yes," he said. "A little banged up around the edges, but definitely
alive."

"The steadfast tin soldier is home again. Down the drain and out
of the belly of the fish. Was it bad?" *It's always bad, but as long as he
lives through it, nothing else matters.*

"It was . . ." He hesitated, unsure. "Yes. Bad. I guess that's the
word. I couldn't begin to explain it. At least not yet."

"You'll tell me when I get back, I want to hear everything. The
important thing is that you're home and you're all right. I've been
worried, I'm always worried, but this time it was worse, the way we
left it . . ." She stopped, laughed, made an effort to slow herself down.
"What I mean is I love you, and I'm sorry I acted the way I did that
last night. If you're still asking, the answer is yes, let's get married,
to hell with the problems, the problems are what makes us what we
are." She glanced up and saw herself in the mirror. She ran a hand
through her thick hair, pulling it back as she waited for him to speak.

"Of course I still want to," he said. "Nothing's changed as far as
I'm concerned. As far as we're concerned. It was only bad luck that
I went back that night, before we had a chance to make it up. But

that's over, we'll go on from here, everything's going to be all right."
She thought he sounded tired, but that might have been the connec-
tion. "Harry told me you're there with Tommy Fellows," he went on.
"What are the two of you up to?"

"We started out trying to link up his work on terrorism to my
research on the germ warfare unit. Japan is incredible, Alex, a weird
mix of sophistication and childishness. There's a sign in the lobby of
our hotel asking Japanese men not to walk around the halls in their
underpants. The whole country is just amazing, you should see it."

"Yeah, well." He laughed shortly. "Maybe someday. I'd rather you
came home. How much longer will you be there?"

She frowned. "I don't know. We're working on a whole new angle.
The anniversary of the bomb is day after tomorrow and that's when
we're going to get our major interview. We've found a guy, an old man
who wants to talk about the Japanese scientific efforts during the war,
he says he was part of it, the germ stuff, all the research. The Japanese
press is much further along on the biological warfare aspect than we
are. There was a major program on television here about the testing
during the war. They debated it in the press for months. But there's
something else going on that we haven't caught on to yet, I can feel
it. There are a lot of secrets here, Alex."

"Maybe you ought to let them stay secret. You're not going to
change anything that happened more than forty years ago."

She silently noted that it hadn't taken them long to get back to the
argument they had the night he disappeared. "I'm not trying to change
anything, I'm just working on a story. Bringing things out in the open
can be a worthwhile goal. Look, we're just going to get in trouble if
we keep on this way. I miss you, I don't want to argue about things
that don't really matter to us."

She listened to several seconds of long-distance hiss. "I know," he
said finally. "I'm just worried that you'll get into something that's
dangerous."

"And this is the same argument we had the night I left. I can take
care of myself." She stopped and lightened her tone. "Besides, I've got
Tommy here to protect me."

Alex laughed. "That's good. Just stand behind him. It'll take a lot
of Japanese to move him out of the way. Now, how long is it you have
to stay?"

"At least two days, until the anniversary. That's when we meet with our informant. People are very big on form and symbolism over here. Old Colonel Udo insists that we meet in some special place on the same day and at the same time the bomb was dropped . . ."

"Who did you say?"

"Who what?"

She could hear a curious strain in his voice. "Who are you meeting with? Colonel someone?"

"Our source. Colonel Udo, he calls himself. We haven't met him yet but Tadashi says he's very colorful. The old guy was crippled during the war—"

"Don't go," Alex interrupted. "Don't meet with him. He's dangerous, Molly. You've got to trust me."

What was he talking about? "Alex, what do you know about it? What do you mean he's dangerous?"

"I know him," Alex's said, his voice level but insistent. "I had trouble with him back . . . in the past. It's too complicated to explain over the telephone, but I'm telling you, he's dangerous. Stay away from him."

She tried to laugh it off. "Alex, dear, he's a crippled old man. Even if you did know what you were talking about, he couldn't hurt us now. Anyway, I'll be with Tommy and Tadashi, I won't be alone. And I promise to be careful. If you want me to get this story and get out of here, I've got to follow up on the leads."

"When and where are you seeing him?" *Maybe it wasn't Udo.*

"As I said, day after tomorrow. At seven o'clock in the morning. We're not sure where, yet. He's got some special place but he wouldn't tell us ahead of time. Someplace he wants to show us. He says it's where they used to work, some sort of laboratory. He's going to call and give us directions right before we meet."

Where he used to work? A laboratory? The Nichi. It sure as hell is Udo.

"Goddamnit, Molly, now listen to me. I know that bastard. He's dangerous. Stay the hell away from him, do you hear me? For once in your life, knock off the women's liberation shit and take some advice. I know what I'm talking about. Stay away from Udo!"

He could hear his breath in the telephone, feel his pulse beating against the receiver. *She doesn't understand, she won't understand.*

"Alex." Her voice was controlled but he could hear her anger. "I'm doing my job. It has nothing to do with any women's liberation shit, as you call it. I don't know what you know, but I fail to see how it could affect my situation. I'll say it one more time: he's old, he's crippled, and I've got two men with me to protect my poor weak self. I'll be home in less than a week. Just let me do my job."

He felt the dam break. He knew Udo. "Fuck your job! You haven't the slightest idea what you're getting into. This is not a fucking story, this is real life . . ." He listened to the click, then the hissing of the broken connection. Another series of clicks, and then the finality of the dial tone. He placed the receiver back on the cradle. He sat on the edge of the bed and listened to more silence, and heard his own words in his mind, and her response, and knew that he had to do something, he couldn't let it go, he had to stop her.

48

THE EDGE OF THE HOTEL BED SAGGED UN-
der Tommy Fellows's great weight. Molly held her breath as Tommy
swung his feet up and leaned back against the carved wooden headboard. The hotel room was spare and functional, but at the same time
graceful and aesthetic. Both she and Tadashi Ishikawa were sitting in
delicate lacquered chairs that would have collapsed under Tommy.
Beside her was a black writing desk with ivory inlay depicting two
children playing and a flock of geese.

Tadashi marveled at the quality of Japanese bed construction, feeling a stab of pride for his countrymen, the *oyakata*, the artisan carpenter
who had built this sleeping platform that would remain stable under
the bulk of the American. They were in the hotel room of the very
fat American, which adjoined the room of the woman reporter. Tadashi
found the fact that the rooms shared a common doorway faintly dis-
turbing.

"Just where are we supposed to meet him?" Tommy asked. "I don't
fully understand." Tadashi had been recounting his evening with Mr.
Udo. He had left out the more explicit parts.

"At an office building near the old Children's School. They still
call it that, though the school was destroyed long ago. It is now a
modern complex of science-oriented businesses. For many years Udo
worked there for the Green Cross, they are similar to your Red Cross.
He made great progress in the field of artificial blood. The Green Cross
has laboratories in this complex. It has all been built since the war."

"You mean since the bomb," Tommy said.

Tadashi nodded. "Yes. Very little remained after the bomb."

"But what exactly is it he's going to give us?" Molly asked. "And why can't he just meet us at the hotel?"

"I do not know, exactly. Certainly he has information for your germ warfare story. As to why he is meeting us at this laboratory, I do not know. I think, though, that part of the answer is that he is not completely right in the head." He tapped his temple. "This is not unusual, especially in the *hibakusha*. He seems to have been badly injured. Such injuries often damage the mind. It should not affect the information he says he possesses, though we must be aware of that possibility."

"And he says he worked with the 731, the germ warfare group," Tommy said. "Why didn't you guys turn him up before this?"

Tadashi smiled. "I appreciate your high estimation of our investigative capabilities, Mr. Fellows. We fashion ourselves in the mold of your famous Watergate reporters. Woodstein, yes? But there are many old soldiers, and the ones who have the most to lose, and the most information, are the most secretive. I myself did not work on the 731 data when the story was under consideration by our national media. In your country this may be a new story, but here it is several years old, and as such is considered largely settled. Mr. Udo was certainly aware of the controversy over this subject, and for his own reasons has now decided to come forth with his information. I believe he is doing so as part of a national resurgence of sympathy for the days of the Empire, a nostalgia for the days of glory, rather than in a spirit of contrition. And as I have said before, all of this is connected with a mental disturbance."

"Could he be dangerous?" Molly asked. She felt foolish for asking the question, but she also felt she owed it to Alex to at least ask. *Forgive me, Alex, I know I hung up on you, but this is my life. I'll be home soon and things will be all right.*

Tadashi smiled. "No, I think not. He is old and crippled. I believe either Mr. Fellows or myself will be adequate guards to protect your body."

Tommy smiled at the thought. "You say there is a resurgence of sympathy for the Empire. Stories on your textbook controversy are widely reported in American newspapers. As well as reports of various officials coming out with statements that would indicate more than just sympathy with Japan's militarist ideals of the time. Do you think

Mr. Udo is part of this trend, that he's actually *proud* of what he did during the war? Whatever that was."

"It is certainly possible, Mr. Fellows. And in your question I note your disapproval. You must understand that there is no upswelling of militarist ideology among the masses. We are not readying ourselves to take over the world, once again. At least not militarily. A fascination with romantic *kamikaze* films among our youth is not of particular danger to the West."

"And what about the Red Guard?" Tommy asked. "It would seem to me that these are a rather dangerous group of young people. I have read that many Japanese are at least in sympathy with them as examples of moral fortitude in the face of a corrupt society." He was lying on the bed, regarding Tadashi through half-closed eyes. On other occasions Molly had seen him interrogate sources in this lazy, menacing manner. If it was affecting Tadashi, the Japanese didn't show it.

"The principles of the Red Guard are not those of the militarists. As for public sympathy, that has changed substantially in the last few years. They are no longer seen as heroic. In their last serious clash with the police they failed to kill themselves, or even go down fighting. They chose to surrender, thus effectively removing themselves from the status of heroes. In Japan, you must die if you are to join such exalted ranks."

"What's all this got to do with Udo and what we're here for?" Molly asked. Watching Tommy and Tadashi duel was interesting, but getting them nowhere.

Both men looked at her. "Perhaps nothing," Tadashi said apologetically. "But if I perceive Mr. Fellows correctly, he is thinking along the same lines that I am, concerning Mr. Udo's decision to inform the world of the progress and glory of Japanese science during the war. If we are correct, it would seem that Mr. Udo is preparing to die. Is this your assessment, Mr. Fellows?"

Tommy was lying very still, hands clasped over his rotund stomach. He watched Tadashi for a long moment. Tadashi was reminded of the great statues of the Buddha. Tommy closed his eyes and nodded.

49

ALEX STRIPPED OFF HIS SHIRT AND THREW it on the gray canvas travel pack by his feet. He turned on the hot water tap. The small porcelain sink, in the center of a long line of identical sinks, began to steam and fill. The Japanese men's room attendant stared at Alex as he punched up a handful of pink, scented soap from the egg-shaped dispenser and began to lather his upper body. The attendant was wearing a crisp tan uniform, spotless white gloves, and an air of superior disapproval. Other men walked into the room, glanced at Alex, and took up positions at sinks and urinals as far away from him as they could get. Alex didn't give a shit what they thought. He didn't give a shit what the attendant thought. It was nine o'clock in the evening. He'd been on an airplane for seventeen hours and he was dirty. He was going to wash, get something to eat, and find his way to the Shinkansen, the famous bullet train. He still had to get to Hiroshima, and he had to do it by six o'clock in the morning. He'd make it, but not by much, and not if he had to stop and get a room so he could shower and change his clothes in a more civilized manner.

"Towel, please," Alex said, pointing to the pile of snowy white towels the attendant was guarding. The man ducked his head and brought Alex a towel. Alex fished a ten-dollar bill out of his wallet and handed it to the attendant. The man bowed, his disapproval vanquished by American money, and stepped back to his pile of towels.

Large amounts of that same money had brought Alex to this location—the men's room of Japan's Narita airport—and it had brought him here about as fast as it could be done. After his phone call to Molly, he'd thrown some spare clothes into his pack and flagged down a cab. At Kennedy he'd had to wait only two hours for a West Coast flight with good connections straight on to Tokyo. The convoluted Japanese airline system could get him from Tokyo to Hiroshima, but no faster than the bullet train, so he'd opted for land travel. His body was sick of the smell of canned airplane air, the nontaste of bland prefab food, the scratchy seats, and the numbing vibration.

He stared out the window as the taxicab drove him to the train station. Tokyo didn't interest him. Even at night it looked crowded, cramped, and incomprehensible, like Cleveland on steroids, though a quantum leap more colorful and confused. There were masses of pedestrians, and rivers of jammed blaring traffic, complicated neon messages in exotic shades of electric color, a forest of bright banners and signs, and all of it in Japanese and he was goddamned sick of things Japanese.

All he could think of was Molly and Udo and how it could be, and how it could not be, except it was, he could feel it, a cold dead wrong feeling down in his gut that radiated a steady pulse of fear and danger. And through it all, anger at how such a thing could live all these years to follow the twisting timeline to intersect with his own life, Molly's life, like some malevolent slow virus that had infected him, and through him, her. But he would not let it hurt her. He would stop it. He leaned forward and dropped two twenty-dollar bills onto the seat beside the driver. "Faster," he said.

"**I HAVE THE ADDRESS,**" Tadashi said, his voice reedy and breathless over the telephone. "Remember, we are to be there at seven o'clock in the morning, without fail." Molly wrote down the street name and number, asking him to spell it so she could get it exactly right. She was at a telephone at the desk in the hotel lobby. While she listened, she watched Tommy standing by a large potted palm. Tadashi explained the directions for them to tell the cab driver, repeating how they must leave early as the streets would be crowded with masses of people attending the Atom Bomb Day ceremonies. She was well aware of the possible problems. The lobby of the Grand was filled with people from all over the world, jabbering and laughing and lecturing each other, all of them swirling around the great bulk of Tommy, who stood observing everything through interested and amused eyes.

"We'll be there," she assured the anxious Tadashi. She hung up the telephone and held up the slip of paper and smiled. Tommy nodded and smiled back.

ALEX FOUND an aisle seat, pushed his bag beneath it, and nodded to the young woman beside him next to the window. She didn't notice him. She was wearing blue jeans and a purple sweatshirt with the words KING OF SHIT in large white letters across the front. She was reading what seemed to be a pornographic comic book. Alex leaned back and closed his eyes. *Just another typical Japanese housewife.* The train accelerated smoothly out of the station.

THEY LEFT an hour early for what should have been a ten-minute taxi ride. The driver carefully explained his route in extremely broken English, showing more by gestures than words that the roads were filled with crowds of solemn marchers. Molly and Tommy could see that for themselves. Molly was nervous, which was unusual for her. It was only an interview. She was glad Tommy was with her. She decided that she was apprehensive because of the way it had all been arranged, because of the crowds of people surrounding them, bumping against the slowly moving taxi. Then there was the fact that Tadashi was so jittery on the telephone, and Alex's crazy reaction to Mr. Udo, whom he could never have known. All of it combined into a lump of uneasiness that grew as the cab inched along.

ALEX SILENTLY CURSED the taxi driver, and the mob that pressed against the car. Gusts of claustrophobia and impotence swept over him. He had told the driver to get him into the center of town—he would have to find his way from there on his own. He threw a fistful of money at the driver, pushed open the door, and squeezed out into the throng. They had made it across the Aioi bridge, the T-shaped crossing that had been the bombardier's aiming point from the *Enola Gay*. The bombardier had missed, but not by much. Alex peered over the heads of the marchers. He climbed up on the back of the stalled taxi. In the distance he could see the ruined dome of the Peace building. He jumped off the cab and began pushing his way forward.

"WE SEEM TO BE through the worst of it," Tommy said, as the cab began to pick up speed. They had traced their way through a complicated series of twisting narrow side streets, skirting the crowds until the main thoroughfares were clear. The address they were looking for was approximately two miles away from the park and the demonstration. Molly wondered if they would have time to hear any of the speeches after they finished with Mr. Udo. The city outside the car windows was modern and Western-looking. Much of it was made up of blocks of apartment and office buildings built in minimalist Bauhaus style. Unadorned square cubes for the offices and unadorned square cubes with attached balconies for the apartment dwellers.

They rode in silence until the driver slowed and pointed to several buildings in the center of a broad lawn surrounded by a low wall. He pulled up in front of a driveway and stopped. Tommy paid him and they climbed out into the bright warm morning sun and stood on the sidewalk looking up at the two ten-story gray concrete office buildings set back from the street. It was Sunday, no workers were in evidence, and even the nearby apartments seemed empty, almost abandoned. It was very quiet. Tommy checked his watch. "We're a few minutes early."

They walked up the driveway. To their left was a raked stone garden with several ancient rock mountains isolated in the center of a miniature beige-pebbled landscape. The pebbles had been raked in a series of circular swirls. "Where are we supposed to go?" Tommy asked.

Molly fished the directions out of her purse. "Enter on left side of building," she read. "At stairwell on left of entrance, go through fire door and descend two levels. Walk down hall until reaching heavy metal door at end. Go through door. Continue on until coming to lighted room."

"Where the hell is Tadashi?"

"He's supposed to already be here."

Tommy smiled. "As one of us pointed out yesterday, the Japanese have a great attachment to symbols. Udo's insistence that we not meet until the anniversary of the bomb, the directions, all of it has a point. And now we shall see just what that point is."

IF HE COULD get to the Peace Dome, the Japanese symbol of the atom bomb, the building that was the prewar Industrial Exhibition Hall, the same building he had seen and recognized that evening when he and Amelia Earhart had stood by the wall surrounding the Nichi, if he could get there he could get his bearings, find his way. *He's taking us to where they used to work. To some laboratory.* The Nichi. It had to be.

After the bomb, after the surrender, the Japanese had been given twelve days before the occupation forces were in place. Twelve days to burn their papers, hide their shame, and conceal the past. They would have sealed off the Nichi, and if no one gave it away, the secret would have been kept. The Nichi would have remained hidden. Until now.

He could see it. The Dome. Across the park, through the arch of the Peace Monument. Around him the crowd spilled onto the wide grassy mall of the park. He began to run.

THE OUTSIDE DOOR opened easily. They hesitated for a moment, half expecting a shout from a building guard, the ringing of an alarm bell, but there was nothing. They stepped inside. The fire door was right where it was supposed to be. The stairwell echoed hollowly as they started down. Neither of them spoke, concentrating on finding the steps in the dim light of a single bulb high overhead. The door at the bottom creaked and scraped as they pulled it open. A chain with a massive opened padlock lay on the floor beside the door. They walked down a hallway lit by only two small bare bulbs. The floor was gritty; cracked and buckled.

They stopped at the end of the hall. They were facing a heavy gray metal door reinforced with steel plates riveted in place. It had a sign in Japanese and a thick crossbar that locked into the wall. The bar was raised. There was no handle. Tommy grasped the bar and pulled the door toward them.

■   ■   ■

THE PEACE DOME was surrounded by a low iron fence. Weeping willow trees stood in the small grassy area between the fence and the building. The paths around it were crowded with demonstrators, standing shoulder to shoulder, staring quietly up at the spidery metalwork of the building. It drew the eye, the dome. The ruined walls could be any building under demolition, but the dome with its skeleton of delicate steel testified not to the power of the bomb, the *pika don*, the flash boom as it was called in Japan, but evidenced the extraordinary *strangeness* of the event. All the structures in this area had been flattened. As if the hand of some terrible god had come down from above and completely, totally, irrevocably destroyed all trace of civilized man. The very earth had fused. And yet the few walls of this building had stood, and above it the fragile dome traced its silhouette against the bright blue sky. The question that came to the mind was why had this survived? Which then led to the next question: why, how, could such a terrible thing have ever occurred?

The area around the park had been rebuilt. These tall buildings blocked his view. Alex elbowed his way through the crowd, ignoring the disapproving stares.

He aligned himself with what the dome looked like when he was with Earhart, and headed in what he hoped was the correct direction. He had at least two miles to go, he thought. He was already late. He reached the edge of the crowd and trotted down a street bordering the park. He glanced back to make sure of his direction. The crowd was still staring up at the dome.

THE HALLWAY WAS completely dark. Fifty yards away a pool of light spilled from an open doorway. They walked toward the light. The air smelled stale and old. The floor was cleaner here, as if the hallway had been sealed against dust and time. A man stepped into the light and faced them. Tadashi.

ALEX RAN THROUGH an empty intersection. The farther he went from the park, the fewer people he saw. He was heading on instinct now, no longer able to see the dome. He ran along the blocks of buildings, hoping for an open space where he could get his bearings. *A mile. If anything is left, I'll recognize it.* He cast his mind back to the night with Earhart, remembering every detail, sifting the memory for useful information. The only sounds were his own running footsteps and the slap of the canvas pack on his back. He checked his watch. Seven-ten.

TADASHI ESCORTED them into the room. They stood blinking in the light, facing the old man. "Molly Glenn, Mr. Fellows, may I present Mr. Udo."

50

THE OLD MAN IN THE BLACK KIMONO STOOD
and looked at the three figures. They were lined up before him like
blinking sleepy children. He looked at them and knew that what he
had done, that what he was doing, was correct. A feeling of peace
settled within him, cloudlike, a calmness that suffused his body with
a misty purity. He understood the blameless joy of the condemned.

He examined the two Americans. The fat one was as large as a
sumo and had the round head of a Buddha. The woman had hair of
fire, and that was fine, an indication of her spirit, of her inner strength.
She would need this strength if she were to carry his message to the
world. She was dressed conservatively, not half-unclothed like most
American women he saw on television. She wore a severe black suit
with a white shirt. He noticed her hand. The small finger on her right
hand was missing. This was the best omen of all—a missing finger is
a sign of great seriousness and purpose.

"Tadashi," he said in a gruff voice, speaking in Japanese. "You
must go. You have done well, but now I must ask you to leave us."
The Japanese reporter had indeed performed just as planned. But he
was Japanese, and the old man knew that could mean trouble when
the secret was disclosed. There might be an argument, and any discord
would be hazardous to the effect he wished to achieve. There must
be no uncertainty. The secret had been buried too long.

"But, *sensie*, teacher, I wish to stay and hear. I have gone to a
great deal of trouble, and I must respectfully—"

The old man waved a hand. "I understand perfectly, Tadashi. Your two colleagues will undoubtedly share my material with you. But I need you to guard the entrance to this building. In fact, I order you to do this. We cannot be disturbed. This is of the utmost importance. You will do me this last great service." His voice had grown softer, but there was an undertone of authority and command, as if the old man's kimono had been pulled back to reveal the hilt of a sword, the butt of a gun. "You will go. Now."

Tadashi bowed, turned, and left the room. Even though the exchange had been in Japanese, the sense of it had been easy enough to follow. Molly was surprised that he had given up so easily. Tadashi had obeyed his superior; the Japanese weapon of authority still ruled. They listened to his footsteps recede. The door at the far end of the hall opened, and then it was quiet.

"Where are we?" Tommy asked, breaking the silence. The brittle atmosphere of strict formality had been somehow eased by Tadashi's leaving. The old man appeared to relax. His face was terribly scarred. His smile twisted into a mass of ridges. "This is my laboratory," he said with a trace of pride, gesturing around the room.

The room was lit by a row of lights in the ceiling. They seemed to be burning at less than full power. The light they cast was pale and fluctuated slightly at uneven intervals, like the erratic contractions of a damaged heart. The room was large and bare except for several pieces of machinery, one of which Molly recognized as a cyclotron. She'd never done much science reporting, but she knew what a cyclotron looked like. This one seemed out of date, even to her. The front part of the room was lined with long, waist-high worktables, all spotlessly clean. At the far end of the room was a sort of conversation-pit area with a large silo-shaped machine that extended upward to the ceiling. The right-hand wall was lined with small partitioned offices.

The old man waited patiently while they examined their surroundings. He was dressed in a traditional kimono, deep black with a white, intricately embroidered Japanese character on the shoulder. Molly found it difficult to look at his face, though in the few minutes she had been in the room the shock at his scarring had lessened. His mouth was smeared upward on the right side, as if the skin had been melted and then jerked and pulled and allowed to cool and fix in this new position. A crablike, rough, rutted keloid scar crawled over his shoulder and embraced the entire side of his head.

"This is my laboratory," the old man said again, bowing slightly.

"Or at least it was. And in a sense, it has remained so. I have not done serious experimentation here in many years, I am more of a . . . what should I say? We have a word that is somewhere between your idea of a maintenance man and a keeper, a worker at a shrine. That is close to what I am. More of a keeper. I have kept the small flame of our triumph alive." He gestured to the far end of the room. "Perhaps we might move down to the lower area. There are chairs there. It will be more comfortable." They walked the length of the room, the old man stepping forward with his left leg and dragging the right along behind. Next to the base of the silo-machine a wooden folding chair had been placed, with a stack of papers on the floor beside it. Ten feet away, two other similar chairs had been positioned side by side. "Please sit down," the old man said, moving to the chair by the machine. As they arranged themselves, Molly rummaged in her purse and came up with her reporter's notebook. She was glad Udo spoke English so well. There was an accent there, though, that she couldn't account for. A hint of clipped British consonants.

"Mr. Udo, will you tell us what sort of laboratory this is? Or was. What was the work done here?" Tommy asked. Molly could see and hear him assuming his air of patience, settling in for the questioning. "And what is the connection with what you are here to tell us? And why has it been sealed off?"

The old man nodded and smiled faintly. "Yes," he said, "I will tell you these things. Allow me to begin at the beginning." He lowered himself carefully onto his chair and began.

"During the Pacific war this was a secret research laboratory. Our job was to examine and develop specialized weapons for the military. This complex was called the Nichi, which means the Sun, and was built far underground to protect our work from bombing by your B-29s. We expected a protracted air war in which all of our cities would be mercilessly bombed. This came to pass in all of the country except a few isolated areas. Hiroshima was one of these. During the war we never knew why, though many reasons were given. Rumors circulated for several years. It was thought we were spared because our city was so beautiful the Americans would want to build their villas here after they had defeated us. Perhaps, it was said, so many of our citizens had relatives in America that some sort of influence was being exerted in our favor. And then there were the prisoners of war who were being held here. There was even a rumor that some very important person was living secretly in our city. That person was thought to be President Truman's mother. You see how absurd our people can be on occasion."

"That's not a trait confined to the Japanese," Tommy said dryly. "In our country there was a rumor that Japanese saboteurs disguised as salmon were swimming up one of the major rivers in our Northwest. Supposedly one of them had been caught by federal agents. Wartime breeds rumors."

The old man smiled at the idea of men disguised as fish. "Perhaps it is our constant search to explain the unexplainable. To understand forces that are beyond our understanding."

"I believe that is a condition of all mankind," Tommy said.

"Yes, I agree. But in the end, as you know, even the possibility of President Truman's mother did not save us. But as you see, this laboratory withstood even that destruction. You used the word 'sealed' earlier. That is a good description. We have our own generators, a separate engine for each laboratory, and they not only worked well then, they are still functioning. I have maintained them over the years, and they remain quite serviceable. They give us light, circulate the air, and free us from any dependence on aboveground facilities." He stopped as if thinking, choosing his words. His hands were clasped in his lap, long graceful fingers intertwined. He stared down at his hands.

"We worked in many areas. Radar, jet aircraft, electronic rays . . ." He paused.

"Biological warfare?" Tommy asked gently.

The old man looked up at Tommy. "Yes," he said evenly. "Some of our people worked on this aspect. And nuclear weapons, as well." He waited for a reaction. Tommy's eyes were half closed. He nodded slightly. Molly was writing in her notebook. She had a tape recorder in her purse, but she didn't trust it. Machines had a habit of running out of batteries or tape at crucial moments.

"This laboratory was the nuclear weapons research group," the old man went on.

Tommy interrupted. "The Allies were aware, during the war, that the Japanese were working on nuclear weapons. Obviously, it came to nothing. The Germans were also experimenting. Neither country was successful." The old man smiled faintly and began to speak, but Tommy moved on. "Tell us about the major projects. Tell us where you did succeed."

The old man sat without speaking for a moment, then continued patiently. "There was a measure of success in all areas. Our problem was not expertise, or even industrial capacity. Our real enemy was time. With so many resources involved in traditional weaponry, there was little money and material left over for our research and particularly our development. The so-called death ray, though we referred to it as an electrical microwave weapon, was a partial success, but adequate power supply problems were never solved. Its range was too limited to be of use.

"The biological studies here at the Nichi were successful on an individual level, most of these formulae having been worked out years before. There were some moral considerations, but the primary nonuse of these weapons was tactical. I believe that held true for all belligerents. In the end it was not morality that held them back, but efficiency. Although they were used against the Chinese.

"Our radar was deficient in comparison with the Allies. That was extremely unfortunate. The radar in conjunction with the jet aircraft would have been a deadly combination."

Molly looked up from her notebook. "I thought your forces had jets in production by the end of the war," she said. She had browsed through enough of Alex's World War II books to have learned something about most areas of the war.

"Yes, that is true. But we would have been much further along had not a serious accident severely curtailed our aviation staff. We, with German help, had built several prototype jet fighters. The fastest and the most deadly was readied for flight in early 1944. The test took place at a secret airfield on the outskirts of Hiroshima." The old man stared over their heads, remembering. "As an official of the Nichi, I was present at the test flight. The pilot was a woman of great expertise. I was not with the aviation workers who had built the plane and were conducting the test. They were under a large tent out on the field. Those, like myself, who were simple observers were on a grassy area at the end of the runway. Many high-ranking officers of the Air Corps were present in the tent. The plane tested was the Shusui fighter. It was a beautiful spring day, shortly after the cherry blossoms had appeared. The plane took off at high speed and went into a steep climb. I was told later that the engine failed at nine thousand feet. The problem was in the fuel tank, the outlet leading to the engine was positioned too far forward on the tank. With the steep level of climb, after the fuel dropped below a certain point, the engine simply quit.

We watched it happen. The plane slipped over and for a moment it seemed as if the pilot would be able to maneuver the craft, or at least control it to some extent, but that was not to be. By some strange twist of fate, the airplane dove straight down into the tent where the experts and the generals of the Air Corps were watching. There was a terrible explosion, and the entire group was wiped out almost to a man. This, perhaps, was the greatest blow our Air Forces could have received and went far in reducing our capabilities in the air. Ultimately, I believe, this one event had as much effect on our losing the war as any loss suffered at sea or on the field of battle." He stopped. Then he looked up at the two reporters as if he were waking from a daydream.

ALEX WOULD HAVE missed it were it not for the rock garden. He was running down a sidewalk next to a low wall, becoming more and more worried that he would never find the spot, when he looked over the wall. The clear area caught his eye and memory clicked into place and he realized he was looking at the piece of ground where the prisoners had been subjected to the biological bomb explosions. The carefully placed grove of thick wooden stakes. Only now it was a rock garden with raked pebbles. He looked up at the two buildings inside the walled grassy area. If he could get into one of the buildings, he could get to the top floor and be able to clearly see the Peace Dome. If he could see the dome which was now behind a screen of intervening trees, he'd know for sure if he was in the correct place. He vaulted onto the wall and over the other side. He hesitated—*could it still be contaminated after all these years?*—then walked out onto the plain of pebbles, past the large mountain-rock in the center. He remembered the rough feel of the wooden stake. He remembered Amelia Earhart beside him. He walked to the wall and leaned against it. In the distance he could see sunlight glinting from the surface of water. He turned around. The building to his left was situated where the administration building had once been. Which was right on top of the Nichi. He was here, he could feel it; there was a kind of resonance in his bones.

TADASHI SAW the man wearing a pack jump over the wall and walk out onto the meticulously arranged pebbles of the rock garden. The man turned, shaded his eyes, and looked toward the building where Tadashi was standing in the doorway. *American tourist? What's he doing all the way out here?*

Alex trotted up the horseshoe-shaped driveway. As he neared the building, a young Japanese man in white shirt and black pants stepped out of the doorway. The man waited as Alex approached. "Sorry, sir. You can't enter this building," the man said in barely accented English.

Alex glanced at the building then back to the man. "Well, I just want to go up to the top floor and look through a window. I'm visiting here from America. I won't disturb anything."

"Sorry, it's Sunday, and I'm the only one here. It's really not—"

Alex punched the man in the forehead. He hit him with his fist as hard as he could. The Japanese went down and rolled onto his back. His eyes were open, only the whites showing.

Alex knelt, gathered up the man, and threw him over his shoulder. He walked the few steps to the building and pulled open the door. He stopped inside and waited while his eyes adjusted to the dim light of the corridor. He supposed he ought to feel shame or guilt but he felt nothing. He would have time to repent and make apologies and amends when it was over. He found an unlocked door, opened it, and looked into what was obviously a maintenance storeroom. Rows of buckets and mops alternated with stacks of bright green cans of cleaning fluids. Alex lowered the unconscious man to the floor. He quickly ripped a cloth towel into strips and tied the man. He tried to make the knots so that the Japanese would be able to free himself in a reasonable amount of time. If not, the maintenance staff would run across him before he starved to death. He stepped back into the hall. He walked to the end of the corridor where he had entered. Next to the door to the outside he found a heavy fire door. He pulled it open. A set of stairs disappeared downward. *There's got to be a way in. If I keep going down I'll find it.* He stepped in, closed the door behind him, and started down.

"THIS IS very interesting, Mr. Udo," Tommy said, "but I don't think a general history of this secret complex is what you called us down here for. Molly, Miss Glenn, is interested in the workings of the biological warfare group, the Unit 731 people. In particular, we need proof that American POWs were used as guinea pigs. This is an important issue in our country. We need this information to redress a wrong perpetrated by our own government on these returned POWs. We need names and numbers. We had hoped that you could help us find this material."

"Yes, Mr. Fellows, I am aware of your interests. Tadashi has passed them on to me. And I am sure that material is here. Not in this room, but in one of the other laboratories. The Japanese worker is a very meticulous and careful record keeper in whatever industry he is employed. Everything has been preserved here. On the day of the bomb the workers hurriedly left the complex and the entrances were then blocked by the debris from the firestorm that followed. When the building above us was constructed, shortly after the war, it was known by only a few principals that there was an extended series of rooms on the basement level. But it was also known that these rooms held matters that were important to Japan during the war, and having no desire to bring these matters to light, especially as the Americans were still occupying the area, the builders walled up the access and installed the heavy doorway. It was kept a secret. The sign you may have noticed on the door warns the curious to keep out because of radiation danger. That is a warning that is taken very seriously here in Hiroshima. If your material exists, it can probably be found. But when you hear what I have to tell you, I believe you will have found a story that will be of greater interest to your readers."

Tommy lowered his head in acquiescence. "We are always interested in stories of great interest, Mr. Udo. Please continue."

"As you have said, it was thought that Japan had made little progress in achieving nuclear capabilities. This is a fact known to the world. The truth is, Japan achieved a nuclear capability far greater than anyone on the outside has ever guessed, Mr. Fellows. Miss Glenn, I wish to tell you that you are sitting in the birthplace of the Japanese atomic bomb."

"NO!" Alex walked into the room. All three of them at the other end stood up. Molly made a small sound and dropped her notebook and pencil. Alex walked toward them. "Bullshit. What kind of new lie is this?" *Good God. His face. Not Udo. Another lie.* "What are you trying to pull now, Tubbs? What is the point of this? Why did you tell these people your name was Udo? Just what the hell is going on?" He stopped at the step that led down to their area. The old man was standing, facing Alex, eyes closed. He opened his eyes and looked intently at Alex. "You are a devil," the old man said quietly. "A spirit. You have come from the past. You cannot be."

"No, I am here. Believe it. I am the truth, but you are a lie."

"Alex?" Molly said, moving to his side. "How did you get here? How did you find us?"

Alex put his arm around her and pulled her to his side. He didn't take his eyes off Udo. Tubbs. The old man. "I took an airplane, just like regular people," he said with a grim smile. "I found you because I've been here before. A long time ago." He looked down at Molly. He could smell her clean hair. Her warm body was pressed against his side; it had been a long time since he had held her. He would hold her soon, but first he had to know what Tubbs was up to. *It was all a lie, a series of lies. From the very beginning.*

"What's the truth, Tubbs? No more bullshit. We'll stay here all night if we have to. Your guard is tied up in a closet upstairs. We won't be bothered. Come to think of it, we'd never be bothered anyway. No one knows where we are. No one would ever think to look here. We'll stay until this is over. Now talk." He turned to Fellows. "Nice to see you again, Tommy. It looks like you've got things pretty much under control here."

"Yes, Alex. Mr. Udo here, or Tubbs as you call him, was just telling us about Japan's nuclear capabilities. A very interesting story, if true, and one that we definitely want to hear. But first, might you explain how you know this man?"

"The explanations are going to have to wait. You're going to hear some pretty strange stuff. His name is Saburo Tomishiro. I know him as Tubbs, nicknamed after a comic strip character that he used to resemble. He's lost weight and added a few years since then, plus the scars. But he's definitely not Udo. Udo was a colonel in the Japanese Army, a particularly nasty character. Tubbs, if you were going to take a name, why take his? What on earth could you gain?"

Tubbs sat down in his chair and arranged his kimono before speaking. Alex hesitated, and then sat down on the step. Molly sat beside him and Tommy re-took his chair.

"You did not know Colonel Udo. You knew only the man you saw. There is a difference. He and I were standing together when the *pikadon* exploded. He was facing the explosion, I was turned away. As you can see. Udo died a very painful death, which he bore honorably. I spent many weeks in a hospital. Since then I have spent many more weeks in other hospitals.

"Why did I take his name? Because my own name was known to your Colonel Donovan. Do you not remember that? As I lay in my hospital bed I had little to do but think. My mind was confused in the beginning, but later I realized that the Americans were going to come to Japan and search for any possibility that we were involved in nuclear bomb construction. As they then did. They destroyed all the cyclotrons in Japan, cut them up and threw them into the sea. Any piece of equipment that would seem to have any use in studying atomic theory was destroyed. They broke up our laboratories with axes. This cyclotron was the only surviving piece of such equipment, as was this lab. I knew that Donovan, your OSS, would come looking for me. They did. But by then I was Colonel Udo. If Donovan had looked at me, he would not have recognized the man he had seen on that island in the Pacific. If you think my infirmities are extreme now, you should have seen me then. As you did, if you remember."

"But why Udo? His crimes were such that he should have been hung with the other war criminals. How could you take that chance?"

"It was known that he worked here, yes, but his role was not generally known outside the lab. Besides, as I said before, the Colonel Udo you knew was not the real man. The real Udo was honorable, a soldier of great courage. The man he became for you to see was in many ways as repugnant to him as it was to you. That he achieved such success with his performance is a testimony to his prowess and determination. It was no dishonor to take his name."

Alex tried to keep the confusion off his face. Tubbs wasn't smiling, but Alex could see he was taking pleasure from his explanation. "It was an act? Cutting a man's lungs out is an act? Johnny Jump was just part of a ruse?"

"In a manner, yes. The unfortunate Mr. Jump was created by the doctor who performed the surgeries, not Colonel Udo. And as you remember, the doctor paid dearly for his strange research. Mr. Jump was able to effect his revenge adequately, despite his having such limited mobility. But essentially, yes, it was all an act. For your benefit. You should not take this personally, if it hadn't been you it would have been some other American. The plan was intricate, but it accepted many possible variables."

Alex felt defeated. Suddenly tired. "How much of it was a lie?"

"All of it. Everything. From the beginning to the end."

"And what is the truth?"

"The truth is here, Alex-san." Tubbs bent and picked up the stack of paper from beside the chair. "The truth is that we, the Japanese, did not fail. We, too, built an atomic device. Two of them. They were exploded off the coast of Korea two days before the Hiroshima blast. They were built in Korea, everything was in Korea. This particular room was always part sham, designed to impress you. It is true we did theoretical work here, but the real work was done in Konan, Korea. We had to convince you that the danger was here. If it meant the destruction of Hiroshima, then that was a price we were willing to pay. Your attention had to be kept from Konan. It worked. Time, once again, was our enemy. Had we been a few weeks earlier, who could predict the outcome? I know you do not believe this, but it is true. These papers are the proof. Over the years I have written the final report on our success." He stood and carried the papers to Alex. Alex accepted them. He picked a photograph off the top of the pile. It showed a familiar mushroom-shaped cloud, over water.

"It can't be," Alex said.

Now Tubbs allowed himself his small smile. "As you said, my old friend. Believe it. It is the truth."

51

"IT IS," TOMMY SAID, BREAKING THE SI-
lence, "not impossible." All of them looked at him. He was leaning
back in his chair, arms crossed over his chest. "I don't understand
what the relationship is between you two." He nodded at Alex and
Tubbs. He frowned and then raised one eyebrow and looked at Alex.
"And I don't quite understand how you've suddenly appeared. You
seem to be Alice, and you have followed us down the rabbit hole."

"No," Molly said, looking up at Alex with a thin smile. "He's the
tin soldier. I told you about him on the airplane."

Tommy shook his head. "Be that as it may. If we could return to
the topic of discussion? I have read certain documents relating to this
question of the Japanese atomic bomb, though I never gave them any
credence. The National Archives has a warehouse full of source material that has remained almost inaccessible. It has never been organized or catalogued. In fact, there were news reports immediately
following the war to the effect that Japan had indeed tested a nuclear
device. One I have read was written by David Snell for the Atlanta
Constitution. This account and others were quickly and firmly denied
by the United States and Japan. Let's hear your Mr. Tubbs out. If he
is about to supply us the missing link, then we have ourselves a story."

"You have yourselves a story if it's true," Alex added. "And in my
experience, the truth is the last thing you're going to get from him."

If Tubbs was bothered by Alex's words, it did not show on what
was left of his face. He seemed as imperturbable as the large rocks in

the garden outside. "You forget, my dear Alex, that when we last met, we were at war. You and I. My business with you was planned."

"Just what the hell was I supposed to do? Was I supposed to tell Roosevelt that you *did* have a bomb? Or was the trick to get me to tell them that you *didn't*? At different points I was being sent back with both of those messages."

"That was the beauty of the plan. It did not matter which conclusion was eventually arrived at, both were beneficial to us. It was all Colonel Udo's strategy. You *did* send a message that the Nichi existed, and that it was located in Hiroshima. That was when our colonel caught you. Conveniently allowing you to get your message through first. If your country decided that we were no threat, even though the laboratory existed, then that was fine. If your country decided that we *were* a threat, then their efforts would be aimed at us here. Which was also agreeable to us. The point was, we were making a bomb, *but we were making it in Korea.* You had to be kept from ever arriving at that conclusion. There was some evidence for it, but by concentrating your efforts on us here, you overlooked or discounted it."

"So you allowed Hiroshima to be destroyed and hundreds of thousands of people to die," Alex said disgustedly. Tubbs gave him a slow nod. "Yes. I will admit that we underestimated the strength of your weapon. Neither of ours was as powerful. But our cities were already being destroyed by your fire bombs. Our people were already being slaughtered in the hundreds of thousands. If we could have finished our bomb even a month earlier, or if our government had not capitulated when it did, the outcome might have been very different. Even knowing what was to happen, even knowing that I would be left with this"— he touched the right side of his face—"even knowing what happened to our people, I would have done the same. We would have won. Or fought you to a draw. It was worth it."

Tommy leaned forward and rested his enormous elbows on his knees. His eyes were narrowed. "And what happened to the factory where you built your bombs? You need an enormous industrial capacity to produce a nuclear device. At least you did back then. Why didn't the occupation forces stumble on something that size and figure it out?"

"You did. Or at least the Russians did. When they entered the war, they swept down through Manchuria. Most of our scientists and workers had already fled, but some were captured. The entire factory was dismantled and shipped back to Russia. That was how the Russians were able to assemble their own bomb. They utilized Japanese technology and Japanese equipment."

"Was your factory near the Chosin Reservoir?" Tommy asked.

"Yes, how did you know that?"

Tommy sat back and smiled. "During the Korean War the Russians sealed off that whole area. No one on our side could ever figure out what they were doing there."

"They were hiding everything that we had left behind," Tubbs said mildly. "Everything that they had not already dismantled and shipped away. Now I have a question. Do you already know all of this, Alex-san? I wonder if spirits know all the affairs of men."

As near as Alex could tell, Tubbs was perfectly serious. "I'm not a spirit; I'm a man."

Tubbs laughed shortly. "No, that is not true. You do not age. You are not a man. You came to me before, with a spirit child, when I was in the hospital. You spoke to me, but I could not hear you, I was deafened by the blast. I thought it was a dream, but here you are. Now. I see that it was not a dream."

Alex stood up. He was tired. He didn't know what Tubbs was talking about. Fear of what might happen to Molly had been keeping him going. And now she was safe. He had no interest in one more round with Tubbs. The man had beaten him, every time. *Let it go. Let the New York* Times *handle it from here on out. I screwed it up from the very beginning, I didn't change anything.* But he couldn't leave it alone. He needed to touch the sore spot one more time. "I was trying to stop it," he said. "I was trying to stop it all. Us. You. I didn't want anyone to use the bomb. It wouldn't have been necessary. You don't need to be a spirit to see that. But now, having seen it all, I can't really blame the Americans for using it on you. The lesson of that war, as you have so ably pointed out, was that Japan would have stopped at nothing. We were lucky. We were lucky we got ours finished first. We were lucky your emperor decided to quit. Did he know about your bomb?"

Tubbs nodded. "He knew. And in the end he was weak. Hiroshima was a terrible shock. Nagasaki broke him. You are correct. Luck was truly on your side."

Alex shook his head. He pulled Molly to her feet and looked at

Tommy. "I don't want to hear any more of this. Do you two want me to take this stuff?" He touched the stack of papers on the floor with his foot.

Tommy nodded. "Yes," he said, continuing to speak while Alex stuffed the papers into his pack and slung it over his shoulder. "I can understand, Alex, why you might be less than enthusiastic about Mr. Tubbs's story. At least I think I can understand. Though I am going to have quite a few questions for you as well. But for now, I will stay here and chat. Do you wish to go, Molly?"

She looked at Alex then back to Tommy. Alex could see her conflict, could feel it in the tension of her body. He still needed to convince her. He still did not trust her with Tubbs. "Please, Molly. Just this once. I'm sorry about my women's lib crack on the telephone. I'm sorry about a lot of things. Come with me and I'll explain."

And then he could see that it would be all right. That they had turned some corner, where each was willing to give in to the other. There would be a future.

"All right," she said. "You get the story, Tommy. I'll work on it later, but you don't need me right now. Before we go, though, I'd like to ask Mr. Udo or Mr. Tubbs just one question." With her arm still around Alex's waist, she turned to Tubbs. "Why? Why are you telling us this? Why now? What is your purpose? Japan has successfully lived down the Second World War, why bring it all up again? Because of Hiroshima, the world feels sorry for you. America feels guilty. Why change all of that?"

The old man reached into the folds of his kimono and pulled out an old, long-barreled revolver. He pointed it at Alex.

"Because," he said, "the war is not over."

52

THE GUN WAS STEADY. "MR. FELLOWS," Tubbs asked, "What time is it?" The presence of the weapon seemed to deepen the silence. Voices suddenly seemed louder, more significant.

Tommy looked at his watch. When he spoke, his voice was rough. "Almost eight," he said, clearing his throat.

"Will you tell me when it is twelve minutes after eight o'clock? Exactly."

Tommy looked at his watch again. "Yes. I can set the alarm. Why don't you put the gun down?"

Tubbs smiled. "The gun is not for you, unless you try to interfere. I would have preferred other means, but my ancestors were all shop-keepers. The more elegant, traditional methods seemed excessive. Now I am glad that I chose this weapon. It is, like myself, a relic of the war."

"What the hell are you talking about now?" Alex asked. He had his arm around Molly. She was pressed against his side, her body rigid with tension. "What do you think you are? Some old soldier coming out of the jungle after fifty years in hiding?"

Tubbs shook his head. "No, I'm just an old soldier who is dying of atomic bomb disease. The same as many other men and women. An old soldier who hopes to make a point. I am trying to help my country."

"You've made your point," Alex said. "Shooting us won't do anything for your country."

"Oh but it will. This is Japan, Alex-san, death is an honorable and respected method of showing a person's sincerity. It is a way of underlining one's statement. The point must be made, and quite emphatically. With the information I have given you, Japan is now about to abandon her course as the atomic victim. She must join the ranks of the rich and confident. We have too long expected and solicited the world's pity. Japanese science is through being thought of as the handmaiden of electronic amusements. We shall assume our proper rank. Our country now controls the economics of the world. It is time to cast off the shame of our past. We did not lose the war. We lost the last battle because of a trick of time, but now we have won. Let us accept our rightful place."

"Fine," Alex said. *Crazy. Humor him, keep him talking.* "Just let us walk out of here, and you can do whatever you want. We've got the story, you can rest assured it will make the front page of every newspaper in the world. You don't need to shoot anyone."

"Yes, I do. I'm afraid I must. In the last few moments my course has become very clear. I came here with the intention of destroying myself. But think of it. If my death will emphasize my point, think what two or even three will accomplish? Tadashi will write the story, the material is all in the papers you have in your satchel. They will find our bodies and the world will know everything. It will be glorious. Besides, you need not worry. You are a spirit, you will not be harmed. If you were a man, you would be dead. You could not be here. You died on the *Osaka Maru*. But after your death you came to me in the hospital. In any event, you did not fulfill your promise to alert your countrymen to Japan's plight. There was no need to drop your bomb on us. The blame is yours. You will live your spirit life, but we will die. The blame is yours."

"Goddamnit, you had a bomb as well! That's your whole point. You would have used it!"

"Yes. But there was no time."

He pulled the hammer back. The double click electrified them.

Just as he moved to leap at the old man Molly clutched at him, burying her face into his chest, turning her back. Alex tightened his grip on her shoulder and began to turn her away when the explosion clanged off the metal walls of the underground room and he felt the bullet slam into her, tearing her out of his arms.

Alex knelt beside her as Tommy levered himself up, his chair clattering over. Out of the corner of his eye Alex saw Tubbs turn and shoot Tommy in the stomach.

Alex leaned over Molly, trying to shelter her with his body, waiting for the bullet that must surely come.

Another shot. Alex turned and saw Tommy standing with both arms outstretched. Tommy stood as if perplexed, accepting the bullets. Two bloodstains began to spread on the snowy white expanse of his shirtfront. He lumbered forward.

Tubbs shot Tommy again. It did not stop him. Tommy shuffled on, moving like a robot, a zombie. He reached the old man and put his hands around his throat. Tubbs grimaced and with both hands pressed the gun against Tommy and fired one more time. Grains of black powder flared across the broad expanse of Tommy's white shirt. Tommy looked surprised but even more determined. He began to throttle the old man. Tubbs put the gun to his own head and pulled the trigger, the twisted scarred right side of his face disappearing in a spray of blood and bone. The old man and the very fat man collapsed together.

Alex turned back to Molly. Still kneeling, he slipped his hand down her back. It was warm and wet. He tried to think of what to do, how to help her, how to stop the bleeding. He gently removed her jacket and made a pillow for her head. Her blouse was smeared red on the right side where the bullet had taken her. Her back was a solid wet red. She made a small cry and her eyes fluttered open. The blood was pooling beneath her. The air was weighted with the smells of blood and gunpowder. He could see, feel her dying. He knew of no way to help her, and his helplessness was an agony.

"It doesn't hurt," she whispered. "I know it's bad."

"I'll get help."

She lifted a hand to his arm. "No, don't go. You can't rescue me this time." She smiled faintly. Her voice was soft and breathy. He had to bend close to catch the words. Her lips brushed his cheek. "Stay with me. You're the soldier. I'm the ballerina. Tell me the story. Tell me the end of the story."

"Molly . . ."

"Tell me the end of the story," she said, her voice catching. "There must be an end."

He tried to remember it exactly. At that moment it seemed very important to get it right. He closed his eyes and tried to calm himself.

"The soldier had been on many adventures. You know that part." He looked at her. She nodded. Her eyes never left his face.

"The soldier was home, on the table with the other toys. He was with his ballerina again." He touched her cheek. "The ballerina was also steadfast. The soldier was so moved by her, by returning to her, he thought he might cry. But that would not have been proper. He wanted to tell her of his adventures, and of his love for her, which had helped him to be brave when he was afraid. But neither spoke a word."

"I can't breathe," she gasped, her voice rising. Her eyes opened wide with pain and fear. "I can't breathe!" He felt her stiffen. Her skin was bloodless, almost transparent. She stared at him still. And then her body seemed to relax.

He waited. She did not move. He slowly eased himself down on the floor beside her. He lifted her head onto his lap. He gently closed her eyes.

"This is the part we never understood, Molly. We used to talk about it, you remember." He was speaking very quietly.

"One of the children, no one knows why, grabbed the tin soldier, opened the door to the wood stove, and tossed him into the fire. It was probably the evil troll who made the kid do it, but I don't know, maybe the kid was just bad. Anyway, the tin soldier stood, steadfast, while the flames leapt and danced around him. He felt the great heat, but he wasn't sure if it came from the flames, or from the love that burnt inside him. He kept his eyes fixed on the ballerina, through the open door of the stove, and he thought that she smiled at him. Oh, Jesus, Molly." He brushed a strand of hair from her lips.

"A sudden breeze caught the paper figure of the ballerina and lifted her up. She whirled in the air, her spangled necklace glistening as it caught the light, and like a tiny fairy she flew, right into the stove. She flared up for a moment . . . oh Molly." He felt himself begin to cry. "Then she was gone."

He leaned over her. Put his cheek to her lips. There was no breath. No life. She had left him. He tried to stop crying, *the steadfast soldier never cries*, he smoothed her hair back. She was so still. He felt a great emptiness. He wiped his eyes. He looked at his hand on her hair and he saw that he was beginning to fade. *Finish it. Finish it. There has to be an end to the story.* He cradled her in his arms. He spoke, softly, quickly.

"The next day, when the maid was cleaning out the ashes from the stove, a sparkle caught her eye. She pushed aside the ashes and discovered a little tin heart, all that remained of the soldier. She turned the heart over in her hand and there was the spangle from the ballerina's necklace. It had melted against the soldier's heart and become part of it." He rocked her gently, back and forth. "Molly . . . Molly . . . Molly. It had become part of his heart."

He looked up. He heard a soft chiming. Tommy's watch. Twelve minutes after eight. Exactly.

He looked at his hand. It was paler still. He was almost gone. He could see through himself. It seemed as if he were already far away. But he felt no fear, he had no room left for fear. There was only sadness, a great loneliness.

Finally, it seemed as if he stood, but there was nothing left of him, truly nothing left of him. He could see her, for just a moment longer, on the floor, pale, in a pool of red, alone. But Molly had gone on, she too was somewhere else. And as he left, he heard the soft continuing chime of the watch, the measured count of time. "She had become part of him," he whispered. "Part of his heart."

53

past. Several technicians in white lab coats looked up from a set of
blueprints, incredulously, as he appeared before them.

A strange phosphorescence, felt more than seen, flashed through
the room. A feathery wave of heat rippled over Alex. The hairs on his
arms and the back of his neck rose with the prickling of his skin. The
room trembled and then suddenly bucked, as if the floor had been
punched from underneath. Fine grit sifted down in streamers from
the ceiling. The technicians looked at each other, dropped their blueprints, and began to shout. All around the room men and women began
to shout. Then everyone ran through the doorway. Alex stood still,
knees flexed, waiting for aftershocks.

Twelve minutes after eight. Exactly.

Pika-don. The flash-boom. The atomic bomb.

Alex walked to the open door. In the hallway, people were streaming past. Alex closed the door. On the back, facing him, was a heavy
iron bar that locked the door from the inside. He lowered the bar and
rammed it home. He stood for a moment, hands on the door, feeling
his heart pound, trying to imagine the hell that was swirling twenty-
five feet above him. He was approximately two miles from the epicenter
of the blast. Close enough to knock down buildings. Close enough to
go blind, to burn, to die in any number of horrible ways.

All the lights went out.

He stood absolutely still, in total darkness, listening to the muffled
screams of panic through the door. In just a few minutes it had grown

hotter, and the air was stale, faintly tinged with an ozonelike smell. He turned around and faced the empty room. The darkness had heightened his perception of his own being, his body seemed to tingle. Beneath the immediate sensations of his body, the pulse-thumping knowledge of what was occurring, he was strangely calm. He had returned to the past. His future had been withdrawn. Molly was dead. And with that realization came anger, a high keening thread of hate and anger.

A thumping came from the right side of the room. A dull thud and a voice, speaking in Japanese, raised in question. Alex didn't know exactly what the man was asking, but the sense of it was obvious: What the hell is going on?

Someone left behind. Must have been asleep. They dropped the bomb on you, buddy, and you slept through it. No one here but us spirits.

The frightened voice asked his question again. There were sounds of stumbling. Alex knew that whoever it was would find his way to the door, eventually. *Come on. Right this way.* He stepped back, put his hand on the edge of the door, and waited. An odd child-memory traced its way through his mind. As a kid he and his friends had built balsa wood airplanes with rubber-band motors. They would wind the propellers, watching the bands knot, double knot, triple knot, watch fascinated to see how far they could go until the bands would finally break.

There was a moment when he could have remained hidden while the man found the door, opened it, and ran out. But that moment passed, and he remembered Molly, on the floor, dead, and the howl of anger seemed to swell. Alex felt the last strands snap.

Now the man in the dark was talking to himself. Coming closer, cursing, grumbling, wanting to know why the lights were off, where the hell everyone was, why he'd been left alone.

Alex waited.

The man finally made it to the door. He pulled on the handle. Locked. More grumbling.

Alex reached into the darkness and found the neck of the small man. There was a quavering wail of fear as Alex pulled him close. He wrapped his arm around the man's head. He held the man's arms tight against his body, held the man's mouth shut and twisted his head, the bristly close-cropped hair stiff against his cheek, twisted it as the man squirmed and thrashed, twisted until there was a wet snap, loud in the darkness, and he held the man with the head twisted backward, and then he dropped the dead man and stepped back. His chest was heaving. Sweat was dripping off his face, running down his sides beneath his shirt. He stood with the man lying against his ankles, and felt for an emotion—guilt, sorrow, shame, anything. But there was nothing. Only the anger, and even that was now blunted. The insanity that had gripped him eased. What was left behind was a strange hollowness, a feeling of endless loss.

He walked back to the other end of the room. Even in the absolute darkness he was able to move without running into anything. It was as if his mind had become emotionally dead, but his body supernaturally aware. He could almost see in the dark, or rather feel in the dark, sense the presence of objects before he touched them. He stepped down into the lower portion of the laboratory. He found that he still had his pack on his back, had carried it here from the present. He took it off, and laid down on the floor. If he were going to die, it would probably be soon. The firestorm from the bomb should be overhead. He considered the possibility of his air supply being sucked out by the flames. He didn't care.

HE OPENED his eyes. The lights in the ceiling were back on, flickering weakly. He looked at his watch as he sat up. Twelve o'clock. He'd slept for four hours. His first thought was that it had been a dream, all of it, maybe all of it back to the beginning, back to Pearl Harbor. But he stood up and saw the crumpled form of the man by the far door, the poor fool who had stumbled into the path of his madness. It hadn't been a dream, none of it. Molly was dead. That was why he had come back. The lifeline was broken. There was no one left to hold him to his own time. She was gone, and now so was he.

The air was much hotter, but it wasn't as stale as it had been earlier. The lights meant that either power had been restored from the outside or someone had gotten the Nichi generators working. Since everything above ground was surely still burning, the likelihood of service being restored from that direction was slim. That meant that he was not alone down here. There were others still alive, working to stay alive. The Nichi had been built to protect the work and workers from air attack. There would have been some sort of plan established for air raids. That plan would now have gone into effect.

He walked back to the front of the room, stepped over the body on the floor, and put his ear to the door. He couldn't hear anything, but that might have been simply a testimony to the efficacy of the door. He sure as hell wasn't going to open up it up, stride out in the hall, and ask what was going on.

He checked the lock on the door one last time. There didn't seem to be any way to open it from the outside as long as the bar was secured. The door itself appeared strong enough to withstand a sustained assault. Alex turned to the dead man on the floor.

"Looks like it's just you and me, buddy," Alex said. "I've got to stow you somewhere. We might be in here for a while." His words were thin and strange in the empty room. He bent down.

The middle-aged Japanese had a wispy mustache and a look of aggrieved surprise on his face. The eyes were wide open. Alex picked him up easily, slung him over his shoulder, and carried him to the back part of the lab. He put the body down, found a wrench on a workbench, and unbolted the metal plate that was inset into the metal silo, the machine that was supposed to be the uranium separator. The door slid off and clanked to the floor. Alex pushed the body inside and bolted the door back on. He straightened up, looked around the lab, and felt relief now that he could no longer see the dead Japanese.

Alex sat down on the step. He carefully refrained from thinking about Molly or the future. His alternative to trying to stay alive was to die. His mind would not allow that as an option.

He was alone in a room twenty-five feet below an atomic bomb explosion. His most serious short-term dangers included death from starvation and thirst, radiation poisoning, loss or contamination of the air, and discovery by the Japanese. The long-term problems were too nebulous and numerous to come to terms with. He had to force himself to think of possible solutions. Not that there were so many to choose from, or they were so difficult, but simply because he didn't much give a damn. His instinct for self-preservation, some cellular genetic imperative, was keeping him alive. His conscious, emotional side wasn't terribly interested.

He listed his tasks. Secure the door. Explore the room. Look for food and water. Trace the air circulatory system. Set up toilet facilities. Check for alternative modes of exit. Figure out what was happening outside, and what would happen there in the immediate future.

He started out by maneuvering one of the wooden, waist-high lab tables against the door. This took a half an hour of inching the table along with a crowbar. He didn't mind; it was difficult and mindless. He considered piling another table on top of the one he'd scooted into position, but he didn't think he was capable of lifting it. And anyone trying hard enough to get past one table was going to overcome two. A small charge of gunpowder would probably do the trick on the door. The tables then could be levered out of the way.

He began searching the offices. There were seven of them. He worked methodically, starting at the closest office and looking through every drawer and storage space.

The offices took two hours. It might have been his imagination, but the temperature in the lab seemed to have dropped to almost normal. Most of the drawers and boxes were filled with, for him, indecipherable papers, undoubtedly scientific reports. The desks held the usual assortment of family photos and nicknacks.

He gathered everything useful together and assembled his findings on one of the lab tables. Five plates of partially eaten rice; six tall stoneware bottles of saki, each bottle carefully hidden away; a rifle with fixed bayonet; and a small pistol with two bullets. The rifle looked as if it had been left over from the Russo-Japanese War of 1905. And that was it. He hadn't really been hoping for anything specific, so he wasn't disappointed.

He piled all the rice onto one plate. It made a grapefruit-sized pile. There was the usual garnish of pickled radish.

He started on the lab itself, beginning in one corner and opening every drawer and cupboard, sifting through the contents. This took him four hours, at the end of which he allowed himself an ounce of saki, measured out in a calibrated beaker. His meager finds joined the rest on the table: a large box of biscuits, hard as rocks but probably edible if he was hungry enough, a tin of loose tea, and another bottle of saki. He filled a sink with water, topping it off just as the flow spluttered to a stop. A small refrigerating unit held several racks of test tubes with a clear liquid. He removed the test tubes, wrapped his rice in a sheet of brown paper, and put it into the refrigerator. In a pile of electronic equipment he found a Geiger counter. He flipped it on and tested the water in the sink, and was rewarded with a very slow ticking that indicated, or at least he hoped it did, that the water was safe. He made another exploratory sweep of the lab and found two more Geiger counters, from which he removed the thick, heavy batteries.

A loud thumping on the door startled him. He walked to the door and listened. The thumping continued, and he could hear shouting, but the door didn't budge. After a while the pounding and the shouting stopped. *Just checking to see if anyone's alive in here. Yes and no. Go away.* He went back to his pile of treasures and poured himself another ounce of saki. He pulled himself up and sat on the table, sipping the rice wine. He climbed back down and went to a wide free-standing blackboard. He erased a series of scientific formulae, picked up a piece of chalk, and began to write.

AUGUST 6: ATOM BOMB, HIROSHIMA. 8:12 A.M.

He looked at his watch. Six forty-five P.M. Day one. He wandered back to the table while he thought, fishing out one of the round white crackers and gnawing off a corner. They were the same crackers he had eaten back on the island after being left behind by the PT boaters. Some sort of Japanese survival food. He chewed, looked at the blackboard, and began writing again.

AUGUST 8: RUSSIA DECLARES WAR ON JAPAN. ATTACKS MANCHURIA.

AUGUST 9: ATOM BOMB, NAGASAKI.

AUGUST 14: JAPAN SURRENDERS.

AUGUST 27: U.S. THIRD FLEET ARRIVES JAPAN.

AUGUST 28: FIRST U.S. TROOPS LAND.

He dropped the remaining piece of cracker back in the box, poured another ounce of saki into the beaker, and drank it down. He went back to the blackboard and finished the appraisal. He wrote the numbers and underlined them.

TIME UNTIL POSSIBLE RESCUE = 22 DAYS.

That's twenty-two days on a box of crackers, a mound of old rice, and a couple of gallons of saki. If the air stays clean. If the Japs don't decide to see why the door is locked from the inside. If I can figure out a good reason to stay alive. If my luck holds.

He knew there were other Americans not far away. There were several POW camps around Hiroshima. In fact, as Alex knew from his research, there were seventeen Americans in downtown Hiroshima, fliers shot down in earlier bombing runs. Of these seventeen, none would survive. Civilian reports after the war told of seeing one airman torn to pieces by a mob on a bridge after the blast. Another, who later succumbed to wounds, was reported alive in an aid station the day after the bomb. The rest were killed by the blast.

But not me, I'm alive. Molly wasn't so lucky. She had to be wiped out by a crazy old man with crazy notions about his homeland. Fucking Japan. Fucking Japanese.

54

THE KEY BECAME THE METICULOUS RA-
tioning of the saki. The idea was to keep his brain functioning but
disengaged from what had been and what might be, from the loneliness
and fragility of his future, and from the precariousness of his present.
He had to consume just the right amount of the high-octane rice wine
to stay mildly intoxicated, yet not go overboard and end up making a
stupid and possibly fatal mistake. The lack of food helped maintain
his state of mild drunkenness. The crackers were dry enough to soak
up anything liquid, but they didn't affect his constant state of inebri-
ation. He was beginning to think that the crackers weren't real food
anyway, that they were manufactured out of dust, floor sweepings, or
some other nonnutritive fiber that filled the stomach but added no food
value.

He spent an entire day reading Tubbs's report on the Japanese
atomic bomb. The two-hundred-page report was thorough and meticulously documented. Virtually all of the primary technical work had
been done in Konan, Korea, in the Noguchi industrial complex that
spread up the banks of the Yalu River toward the Russian border. Vast
supplies of raw materials, and more than a million kilowatts of power,
were at the disposal of the atomic builders. Five giant uranium sep-
arators were shipped from the Amagasaki Steel Works to Konan. Uranium hexafluoride was supplied by a laboratory in Tokyo which in
turn procured the raw ore from mines in Manchuria excavated by
Chinese prisoners. The whole line of progression, from experimen-

tation to final assembly, complete with charts and diagrams, ended with a series of photographs showing the finished bombs, ships at anchor, ships being loaded with experimental animals, then a series of remarkably sharp shots of an explosion, ships burning, and the signature mushroom cloud. Alex placed the last photograph back on the pile, stacked the papers carefully, put them back in the pack, and spent the rest of the night contemplating what was, and what might have been.

He stretched the rice out over three days. He saved the pickled radishes to eat with the crackers. He was constantly hungry, but the dull gnawing in his gut settled into a permanency that he accepted as part of the pain of being alive. In only a few days he could feel himself growing progressively weaker. He knew if he tried to stay in the room for the full twenty-two days he'd never make it. He and his Japanese partner in the silo would become permanent residents. On the fifth day, in a mood of mild, boozy interest, he made his first foray into the ventilation system.

His attention had been drawn by the fact that the air in the laboratory had continued to circulate and continued to be radiation-free. He unbolted a ladder from the side of the tall silo and leaned it against the back wall where the metal grate of the exhaust system was situated. The setup was simple but effective. The air came into the room at the front, and exited at the back. The metal ductwork was square, made of sturdy metal, two feet wide and two feet high, large enough to deliver the self-contained volume of air needed to cool and aerate the extensive underground network. And large enough to crawl through. If he was going to stay alive, he needed food. To get it he would have to leave his room. To simply walk out the front door could prove deadly. So it was into the ventilation system for several reasons: to see if there were others trapped in the Nichi with him, to find any existing food and water, and to give him something to do, to keep him from thinking about Molly.

He made a small leather pack for the Geiger counter and strapped it around his waist. He fashioned a miner's helmet out of a tin pot and riveted a rather cumbersome flashlight to the top. Straps tied under his chin kept it in place. Screwdrivers, a pair of pliers, a small hammer, and two wrenches fit neatly into a leather holster lashed to his chest. He took a large test tube of saki, capped with a rubber stopper, and tied it to the back of his wrist and forearm. He stood at the bottom of the ladder and waited for a moment as a wave of hunger-weakness washed over him. Then he climbed the ladder to the waiting duct.

He pulled himself into the hole. He had five feet of straightaway before the system made a sharp right L. He lay stretched out in the duct, catching his breath. The metal surfaces were coated with a layer of dust that tickled his nose. He waited until the impulse to sneeze and cough had passed, then began to pull himself forward. He squirmed around the L into a long dark tunnel and switched on the flashlight.

He pulled himself along on his elbows. The dust made the metal slippery, which eased his progress, but he was soon panting from exertion. Five days on reduced rations and a steady inflow of saki had left him weaker than he'd thought. His breathing was loud and strained. He made another right turn and saw a faint light ahead. He moved along, taking care to keep his gear from banging against the duct. He came to a small grate and looked out onto the main hallway of the Nichi. It was empty. He pressed his face against the grate and inhaled the dust-free outside air. After a few minutes rest he pulled himself onward.

He crossed over the hallway and into foreign territory on the other side. The weak beam of the flashlight showed what seemed to be a dead end but turned out to be a T-joint with ductwork running off to both the right and the left. Faint light filtered through from the right, so he turned that way and continued on. This time he was rewarded with a much larger grate. He lay on his side, and looked down on another laboratory. It, too, was empty. From the appearance of various paraphernalia scattered around, he decided it was an electronics lab, maybe the home of the infamous death ray. He didn't see anything that looked edible. He flopped over on his back and looked up at the metal ceiling a few inches above him. He untied the test tube of saki from his wrist and took a sip. Part of it spilled and ran down his cheek.

So where the hell is everybody? He wiped the saki off his cheek and saw that his hands were black with dust. The possibility that he was alone both cheered and depressed him. Being alone meant he didn't need to fear being caught, but it could also mean he was trapped, sealed in. Alex imagined Tubbs coming across his bleached bones sometime in the future. Thinking of Tubbs brought back Molly. When he thought of Molly, it all began to crumble, all the little stratagems for staying alive, all the *reasons* began to disappear. He drank off the rest of the saki and held himself very still while he emptied his mind and relaxed every muscle. The hate he had felt the first few days had begun to dim, but he brought it back, nursed it into full force, letting it overcome his thoughts of the past.

He made himself consider only the here and now, the dark world of the duct. *Let's see, go back? Go on? Stay here and starve to death? Who gives a shit?* But in the end he rolled over and moved on to check the next room. That's where he found them.

Twelve of them. They were in a small storage area off the generator room. He could hear motors chugging away nearby, could just see the corner of one of the gasoline-powered engines. The Japanese, eleven men and one woman, sitting and lying on blankets and sheets of canvas that had been spread on the floor. A few of them were in military uniform. One man seemed to be injured. Alex pressed close to the grate and examined the men carefully, looking for Tubbs. He knew that Tubbs had been aboveground when the bomb was dropped, or at least that was what he had said. The condition of his face certainly verified it, but what was one more lie in the scheme of things? What if he *is* here? *If he's down here, I'll kick out the grate, jump down, and kill him.* Alex was suddenly flushed by the idea. His heart thumped with excitement. If he could find Tubbs and kill him now, then Molly wouldn't die in the future. He pressed even closer, peering down. The men were talking and arguing. Several were chewing something that looked like beef jerky. Alex felt his mouth watering. He made himself back away. If one of the men happened to glance up and see his face mashed against the grill, he would be in serious trouble.

He laughed at himself. *Serious trouble? What am I in right now? If there are twelve of them here, does that mean there are more elsewhere? No, they would tend to bunch together, safety in numbers. The generators are the most important survival factor; they have to be tended. How long will the Japanese stay? Can I get food from them? Kill them? Are they in contact with the outside?*

His neck was beginning to tire. He put his arm under his head so he could see without holding himself up. He wished he had some more of the saki. The more he watched, the more he thought they were arguing. There was a fair amount of arm waving and raised voices. After a while, as he began to grow bored, he realized he was sobering up. He carefully began sliding back down the duct. When he reached the T-joint he maneuvered himself so he was moving headfirst again.

Finally he poked his head out in his own room and breathed deeply. He now noticed that there was a definite unpleasant odor in the room, undoubtedly his roommate beginning to decompose. He climbed down the ladder, unbuckled his gear, and allowed himself a double measure of saki to make up for his time in the duct.

When he awoke, it was dark. For a moment he lay on the floor and wondered how he had slept so late into the evening. And then it dawned on him that the reason it was dark was because the lights had gone out again. He sat up and felt around until he found his miner's helmet. He strapped it on and switched on the flashlight. The beam was weaker than it had been in the duct. The batteries wouldn't last much longer. He had scrounged four more batteries out of various drawers in the worktables. He found them and slipped them into his pockets.

He turned off the flashlight to save the batteries. The air was dead again, the odor of decay much stronger. That, coupled with the failed lights, meant the generators must have stopped. Either the Japanese had run out of fuel or had abandoned the Nichi. Either way, he had to find out. He couldn't survive without air. He might be able to sit in the dark for two weeks, but he doubted that in the end he would come out sane. He fumbled around and found his jug of saki.

He'd have to go see what had happened. Back to the ducts. He turned on the flashlight and began his preparations.

If the Japanese were gone, he would have to move his center of operations to the generator room. Besides, his roommate was beginning to make the lab untenantable. He supposed that it would have been physically possible to move the body somewhere else, but there wasn't enough saki in the world to get him through that.

He gathered up everything he thought would be useful. He had four full bottles of saki left. He found some graduated cylinders with wide stoppers, filled them up with water from the sink, and wrapped them carefully in strips of dark blue cloth from one of the storage cabinets. He located the extra batteries he had taken from the two spare Geiger counters.

He loaded everything into the pack on top of Tubbs's report. The pack was extremely heavy and clanked and gurgled as he lifted it to his shoulder. He crammed his pockets with biscuits and ate the last shreds of pickled radish. He drank off the dregs of a bottle of saki and climbed the ladder.

The batteries for the flashlight ran out halfway through the duct. He had to stop, fumble out the extra batteries, and replace them in the cramped dark. His breathing sounded like a set of bellows before he was finished. He rested for a few minutes, trying to calm himself as a claustrophobic anxiety began to set in. He squirmed on, dragging the heavy pack behind him.

He turned out the flashlight and worked by feel after turning the corner at the T. He found the second grate and lay quietly, trying to hear some sound of movement or sleeping people. After ten minutes of waiting he flicked on the flashlight and shined it around the room. Empty. Even the canvas and blankets they'd been using for bedding were gone.

He shined the light on the inside of the grate. It was fastened by six screws, just like the one in his lab. He located the pliers in his tool belt and began unscrewing the screws from the inside. He held on to the grate as the last screw dropped into the dark room. He lowered the grate as far as he could reach and let it drop.

The ventilation system was twelve feet from the floor. He squirmed around and got his feet over the edge. He tried to lower himself carefully, but he was too weak and he slipped and fell, landing with a dull smack on his side as he clutched the pack to his chest. He lay on the floor, panting, thanking the gods that he hadn't landed on the pack and smashed the saki bottles.

There were seven generators. In the light of the flashlight they looked like a line of monstrous green toads waiting to be fed. He unscrewed the caps of the gas tanks on each and pointed his head so the light shone into the tanks. They were all empty. Stacked neatly next to the last generator were a half-dozen five-gallon drums that now contained only the smell of gasoline.

The rest of the room was empty. The flashlight beam played along the walls as he looked for an answer that wasn't there. He sat down on one of the metal gas cans, pulled a bottle of saki out of his pack, and took a long drink. The liquid gurgled and sloshed as he shook the bottle, checking the level.

He was aware that his continual drinking was taking a toll. His thinking was becoming dulled. He had to break each problem down to its basic elements and line them up so he could turn each fact over while he contemplated its meaning. The reason the Japanese had abandoned the generators was because there was no more gasoline.

Without gasoline there was no light, no air, no hope. He pointed the beam of light at his watch. He was now into his sixth day without adequate food. He could stay down here and die, or he could go above-ground and probably die. Besides, he had to find Tubbs, had to kill him, had to save Molly. He stood up, watching the light skitter across the floor as he staggered and caught himself. He very carefully pushed the cork into the neck of the saki bottle. He found, to his surprise, that he was tired, but hopeful. First he would sleep, then it was on to the rest of the plan. Find Tubbs. Kill Tubbs. It was enough.

55

HE FLINCHED AT THE SCRAPING SOUND AS
he opened the door. He looked out into the hall. The light from his
helmet flitted over the walls. He was on his feet again, out of the
ducts. He looked both ways and saw the shadows of Japanese soldiers,
lurking forms waiting to pounce. *Jesus Christ. Take it easy.* Now that
he had a purpose, the thought of being kept from it made him jumpy.
When he'd had no reason to live, he had not been particularly afraid.
Now, fright, the self-preserver, had come back to him. He walked
down the dark corridor in the direction of the stairwell. His footsteps
echoed in the darkness. He turned the corner at the end of the hall.
He could see that the door to the stairs was open.

Debris spilled through the doorway. Alex stared at it, the flashlight
illuminating the pile of rubble in a weak pool of light. His gaze, and
the light, followed the drift as it sloped through the door. He looked
up with a feeling of awe, as if he had come upon some natural cave
formation of exquisite beauty, of infinite complexity. The stairwell
was jammed with wooden boards, beams, huge chunks of cement,
blocks of stone, chairs, desks, papers, twisted lengths of pipe, and
spiderwebs of electrical cord. Stalactites of reinforced concrete dangled
from the mass. The debris was crammed together in such a way as to
be self-supporting. For just a second, he felt the coal of hope within
him flicker and weaken. He tightened the straps on his pack, adjusted
his helmet so the light shone at a higher angle, and waded through
the doorway into the stairwell.

There was a passage, of sorts. The Japanese who had been trapped down here with him had tunneled out. But it was a small passage, and the rubble had silted in after they had climbed through. If anything, their exit had weakened the stability of the structure. Before he could consider the danger and lose his nerve, he began to carefully climb the shifting slope.

As he worked himself upward, the mass shifted around him. Each piece removed was a possible keystone, every element threatened the whole. The tunnel closed up behind him, he could not go back. He would climb forward, ease away an obstruction, climb over it, push it behind. He pulled a desk chair free and found himself face to face with a dead woman. Her face was a bloated kabuki mask, plaster-dust white streaked with webs of mud-brown blood. He burrowed away from her.

At one point he found himself in a sort of cavern, the concrete steps miraculously free. He rested on the steps, like a tired spelunker taking a break, drinking his saki, keeping his mind on hold, careful not to think. The crazy jumble that loomed around him was a reflection of his mental state. Each memory, each scrap and shard of his past, was tumbled together, the beams and supports precariously situated, any piece of it able to bring down the entire structure if unduly disturbed. He leaned back on the steps. A lone foot projected out of the ceiling of wreckage above him.

It took him eight hours. His hand were scraped and cut, gloved with bright blood. His clothes were torn. He was filthy, sweating, covered with a coating of dust and dirt.

It was night when he came through, when he pushed aside the last obstacle and stumbled out. His mind expected a release, the smell of clean air, a sense of freedom, but the warm outside air was thick and close with the sharp stink of burn.

This was not the odor of wood smoke, the pleasant smell of an open fire, but the stench of objects destroyed. Not just wood, but clothing and appliances and paper and roof tiles and metal and bodies, of men, women, children, animals, of all things having been consumed, cremated. This pungent smell was laced with the sweet stench of decay.

He emerged from the basement, turned, and looked up at a dark mountain of rubble that had been the administration building. A faint glow from the cloudy night sky lit the scene dimly, showing the mountain as a tangled heap. He stood in front of the ruin and tried to locate some point of reference. It was too dark, the landscape of twisted wreckage too confusing. He climbed a low hill of debris. Smoldering fires glinted red, eyes in the darkness. He climbed back down, realizing that he had nowhere to hide, no direction or place he knew was safe. If he was going to find Tubbs, he would have to do so as soon as possible. Once the Americans arrived and organized things, Tubbs might be easier to find, but a hell of a lot more difficult to kill. He rummaged around and found a small cavelike opening between two pieces of upended concrete. He dragged himself in. He took off his helmet and wiped his face with one of the blue rags he used to wrap his water beakers.

The night around him was silent. He sipped his saki and pondered the possibilities. Since Tubbs had been caught in the initial blast, he would have been taken to the nearest medical facility. *Locate the hospitals, work my way through. I'll say I'm a German. A friend.* He corked his saki bottle and tried to make himself comfortable. He emptied the pack of everything except Tubbs's papers and used it as a pillow. Eventually he slept.

SOMETHING TUGGED AT HIM. Alex opened his eyes and jerked his foot back in his cave. He heard the sound of scrabbling, sliding debris and running footsteps. He sat up slowly, peering out at gray daylight. He rubbed his eyes. He sat very still and listened, but after the footsteps there was no sound. He unwrapped his beaker and poured an ounce of water onto a rag and wiped his eyes. He took one sip of the water. He took a biscuit out of his shirt pocket, gnawed off a corner, and began to chew.

From the triangular-shaped opening of his cave he could see only another pile of rubble. He forced the entire biscuit down before rewarding himself with a mouthful of the saki.

He crawled out and stood up stiffly, his bruised and scraped body protesting. He faced a scene that his mind had difficulty accepting. He looked out over a plain of utter destruction. A gray mist was lifting from acres of rubble. The ground was covered with a layer of debris that rose into house- and building-sized mounds. He knew from photographs that this was Hiroshima after the atomic bomb, but there was no previous experience that could have prepared him for the sight. He had seen men die, he had seen them blown apart, had seen the pieces of bodies strewn around like so much trash, but seeing an entire cityscape transformed into nothingness was beyond comprehension. He remembered the line from the *Bhagavad Gita* that Oppenheimer had recited after the first test of the bomb at Los Alamos, "Now I am become Death, the destroyer of worlds." Now he understood.

He went back to the entrance of his concrete cave and began putting his bottles and gear away in his pack. He kept glancing over his shoulder at the missing city. He stopped as his hand fell on his Geiger counter. *Holy Christ, I forgot.* He turned the counter on and sat back and listened to the rush of clicks. A needle on the top of the machine registered three quarters of the way across the dial. The lower end of the scale was marked in green, and the needle was sitting solidly in the red zone.

He turned the machine off and slipped it into the leather holder at his waist. He stood up, put his tin pot helmet on, slung the pack on his back, tied a piece of blue cloth over his lower face, and stumbled down to the street. To where the street had been when there had been a street.

Today is August the thirteenth. Soon the Japanese will surrender, Soon the Americans will come. But today I am a German. Today I must find Tubbs. Today I must kill him. I will not be swayed by this horror, I will not be moved from my purpose. I will not be afraid.

But he was all of those things, afraid and horrorstruck, because he was alive, and around him there was only death. He could see it, smell it, and even taste it with every breath. The sun had come up somewhere in the sky, masked by a pall of mist and smoke. Around him and in the distance, Alex could see humans moving and standing on mounds of rubble, like prairie dogs watching over a colony. Figures dug and pulled at the piles. Some of them stood looking down at household objects, pictures, possessions culled from the wreckage. And bodies. When the living saw him coming they moved away, hiding behind debris. They were mostly women, heads wrapped in shawls. By their sides were silent children. The few men squatted on their heels and stared at what had once been homes.

In the far distance Alex could see green hills. He walked away from the center of destruction, toward the hills, toward buildings that had not been completely flattened. He passed a brick cistern and stopped to wash. The cistern was ten feet wide, the water covered with a skim of ash. He swept back the ash and looked at his reflection.

He was dull and gray, his clothing torn and filthy. He was wearing a bandit's mask on his face and a cooking pot with a flashlight eye on his head. *No wonder they move away from me.* He bent close to the surface of the water.

At the bottom of the cistern, staring up toward him, was a layer of bodies. Squeezed in together, solid from side to side, bloated, their arms floated free, hands opened, beseeching him. Their flesh rose in tattered sails, pale seaweed, swaying slightly in the small current he had set in motion when he cleared the surface. He backed away, breathing quickly, trying not to retch. His eyes skittered over the destruction around him, seeking some spot of relief, but there was none. He stood alone in the road, facing the cistern, feeling the drowned men and women reach toward him, feeling the cold touch of their outstretched hands. *I am Death. I am Death.* The only sound was the occasional sliding thump of rubble breaking apart and falling. There were no birds singing, no dogs barking, no people talking, not even the whisper of a breeze. He was sick, and weak. He walked on.

The streets became actual streets, identified as such by the lines of buildings that were not entirely demolished. More people began to appear, ragged and torn, none of them unhurt or untouched. Some of them were almost naked, bodies barely covered with shreds of clothing. He joined them as they shuffled along. No one spoke. They edged away from him.

They came to a large building that had been only partially destroyed. A crude red cross had been painted over a gate. Four intact walls around a courtyard fronted a three-story brick building with half the roof blown away. The courtyard was filled with the injured, sitting and lying on the ground. Those less hurt helped those with more serious wounds. A nurse in an immaculate white uniform moved among the wounded, dipping water from a dented pan into waiting mouths. The absolute whiteness of the woman's clothing, bright against a world of mud and blood-brown, ash-gray, and black, came as a visual shock, a glimpse of some past life where all was not pain and dirt and death. The woman moved with a dancer's grace, her face calm and composed. On the ground, the wounded lifted their arms to the woman and cried out for water. She talked to them, Alex could hear her speaking in German, a steady murmur of consolation and solace. Some of the people stared straight up into the sky, unmoving. Alex realized that the staring ones were dead. Some of them were beginning to swell.

He braced himself against the sight. *I have a purpose.* He stepped over and around the wounded until he was beside the nurse.

"Excuse me," he said in German, "I am looking for a Japanese friend. He has been wounded." His words sounded odd to him. He had not spoken in so long that his voice was rough. He hoped his German did not sound as unusual to the woman as it did to him. She glanced at him and knelt by a blackened figure. She felt at the figure's neck then pulled the remains of a blanket over the charred body and stood up. "Yes," she replied, also speaking German. "And what do you want of me?"

"Is there a listing of those who are here in the hospital?"

She cast her eyes over the assembled injured as he spoke. Then she turned toward him. Half of her face, the right half, was bright red. Her right arm and hand were bright red. As if she'd been held to a fire on that side. "This is not a hospital, it is a convent. Or at least it was. Most of the nuns are dead. The Sisters came to this country to help the people. I came to help the Sisters. None of us realized . . . no one ever . . ." She stopped and looked down at the ground. When she looked back up, her face was calm. "There are no lists of those who have come here," she said. "There are no doctors, just a few of us who were not killed by whatever it was that exploded. You appear able-bodied, if a bit strange. Stay and help us, perhaps you will find your friend." Alex looked at the scattered bodies. *How the hell am I ever going to find him? I'll have to look at every one of them, just to be sure.* And then he thought of Molly. If he could find Tubbs and kill him, Molly would live. "All right, I'll help you. At least for today. Are there many more places like this?"

She shook her head. "We don't know. There's a hospital near the edge of the city that's functioning, but they have no room for any of ours. The entire city is in need of medical help. There are aid stations run by the military. Some soldiers came and told us to keep everyone here. There are no more medicines. There is nowhere to take the wounded. Go inside and put your things down. The dead must be removed, place them in the street outside, then find a pan and fill it with water from the cistern inside. When we run out, I don't know what will happen. But for now, give them something to drink. They are suffering. They have an intense thirst." She moved away from him and bent to the next patient.

He put his pack and helmet on the floor inside the doorway. The doors and all the windows to the convent had been blown out or burned away. The top floor of the building had been abandoned, but the second and first floors were relatively intact. The floors had been spread with thin mattresses and the wounded were lying on them, two to a mattress, almost wall to wall. Three Japanese nuns offered water, and what little solace they could provide.

Alex found a bucket and a deep spoon, which he bent to make a dipper. He began on the top floor, determined to look at every person there. On a stairway he found a small book, a half-burned Japanese hymnal or prayerbook, which he slipped into his pocket.

The worst of the wounded had been brought inside. He forced himself down on his knees, making himself look and touch each of them, ascertaining if they were alive or dead. If they were dead, he tore off a page of the prayerbook and laid it on them so he would know which ones to carry outside.

It was difficult to tell the men from the women. Some of them had paper nametags pinned to the remnants of their clothing, but he couldn't read them. He ignored the names and looked at their swollen, blackened, torn, disfigured faces, and tried to imagine each mutilated person as Tubbs, tried to overlay his features on what remained of theirs. He placed the dipper between their lips and gave them water. When he had finished seeing to everyone on the floor, he began carrying the bodies down. Each of them was lighter than he'd thought men and women could be, but each of them possessed a weight that grew and grew as he worked, a combined mass that began to smother his anger and his purpose. He worked his way down from the top floor, and by late afternoon, outside, when he came upon the woman with the child, he was working in a daze, a kind of functioning trance, unable to remember what Tubbs had looked like, and only barely able to remember why he cared in the first place. He moved among the people, kneeling, offering water, standing, kneeling to the next, until his movements became a mindless ritual, his existence tied to the slender memory of his purpose. His touchstone remained Molly, but now her name called up only a distant feeling of love and loss.

The woman was lying on her back. He could not tell if she was young or old. She lifted the child to him. A little girl. *"Hanako,"* the woman said in a rough voice. *"Hanako."* Alex took the child and held her clumsily in the crook of his left arm as he scooped up a dipper of water. The child had solemn black eyes and short hair cut in bangs.

Alex thought she must be around two years old. She weighed less than the bucket of water he had been carrying. She held herself stiffly, pushing away from him. She was wearing dirty white pajamas. The right shoulder of her shirt had been burned away, and the skin beneath was raw, ugly and swollen under a layer of soot. The burn was weeping a straw-colored fluid. The child did not flinch when he dribbled the last of his bucket of water over her burn. She allowed him to gently clean her face. When she saw that he was not going to hurt her, she relaxed slightly. "Nurse?" he said to the German woman, who was kneeling nearby. "What does *Hanako* mean?" She sat back on her ankles and pressed her hand to her back. Alex could see that she was ill. "Flower," she said. "The child's name is Flower. They have been here for several days."

Alex started to put the child back in the mother's arms when he saw that the woman was dead. A thin stream of black fluid dribbled from the corner of her mouth. Her eyes were open, fixed on Alex.

He turned the child away from the woman on the ground. "Please come here," he called to the nurse. "Quickly. We need you."

The nurse pushed herself up, wiped her hands, and picked her way to them. She knelt, checked for a pulse, then closed the woman's eyes. "I think she was the grandmother," she said. "She said the rest of the family was killed."

"What do we do with the little girl?" he asked. The child sat in the crook of his arm, looking back and forth between them as they spoke. She seemed to understand that they were talking about her. The nurse stood. She looked at Alex and the girl. "You'll have to take care of her. There's no one else to do it. You're healthy, one of the few healthy ones I've seen in the last week. You take care of her."

He stood up, holding the child in his arms. He gestured at her wounded shoulder. "I don't know how to take care of a child. She's injured. Besides, there's something I have to do. I can't."

The nurse turned to face him, eyes narrowed, hands on hips. "I guess you'll have to learn then, won't you? And whatever you must do, whatever is more important than saving a child, will have to wait. There are thousands of children who need to be helped. This is just one of them. Anyway, you're an American, not a German. You fooled me earlier, but now your accent is not as good as it was this morning. I can understand why you're pretending to be a German; you must be an escaped prisoner. You don't have to bother any longer. A soldier came by while you were working inside. We were told to listen to the radio tomorrow. There's to be a special announcement by the Emperor. It can only mean one thing. You've won. Now all of this"—she swept her hand around the courtyard—"will be yours to clean up. *You* visited this upon these people. *You* are responsible. You take care of the child. Your countrymen will be here soon enough. They'll relieve you of the burden." For a second she seemed to sway, rocked by a wave of pain. "I'm busy," she continued, calmer. "You've been a help, and we thank you. Now I must get back to work." She picked up her water pan and Alex's empty bucket and turned her back to him.

Alex looked at the men and women scattered around the courtyard. None of them were well enough to take the child. The little girl was looking up at him. *She's right. I am responsible. In more ways than she could ever know.* "All right," he said to the little girl, feeling slightly foolish. "Later we'll find a home for you." She looked at him solemnly. He smiled at her. She reached out and touched his lips, then put her head down on his shoulder.

56

THE FIRST NIGHT THEY STAYED IN A DRY
corner of a destroyed temple. Two stone walls and a portion of roof
formed a lean-to that kept off the rain that began to fall soon after
dark. Alex knew that the thick, heavy drops of rain probably contained
significant radioactivity. He ran the Geiger counter over Hanako and
found that she registered just into the red zone. His own body had
dropped down into the green. He remembered reading that the worst
of the radiation had been over fairly quickly. He knew that he should
get out of the city as soon as possible. But there was still Tubbs.

A squad of Japanese soldiers with rifles set up a steaming cauldron
on a street corner and dished out balls of rice. Alex dug a begging bowl
from the rubble of the temple and, carrying Hanako, joined the silent
queue that formed. He had to eat, and he had to get food for the child.
The soldier behind the rice pot stared at him, then asked a question
of another soldier nearby. The second soldier walked over and looked
Alex up and down. For a moment the two of them stared into each
other's eyes, then the Japanese shrugged, barked an order, and walked
away. The man at the rice pot spooned up a ladle-full and plopped it
into Alex's bowl. Alex took Hanako and went back to their shelter.
She sat with her mouth open, like a baby bird, while he fed her with
his fingers. After they finished the rice he gave her a cracker, which
she thoughtfully contemplated until he ate a piece of it to show her
it was food. The two of them sat and ate their crackers, and sipped
water from the beaker.

When the rain began to fall, Alex made a small fire which he fed with splintered chunks of wood from the temple. From where they sat, out of the rain, he could see a life-size statue of a seated Buddha, exposed to the outdoors, rubble strewn around his legs, serenely smiling, glittering gold in the firelight as the rain pattered down. They slept. The child lay curled against his chest; both of them huddled in the corner of the stone walls.

In the morning the soldiers were back at the rice pot. This time there were flecks of fish in the rice. As Alex waited, a wave of dizziness swept over him, *don't faint, you'll drop the kid.* He stood perfectly still until his head cleared. He realized that his steady diet of rice, crackers, and saki had seriously weakened him. His torn clothing flapped around his skinny limbs. He clutched Hanako and his begging bowl, and the thought came that if he didn't find Tubbs soon he would never have the strength to kill him. He must finish it. He had to get Hanako away from Hiroshima. If either of them were to survive, they had to get away. He was surprised at the idea of his own survival. He thought he had lost any overt will to live, beyond what he considered his mission. Now he found that he had another purpose. He would get the child to safety. After that, it didn't matter.

He and Hanako squatted on the ground and ate. Nearby, a large radio hooked up to a car battery was carried in and placed on a low table. Alex picked up Hanako and walked closer to the table, towering over the group of neighborhood people gathered there. The soldiers were standing on either side, one of them holding a gold-framed picture of the Emperor. Everyone who could stand did so, with bowed heads. Those who could not stand sat or lay on the ground. Everyone faced the picture.

An announcer's voice came on and after a moment of silence, through an atmosphere of static, came a high, thin voice, that Alex knew was the Emperor, telling the Japanese people their country had surrendered, the war was finished, and asking them to bear the unbearable. After the announcement, the radio was turned off and the people stood awkwardly, most of them weeping. Alex couldn't tell if the tears were for the loss of the war or from relief that it was finally over. He turned to go when one of the soldiers marched up and stood in front of him. The soldier made a statement, then held his rifle out to Alex. The soldier was joined by the rest of the squad, all of them offering their rifles.

"No, I can't take them," he said, shaking his head. "I'm not interested. Let me alone. Someone will come soon." He turned and walked away. He stopped and looked back. The soldiers were still standing at attention with the rifles outstretched. Some of them were crying.

HE SEARCHED THE AREA, visiting aid stations and makeshift hospitals. Each night he and Hanako returned to the ruined temple, where they ate and slept. The neighbors had joined together in pooling their foraged supplies and preparing the evening meals. A soup was made of dandelions and wild grass. The government passed out sacks of flour made from acorns and dried pumpkin stems. This was made into dumplings that Alex forced himself and Hanako eat, though they were even less palatable than the crackers. His remaining crackers were added to the communal stockpile.

Hanako did not speak, but she had accepted him as her protector. She made her few needs known to him with graceful gestures and a wide range of facial expressions.

Their days were spent with the wounded, the dying, and the dead. As he walked between the rows, he still forced himself to inspect every face. But he found his mind drifting, and he would sometimes finish an entire room of people and realize he had really seen none of them. His mind seemed, at times, unable to process the information. He would walk back and forth between the blankets and cots and stop at the end of the last row and stare at nothing, perhaps a wall, or the faraway hills, until Hanako tugged at him and he returned to the world.

She became life to him. In the presence of death, constant death, her small warm body, her arms curled round his neck, her head resting on his shoulder, became his reason for living. His purpose—to find Tubbs—remained, but without her, as the days went on and the task seemed endless, he doubted he would have gone on. He thought he would have lain down and simply died. He would have found Molly in death.

At times one of the old ladies in the neighborhood would take Hanako and give her a bath. When she was not with him he felt cold and alone. He missed the feel of her head against his cheek, the good smell of her, somehow clean in a landscape of dirt and ash, her eyes the only brightness in their gray world. She trusted him, depended on him, and he found that he was dependent on her. He had very little experience with children so he was not really aware that in a few short days he had grown to love the child. Under other circumstances he would have marveled at the strength of the bond, and the speed at which it had been formed. But here, in the ruins of the city, his mind was little given to reflection. He knew only a fierce protective urge to keep Hanako from harm. And so, they continued on.

He found Tubbs on the fourth day after the surrender.

Alex was carrying Hanako, walking through the crowded wards of Hiroshima's only functioning hospital, when a man's eye caught his, and he moved closer and looked down and knew that he had found him. Tubbs was wrapped in bandages, only half his face showing. His body was covered by a light sheet. As Alex bent close, the eye that peered up at him showed recognition. Almost never had anyone looked back at him in the days of his search. The wounded were lost in their own terrible world. But here was a man who looked back.

"Tubbs?" Alex said, getting down on his knees next to the cot. He shifted Hanako to his hip. He glanced around the room. No one was paying any attention to them. "Tubbs, goddamnit, it's me, Alex." He was breathing quickly. The wounded man's mouth was under bandages, but there was a small opening in the gauze mask. "I found you, you son of a bitch," Alex whispered. The man said nothing. His eyes followed Alex's movements. Hanako reached over and patted the sheet. Alex put her on the floor. She began to cry so he quickly picked her back up.

"Listen," he whispered, leaning close. The stench from the wound was almost overpowering. "Listen, I've got to do this. You've cheated and tricked me from the very beginning. You're going to live, and in the future, you're going to kill someone, and now . . ."

"Does he speak English?" a voice behind him inquired. Alex turned to find a Japanese doctor in a dirty, torn lab coat. The doctor's face was haggard, his eyes dark with exhaustion. A gauze dressing was wound around his right hand and wrist. "Is he a friend of yours?"

"Yes," Alex said. "Yes, a friend. You speak English."

The man nodded. "I'm his doctor. I studied at the University of Southern California." He took his wire-rim glasses off with his left hand and cleaned them on his bandage. He put them back on. One of the earpieces was bent. "He's badly hurt, but I think he'll live. You must know his name. He had no identification when they brought him in. We try to find out who they are so their families can be notified."

"You don't know who he is?" Alex asked. He looked back at the wounded man. *It's Tubbs! Isn't it? It's got to be.* "He knows me," Alex said.

The doctor nodded. "Perhaps. He's been delirious. It's possible he knows who you are. Leave his name with the soldier at the front desk on your way out. I'll leave you alone with him, but don't expect much. I don't think he can speak yet." The doctor turned and slowly walked away.

The room was quiet. Alex looked around, but there were no hospital personnel present. Only the patients, all of them sleeping or staring at the ceiling. *I can do it. No one will know.*

Hanako still clung to his left side. He'd have to do it with one hand. Strangle him. Lean close, as if they were talking, get hold of his neck and squeeze. Even if he got caught, it wouldn't matter. Kill Tubbs now, and Molly lives then.

"I've got to do it," he whispered. Hanako patted him on the shoulder. "Not now," he whispered to her. He reached over and put his right hand around Tubbs's neck. The bandage was thick and rough against his hand. She patted him again, and he turned to her and snapped, "Not now, Hanako, I'm busy!"

Her eyes widened and she looked at him as if he'd slapped her. She began to cry. The sheer stupidity of what he'd just said rolled over him. *Not now, Hanako, don't bother me, I've got to kill a man and I've only got one hand free.* The wounded man's eye stayed fixed on him. *And I'm not even sure I've got the right guy.* He started to laugh and at the same time he felt tears come to his eyes.

Not now, God help me, I'm busy.

He knelt on the floor and tried to blink the tears away. Hanako was sobbing softly. He got up and sat on the edge of the cot, holding Hanako close against his chest. He felt all his frustration and helplessness softly explode inside him and he was suffused with guilt.

They came to him, then. The dead. All those men he had killed. He saw them in his mind as their deaths quickly flashed by. The pilot he'd killed at Pearl Harbor, dying in a quick burst of tumbling flame; the enemy soldiers on the island, Lord knew how many there were of them; the two guards he had coldly murdered back at the Nichi so that he might escape; the last of them, the poor dumb clumsy man in the lab, stumbling toward the door in the dark, whose only crime had been in being in the same dark room with a man driven mad by the death of his love. And now he was faced with another, Tubbs, lying helpless, waiting. It was too much. There had been too many. The cistern was full and the bodies lay just below the surface staring up at him, and he found that he could not do it. He found that morality can come not with a bang, but with a whimper, not with the hot flame of determined righteousness but with a simple surrender. He was sickened by the thought of death. He no longer had the strength for it.

Hanako stirred in his arms and he knew that she was the answer. He must use his strength for life. Her life.

I can't do it, Molly. I'm sorry. I'm sorry.

He wiped his eyes with the back of his hand, and looked around the room and saw that it did not matter. Death was a solid, irrevocable presence. Somewhere, in the future, Molly, his Molly, was already dead. Killing again would not save her. Putting his hands around this ruined neck and choking the life from this man would not bring her back. He could not undo what had been done, Time was not a film that could be run backward. Molly's blood would not flow back into her veins, she would not spring up from that concrete floor. That future was fixed, because he had already lived it. He supposed that there might be another future, one that led from this moment onward. That perhaps there was a line from the past to this present and on, where another Molly would be together with another Alex. But she would not be his, never again.

He would do what he could for that other Molly, for that other Alex. He leaned over. "Listen to me, Tubbs. I can't kill you, I'm not going to do it. Listen, and remember. In the future, when you're old, remember that there has been enough death. Remember that I let you live. There is no answer in killing. It cannot change what you will wish to change. It will not help your cause." He stood up, shifting Hanako to his left arm. He leaned over and adjusted the sheet on the wounded man. "We are not spirits. I am only a man. This is only a child. Remember."

He turned and walked from the room, through the rows of wounded, past the soldier at the front door, into the sunlight. Hanako had stopped crying. He looked into her clear bright eyes and saw that he had been forgiven. He felt his spirit rise. He would go on. They would go on. He had reversed Oppenheimer's terrible curse, he had added a line to the *Bhagavad Gita*. No longer was it necessary for it to end with *I am Death* . . .

There was another choice, another path to be taken.

I am Life, Healer of Worlds.

As they walked away from the hospital, Alex glanced back and saw the Japanese doctor standing in the doorway, looking up at the sky, looking up at the sun that had finally broken through the heavy gray layer of cloud and soot. Hanako saw the doctor and waved good-bye. The doctor smiled at them.

Alex held Hanako close against his side as they walked away, toward the green hills.

Afterword

He stood on the hill, overlooking the bay. A large, flat landing boat carrying American troops moved away from the side of a U.S. Navy destroyer. The landing boat motored toward the main dock. Two trucks and a jeep had already arrived on shore. Alex watched as the troops put in at the dock and climbed onto the trucks. After a minute of arm-waving confusion, the convoy moved off.

The trucks drove toward what remained of Hiroshima. From the hill, Alex could see what awaited the soldiers. The center of the city had been crushed flat by the blast. It would still be radioactive, still deadly. He knew that there were people there, picking through the ruins. People who would die of leukemia and cancer and other illnesses known collectively as atomic bomb disease. The rest of the city, seen from his vantage point, lay spread out in broad fans of destruction. Ruined. Burned. All of it layered beneath dust and dirt and soot. Desolate.

He turned away. He walked down the other side of the hill. He stopped and took off his shoes and tied them to his belt. The dirt of the path was warm beneath his feet. His pack was full, heavy on his back.

He walked down into a valley. Hanako sat on his shoulders, her hands clasped in his hair. The road wound through the hills northward, away from Hiroshima. He would follow the road.

He had traded his last two bottles of saki for rice and vegetables. He had several blankets, issued by the remnants of the Japanese Army.

An old lady had sewn a set of new clothes for Hanako. It would be cold in the north, in the wild areas. They would make their way to Hokkaido, the northernmost island of Japan. They would be left alone. The occupation would stay in the south. He had thought of going back, but to what? To sit on the porch and argue with Surrey? To know that not far away another Alex was growing up with a father he hated, and a mother who would die? Would he be able to stay away from that boy? To keep from warning him of the dangers ahead? To try and save Molly once again?

Besides, they would never let him take the child. The authorities, Japanese and American, would shake their heads and cluck their tongues and they would take Hanako away from him. He would not allow that. The solemn little child was a part of him.

They stopped for lunch by a small stream. He built a fire. As his rice boiled, he sliced a sweet potato into the pot. He fed the fire with the pages of Tubbs's report. As each page crinkled black and burned, he felt the day grow brighter.

Hanako sat by the clear water and played with pebbles and sticks. Alex took off his clothes and waded into the cold stream. He washed, rubbing himself with fine sand until his skin was flushed and clean. He sat on a rock and let the sun dry him. He closed his eyes and listened to Hanako at her game, and the birds in the trees and the hum of dragonflies. When he was dry, he put on clean clothing: a white shirt and a pair of black, loose cotton pants. The old lady had made his clothing as well. His shirt and Hanako's outfit had been sewn from the remains of an American parachute. He had left his Geiger counter and extra batteries with the old woman. He kicked out the fire, making sure every scrap of paper was burned. He scattered the ashes. He picked up the pack and shouldered it. He lifted Hanako back up top.

In the late afternoon they walked along the road and the sun lowered toward the horizon. The farther they walked, the greener and more alive the landscape became. It was as if the gray, black, muddy monochromatic veils of the past were being lifted. He found that he was happy. At peace.

The child patted him on the head and laughed. Her feet bumped against his chest. The sun was warm and cast a long glow on the road and the trees and the grass. The birds sang. Hanako leaned down and patted his face. She pointed at a yellow bloom, almost lost in a thorny bush at the side of the road. She laughed again. "Hanako!" she cried. "Hanako!"

"Yes," he said, surprised and elated at the sound of her high piping voice. "Flower. Just like you, Hanako-chan. Little Flower. You have survived. We have survived." He held her small feet in his hands, and felt her tug at his hair, and the sun was warm on his back.

BOOKMARK

THE TEXT OF THIS BOOK WAS SET IN THE TYPEFACE
FAIRFIELD MEDIUM BY CRANE TYPESETTING SERVICE
INC., WEST BARNSTABLE, MASSACHUSETTS.

IT WAS PRINTED AND BOUND BY BERRYVILLE
GRAPHICS, BERRYVILLE, VIRGINIA.

DESIGNED BY MARYSARAH QUINN

FOR THE ANSWERS TO THE CROSSWORD
PUZZLE ON PAGE 59 SEND A
STAMPED, SELF-ADDRESSED ENVELOPE TO:
ALLEN APPEL
C/O LUCY HERRING
DOUBLEDAY
666 5TH AVE.
NEW YORK, NY 10103